Stewart Hennessey was born and educated in Scotland. He worked as a journalist in Glasgow, Edinburgh, London and Moscow, contributing to the *Observer, Scotland on Sunday, Independent, Times,* BBC and sundry others. He enjoys poker, para-gliding and graveyards. He and his English wife, Maisie, also a writer, live in Edinburgh.

stewart hennessey

drowning in the shallows

review

Extract from 'The Man Watching', *Selected Poems of Rainer Maria Rilke*, edited and translated by Robert Bly, 1981, reprinted by kind permission of HarperCollins Publishers.

First published in 2000
by Review

An imprint of Headline Book Publishing

10 9 8 7 6 5 4 3 2 1

ISBN 0 7472 6339 6

Typeset by Letterpart Ltd
Reigate, Surrey

Printed and bound in Great Britain by
Clays Ltd, St Ives plc.

HEADLINE BOOK PUBLISHING
A division of Hodder Headline
338 Euston Road
London NW1 3BH

www.reviewbooks.co.uk
www.hodderheadline.com

For encouragement, help, sarcastic emails, inspiration and textual feedback: Bella Bathurst; Jo-Ann Goodwin; Peter Jinks; Eilidh MacAskill; Andrew Mackenzie; Norman MacLeod; John Mackenzie; Gloria Mete; Francis Murphy; Ruaridh Nicoll; Theresa Ratcliffe and Georgina Wroe. For faith, labour and tolerance: my agent, James Hale and editor, Bill Massey. For wisdom: Steven Briggs and Roger Gard (RIP). For knowing how to throw a man out of a nightclub repeatedly without damaging him: the bouncers at Po Na Na. For everything and so much more: WT.

What we choose to fight is so tiny,
And what fights with us is so great.
If only we could let ourselves be dominated
As animals are, by the immense storm.
We would become strong too, and not need names.
When we win it's with the small things
And the triumph itself makes us small.
What is extraordinary and eternal
Does not wish to be bent by us.

Rainer Maria Rilke (translated by Robert Bly)

'How would you feel if we came over and chatted you two girls up, just for fun? I mean, how would you girls feel about that?'

I would venture you'd feel fine. I would further venture it's pretty darn tricky to turn down such an open, honest, humorous and self-deprecating young man. Who's bloody sexy to boot.

'Well, you can try.'

Most excellent, that'll do nicely. When they've no boyfriends about they so often say those precise words. And what better opening could a man ask for?

'I'm Rich, that's my name, you know, I mean I'm not rich as such. And this is Simes. He is very Simes as such.'

I think I just managed to avoid sounding contrived there, especially the way I made the last phrase sound like an afterthought.

'You use that line a lot, don't you?'

Oh dear, smartarse alert, smartarse alert . . .

'Oh no, no, no, good God no. No, I only use that line when I'm chatting women up in nightclubs . . .'

Hey that was quite funny. She's smiling. She's smart. Good; smart ones are the easiest for me. Simes struggles with them. Hopefully her friend is the kind of dumb fuck that falls for his pish.

'. . . I think it's a good icebreaker line, and it subtly implies that I am quite rich, because I say I'm "not rich as such", rather than "not rich at all". Also Rich and Simes are

1

informal, friendly names, unlike Richard and Simon, so already you've got mate status. Furthermore it beckons forth your names, does it not? And thus potentially opens up a discussion about names.'

'I'm Ruth, and this is my sister Paula. Have we deviated from the script yet?'

'No, not at all. This is going very well, all according to plan. However I cannot help but notice that your glasses are rather full so I can't offer to get you a drink which is always a good next move; you know, offering after contact has been established, rather than before, which is crude, old-fashioned and makes some women feel like you're saying "Your company can be bought". What do you think?'

'I think you're a chancer.'

That's a bit bleedin' obvious, honey. Maybe she's not so smart?

'Tut tut, "think I'm a chancer". I'm obviously a major chancer, I make Jeffrey Archer seem sincere. In point of fact, my dear, my chancing hardly merits mention. Now, is that really the deepest perception you have so far garnered from our limited – and yet charged – interaction?'

'Oh, this is charged? Glad you told me . . .'

It's OK, she's smiling, likes a little bit of touché. So do I.

'. . . I could tell you more, including the fact that while you think you are wonderfully ironic and upbeat and charming a lot of people probably think you're a show-off, tacky bastard. Your mentions of money – two already – seem inappropriate and insecure. I bet you have a decent enough job but couldn't manage a piggy bank.'

Oh Christ, there's one in every club; a sarcastic cow that's as verbose as me.

'No please, don't hold back. My fragile male ego wants more of this.'

'OK. I think you would be well-advised to concentrate less

DROWNING IN THE SHALLOWS

on your irony which can make you sound smug – though I sense you're not – and pay a little more attention to your clothes. That shirt badly needs ironing; it's expensive but you look cheap in it. And those shoes don't go with anything you're wearing. Shall I go on?'

Christ, really do have a right one here. She's checking I can take this. No sweat honey, anything for sex. Lovely tits, I determine to lick them before this night is out.

'No need. I can see you are a woman of considerable perception who can advise well and talk eloquently. However, I suspect you would make a crap Samaritan. And don't you think the crumpled shirt might appeal to the maternal side of women?'

'Nope, it wouldn't. And I work in charity.'

'Really?'

'No. I just like lying about what I do.'

God give me a break!

'Oh. So what do you really do?'

'I'm a lap dancer.'

Brilliant! Sex. First mention of sex, and she made it. Of course she's not a lap dancer but that's such a wonderful moment, that incidental revelation that sex is on your mind. And sexy dancing, that's my favourite, and when they're feeling sexy and decadent having a one-night stand you can get them to dance for you, alone at home it's amazing how erotic they'll get. Simes never believes, but the old cliché's true; inside every woman there is a stripper dying to get out. And I'm here to help. Ruth baby here, she even expects me to be picturing her lap dancing right now. Oh honey, I can picture so much more than that. But be patient my yearning loins, we're still a long way from home.

'That is a porkie pie, Ruth. If you're a lap dancer, I'm a llama. So, rather than give you the opportunity to wind me up with a succession of lies about your occupation, I'll tell you straight what I do: I'm a copywriter.'

3

'What do you write for?'

'Advertising mostly, though recently started doing political speeches; big words, big visions, big loads of rhetorical, rabble-rousing tosh – great fun though. I like doing book covers the most.'

That was good, a little bit of honesty while revealing a creative nature. Now she feels a bit silly not revealing her job.

'What do you really do?'

Nice and low-key again. She will reveal it surely, and thus be surrendering in a small but still encouraging way. Please be a nurse.

'I'm an academic.'

Yeuch. She'll know everything about one tiny slither of something and fuck all about anything else.

'Really, what area?'

'I'm a social scientist.'

Yeuch again! I know this trip; society's a shambles, life's a worry and sex should be sound. I hate these earnest gits.

'Really, what area?'

'Sociology.'

The worst. Please God say it ain't so. Anything but a sociologist. Didn't that bollocks die in the 1980s? I'm sure Thatcher and Reagan rounded them all up into a sports stadium and had them shot. No? Damn, that was just a fantasy I had. Now I'm not pandering to her bloody earnest treatises, but only because I can't. Actually maybe I can. This is going to be tricky. Christ, she's not even embarrassed. Here goes.

'Really, I used to read a lot of Weber and early Marx. I veer to anthropology though, particularly Malinowski's stuff, and especially on the Trobriand islanders; now that was genius, what's your speciality?'

Because you have to talk now. I've just burned up my entire knowledge of your dreary subject.

'We're looking at hardcore industrial communities . . .'

4

There's a surprise. God, why dost thou want so much to extrapolate the Michael tonight?

'. . . in the information age, really the way these communities have no way to develop in the 21st century since they were created for such a singular purpose which is now irrelevant.'

Yes, but you're going to take two years and 70,000 dull words to repeat that bleedin' obvious statement.

'That's interesting, but basically if they have absolutely no *raison d'être*, what can be done about it?'

Shit, sounding dismissive; meant to sound concerned there.

'Nothing, I suppose. Who gives a shit?'

'What? You mean you don't care?'

'No, I do . . .'

Thought that was too good to be true.

'. . . but governments now don't have long-term social planning programmes, so it's pointless studying it. Nobody cares.'

Yes, shame about the demise of those long-term social planners like Josef Stalin, Mao Tse Tung, Adolf Hitler, Pol Pot, sociologists and other omnipotent plonkers who mistook themselves for God at the drawing board planning 'The Society of Man'. Oh how the world misses them.

'That's a shame. I don't mean for you, I mean you've at least still got a valid job, albeit a frustrating one, but it's a shame to think there simply isn't any serious social planning from government any more. I hadn't considered that.'

Christ, the clichéd crap a man will spout to get laid. Did I get away with that? Or did I just make myself nauseous for nothing?

'Yeah, that's just the way it is.'

Aaaaargh, patience, Rich, patience. But Christ, she's the type that used to go around the student campus saying she'd never work for the MoD. I never figured out what on earth

5

those pious prats thought the MoD could possibly use them for. Target practice, I suppose.

'Still, you got to look on the bright side: at least communism's over.'

Oh dear, Rich me ole' mucker, tread warily; you're in danger of bringing in reality.

'Where's the connection?'

No. I can take this no more. I am going to have to give it to her good and straight and hope she still thinks I'm a nice guy, just misguided, in need of educating; that should keep her interested. Anyway she'll want to hang in to prove she's right. Bloody academics, always got to be right.

'Well, the commies were all scum who should have been shot except the pretty ones – you know, maybe we could have found some purpose for the really cute ones – but now they're all fucked anyway so it's almost perfect, except that social science, communism's incestuous little sibling, is finally going to have to justify its cult-like existence. All those utterly unheroic heroes of the red-brick campus with their crappy, pseudo-sage beards, woolly jumpers, bad breath, adolescent complexes and penchant for shagging their sycophantic students who are in turn – laughable and incomprehensible though it is – intellectually in awe of said useless deadbeats, well now these beards have to explain themselves. And we want to know why they, despite being self-evidently the devil's spawn, act like they have a right to be so constantly irked with the ignorance of the rest of us who so foolishly believe the world is complicated and mysterious and that society is not some little Lego-like toy for them to trash and rebuild as they see fit. So it's all worked out fine in that sense, dontcha think?'

Well, said it now, but that wasn't as spiteful and witty as I'd hoped it would come out. Damn, you only get one blast when you go for a rant. Still, should have got her back up.

'I don't agree.'

Is that it? 'I don't agree'? Nothing to retort, no anger, no nothing? Oh shit, I've blown it.

'What do you not agree with? That all sociology lecturers have bad breath? OK, I was exaggerating there. I heard about one at Durham who used Listermint. But what else?'

She's smiling, are we friends again? Is this possible? An academic who can laugh at themselves? But that was a stupid risk; it's always a mistake to mock. You must learn patience, Rich. Patience my man. Never forget the four sacred principles of sharking (aka life's purpose). 1. Be happy. Nothing is more attractive than happiness. No jawline, moody pose, clothes, reputation or wealth; nothing beats looking like life's great. 2. Feign respect. If you can't develop any real respect – and they can make it tricky – feign it. No respect, no chance. Even the most drunken slapper wants to believe you respect her. (And this one wants professional respect. Academics are even worse than doctors for taking themselves seriously.) 3. Fuck all worth having comes to he who waits. If you haven't got the guts, technique and charm to shark, you'll just get slappers, drunks, desperados and dullards, but mostly you'll get nothing. So don't bother leaving the house. 4. The whole art of chatting up is shutting up. It is entirely about getting them to do the talking – especially about themselves. Draw them out, crack jokes, be knowing, understanding, always listen carefully and look fascinated. Next thing they know, they feel intimate with you.

'It doesn't matter, you wouldn't listen.'

She's smiling again, hope is not lost.

'I would. I'm just overstating things for fun, I can't help it. Can I buy you a drink?'

'No, I would, but I'm about to leave to meet my boyfriend. Honest.'

Bitch, bitch, fucking bitch! Mention of boyfriend is way too soon. She might as well say 'Away and fuck your mother some more, you disgusting creep.'

'You have a boyfriend? That's OK, I'll overlook it for tonight, but he may have to be chucked if we still feel good in the morning.'

'Rich, it was nice talking to you, a lot more fun that most guys, but I really do have to go and meet my boyfriend now.'

'It's OK, my fragile ego can handle being red-carded, I won't cry for more than a week.'

'You won't cry at all. You'll move in on another two girls the minute we leave, possibly those two there.'

Good idea, the small, dark one looks dirty. I like that in a woman. So fuck off.

'No, we won't. Honest, I am disappointed you're leaving, I'd like to have talked more with you. Here's my number, in case you later realise the terrible mistake you are making by rejecting me.'

'Thanks, I'm not rejecting you, I really am meeting my boyfriend, but thought you looked like fun so I said it was OK to talk. Your opener is a great line. And you are fun.'

'Thanks, I enjoyed talking to you.'

'But I happen to know you couldn't care less for talking more now you know I have a boyfriend . . .'

I'll forget about him if you will.

'. . . It's just thrill of the chase for you. You aren't interested in sociology or me, just sex. Bye.'

Ow. Smart one indeed. Thank God she didn't stay. It's hard to chat up the next ones when you've been so thoroughly red-carded by someone who can still watch you. Most off-putting. Simes hasn't fared any better with her sister. Ah, he's already nodding at the next two. I baggsy the dark cutie.

'How would you feel if we came over and chatted you two girls up, just for fun? I mean how would you girls feel about that?'

I would venture you'd feel fine. I would further venture it's pretty darn tricky to turn down such an open, honest, humorous and self-deprecating young man. Who's bloody sexy to boot.

'You're welcome to try . . .'

Most excellent, that'll do nicely . . .

Tuesday, 1st March

I can't believe I'm having to meet this guy. And having to meet him in my home. And be nice to him. 'Ian's hurting,' says Mike. 'He's missing Marion. So much.' Oh God, I do hope so. I hope he really misses his bitch girlfriend and I hope she died in enormous pain. I wish Iain and Sarah, and some days even Mike, had been on the motorbike too.

I bet they made a cute foursome. I can see them in London wine bars, with super-flashy mobile phones and Gold Amex cards, snorting coke in the toilet and feeling like they'd really arrived. Smug gits. Daily I see them in my mind's eye, Iain and Marion, Mike and Sarah, the men working in one investment bank, the women in another, oh how cute, two sweet trysts defying the battle lines of corporate loyalty, and I see me back in Edinburgh, looking after Mike's and my home, keeping the faith, keeping the fucking faith, waiting, resisting offers no problem, unable to believe my luck that I had a guy like Mike. Ha.

God, will this rage ever end? Four years on and I still want blood. Marion's wasn't enough, oh no, I want Sarah's, extracted from her living body, preferably her hanging upside down, stripped naked, I'll lacerate her, oh so slowly, with a scalpel, while smoking and pouring in vinegar with a pleasant smile. Instead I have to meet Iain and be fucking nice. I can do it. It's just another tiny drop of poison seeping into my rotted heart.

I feel ridiculed in front of Iain and I haven't met him. He'll be here in an hour and the evening will be over by midnight. Then I can return to my furious solace. Of course I don't want to be nice, but tonight I'll pretend. I'll face Iain and retrieve some pride; I'll make out like that summer didn't bother me; like it didn't turn me into a twisted, fucked-up cow a stone underweight, lined and grey and always tired, exhausted from hating.

I looked at my naked body in the full-length mirror this evening, just to savour the physical scarring. How twisted is that? My long, lovely, dark brown hair, always washed and brushed straight. Who is it for? Not Mike, not me. Why do I bother? My hair falls low enough to cover my breasts. I seem to want to cover them, yet they are pretty pert for a thirty-one-year-old, but that small sag; it tells me time is running out, the best has passed and this misery is it. Looking at them, small with small nipples, on my thin-hipped body, all elegance and no earthiness, no child-bearer me, can this be my fate? My green eyes, they lure men, I almost hate them, big beads coming out at you above my shapely mouth and average nose, announcing that I'm some piece of exotica, some novelty act, but they stare out of the mirror at me accusingly. They're not my eyes at this moment; they belong to the brilliant therapist everyone thinks so capable. But, alone in the mirror, they are mine, and they are the eyes of a frightened child – what have I done to her? I looked away, tears were building.

I'll put her through more tonight. I can't get out of this. Mike says I have to meet Iain, and it's his call at the moment; I cheated last. God knows the leaden power pendulum which hangs over our relationship for evermore will swing back to me in due course, just as soon as I find out about his next (current?) peccadillo. Ah, such a charming little word for torturing the person you believed you were on earth to look after.

But for now that pit is in my stomach, that special pit that appears the moment your worst fear is confirmed: he's cheated. And there it is, the pit, that hellish void which you cannot believe you are going to dive into and exist in forthwith. But you are. Oh yes, you are. You won't leave him, oh no, you won't do what you always said to everyone – including yourself – you would do, because now you need him more than ever, because you are obviously a piece of shit nobody else could really want. He is everything; if you can't hold him, you can't hold any man. If you leave him you will be on your own forever, or forever chasing someone who of course doesn't really love (unlovable) you, and you are already lonelier than you thought the saddest fuck could ever be. You are pathetic and facile, left out of everything, far too unattractive to have a proper boyfriend. God how you need him there, as if with his presence he can convince some part of your demented mind that it never happened, or that it doesn't matter, or some such shit, consoling lie you never believe for more than a few seconds. And after those glimmering seconds, after that false hope flees, you are newly devastated, all over again, and you rage harder for a few hours, and then it's back to the aimless misery.

Iain will enter my home soon. He is not human to me, he is a spectre, a membrancer of that summer, scaring me. I don't want that memory because the truth is that summer was the happiest I had ever been – before I knew. Thinking of that now chills more than anything that has happened since that moment, when I found out and my life changed and I became somebody else. All because that prick had to have his cheap fun. 'I don't love her,' he said. That made it worse. Anything he says makes it worse. It's only ever got worse and worse. Four fucking years of breaking up, fights, restarts, cheating, all these revenge fucks, all this hurt and hate just because Mike wanted a shag, four years unlived, squandered on pain.

Sometimes I can't bear to look at Mike. I don't want to see him in repose and register his misery, sense his pain, his defeat and ennui and the regret he cannot bear but has to. Now he needs to cheat to get away from being hated, to get some confidence back. And each time I need revenge, I need to try and escape but I never do, I can never sustain interest in other men, God I try, but I always come back, the idiot institutionalised prisoner of hate (but calling it love, of course). And each time we need to believe it's the last, but we don't buy it any more, not really.

And if I do watch Mike's sweet face – I can hardly bear to even call him sweet, to be sympathetic at all, his pain on top of mine, that's enough for a breakdown – I just want to cry quietly, 'How could you? Why, Mike?' but such tenderness must be banished. Such words can only be screamed in reproach, never shared. We would cry forever if we faced what we've done to each other; we catch glimpses of it, at odd moments, usually during fights, and it gnaws at our hearts more than the spite.

Some couples aren't spiteful, they can handle infidelity. Perhaps after years together they don't need sex to stay close, perhaps they turn a blind eye not wanting the hassle, perhaps they really don't care, perhaps what you don't know doesn't harm you, but we were young, so in love, it was the biggest thing ever, this wasn't our fate, we've stepped out of our own lives, we're living other people's lives, I can't moralise about cheating, I have no real opinions, just anger, I don't know anything any more.

I'll face Iain, I'll be nice, it matters not a jot, nothing matters. Mike and I will soldier on, and pray God give me another life because this one feels over.

Wednesday, 2nd March

Last night was strange. I tried to hold on to my hate but I think it slipped away the moment I met Iain. He looked petrified, not of me, but of life. He greeted me with a confident smile that caught me off-guard. It didn't affect his strange gait – slow, distant, haunted – but, in retrospect, it seemed to say a hell of a lot: 'I know you hate me, and I understand, but, frankly honey, your pain is self-indulgent twaddle compared to mine, so don't bother hating me. Can't you see I'm a wreck who couldn't care less? I'm not worth the effort of hating.'

He had a friend with him, Derek. Normally I loathe Derek, for knowing Iain, but last night I realised he is fine, and nervous of me. I suggested we go to the pub. I was fascinated by Iain. He was in shock, a year on, still unable to accept she has been taken from him, that life can be so cruel. He said to me at the bar: 'I know you are not the person to talk to about Marion, but don't feel awkward, I don't want to talk about her.'

I said I didn't mind, and by then I think I really didn't. I bristled once, as we walked to the pub, when that summer got a mention in passing, but it was a reflex. I knew they wouldn't be crass enough to go on about old times.

'I never understood that anything could matter so much,' said Iain. His voice was soft, hardly any timbre. 'I didn't know it did at the time. If I get better I'll never believe again that all the nonsense we fill our heads with matters. We just use it all to shield us from the biggies, you know, like love and death and time fleeing by unmarked.'

I asked what he meant by better. He smiled, 'get by without Prozac, booze, coke, tears, or a crap one-night stand. Or all five on a really good day. I want to be able to give a shit again.'

There was no self-pity in his talk. I think he was talking

about Marion to get that bit of the evening out the way. He was just trying to inform, he had no interest in getting our sympathy. He knew he was on his own, utterly.

His remark about 'biggies' sparked off a long conversation where Mike showed off his brilliant mind, so lateral, so witty. I wondered if that was some sort of biggie about Mike I shield myself from. I thought about Mike caring about Iain, and spending time with him, caring about him in some male way where nothing is really discussed.

It made Mike happy to see Iain and me getting along, like a war of attrition between me and a significant part of his life, part of him, had resulted in a cease-fire. And Mike being happy made me sad: how rarely I see that.

The conversation wandered back to Marion. 'Your ring, that's nice,' Iain smiled.

'Thanks,' I said, knowing he wanted to steer the conversation away from Marion. 'I used to like it but I'm sick of it. It reminds me of the dreary boyfriend who got me it for my 21st. It won't come off.'

'But it went on and your fingers don't grow as an adult,' he said, amusingly serious.

'No biggie, so I have to wear a piece of metal I don't like.' I shrugged.

Iain took my hand and slowly started to work the silver band over my knuckle. He pulled my hand close to his face. Mike and Derek were watching. We had had three or four drinks and were at that merry, relaxed stage that you spend the rest of the evening trying to recapture.

Iain began wetting my finger, licking it, looking up at my eyes every so often. It was a bit bloody fresh. And I liked it. There was something calm and unselfconscious about Iain; as if seeing the biggies had taken him very far away from normal codes of behaviour.

Out of the corner of my eye I could see Mike smiling into

his pint, maybe half-turned on, maybe thinking of our twisted sex life where we have tortuous videos playing in both our heads of the other with someone else, usually someone we haven't met, and always someone much more attractive than ourselves, of course. That hurt defines the bed.

Iain took my finger in his mouth. I thought about giving Mike oral sex. I do it a lot just now, since I am the one who ruined the latest promise of this being the 'truly last incidence of cheating'. By nature I love oral sex, giving and receiving – to me, both feel like a gift – and Mike does have a beautiful cock, but mostly he is too quick to demand it, so I do it mechanically, without love, swallowing dutifully, bored. Somewhere in the recesses of Mike's darkened mind he knows it. And doesn't care.

The ring was beginning to hurt my knuckle. I groaned, Iain started to lick my finger more and pull gentler. Mike looked concerned, how farcical. Mike likes hurting me, he talks about my latest fling (flingette really, but he can make it sound like a lifelong marriage) and wants to possess me, he tortures himself with the nitty-gritty details, which I sometimes exaggerate. It was actually rather dull, which would never satiate Mike. The thrill of the illicit, of having sex behind Mike's back, was all that charged it for me.

So now Mike hurts me in bed. And mostly I like it. When you're consenting the tables turn; it's the one being tied up and abused who is in control. Mike has all the responsibility, not to really push it. When he grabs me and turns me over to fuck my arse he has to take care not to hurt me too much, he has to check himself. In fact he has to face the truth; that he does care. I just lie there, going with the fantasy. Sometimes I love being the recipient of such strong passion, being forced to be the recipient. And other times it's tiresome, especially since there's no other kind of sex between us, lately.

17

Iain was becoming aware that thoughts were racing through my head, or at least that I was becoming aroused. He stared intently at the ring, very determined to get it off. The strange dynamic was not lost on him. He didn't care. He was detached. He was more interested in the ring than anything else.

He wanted finality, he was wanting to get the ring off, perhaps as if that would end something, perhaps as if he would then be over Marion. I reckon odd things often obsess him, in between caring about nothing. Mike and Derek chatted among themselves, exchanging friendly glances with us, and both buying another round while Iain wrestled with the ring.

He licked and tugged for fifteen or twenty minutes, and for the first time in eleven years the ring came off. I was glad. The dampness between my legs was getting uncomfortable.

We staggered back to the flat. How tawdry our life seemed when Derek and Iain had gone. Sometimes somebody's pain is so grand and pure it humbles your own. Mike didn't push it; he didn't celebrate his victory.

'Thanks for being nice, Denise,' he said.

He rarely calls me Denise, usually Denny.

'No problem,' I answered.

In truth the devil-may-care drink had kicked in. I was imaging shagging vulnerable little Iain some time Mike was away. Then I'd literally be fucking the dreaded foursome. Delightful.

Aren't I just?

'Scary biscuits!'

The *Alma Mater* sailed on. They hadn't heard him scream as he fell. Maybe he didn't scream, just whimpered; he wasn't sure. He shouted now. 'Hey, Simes, anybody, I've fallen in the fucking loch!'

Still the boat sailed on. Bloody stoners. It must be half a mile to shore. They've got to notice. He shouted again. 'Ahoy there, shit-heads, I'm in the fucking soup, come back!'

He was less hopeful this time. He had realised the engine was too loud and they were all huddled below, beside its roar. He watched, incredulous, as the *Alma Mater* continued to sail further away: 30, 40, 50 metres. Stupid boat. Stupid name. Bloody converted fishing boat, what kind of a thing is that to sail in? The frustration was too much. He felt like he might cry. He turned away and contemplated the shore, the fucking distant shore.

Everything looked threatening: the loch, the land, the elements, all bearing down on him.

And it's getting dark. How long will it be? When will the sodden boat turn and start looking? God that boat can shift, can hardly hear it already.

Oh Christ, can hardly see its wake, all this greyness, so choppy. Now if he can hardly see the wake, a sizeable whiteness, what chance have they of seeing his little head bobbing about in this gloom? Shit.

They'll still be toking and laughing, stoned idiots unaware there are now only five docile bodies milling about. It's nice

19

to feel noteworthy. Bloody zombies. He certainly didn't feel stoned now. There's nothing quite like a surprise dip in Loch Ness to bring a man round, no siree.

Oh triff. It's started to rain. Thank you God, that's just dandy, exquisite timing, thank you so fucking much.

This light, it isn't twilight, too dark, shit. It's bloody overcast something awful. And treading this fresh water is knackering. Better kick these shoes off.

He undid the laces. He had to reach down to pull them off, he knew he would sink and spin a bit, no panic.

Rich resurfaced, caught a mouthful of water, spat it out and stared into the rain. Shit, there really is a storm kicking in, Simes was right. And those shoes were from Jones, bloody stylish items to drop into the middle of a dark, Highland loch.

They seem to have sunk. How did that happen? How weird. They're on a long slow journey to the bottom. They should have floated, shouldn't they? But they're sinking through all that darkness. Unseen for evermore. Rich pictured them sinking. He hated the thought of all that blackness, so close, just beneath his wee legs.

What creatures lurk down there? Bet they're ugly.

Maybe one will see his shoes? Maybe one will see him soon? He pictured himself, five feet, ten inches and just over eleven stone of humanity sinking into blackness, bereft of his energetic manner, dead, floating down slowly, his short curls wavering about, their chestnut brown colouring barely discernible in the blackness, his generous mouth and blue eyes both open and gaping, set, as if in stone, an expression of horror, sinking down, ever more down.

What an absurd thought. Jesus, will that fucking boat never fucking turn? Can't wait much longer, this is getting dull.

Rich's mind returned to the reality of his booties. He wished he'd been less rash. He could have tied them together, or one round each wrist, whatever, just somehow kept them.

It wasn't that he liked them that much. It was more he didn't like the way they sank. Now he couldn't stop picturing his little Italian, brown booties sinking further and further into that blackness.

For years the Lockerbie bomb victims had played on Rich's mind. He could never forget the way they had taken several minutes to fall to earth, through blackness. It was 21st December 1988, the winter equinox, the longest night. Rich always thought that was significant, as black as night can be, though he figured the Arab terrorist who planted the bomb probably didn't attach much astrological significance to the matter.

Now if his body followed his shoes it would be a bit like the Lockerbie bomb victims, both falling through blackness, both taking a few minutes. They were probably mostly dead when they fell, but not all of them. Actually, he wouldn't be dead either, not for the whole journey.

God, this is Lockerbie-like. All those passengers relaxing in their seats, an instant later they are in the open sky beginning the long descent; like him, relaxed, next thing tossed to the elements.

Rich knew they would have attained top plummeting speed after a few seconds, about 40 metres. He had reached that speed, when he bungeed 102 metres in Skippers Canyon in New Zealand, the biggest bungee in the southern hemisphere, fan-bloody-tastic, but petrifying.

Rich often pictured the Lockerbie bomb victims in freefall, especially the ones who had moments of consciousness during their descent. What went through their minds? That they were dreaming? Maybe they heard a faint scream or saw a spec of a body or a piece of plane in the darkness falling somewhere near them? What if they fully grasped their situation and saw it for what it was? And still had minutes of falling to go – not even through the clouds yet? What would come to mind during that bizarre journey to death? That this was a strange way to exit this life? Maybe it would seem right, strangely familiar, inevitable. The disbelief in horror films is momentary; this took minutes, something comes after the shock. Maybe they would become calm enough to cry.

Why was he thinking about the bloody Lockerbie victims? He wasn't going to take any sodden journey through blackness. And even if he did drown, well, dead bodies float, even in fresh water, don't they? He wasn't sure. Bloody shoes didn't float. Maybe they floated away and he didn't see?

Who cares? Was he stoned or something? Because it sure as hell wasn't his fate to drown in this dismal place.

But that's how it happens, always desultory, never dramatic. The drama is put in to emphasise the cause of death, to explain the strangeness away. People don't want to really see life just ending; quietly, privately, just exiting the world which spins on regardless. It's the ultimate loneliness, and it's utterly undramatic, in fact the end of all your dramas. Even the soldier with a sabre run through him at Waterloo dies a moment later, in his own perfectly isolated instant.

Familiar thoughts, just babble; he should shut up and get with the programme: destination shore. That fucking boat will be across the fucking world before they notice he's gone.

The *Alma Mater* was barely visible in the waves. And it disappeared regularly. Rich wondered if the waves were rising. He worked his legs hard to rise up and see if the boat had turned. Still it hadn't.

Jesus, will they never notice? Definitely time to make for shore. It's only 600m, maybe, no panic, but Christ he was cold and tired; he couldn't die this way, healthy young man and all that. He can swim, no panic.

Only been in the water a few minutes, no need to get excited. Bloody ridiculous, a grown man falling off a boat. OK, his legs feel exhausted, but they're being weighed down by his 501s, better get them off.

Rich undid the studs in his Levis.

Fuck, going under for a while; that was meant to be mock-panic. Rich forced a smile to himself.

Down he went, concentrating on getting the jeans off. Round his ankles, no going back now, legs can't circle, sinking lower and lower.

God, not treading water at all, you do sink, this is spooky water, it is that Lockerbie journey, in water.

He got the left leg off, and spun half-backwards, unsure which way was up. He started peeling at the right leg, spun a bit more, ran out of breath and made for the surface, dragging the jeans, but he couldn't propel properly, the jeans were making his progress lopsided, he might be moving at a ludicrous angle. He opened his eyes to guide himself to the surface light. His worst fear was confirmed; he was in blackness. There could be a monster two feet away and he wouldn't be able to see it.

With enormous, exhausting strokes he made for the surface. Once there he didn't pause. As he caught his breath, he yanked off the Levis and tore for shore almost in one motion. He wanted away from the blackness he had just visited. He thought about how that blackness was still going to be there, underneath him all the way, until near the shore.

He remembered what he'd read about sailors in the North Atlantic: when a rogue wave crashes on their ship the first thing they do is bolt to a porthole to look out. If they see whitewater they know they're probably sound as a pound; still on the surface. If they see greenwater it's scary, they're in the body of the wave; it may auger doom. And if they see blackwater their boat is a submarine.

But that was a book about a unique event, *The Perfect Storm*. This is just a daft situation. Still, fishing boats and blackness: the stupid *Alma Mater* and where his shoes were.

He swam and swam, with unsustainable zest. It was as if he could swim forever. In fact he was unable to slow down.

His heart beat fast. He knew the danger of hypothermia. He'd learned about it when he worked as a lifeguard; a holiday joke job on Gran Canaria to help some Hotel del Peasantry meet the worries of the local tourist board.

He doubted if he or any of the other fraudulent lifeguards Baywatching their way about the beach would have been any use to a tourist in distress. The lifeguards had been sharks themselves; eyeing up, chatting up, subtly drinking (alcohol tastes even better when you're not allowed it) and posing the vague days away. It was a good time. But now the day of lectures on drowning was back to haunt him.

He knew people usually survive less than ninety seconds underwater. Then they would reach 'break point'. Towards the end of those ninety seconds they would sense darkness closing in. Whatever was in their mind's eye would become surrounded by blackness, and/or become dark and faint itself. For sure, his fear of blackness was wise.

After the ninety seconds, very few people ever return. They open their mouth. The body has accepted there is no oxygen coming; it might as well override the profound instinct to hold the mouth closed in water, and see what happens. The body, barely conscious, already in death's grip, is flooded with water and becomes utterly useless. Life departs.

Clearly then the best plan was to keep your fucking mouth shut and not go underwater for long. Simple. If you can't do that you only have one tiny, utterly crap chance of staying alive; laryngospasm.

That comes after the break point. The mouth has opened, the water had reached the larynx, and the body decides this flooding is even worse than not breathing. Instantly it contracts the muscles round the voice box to keep the water out. After a laryngospasm the person is still said to have drowned, but there is no water in the lungs. It's more like suffocation. Few people have laryngospasms. But they include many of the precious few who have returned from beyond break point.

Well, ain't this head clogged with cheery information? Fact about Drowning Number 57: it's crap, don't do it.

Gradually Rich eased his manic strokes. He seemed to be swimming against the current. In a loch? Or against the wind maybe? Or is it just this tough to swim in freshwater? Christ, this is the largest body of freshwater in the British Isles and he was in the middle of it, in early March, freezing. It doesn't matter. Whatever, he simply wasn't stopping until he reached the shore. And of course he had the physical strength to reach the shore. But, then, most people who drown are perfectly capable swimmers. Rich knew why people drowned in his situation: bad cramps and hypothermia. He did not want to think about them. They were real possibilities and there was nothing he could do to prevent either of them.

His mind wandered back on to the drowning process. He remembered that hyperventilating extends life by 50–60 seconds when drowning; the break point comes when the body is full of carbon dioxide. The hyperventilation process expels carbon dioxide, so the body takes longer to reach break point.

Just supposing he did drown? What would be his final thoughts? Something as bloody stupid as that bloody stupid name for that bloody stupid boat, or something like, 'I can't die; I'm meeting Kate on Friday.'

Rich knew people always felt surprised, as if drowning can't really happen to them, at least not right now. They feel a bit embarrassed and uneasy; they simply don't know how to respond and they feel they should have a response. Faced with death, mind and body blur; neither have a clue how to handle this thing. Both have always known it was coming but never knew when, so they are never ready to greet it.

Rich determined to get his mind off all his knowledge about drowning, which he deeply regretted ever acquiring. He stopped swimming and looked up into the clouds. Patches of them were black. He knew the storm was growing. That didn't take special knowledge, just eyes. He looked across to the overcast land, and could see no shadows in the dark hills. They were a singular mass beneath an ugly, jagged line in the sky. Then he regarded the grey surface of the water. It alone seemed natural from this strange perspective. He became very aware of the vastness of the depths beneath that veneer. He finally accepted that he really might be about to die.

He started swimming again but now he swam without thinking about swimming. Most of his being wasn't involved in swimming; it was waiting, existing in a meeting place with terror. His life was on hold. And he was waiting to see if it was going to be continued. He was powerless. The terror, a far bigger force than him, would decide. And it really might end his life. Therefore all he could do now was wait and hope.

Occasionally he panicked and decided he wasn't going to get cramps. Or hypothermia. He just wasn't. It was merely his misfortune to know those dangers existed. They were not going to happen to him. But most of the time he was brave; he faced the terror and hoped.

He managed to spare a thought for what it might be like if he reached the shore. He thought he would cry.

And he did reach the shore. But he didn't cry. About forty yards out, he found the floor of the loch with his left foot and knew it was over. He swam in a little more and gently beached his limbs on the rocky bottom about twenty yards from a tiny beach. He stood up and stepped slowly over the rocks until he was staggering up the small stones, solid earth just beneath. He realised he had a big smile on his face. He sat down, then lay down, the sweet rain tapping on his front, the solid ground beneath his back, his whole life ahead.

Physically, spiritually and utterly, Rich was exhausted. He lay for five minutes, maybe longer, time didn't matter, then fell asleep. He awoke freezing but it was sound, not cold, that woke him. He lay still for a few seconds savouring the unfamiliar feeling: joy at being alive.

He heard Simes scream again, 'It is him! He's here!' He heard noise on the shingles to his left and sat up. It was comical. They all stopped running and stared, then continued towards him but just a fast walk now; they were obviously trying to regain some composure, to let it sink in that he definitely hadn't drowned. Rich felt enormous love for them all and grinned as they got close: 'Sorry. Didn't mean to scare you.'

'Eh, no, good to see you,' said Simes in his controlled way, and smiled as if it were all a prank. His tension made Rich happy. Simes loved him, it couldn't be clearer.

Everyone was horrified about how far Rich had swum. They all made remarks about the various ways they had envisaged him drowning. Nobody was being terribly humorous. The women sounded angry, Rich noticed and felt amused. He heard it as the difficulty of bearing the huge relief.

'We should talk about this after a few drinks,' said Simes, still sounding tense. 'I'm leaving the boat here for the night. We don't have time to get to Fort Augustus and back up today. And there's something about a friend half-drowning that takes the fun out of a trip.'

'I'm not half-drowned. I'm completely undrowned. Best way to be, I always say.'

They weren't ready for Rich's sarcastic humour yet. They called two cabs from a nearby village and hardly spoke a word during the one-hour drive to Achnasheen. Rich could sense their nerves settling, even hear their breathing getting deeper. He also sensed that their mental images of him dying an unseen death in dark waters were fading, but he guessed everyone would retain one or two images, maybe for life.

Later that night Rich went off to phone his sister. He wanted to stroll through the storm so he went to the public phone box in the village. He danced along the street, loving the storm, the sensual storm, the same one that six hours earlier he felt might kill him. The lonely Highlands felt rapturous.

'Hi, Denny.'

'Rich, do you know what time it is?'

'Nope, and I don't care. How the hell are you?'

'Fine. And tired. Have you been drinking?'

'*Moi*! Drinking?! But of course. Copious quantities. Seriously, how are you? Do you miss your wee brother?'

'Yes, Rich, I miss you. Is that enough? Can we sleep now?'

'You still having that fucked-up relationship with Mike? Course you are. Force of habit. You are wonderful and must get something better. You're such a babe. It'll be no problem.'

'Rich, what are you doing phoning me like this? Are you OK?'

'I'm great, never better. In point of fact, never, ever, ever better. Ever!'

'Really. Well, I'm pleased to be informed of that but I am still tired. And what's more my relationship is not fucked up. And you're my brother, you don't call me a babe.'

Rich put on his John Wayne voice: 'The hell I don't. You are a honey, a catch, pure raw sex and you should feel great to be alive, and grateful. But you don't, you feel like shit.'

'Now let me guess, brat: you've been taking drugs too?'

'Ah sure have sis, and frankly my dear I don't give a damn. I can't wait to see you. I want to see more of you. Since I nearly drowned earlier – it's not worth going into – it occurred to me that we don't see enough of each other.'

'You nearly drowned? What happened? Are you OK?'

'Honestly, never better . . .'

28

'Where are you? You nearly drowned? Rich! What happened?'

'Ah, you're sounding angry: that's because you're panicked because you nearly lost your wee brother, and you love him so much. Anyway I didn't drown and I'll tell you the story another time. But I'll tell you right now, nearly drowning is enough to give you religion.'

'Is it now? What hap . . .'

'Yes. Now, for once, don't be a sad cow, all wrapped up in your sad relationship. And don't snap at me, it bores us both. You should hear the sea crashing here, even just driving through Inverness, it's the sound of beauty and power, life and death, the universe, and all sorts of other wonders . . .'

'Yes, Rich, I'm sure it is, but I hate the sea, it scares me, and it's two thirty in the morning. Are you sure you're OK?'

'Never better – honey! And all that water, all those depths, they don't care it's two thirty, yet they know it is that time, they know everything, they are in touch with everything, the cycles of the moon particularly, and they have to crash at the moment, much like you . . .'

'You're delirious, Rich, maybe it was your near-death experience and maybe it's the shit you've taken, I'm glad you are OK, but I'm tired . . .'

'And the moon says "That's OK waves, you crash on that shore, that boat, whatever your poison," and the moon also decides when fish eat and breed, and even if you, say, take oysters out the sea and stick them in never-changing tanks they will still eat and breed according to the moon, and the moon, the ocean's chum, its tidal mate, is in touch with people, women especially, with menstruation. Did you know that was from the Latin word *mensis*, for month? The regular menstrual cycle and the lunar cycle are the same, twenty-nine and a half days, amazing eh? And we're all born according to menstruation, according to the moon, which is linked to the stars and everything. And then there's Mensa, smart people relate to the moon, OK, that last bit was bollocks, but you get my drift . . .'

'Rich, informative though you are, I'm tired . . .'

'Who wouldn't be in such a fucked-up relationship? You think you can't escape, but that's what I'm phoning you about. I'm here to tell you that you can escape, dead easy. Just leave Mike. So then, that's your life sorted.'

'Oh, so nearly drowning makes you know everything, does it?'

'I know you love me. Did you know that? Ah! You'd forgotten. Remember, we fought all through growing up but hated it when anyone was cruel to the other; nothing made us more angry. Isn't that strange to remember?'

'Eh . . . that's a sweet thing to remember. You must be really drunk if you are being sweet.'

'I can feel you smiling, you don't get much pure love any more, do you? Our lives are passing us by. I nearly died, or at least I though I did, so it had its effect. Anyway, I know about life tonight, maybe just this once, so listen: I love you and you love me and I'm not embarrassed to say it tonight. We should listen to each other, see each other. And you should give Mike the big E.'

'Oh yes, I should listen to you calling me a babe.'

'Why not? What does it matter? What would it matter if I fucked your brains out? I would if I thought it'd help you escape the hell you're in. And I'm sure the pleasure would be all mine.'

'Oh Jesus, Rich! You are disgusting. Mind you, given that you shag anyone who wanders past you, you don't even surprise me. Or flatter me, for that matter.'

'Doesn't matter, I'm too flirty, and so are you. Hey, maybe we inherited the flirt gene? Point is I realise I love you and care about you and wish you would leave Mike to enjoy the rest of your life. I always thought I'd be risking our relationship by saying it – you're so bloody proud – but I know time is short, you know, we are all going to die, we *really* are, so you have to do what needs to be done. And the profound crapness of your so-called relationship is hardly news to you. You could get something that works. You would have tons of choice, you're lovely, my mates all adore you . . .'

'I think I'd prefer a clitoridectomy to any of your mates. Besides, I may have a slightly more positive view, every relationship has tough patches . . .'

'Yes yes yes, tell it to your diary. Hey, that's it! I bet you do tell it to your diary – the truth I mean, not your proud crap. Do you still keep one? Of course you do, you always did, like a secret friend. Remember when you were sixteen you found out I had read it and you wouldn't talk to me for a month? I was angry too, Christ I was raging, I wanted to murder! Everyone, including you. You never understood that: you'd had sex and hadn't told me; I was jealous of Ronnie having sex with you; I was jealous of you having sex at all, and I was jealous of your diary for being closer to you than me; I'd thought we told each other everything. So many things are so clear tonight. I love you, truly, madly, deeply. Even sickly. Any way you want. I love you. Now I've got to go and dance, and you've got to leave Mike. Bye.'

Rich did not go straight back to the lodge. He detoured into the woods, whistling 'Singing in the Rain'. The storm was in full roar. Soon he was dancing, skipping and singing aloud. Twice he fell in the mud. Both times he thought it was the funniest thing that had ever happened to anyone.

He was wearing black dress shoes, all he had with him apart from the Jones booties. As his inappropriate footwear squelched into the darkness and mud, he pictured his booties sinking and the Loch Ness Monster coming across them and putting them on. Then he pictured the seeming reality: his booties, settled on the bottom of the loch, in that blackness stretching back longer than the history of man. It had been there, just beneath his legs, ready to take him. But here he was, alive, and the happiest man in the Highlands.

Welcome to THE SQUIRM SHOW, the funniest show in town. Venue: THE VD CLINIC WAITING ROOM. Featuring: THE DEGRADED.

I love this show. It's full of scum, slappers, puglies, schemies and other arguments for gas chambers. And they all feel ashamed (as they should anyway, VD-ridden or not).

It's a wondrous sense of shame; to be relished. It fills the air; it's stifling, like moisture in the clammy jungle; you can almost touch it. But nobody even wants to acknowledge it. This isn't shared shame. This is deeply personal and very defensive shame; 'Yeuch, I wonder what they've got, bet it's disgusting!'

Everybody must have something that shows how hideous diseased genitals are, except your own of course; 'The doctor said it was just a small infection; it could happen to anyone; it can be treated easily; it doesn't matter [but that bastard/bitch that gave me it should pay!]'

Beyond the waiting room are the AIDS counsellors. Now these are a fun experience: little frumps talking down to you about sex. You can't possibly take them seriously since you catch VD when you go sharking and when you go sharking you give fat, elderly, ugly frumps a wide berth. These do-gooders do not belong in your world, on Planet Sex.

And in the VD clinic we are still very much on Planet Sex: where there are thoughts of VD there are thoughts of sex; where there are thoughts of sex there is frisson; where there is frisson there should not be pious frumps.

33

So you're stuck in a room with one of these frumps offering you sympathy and advice about your predicament when you feel like you should be offering them sympathy for being so ugly and advice about how to cheer up. Why are they always ugly? Is it a prerequisite for the job? Maybe it's a ploy to put you off sex?

But here, in the waiting room, is the best part of the show. Now the girl in the corner, she couldn't be an AIDS counsellor: she's a babe. If she counselled you about condoms you'd ask for a demonstration. She's got her head buried in *Homes and Gardens*; she's determined not to look anyone in the eye. She is dreading someone she knows coming in. Wish I knew her name, so I could shout hello to her.

Such embarrassment; so cute, so sweet, it'd be nice to dirty her up. I can picture my cum dribbling down her serious little face, a tiny stream running by the corner of her mouth, her tongue sliding out to lick it, she savours it, swallowing slowly . . . I bet she hasn't even got a home or a garden, probably a student.

Students are great. They let you do anything to them and they think it is crazy and anarchic and daring of them. Mind you, sex is all they're good for.

This guy beside me, he's grinning away. He doesn't care who sees him. He looks almost proud to be here. I wouldn't go that far, mate.

And the couple over there, they look happy. Wonder who's caught it? Or who gave it to who? Why is one of them not raging about it?

Lordy lordy, how did that catch VD? Surely nobody has been inside it? How could they get their cock through all that flesh? She's so fat she's not fat; she is another shape, something for kids to play with, like the Honey Monster, a Weebles Wobble, a teletubby, a Spacehopper. Must be a phantom infection.

That girl just along from me, don't want to turn to look too much; quite pretty but looks terrified. First timer, I'll wager. How well I recall my first time; feeling like a contaminated, shameful piece of putrefying humanity. I imagine it's similar for women, only more so. So don't worry wee sweetie; it passes. I felt turned off, and like a turn-off, for, oh let's see now, three hours? It's like a second virginity; your very first dose, you poor thing, come rest your weary genitals on my face (so long as it's not herpes).

The two scummy nerds look odd, sort of restless yet lifeless; like junkies waiting to buy whizz. Is one of them chumming the other? Or have they both got VD? They've both certainly got serious cosmetic conditions. That skin is expensive; you have to spend a lot on drugs for that special grey translucence. And his mate, Mr Spotty Sallow, that requires Evostick surely? Bit old for that, aren't you, lads?

Ah-ha! Mr Translucence's eyes. Sorry chaps, I belittled you. Whizz and Evostick? How could I? Those pinhead pupils clearly state heroin, nothing less. Wouldn't mind a wee sniff myself. You two are probably dumbfuck mainliners.

Ah-ha again! I know why you're here together! (As if your type would ever wait for each other; most slow of me.) You shagged the same slapper, didn't you? Probably one after the other? Probably at the same drugs-fuelled party? Eh lads? She must have been out of her face to have you two. Did she even know she was at the party? You don't look like you are above jelly-banging. I can see you, quietly filling her drink with temazepam, then when she falls asleep, gleefully filling her cunt with cockcheese. You'd chew your own foot off for a consignment of Rohypnol, wouldn't you? Oh yes, I have your number. I bet even your parents don't like you.

My turn, I don't like this bit. It's just the waiting room which amuses me. I hope to God he doesn't stick that little umbrella up my cock. It doesn't really hurt that much. It's the

35

anticipation that tortures. That moment you see the cold metal, you urgently want to not be there, you even want to faint to get away. But the worst moment is a few seconds away yet; the doctor steadies your cock with one hand and brings the umbrella close to it with the other, and then it happens, you feel the metal touching, being jabbed in to scrape. That instant is enough to put you off sex. Almost.

The thought that kills me, even more than the anticipation, is: why is this fucking arsewipe of a guy fucking doing this? I mean, gynaecologist! What kind of a fucking job is that? What miserable weirdo fuckwit wants to spend their days looking at diseased genitals? I mean, fine if they went to work on a maternity ward, the miracle of birth and so on, if that's your trip – but seven year's training in order to spend your days looking at warts, smelling discharge, prodding inflamed genitals, messing around with piss, staring at schemies' reproduction equipment and not being allowed to cut it off. What mind chooses to do that?

That mind calls this the Genito-urinary clinic, or the STD unit, or something else again, but it's all messing about with words. We, the punters, cannot avoid the truth. We know we're here because we have good, old-fashioned VD; two resplendent little letters conveying the eternal truth about our grubby condition. There's no getting round it.

This doctor looks sane, very cheerful, a lot of jokes about VD, but he must be mad. He's about to stick a metal brolly up a cock that he has just diagnosed as being surrounded by pubic lice. And he studied hard to get into this situation.

I want to say: 'Wake up and smell the coffee. Wake up and smell anything other than diseased genitals. Live a little. Are you aware, Mr Intelligent Upstanding Member of the Community, that you are spending your life fondling bits of humanity which the rest of the world doesn't want to exist? Are you aware you're a very sick man?' But one doesn't unleash satire on someone who is about to stick a small metal brolly up one's cock.

Like I suspected, I probably just have pubic lice. My old friends. Back for a brief visit. Two days of special wash and they'll be completely gone, hopefully. (Don't want them hanging round for the weekend. Nothing worse than unwelcome guests at the weekend.)

Now as I depart and glance around this waiting room, everyone sneaks a wee glance at me and has one last thought about my genitals. It's the bizarre nature of life; in here we picture strangers' genitals, more lucidly and more compulsively than at any other time, but they are guaranteed to be diseased. They are at their least attractive, never less worth picturing.

And as I exit, I ask myself, 'should I be angry?' Probably. Most people get angry with whoever gives them VD, but I'm not. She's fine, it was an accident. It's just basic animal instinct to be angry, to be protective of one's genitals; the source of life and route to unbeatable thrills and pleasure. Where would we all be without our genitals? We wouldn't even exist. People aren't grateful enough for genitals.

Even when they're diseased we shouldn't be too put off. Lice, gonorrhoea, chlamydia, warts and almost all infections: no sweat. AIDS, Hepatitis B, Hepatitis C and that thing in Cuba that turns your dick green and leaves you impotent: big sweat. I feel grateful for the time my genitals are fine, which is most of the time.

hi eileen, enjoyed the weekend. hope you did too. I have some faintly bad news for you. I don't know how to say this gently: you've got pubic lice. you gave me them on saturday. nona problema. just get thee to a VD clinic. they'll give you malathion which will wash them away in 2–3 days: bob's your uncle and back on the pull by friday. if you're embarrassed to go you can buy it over the counter at the chemist, or borrow some off me (tragically I always have some) but I suggest you go to the clinic and get a full check-up.

yours in flea-bitten affiliation,
rich

Rich, I'm really, really sorry. I'm so embarrassed. I just went to the toilet and checked. It's horrible. I don't know how I didn't notice before. I feel rancid. I can't finish the day at work but I've got a meeting with the MD; I've got to. I'm going to sit in the bath all night. It's disgusting. I've never had anything before. I slept with this American guy in London three weeks ago. It must have been him. I've had this for three weeks! Please don't tell anyone. Rich I am so sorry. Is it really as easy to deal with as you say? Will there be any long-term consequences? I am truly sorry. PLEASE PLEASE don't tell anyone.

With deep regret
Eileen

eileen, panic not. I won't tell a soul, maybe just a wee emailshot, a small website, the odd billboard, but nothing you won't laugh about in years to come. it really is cured that easily and there are no long-term consequences, except for feeling like a slapper for a while. don't feel bad. worse things happen in beds. are you sure you have never caught anything else? . . .

yours in gnawed genital bonding,
rich

Rich, please don't turn this on me. And please don't think I'm a slapper. I did once have NSU but antibiotics got rid of it in a week. Since then I've always used condoms, except a few times, including you. I used a condom with the American guy.

I thought he was too casual, like he does this a lot. I didn't exactly feel special. Christ I could throttle the shit head. I guess condoms don't keep pubic lice off? Honestly I've never had anything worse than NSU and thrush.

Yours with all my regret, apologies and thanks
Eileen

eileen my dearest, so you've 'never had anything before' then you've had 'nsu', then 'nsu and thrush'. that's a lot of progress in two emails. what will you have had in five emails' time? a regiment of fusiliers? . . . 'tis but a jest, it's hard not to be amused at your embarrassment, especially since you are on safe ground. I know you too well and like you too much to judge you about what you've caught or done.

i also know it's none of my business (isn't it great the way that announces 'i'm going to stick my nose in', like the way 'i don't mean to be rude' rings out like 'i mean to be rude'?) but I was under the impression that you returned from london six weeks ago . . . and you have slept with at least one person other than me since your return . . . and honesty is always the best policy, as i'm sure your dour Highland parents repeatedly informed you . . . and if you're caught hiding something, people will assume you have lots to hide . . . and next thing you are rated the biggest slapper in edinburgh . . . and then you get depressed and start sleeping around even more in order to feel wanted and prove to yourself you don't care . . . but this just lowers your self-esteem and the pattern spirals . . . and where would it all end young lady? in suicide? in a brothel? or, even worse, in a marriage? . . .

yours in scratching sincerity,
rich

Rich, that's true, I did sleep with James. Maybe it was him? I thought everyone knew about the American guy; Moira was with me and I knew she would tell people, so I told people. So just now I put the blame on him, but I guess you heard about James. I forgot you were friends with him. I'll sort it out. Sorry again, I'm just so embarrassed.

Yours in all honesty
Eileen

eileen, my lovely, naïve, youthful amateur, I know you are no slapper, just going through a wee phase, boredom, hormones, fun, attention, experimenting, drunk; I know not. and judge you not, but, er, it wasn't james I heard about. i'll not say any names and we can skip the guessing games and further embarrassments.

yours in itchy confidentiality,
rich

Rich, who do you know about?
e

eileen, surely there is only one other?
r

Rich, you cheeky schwein, OK I've been on a roll. I don't know what's got into me. Well, I know four men have got into me since London. Tell anyone and I'll kill you.
e

eileen, this roll you've been on, did it begin in adolescence? mine did.
r

Rich, honest, just recently. I think I regretted a couple so I just continued to sleep with more, maybe a bit like the pattern you describe. I don't understand, I already felt cheap so I sort of switched off and just went with it. This lice feels like my comeuppance. And I feel like shit. So, please, who did you know about? What do other people know? I feel really awful.

e

eileen, search me about what others know. I knew nothing, it was just you said three weeks since london when I knew it was six, so I thought I would try to wheedle the truth out of you. got to pass the time somehow in the office. otherwise I could end up doing some work, and that's against my principles on a tuesday. so, just four eh? not a bad strike rate, so long as they weren't too dreadful a four.

r

Rich! You are lower than the slime on a snail's belly!

But I trust you. Going to Alex's on Friday?

e

eileen, I resent that. a snake's belly maybe, gliding across the ground, but not a snail, right down in the mud, that's too much.

catch you at alex's.

tons of love and trust and confidences,

r

'Hi Denny, how's it going?'

'Good. What is my little alcoholic brother doing in at eleven thirty at night?'

'Denny, I am not an alcoholic, I am not an alcoholic, I am NOT an ALCOHOLIC! OK I'm in denial. Actually I'm sitting here sipping a wee bottle of Chenin Blanc, bit tipsy in fact.'

'Just a wee bottle?'

'Well, wee if you think of a magnum. Normal size really.

41

Got another in the fridge. I'm not a well man, it's these bugs that are going about. You should be sympathetic to your sick little brother.'

'I've long known you're sick. And long run out of sympathy. You don't have to phone me to tell me that. Is it flu?'

'Not exactly. Bugs; I used the plural advisedly. It's pubic lice.'

'Oh God, now you're even more disgusting than ever. I'm definitely not sleeping with you now!'

'You mean you thought about it before? I'm sorry, I was delirious when I joked about that, that night.'

'I thought about it but it made me throw up, so I stopped thinking about it.'

'Thou dost mock too cruelly, wicked temptress!'

'Listen up, Tartboy. Have you got some malathion?'

'Ah-ha! You know the name of it, Miss Goody-Two-Shoes, Miss I'm-too-tasty-for-the-likes-of-my-lovely-wee-brother!'

'But I've never had call to use it . . .'

'Yeah, sure . . .'

'Have you told whoever gave you it, and anyone you could have given it to?'

'Yes, yes, emailed Eileen today. Got quite a confessional out of her; five guys in the last seven weeks, my kind of woman.'

'Was she OK?'

'Tickety-boo, just embarrassed.'

'Who is she? Why is she sleeping with all these guys? Just a slapper?'

'Dunno about the rest. She's really lovely. I think she sleeps with me to avoid regretting the last time she slept with me. You know, to make it seem meaningful, like a quasi-relationship.'

'You must like her, have you ever thought about a relation-ship with her?'

'Goodness gracious me, wash your mouth out! Why on earth would I want to ruin good sex?'

'Sex within relationships is the best.'

'Funny you should say that, because sex within relationships is in fact DEATHLY DULL!'

'You are showing your limited experience, brat. Has it occurred to you that maybe this Eileen is hurt by you. Maybe she wishes you wanted a relationship with her?'

'Of course she wishes that; she's a woman! Therefore she would very much like me to want a relationship with her. But just so she feels wanted. She doesn't want one with me. That's women for you; they want to be wanted even if they don't want you. All bitches.'

'How do you know she feels like that? Have you asked her? *Puer eternus*, that's you.'

'Pray tell, what bollocks are you talking? That was an insult, yes?

'*Puer eternus*; the eternal boy. It's a precious and likeable aspect, which a man carries through life . . .'

'Couldn't agree more, I'm precious and likeable. Is this your way of admitting you fancy me?'

'No, brat. The *puer eternus* should be one aspect among many. It's all there is to you.'

'Oh dear, taking psychology seriously, you must be really depressed. Sorry, didn't realise you were that desperate.'

'I'm not depressed. You are a brat. Simple as that.'

'No, you just say that because you see me as your wee brother, instead of the mature sex machine which I am.'

'All guys think they are magnificent sex machines and pity the poor wretches that can't see it.'

'Absolutely; most men have that delusion. I, by contrast, have no need of it since my irresistible sexuality is an empirical fact. Anyway, women are still all bitches, including Eileen. She might feel rejected by me and she might try to hide from the rejection by sleeping with me again, but truth is she is actually after another guy, some guy called Johnny.'

'Really? It's not going to help her get him if he finds out about the lice. Is she going to have to tell all those other guys she slept with?'

'Probably, she isn't sure who gave her it. Poor thing; she only caught it at the weekend off me.'

'What?! And you blamed her?!'

'Yeah.'

'Richard! You irresponsible, selfish coward!'

'Come, come, dear sis, I had no choice. She would have been mad with me. She might have told people. And people love passing on VD gossip. They would spread rumours, rumours which are true, rumours which could detrimentally affect my sharking chances in Edinburgh. And we couldn't have that, could we? I mean, I live here: this is my town.'

'Rich! You are a horrendous misogynist. Jesus!'

'I'm not a misog . . .'

'You're right, misogyny suggests depth. Christ, after you nearly drowned, you said you were going to be more responsible! Honest, Rich, how could you do that?'

'Piece of piss, this woman, a wanton hussy methinks, from Glasgow, phoned me last night to tell me she gave me the lice two nights before I slept with Eileen, so Eileen is the only person I've given it to. We'll both use the wash. It's all in hand, and in two days' time I'll have unusually clean pubic hairs. Like to see them? . . .'

dear Captain
My name is Nicola im 8
years. old, this is my first
flight but im not scared. I
like to watch the clouds go
by. My mum says the crew is
nice. I think your plane is
good. thanks for a nice flight
don't fuck up the landing
            LuV Nicola
                  xx xx

Thursday, 6th April

Karen emailed me this pic handed to a flight attendant on a Qantas flight by an eight-year-old girl; it was lying around on the net. So I don't know Nicola but she makes me smile each time I look at her drawing. I cherish the idea that I will have a child so spirited and amusing. Obviously you would have to scold her, but it would be hard to keep a straight face. Normally I smile at that drawing anticipating my own little Nicola, except tonight. After what I heard today, I am no longer confident that I want children, at least as long as I'm with Mike. (I heard it when I was 'with' Aaron today; that ought to say it all anyway). I used to think we were heading for children, regardless of the hell. Leaving aside the somewhat tricky matter of me not necessarily knowing who the father would be, what chance would a child have being conceived in this house of bile? I don't think it would be a happy little Nicola handing hilarious letters to air hostesses.

At least I know it. Women are great at denial, but not me. Some stupid cows think having a kid will repair their relationship, all evidence to the contrary. You just end up with a miserable child to boot, feeding off and into your misery. I'm sure your previous troubles seem a mere trifle with this new life in the house, but pretty soon they reinvent themselves, appearing in other guises to fit the new circumstance. You might as well be one of those little schemie slappers; age fifteen and can't wait to drop a sprog. And have, at last, something that won't leave you, something that will – seemingly – always love you, something that will prove you have a purpose. And you'll be terminally pathetic and desperate.

But the fact is, I only now see that before today I still wanted Mike's child. I wanted to believe it could yet work out. I hadn't abandoned hope. There was no real difference between me, the stupid cows and the schemie slappers. But now there is. Aaron told me a true horror story. In so doing he ripped out my beautiful desire for a child. Is that possible?

He told me it in the pub after sex. (He likes me but is disappointed with me sexually. I just want to do fluffy stuff; I get enough kink and gymnastics at home. He laughed, said that it should be the other way round, said he always gets things the wrong way round.) He's a court solicitor and on Thursday this woman came into his office. She drinks too much, does drugs by the bucketload and has shagged half of Edinburgh. She used to give Aaron blow jobs in the office when he fought a case for her two years ago. She sort of tears through life.

However she is not a standard issue loser. She's enigmatic, extraordinarily intelligent, good-looking, witty, confident: quite a trip. Strangest thing is people always react to her.

Often she fascinates them. She has umpteen adoring friends. But sometimes people hate her. They talk of her strange presence quite fearfully. But even those people usually concede she has something special about her. How she's still alive seems special enough.

She often tries to come off drink, drugs, being a slut and so on. She always fails. Therapy, steady boyfriend, detox clinics, moving abroad, even becoming a counsellor herself: nothing ever works for her.

Two weeks ago she was up in court for theft, her third such offence. She pled guilty, no choice, that wasn't a problem, just another fine. But the Sheriff didn't like her. She angered him, for no obvious reason. So the wig, as she called him, deferred sentence until he receives a social enquiry report. In other words he's thinking about sending her to jail. Even the prosecutor was astounded.

He needs a social enquiry report before he can imprison someone who hasn't been imprisoned before. Since this is not her first offence of this type she's eligible for up to twelve months in jail, more likely to get a few weeks or months, but she's still petrified. Aaron had never before sensed any fear – of anything – off her. He says there is an amazing distance between her and everything around her. It's otherworldly, her allure. 'You wouldn't be surprised if she levitated.'

And now she's slightly lost that quality. She's petrified because she knows this enquiry will find the same as all her doctors, therapists, counsellors, lovers and family over the years; absolutely nothing. That is, no mitigating circumstances.

She can't prove to the social worker who'll be doing the enquiry, due in four weeks, that she had a difficult childhood, or has dependant children, or a heroin problem, or a violent lover, or terrible financial woes, or any such thing. She believes she'll go to jail for not having any problems, for not being a bloody victim.

She does have an Achilles heel; a fear of enclosed spaces and darkness. Even as a tot she couldn't sleep unless the light was on and the door or window open. If somebody switched off the light or closed the window when she was asleep she'd wake up almost instantly and wail like the damned. She knows claustrophobia will not excuse her crimes in the report, especially since it has never been formally diagnosed. She senses that jail is her nemesis.

It's all because she nicked a few hundred quid from work. She held down a job, somehow, as a paralegal in a posh solicitor's office. And the firm were throwing the book at her in court. Normally they wouldn't give a shit, just sack her and make her repay the money. That way they avoid anyone knowing somebody dishonest had worked in the firm. But a senior partner loathed her, like the Sheriff, so much that he'd watched and waited, and after a long, patient year he caught her. And he wants her done.

Aaron was a good one for her to go to. He's a deeply disillusioned guy, no professional loyalty. He's got a failed marriage and a great career (again he thinks he's getting life the wrong way round). He certainly doesn't like the way the other lawyer's office is treating this girl. She was a star in the litigation department. Within six months she was politely correcting experienced partners and handling complicated cases herself. She was paid shit of course, and had the gall to notice, and she hated the way some of the snooty partners treated her and the others, so she put her hand in the till. It paid for wild weekends in London.

Aaron is really seized by an urge to help her. To him, it is critical that someone so special should not languish in a scuzzy jail. Also, on a prosaic level, he knows she's a good person. He says he doesn't care 'one iota about nicking off a huge, mercenary company which will merrily absorb your life and crush your spirit for profit's sake.' Also, like all lawyers, he doesn't care about the law, in moral terms; 'Laws are just the rules for the game you're paid to win. Principle isn't in it. Victory is all.' And Aaron is an excellent player.

But this time he is not even involved in the case. And neither her lawyer nor Aaron has any real role to play in the social enquiry report. She came in on Thursday out of desperation, asking for help, which is way out of character. She remembered from two years before how Aaron was always so scathing about law. She wanted to know what she can say to the social worker, if there are any tricks she can use?

He started banging on at her about her parents, and all the usual, and she tried to convince him that she has a sound memory and definitely wasn't abused. And she knows she seems like an abuse case. But it seems like her only chance, so Aaron persisted with questions about her parents and she continued with answers.

Then suddenly Aaron realised he had met her parents. He liked them. He even took their phone number. They were an old couple, New Town types, but not snobs; very bright, cheery and almost well-to-do. He met them at a dinner party, sat beside him.

He remembers a particular conversation with them about work, them talking about how hard they worked, and saying what a sad waste of life offices are. But he remembers their determination to send their kids to good schools, like they never went to, and their joking about loans and extending the mortgage and part-time work in order to pay the school fees. They were partly laughing at themselves, partly celebrating that they made it.

These were good, passionate parents. He remembered them clearly. And they were also parents who sent their kids to boarding school. They talked about how much they missed the kids, but were happy it gave them more time to work and earn money. They were both entirely unselfconscious about

49

their penniless backgrounds; an unusual and likeable trait in the New Town.

Now if two parents work that hard for their kids' education and then send them out the house, where they are unavailable for abuse, of any sort, there is little point asking the child how her parents abused her. However, the doctors, social workers and shrinks had stood by the theory that this was a classic abuse victim if ever there was one, boarding school or not.

Aaron thought not. Once he realised who she was, or rather who her parents were, he asked her to leave. No more questions, but she must return next week when he had thought of something for the social worker.

As soon as she left the room Aaron phoned her mother to see if he could find out anything helpful. Her mother burst into tears. She was so happy to hear about her daughter, to establish contact. She started rambling about how only her brother – not her or her husband – has had any contact with her these last six months. They had a stupid argument and the strong-willed daughter won't speak to them. And now the mother doesn't think about anything else any more. She wants her daughter back.

She loves her daughter. Her birth was the happiest moment in her father's life. Both of them cried, even a few days later they would still bubble. They couldn't believe their luck, that after trying for nine years and after five miscarriages, they finally got a sister for the brother. They were dazed. Nothing had ever been this precious in the world to anyone before. They went to church a lot. She was Catholic, he was Church of Scotland; some Sundays they went to both churches together, just to try to find a way to thank God.

Cynical Aaron was touched by this. He was thinking about that and thinking about his grubby profession and the way the odds are stacked against this strange girl who had such a joyous birth. He's reassured her, but can't see what to do.

Truth is he knows some people in the firm that's doing her, they're nice enough but it's too late to talk to them and try to persuade them to drop the charges. Anyway they're just the usual company morons, not likely to argue about a decision from on top, you know, promotion and all that, five years of grant loans and two years of trainee wages to get to their position and then to risk being frozen out by partners because they defended a paralegal who got caught on the filch. Unlikely. That would require principle.

He has no way of influencing this case and he's on the phone listening to this woman pouring her heart out to him, also needing help, which he feels she deserves but, again, he cannot deliver. Then he feels even guiltier because the mother remembers the dinner party they met at and is gracious enough, amid all her emotions, to accurately recall details about Aaron and ask about his divorce and how such and such a case went. She even says that he was a wise young man, but he's not feeling wise, he feels like a fraud who is part of the profession that's doing her daughter, a fraud who promised this sweet woman's daughter something he cannot deliver.

For once he wants to deliver. He's delivered for scum often enough, and this girl is a one-off, something so strange and strong, so needing preserved.

The mother is still rambling on, still grateful to hear about her daughter. She wants to stay on the phone. Tentatively he enquires if she knows much about her daughter's lifestyle. She does, and she informs Aaron about the porn film, the injecting and the competition with her friend to see who could give the most blow jobs in an evening; she even uses the phrase 'blow job' and adds that her daughter won.

Aaron's quite aghast. He realises that none of it fazes the old biddy one bit. She talks about it all casually, as trite details.

51

She doesn't feel judgmental or reviled. For her that would be like being disgusted with your baby for shitting in its nappy. She just worries and loves her daughter, simple and pure.

That night Aaron couldn't sleep. He phoned an ex-girlfriend very late. He knew her husband was out of town. She was still awake and she likes him so she listened while he told her the story.

The ex kept returning to the five miscarriages the mother had before the special woman was born. She kept saying how traumatic that must have been for her. Then she brought up the abortion she had to Aaron and said that maybe that was one of the things that caused them to drift apart.

She had been determined to get to the end of her Ph.D in Restoration Drama and he was doing the post-grad law diploma. Neither wanted to be led astray. So she didn't want the baby. But she also felt that because she didn't want it she absolutely had to get rid of it; otherwise it would be an unwanted foetus, and unwanted child, and it would know. It's always been something she has had trouble explaining. It exists on another level from the obvious practical considerations. She still feels a bit guilty about it, like she must be a fundamentally selfish and unloving woman, she's never properly got over it.

When she has her first child she knows it will feel like her second, as though the first one died, as though she killed it. But it might help now she's with this other guy; it might feel like only a sort of a half-second child. It was all very spooky for her.

Aaron hung up, with her words ringing in his ears. He set about two bottles of wine, sadly no big deal for him, and tried to figure what's so special about this woman.

He's an inveterate cynic and he hates himself for it. Some people believe in humanity, but he can't. I think he's read too many bleak history books. He always quotes Adolf Hitler in

Mein Kampf: 'Never underestimate the mindlessness of the masses.' Others believe the world is interesting. Aaron says it's on its way down to hell and nothing can stop it; you only have to look at it getting uglier each decade and think of all the destruction man has wrought. The environmentalists are just pissing in the wind, apparently.

The one key word he clings to is life. So he's trying to figure how this girl touches his life, what it is about her unique vitality, her distance, her intelligence.

He is so cynical he has virtually no frames of reference. He can't work her out, but she's really disturbed him. She's made him think about his own complacency, how he doesn't care about anything. He hates catching sight of this, but he has faced it before, that he has no spiritual or intellectual life.

He says he would perish if his spirit were tried, because it's weak from lack of nourishment. For example he says he wouldn't have been a survivor in the concentration camps (more bleak history references). He says he would have been one of the 'proud, glib guys who saw the Nazis for the banal pantomime fantasists they were', and he'd probably have mentioned it to them, on an arrogant ego-trip. He probably wouldn't have been calm and joined in well-planned resistance. He'd just have been hauled off to the camps.

Once there he wouldn't have been able to handle the horror, to remain motivated and rise above the evil. The ones who survived, who ducked and dived and kept their wits and never gave in to the seemingly inevitable, were people of faith. It wasn't remarkable individuals or even particularly good individuals such as in the films, though they might be those things too. However historians discovered it was hard-line communists, orthodox Jews, strict Christians and so on who were far more likely to survive than the natural rebels, criminals, self-appointed Nazi haters and all the other people who fell foul of the regime. At the outer limits of human endurance, faith triumphs.

Aaron hates knowing that. He hates knowing that faith and strength are the same. Life has its trials and leads to death, he says, like the concentration camps. It's just there's good stuff too, but it's all relative. In the camps they would laugh and feel joyous at the sight of fresh fruit, which we take for granted. So, even in normal life – in all life – faith is critical.

He's drinking and turning all this round in his head, still searching for an understanding of the special woman and her life-force; that's the only word he can find for it. And how it's led him to thinking about himself. Maybe it's the way she couldn't survive in a concentration camp either? Maybe not even in jail? And he's her last chance.

He has a final thought about his ex's abortion, thinks how the child would have been eight now. Then he thinks of all his friends' abortion stories, all those ghosts, all those good people carrying a sadness.

About 5.00 a.m. he gets to sleep. He dreams there are zombies stumbling around his flat, wailing and looking for him. He takes cover beneath the bed where it's warm; he's lying in goo, bloody afterbirth goo, then he's escaped to the street, a foreign street with lots of stucco architecture: it's exotic, maybe the Spanish interior; he's running along, passing people standing in arches and wearing garish clothes like a festival is on, and they all glance at him, surreptitiously, and then at each other, knowingly; but he saw the glances, he knows they're zombies, and he has to escape before they know he knows . . .

He woke at 10.00 a.m., late for work. He phoned in and went to shave. Watching his face in the mirror change into a slightly different face as the foam and bristles come off, he muttered in a hammy 50s horror voice: 'The undead. The undead. And the unborn. And let's not forget the unlived, too, boys and girls. Oh yes it's a full horror story tonight.'

Then he got dressed and put the coffee maker on. The switch clicked, the light went on and that instant he knew all about the special woman. Just like that. Something inside. He was excited but petrified. He had to check.

He phoned the mother and asked how she felt about all those miscarriages before the special woman was born. For the first time she was defensive, and asked what he thought she felt? He apologised but wouldn't be put off. She said she never really talks about it. It just slipped out last night when he phoned.

Then she said it was a terrible time before the special woman was born. She started to cry and say how wonderful her husband was during it all, how most men wouldn't have been strong enough. Aaron listened but he was just waiting to push her, carefully, to where he could pin her down. He knew what she was going to say, but still, he had to hear it, coming out her mouth.

She slowed crying. Gently, he pushed her: 'Sorry I don't mean to pry, I just wanted to know how you, personally, felt. It sounds extremely traumatic.' She paused, and then she said it: that she felt nervous and scared and unworthy, more so each time she got pregnant. By the time it got to being pregnant with the special woman she was exhausted. She really couldn't bear to hope. 'I only wanted to miscarry and get the trauma over with. I hated the pregnancy, hated the foetus, hoped it would die, soon! I felt like it had invaded my body and was making me mad.' Right up until she went into labour she was convinced it would die. For nine months she had willed it to die. That's what the pregnancy amounted to: a battle of wills between her and her unborn child.

The spirit of the special woman had fought hard for a life inside the mother, where five had died. And, more than the previous five, the special woman was unwanted; the mother said, 'It was more distressing, more hateful each time.' The special woman's first experience of life was fighting to exist.

Aaron thought about her passion for life, her claustrophobia, the distance between her and everything, the way she could only depend on herself, but boy could she do it. Suddenly it seemed so basic and obvious. But it was also scary, too real. He felt close to some strange realm, some place where life comes from.

And to Aaron, and me, it shows that the rot can start in the womb. As soon as life is released from that strange realm into the womb it is available for humans to affect, define, nurture or corrupt. Aaron says the strange woman makes him think that we don't create life at all; it is just our responsibility to look after it, whether it is our own lives or the lives of our children. It just passes through us.

I can't have a child with Mike. It would have nothing in common with the special woman (he wouldn't reveal her name; client confidentiality, he can't break the habit, not even during pillow talk). But it would arrive from that other place to soak up Mike and my's sad and troubled world, while just a foetus. What a welcoming.

Friday, 7th May

Aaron invited me for a celebratory drink with his 'special woman' tonight. Her name is Lucy and she 'got off by seducing the social worker and telling a pile of lies'. I was awestruck by her, hardly noticed her strong, handsome face at first; so struck by her penetrating eye contact and – dare I use that horrible hippy word – aura. She knew I was a therapist and didn't mind all my questions. Not a complex or insecurity in sight. I asked about her parents and she said; 'Yeah, I've rung them now, just couldn't be bothered before, they're so needy.' I finally understood, a little. Neediness is what she can never understand. She has never needed anyone and cannot believe anyone might really need her. For all her mesmerising presence, *joie de vivre* and friends, she may be the loneliest person I have ever met. Fated to be lonely from birth.

There is a moment which is so beautiful and pure, it eclipses all other moments and all other memories of all other moments. This moment is so absorbing that it is difficult to recall later.

The Moment does not come easily. A lot of money and time must be invested to attain The Moment, yet it cannot be planned, nor foretold by any means. Theoretically, all mankind can experience this moment but, in practice, only the serious drinker will do so.

The Moment happens when the serious drinker has purchased, but has not yet tasted, a drink; a particular drink, particularised not by type or brand, but by timing and the drinker's state of being.

It is the first drink of a certain evening. This evening, or more precisely the wondrous moment within it, has taken days, if not weeks, to build up to; not that the drinker has been abstaining during that time, for that would yield a different moment, an expected, lesser one.

Similarly, this mysterious moment has nothing to do with the facile appeasement of the shakes or the monotony of clicking into familiar drunkenness. The shakes are not present at any point and immediate drunkenness will not be forthcoming. This moment is all about extreme pleasure, indeed rapture, and it is the sole province of the vastly underrated borderline alcoholic. That condition is the key. But the name is all wrong.

The word alcoholic should not be associated with those who achieve The Moment. An alcoholic is permanently drunk. Thus he (or she) sustains the subconscious belief that alcohol is an ever-replenishing antidote to anguish. If he remained sober for any length of time, this ridiculous belief would burble up to his consciousness, making him feel bereft and silly. That is the only interesting moment an alcoholic, with luck, can expect.

Furthermore, nobody on a borderline experiences wonderful moments. A border is a constricting space around an invisible line which will be crossed, dully, inevitably. The only interesting moment that can happen to one at a border crossing is the moment of arrest, which is distinctly lacking in wonderfulness. The man who is known as a borderline alcoholic is not confined to such a narrow space. On the contrary, he leaps across that space, from sobriety to drunkenness, back and forth as he pleases, taking what he chooses from each state each time, returning over the border when he gets fed up. His drinking is not a problem. It is a spiritual visa.

With this visa, the serious drinker can get to The Moment, but the visa is just one of two necessities. The other is the journey to The Moment, and that can only be embarked upon unwittingly.

Arrival at The Moment comes after an indefinable struggle has taken place over an unknown period of time. In so far as this prelude battle can be understood, it is assumed to be, primarily, between chemicals inside the drinker, but it may also be between chemicals inside the drinker and things outside the drinker and therefore between moods: moods affected by the world around the drinker, moods in the widest and therefore most incomprehensible yet most influential sense. And so on out, further and further, into the physical and metaphysical worlds, on into the alignment of the stars: this is a big moment.

All that is clear is that the chemical and spiritual equilibrium needed for this moment cannot be contrived. There are a few, mostly vague and unhelpful, guidelines. The drinker may or may not use drugs; help or hindrance, drugs do both and it's often difficult to detect which. The drinker must not have had a recent big life event; it would bear down and intrude on The Moment. He has probably been busy the day The Moment is achieved and he has certainly been drinking heavily for at least two weeks, yet he did not have a hangover this morning, even though he possibly seemed to merit it. His life will surely have been a blurry but manageable affair of late, up until The Moment, which is of poetic clarity.

The drinker feels good, no panic, even before the drink is purchased, so this moment is not begot from any craving. The drinker may even have had a couple at lunchtime. Perhaps he then had to return to work, and then work late, so that he has arrived in the pub after 8.00 p.m. to discover that he has had the divine moment bestowed upon him. Good fortune and an absence of planning are the mysterious forces behind The Moment.

The Moment can occur in pubs or at home. With the latter, loneliness, the eternal dampner, lurks. Yet the drinker should, ideally, be alone, perhaps in the sanctioning pub but without a social context holding him back from full immersion in The Moment. If he is with friends, he will have to become oblivious to them to experience The Moment.

You can tell when a man has attained this higher state; he will regard his alcoholic beverage before imbibing, but not in the usual, ritual way, with an appreciative smile. He gazes for a few seconds with wonder and respect at the glass of alcohol, which he does not touch; it sits there in isolated glory, on the bar or table, while he savours The Moment. He looks far away yet very alert. Worries are gone, memories are accessible but unwanted, plans unnecessary. He is emptied of everything pertaining to the rest of his life. And excitement is infusing

61

his entire, tingling being. He is pausing in order to relish that powerful but delicate feeling and to give it time to do its beautiful utmost. At this moment, in the pub, the drinker has achieved the perfection of alcoholic consumption.

It is a state of being to which few other moments in this frustrating life can aspire. Even that thrilling moment when one's long lusted-after love object has finally succumbed to a bout in bed has elements of impurity, of doubt; performance, disappointment, disease, pregnancy and the knowledge of experience whispering in your ear 'It never works out', even as you undress. There are no such taints on The Moment. This will work out.

It already has done. The desire is itself the contentment. The actual drinking is only necessary in so far as it will be done. The process of doing it is of no consequence. Before that first guaranteed mouthful, yearning, a seemingly omni-present aspect of being alive, is finally absent.

And for the rest of the evening anything seems possible. But it will be good; from this high it would take more than an evening to reach a low.

All this, Simes contemplated while staring at his cold, brown bottle of golden Pils lager. He thought about what would happen if this moment could be extended to everyone and prolonged indefinitely. He imagined the entire human race sitting in pubs gazing silently at bottles of Pils, suspended in the glow of anticipation; wars cancelled, work stations deserted, no needs, no desires, no sex, eventually no people, and no matter; the human race closed down in bliss.

He stretched out his hand. He touched the tantalising bottle. He brought it to his lips. He let it touch his lips. He cocked his wrist. He heard the quiet glug of liquid as it flowed into him. The moment of perfection was passing. He put the glass back down and decided that, since he was alone, he would answer his mobile phone after all.

'Hello.'
'Ur you Simon McAllister?'

No, I'm Lord Bucket-head. Why is an ape phoning me on my birthday?

'Indeed, have been for precisely thirty years. Of what service can I be?'

'Right! Ah want tae hear yir side ay this story.'

Trouble.

'Excuse me?'

'Ah says Ah want tae hear whit yuv goat tae say fir yirsel.'

Bad vibe, very bad.

'Well, that depends on what you want to talk about.'

'Ay, weel, I want tae talk aboot ma daughter.'

It's bad.

'Sure.'

'Ma daughter says you goat hir pregnant.'

Oh no. Oh fuck. Oh fuck, no!

'No, there's surely some misunderstanding here.'

'Look, yir name's Simon McAllister?'

So what? Proves nothing.

'Yes.'

'Ye live at 45 Trevant Lane? Awright?'

Shit, he's got me. Oh Jesus, I've got some slapper up the duff. Oh God, and she's told her father. When? When? Who the fuck is she? Who the fuck is she? When did this happen?

'Aye, weel, Ah want tae hear yir story, yir ain side ay whit happened, before wi aw git carried away. Now ma daughter

63

says ye met her at The Kitchen nightclub doon the Cowgate and that ye took hir back to yir hoose.'

Oh no, not The Kitchen, only go there blootered. Shit, adds up, been there a few times lately. Oh fuck, fuck, fuck, can't remember it. Who the fuck is she? Oh hell. Stall the nutter.

'I'm sorry, I think there may be a mistake.'

'Look, she goat yir address. Nay mistake. She kens whir she went!'

Oh God, this can't be happening.

'And the situation's this: the lassie's pregnant and yir the father.'

Oh Christ, better get out into the street to talk about this. The little slapper! I want a DNA test. It's a lie. She's pregnant to someone else but I'm the only guy with cash that shagged her. Hope to God it's not mine. Oh God, probably is. When? Fucking when? There was that Helen girl, but that was ages ago, wasn't it?

'Well, perhaps we should get medical tests.'

Tell me her name, you bastard, give me some clues.

'Whit ye tryin to say? Ye callin ma daughter a slapper?! Yir no getting oot ay this!'

Right, I can hear myself think out here. And that was stupid, offensive. But I don't remember a fucking thing about it, including what the stupid slapper looked like. When was it? Vague memories of people back after The Kitchen, a couple of times. Who were they? When was that? Oh God, I feel queasy. Only shagged Silvia in the last few weeks, haven't I? Christ, not even sure. This one must be from weeks ago if the bitch is so sure she's pregnant. But Helen was months ago, wasn't she?

'Sorry, I wasn't trying to infer anything. I appreciate this must be difficult for you. Please understand it's also a shock to me.'

Oh Jeeze, this is going to fuck up my whole life. I've got to stop drinking. This ape is the grandfather of my child. I feel really ill.

'Ay, weel, she says white happened wis yous went back to yir hoose and she goat pregnant. Awright, that's her story. Whit huv ye to say for yirsel?'

Think of something. He's not that unreasonable. All those vague nights. Why do I do it? Something was bound to happen, something had to give, but, oh God, not this, please not this. It's like that time that girl phoned and said she slept with me the night before but had left in the morning before I got up and I said 'no way' and she described my cock and stretch marks and, oh God, that was worse than waking up with a strange bint in the bed and, oh Christ, I'm a useless, tacky bastard who had this coming.

'Well, obviously this is serious, we need to discuss it.'

'Ay, right, 'cos ma daughter's keepin the bairn, she's a good lassie.'

Yeah, I'm sure she's the Virgin Fucking Mary. Right, sound cool, keep cool, I could skip the country. Maybe hang out in Spain, or France, I could work in France, French isn't too bad, I'd pick it up, would have to live somewhere there's plenty of galleries, don't need great lingo for picture-framing, probably a big city, probably Paris, maybe Toulouse, that's sunnier, or Nice, yeah, Nice, lovely Old Town, probably too small, maybe should meet this slapper before I split? No.

'I'm sorry but I can't recall the night in question.'

'Can ye fuckin no? Weel, she does!'

Shit, offended him again. Calm him down. Stall, think! Oh God this was inevitable, it was all bound to catch up with me one day, and this is it. Oh, my stomach, need to breathe slower.

'I appreciate that. I'm sorry.'

'Ye canny jist take advantage ay a wee lassie when she's

drunk, ye ken, yir no getting away wi that! Noo, c'mon, Ah'm talkin tae ye man tae man here. Ah want to ken whit you say aboot this. Whit ur ye gonna dae aboot this?'

Ad-fucking-vantage! *I* took advantage, did I? Christ, how quaint. I can't even fucking remember a thing about it. Maybe she took advantage? How the hell do I know? I've got some advantage now, haven't I, you old bastard. Advantage McAllister but game set and match to the nameless daughter of a rough-sounding thug. Oh God, can this really be happening?

'Well, clearly we will have to do something here. Perhaps we should meet to discuss this?'

Since I've no sodden choice as you know where I live, you cunt. Then I can size you both up and see if the mother of my child – I really might be sick – has a face I recall. It's probably so ugly I'm repressing the memory.

'Ay, Ah want to know yir plans, whit yer gonna do?'

He's not stupid, not giving much away. And not really wanting to be enemies either. Christ, that's it! He's open to the idea that I'm some future son-in-law. No fucking way, keep cool. Who the fucking hell is she? Some birthday present, this.

'So whit do ye think aboot it? Have ye any plan?'

I'm working on one matey, no fears there. I could stay and pay for the child's upbringing. Oh Jesus, she'll bring it round to the house and try to get me attached to it. Oh God, I don't want a child, definitely not now, not this one, Jesus, I'm a drunk and I don't know the mother. Oh God, it's punishment. Paris it is. A new life starting in a few days, got to leave soon, don't want to see them, they'd know what I looked like, get a haircut, how well can she remember me just now? Credit cards are working, can run up a few thousand. When would I come back? Don't want to live forever in Paris. Travel about? Far East? South America? Years of travel, not so bad. Can I make the cash in France? Take the van. Could I sell the house fast enough? Pay off the mortgage? Make a few thousand? Stay in Edinburgh and move house? No, nerve-racking, waiting to be caught, scared to go out. Would she find me? See me in the street? Would she remember what I look like? What's the legal situation? I fucking pay, that support thingy agency, tracks guys down, read about it in the papers. How long will I be away for? Years.

'I'm waitin to hear whit yiv got tae say for yirsel?'

'Yes, sorry, you know, it's just very surprising news to have sprung on you. I'm just letting it sink in.'

What about I pay them off, maintenance? I earn thirty-one with all the private work. Taxman knows about eighteen, then there's tax-deductible expenses off that, so show psycho and daughter final profit in taxman's eyes, could maybe convince them I've still got expenses to come off that, show them receipts. No, he'll know, probably self-employed himself. Christ, he'll even know the taxman's figure is a pile of shite.

'Yir gonna have to meet yir responsibilities, ye ken. Ye huv to face up to yir situation here . . .'

'Mm.'

Come on, Arithmetic Man; pretend to be levelling, say really earn twenty-two, taxman knows about less than eighteen, so under fourteen taxed at twenty-two per cent means say less than eleven and a half plus personal allowance four is just over fifteen in hand a year which is, eh, one thousand two hundred and fifty a month, plus undeclared four is another, eh, third a month, so that's three hundred and thirty-three, so a total of one thousand, five hundred and eighty-three per month, shit missed out ten per cent tax band, that's twelve per cent extra I get on one and half grand, which is one hundred and eighty quid, which is fifteen a month but was under so total about one thousand, six hundred per month; how much do these things cost? What the fuck does a child cost? Also self-employed so don't earn during holidays, juggle that in, no, leave it out, he'll say I shouldn't go on holiday since I'm taking fuck all to do with the sprog. I can hear it now: 'Yir oan yir holidays aw the time!'

'Ah mean Ah want tae be reasonable aboot this, but yir gonna huv tae wake up tae reality, son.'

Oh, 'son' is it now?! And 'reality', Jesus, that was a big word. Got your Thesaurus out, you fucking git? Go for sob story about paying five hundred a month to my dear old mother, so offer six hundred per month, that's more than half my income, after mother's taken into account; reasonable, surely? Oh shit, mother will go ballistic, might not play ball, might adore the brat, Jesus, going to be poor. Will they accept that? Is it too much? What the fuck is she like? Should I ask her name? I'm going to France.

'I'm listening and I understand what you mean Mister, eh, sorry, what is your name?'

'Ma name's Davie. Ah suppose ye dinnae ken her name either, for Chrissakes.'

'Well, to be honest I think I recall the evening now, but I'm terrible with names.'

'Ay weel, yir gonna have to think ay yin for the bairn, aren't you?'

Am I fuck! But that was quite witty. No name for the daughter, though.

'Davie, can I just check, your daughter has brown hair, yes?'

'No, she husnae!'

Shit, now he's raging.

'Christ, whit ur ye like? Ye dinnae remember her at aw! Her name's Margaret!'

Shit again, no bells whatsoever. Margaret? Margaret? Not unfamiliar, but no, can't place the fucking ugly cow.

'Right, well, why not us three meet up? I'm away for three days but back on Friday. Is Saturday OK for yourself and Margaret?'

And I'll have cleared customs the night before. God, new life. Oh Jesus, I knew I would crash, but not like this.

'Whit the fuck ye gaun away fir? Whit's mare important than a new bairn?'

My Channel crossing on Friday, you piece of shit.

'To be honest, I'm keen to work this out too. But I'm going away for work reasons and I think I should be thinking about finances, Davie. It'll give us time to get used to the idea. It is a shock after all. Why not bring your wife too? Might as well all meet.'

'Awright, whit time and whir'll ye be?'

Paris all day.

'Do you know Stac Polly? The one in the New Town?'

'Nah.'

Course you don't, it's nice.

'Do you know Café Rouge? It's on Frederick Street, very easy to find. Why don't we meet for lunch at two o'clock on Saturday?'

'Awright. Ah ken that place. We'll be there.'

Have a nice meal.

'I'll see you then, Davie.'

'Ay, see ye.'

Only in hell, you old bastard, who's just ruined my life. Oh God, it had to happen, inevitable, you only get away with drinking and sharking for so long. Christ, why did I do it? When did I do it? Oh God, I want to stop drinking. I want my life back. What does it matter now? Oh Christ, I want a drink. A life in penury with a hellish brat or a life on the run? No, calm down, a few years and it'll blow over. Send money back for the kid, got to be decent, how will I send it? France, good wines, good place, lots of tourists to shag. New life, think positive. Christ, it's the phone again, might be my new family again, switch the bloody thing off. Oh Christ, Simon, you stupid, reckless twat, you've really done it this time. Right, money is first problem, phone estate agents in the morning, see how fast the cottage can be sold. Wait, shit, if that's not them on the phone just now, then I can't one-four-seven-one to get their number. Shit, got bleeped in the middle of Davie's little chinwag anyway; that's probably same person calling back. How will I contact them to send money? Should send some. BT could maybe trace the number he called from; sounded like he was at home. I'll ring from France, from a phone box, and present them with a *fait accompli*. Who the fuck's number is that on the display? Oh, it's Fiona's, probably Rich. Better get back out the pub.

'Rich, man, don't hang up, I'm here.'

'Oh, hi, thought you'd have left . . .'

'Listen, I got a problem, major problem. Got some slapper up the duff, her father's on my case; ain't gonna get to walk away from this, might have to leave Edinburgh for a while, it's looking fucking . . .'

'Hold on, talk slowly, don't panic. Where are you? Who have you got up the duff?'

'I'm in Howe Street. And fuck knows who I've got up the duff. Don't remember a thing about it.'

'What? Don't remember?'

'Not a fucking thing.'

'You don't remember having sex?'

'No.'

'Shit, it can be done. I know. Wait, what was she like?'

'Rich, I don't remember even meeting the bucket-cunted bitch! I don't *know* her.'

'Oh Christ, then how do you know it's not a mistake?'

'No, no, listen to me . . .'

Simes conveyed more about the tone and details of the conversation to Rich. He could feel Rich's frown emerging at the other end of the phone as his protests subsided. It stoked Simes' panic. Eventually Rich spoke, lamely; 'Hmm. Maybe she can be persuaded to have an abortion?'

'No, they've already decided; her father told me that before I even got the chance to suggest it! She must want the fucking brat or she wouldn't go and get her father's help. They mean it, I could tell.'

Rich was all but silent now. Then he spoke suddenly; 'Wait. You said the Kitchen? When?'

'Dunno, do I?! Must have been over a month ago if she's so sure she's pregnant.'

'Eh, oh, hang on. It wasn't that wee one with the big tits, was it?'

'How the fuck would I know? Who are you talking about? When was that?'

'Eh, more like a couple of months back, I think. You don't remember her?'

'No, I fucking don't and I don't want to. No, wait, what was she like?'

'Surprised you don't remember. Mind you, we were wrecked that day. You'd started at lunchtime, I hooked up with you later, after . . .'

'Yeah, yeah, what was she like?'

'Eh, like I said, small, quite chunky I think, big tits, dyed blonde hair; I remember her hair because it was really long and because she was so small it kind of made her look like a dwarf, ch, that's all I really remember.'

'Great. Bloody wonderful.'

'Eh, also, I think I remember now; I emailed you the next day and you said you'd just gone home alone or something, but you couldn't really remember leaving or anything.'

'Oh Christ.'

'But, eh, you know, I think she was OK, looks-wise, honest, seemed like sort of fun, you know.'

'Oh Christ, sounds beautiful. You know, I do have a hazy memory of meeting some small girl in some club. Shit.'

'Name was Maggie, I think.'

'Yes! That's her!'

'Oh. Well, eh, I have to say, end of the night you two were sort of lumbering into each other. I poured you both into a cab, and she was, you know, well, rough as you like, to be honest, though I don't really remember much myself, it was . . .'

'Oh God. It really has happened. I'm fucked. I'm going to go to France, start afresh, clean up my act. You know, man, something like this had to happen. I'm going to use this to change my life.'

'Look, stay cool. Let's talk about this. Everyone is expecting you round at Fiona's for birthday drinks in ten minutes. Come along and have a drink; you and I will trap off pretty soon and discuss your options.'

'I can't face anyone.'

'Life goes on mate. We'll just have to deal with this.'

'Yeah, but I can't stop thinking about it and I don't want anyone to know; oh shit, everyone will know eventually.'

'Come to Fiona's. We'll work out a strategy.'

'This is my whole life fucked.'

'No, it's not. France is an option. I'll visit, maybe join you for a while. Maybe meet Maggie and family and see how you feel . . .'

'Ill! That's how I'll feel.'

'You might be able to negotiate; sort of Maggie gets an allowance and an unofficial interdict not to come within seeing distance of you? Look, let's just discuss this tonight. See you at Fiona's, OK?'

'Yeah, sure, got to come up with a plan. I'll get a cab, see you there in ten mins. Don't tell anyone yet.'

'No probs, see you soon.'

Simes was able to breathe a little easier after the conversation. Rich was always good in a crisis, grabs the nettle quickly. Now

Simes was aware that his hair was sticky with sweat, just above his aching neck. He returned to the pub and downed the rest of his Pils. It might have been water or a gallon of meths for all it intruded upon Simes' daze. It's all over, he thought; all over, this easy life has ended. After umpteen pregnancy scares, one abortion in his honour, another where he was a keen suspect, and one miscarriage, he had finally fucked it up big time. That's what you get for feeling emboldened by warning shots, for feeling ever more invincible with every scrape you survive. Arrogant prick. A somnambulant stroll took him into the street.

He waited for a cab on the corner of Howe Street. A young mother let herself and her baby out of the gate of the private gardens, on adjoining Heriot Row. Simes stared across the road into the pram, transfixed. The woman was pushing the pram in Simes' direction: it was the future, coming his way, unstoppable now; he continued to stare; he blinked as if hoping to vanish this portent. The woman became aware of him gawping and returned a wary stare. It broke through and Simes came back to the present, smiled at the woman, as if in appreciation of the baby, and then looked away, down Howe Street, still picturing the baby and not seeing an empty taxi until it was almost past him.

In the taxi he thought about how often he had made a fool of himself when drunk, all the crass things he had done, the ones he could remember anyway. Normally he didn't care. He learned a few years back that generally everything passes and fades. Rich feared fallout more. Rich always defended his partying lifestyle and image: 'Disapproval is the province of the jealous, the dull and the cowards,' he would say. But Simes didn't need to contrive a proverbial refuge; his belief in the dissolute life ran so deep that words were unnecessary. So some people mocked him? Big deal, they didn't know him: blinkered by righteousness, they mistook a persona for a person and enjoyed judging. Subtle sneers could lash Rich's confidence, but not his. He was, simply, more reckless than Rich. That was why this had happened to him and not Rich. But now he cared; more than Rich, more than anyone, and he hated his lifestyle for what it had wrought, a baby for God's sake, a person, an unwanted life unknowingly conceived.

The regret was tortuous; it had always been there, loading, building, awaiting its moment, a trigger, this. And now he is lost, it's all his fault, he's always pushed it, as if goading the world to bring something down on him and now it had; pregnant Maggie, his inevitable retribution.

By now the cab had pulled up at Fiona's flat in Marchmont. He clambered out, feeling sad, thinking how he would miss the friends he was about to see when he slunk off to France, shamefully.

'£4.20,' said the podgy old cabbie out the window.

Simes, gearing up to put on a face for the party, smiled and gave him a fiver. 'Keep the change!' He turned and tried to breeze up the path of the freshly blasted tenement. He glanced up into the drizzle and saw James waving from Fiona's flat on the second floor. He smiled and, again, felt extraordinarily appreciative of his friends; the friends he didn't feel up to facing. He tried to steel himself; he thought about how himself and Rich were 'the only ones who really go for it', as Rich said. He tried to tell himself that he was too old for all this going for it, all this clowning around, but he didn't care if he was or not. It came easy and he was happy; 'was' being the all too apposite word.

Fiona spoke on the intercom: 'Hey, at last birthday boy!' The buzzer sounded and he pushed through the door and plodded up the cold, stony stairwell, feeling like he was, right now, entering his new miserable life of shame and hiding, his new reality, served up on his thirtieth birthday. Suitably ominous.

At the top of the stair Fiona was waiting at the door. She kissed him on both cheeks. He was aware of her big, pretty eyes and small nose, a babyish face, he thought, not taking in her long black hair and emerging wrinkles. 'Everybody's through in the living room,' she said, and led him along by the arm. The physical strain of smiling made him worry that he looked like he was smiling sarcastically.

He let her lead him along the hall, where he took nothing in, and into the elaborately furnished living room. The red curtains were the only furnishings to register on his consciousness. He kept his smile on and seemed to be regarding everyone from a great distance. He was aware that daylight still lit the room and he heard voices but couldn't engage with the meaning of the words. He could just smile, while weeping inside, 'This can't be happening, not a baby: I'm only thirty.'

His hysteria was building rather than diminishing in company. He couldn't recall ever feeling lonelier. He resolved to pretend he was ill soon and leave to go home, but he had only been here a few seconds. He would have to bide his time for an hour or so. This was it, he thought. Should concentrate on dealing with people, on overcoming these new circumstances.

Fiona was calling him. So, er, he ought to respond. 'Simes? Simes. Sye-ims! Listen to this,' said the baby face, the alarming baby face. He looked round the room: they had all been babies some time; babies; people-to-be – oh Christ. Rich was pressing the play button, for whatever it was he was supposed to listen to, Rich, his best mate, his favourite overgrown baby; oh Christ, he was only a big baby himself, only thirty, can't have a baby, this can't be happening.

While his mind raced, a voice came to him, 'Whit ye tryin to say? Ye callin ma daughter a slapper? Yir no getting oot ay this!'

Simon was back in the phonecall. The room had gone

silent. Rich shouted, 'Here's the best bit!' and Simes heard himself speaking, very tensely through the speakers: 'Sorry, I wasn't trying to infer anything. I appreciate this must be difficult for you. Please understand it's also a shock to me.'

The room had convulsed into laughter.

And joy was flooding through every facet of Simon McAllister's being.

S oft morning light. Hell. Clock? Fumble. 8.00 a.m. No. Say it ain't so. To be woken this early, by demonic pain, means a lot more demonic pain is on the way. Hours and hours of it.

Rich forced his legs to flop over the side of the bed. He made unsteady progress over to the shutters and slammed them shut; hellish noise; he did it again, and twice again, until the room was in complete darkness. Then he banged himself into the dresser. Christ, still drunk. Forget work. Phone to cancel appointments? No. Talking, an unfeasible effort.

Bathroom. Right index and forefinger down throat. Thin, watery puke, no solids. Never ate last night, always makes it worse. He liked puking – the strain, particularly that concentrated instant before expulsion from the stomach – it vanquished the headache for a few precious moments. But it was exhausting. A few pukes later; aching guts, legs shaky, feeling weak enough to cry. Slow breath and one last puke? He had a brief thought about the way he always shoved his two most nicotine-stained fingers down his throat. Can't be good. He shoved them down as far as he could. His stomach retched. Out of puke.

Puking over. Zero response. Disaster. Once poison has been expunged one expects some kind of gratitude from the body. Somewhere inside something should relax, even just incrementally, surely, some part of the head, some region deep in the guts, just some easing off. Today, nothing. And now that he had stopped, the headache was worse than before. The demon was stronger or he was weaker, same thing. This was a fight in the soul. He caught sight of his haggard face in the mirror. A fright. 'You're clever,' he mumbled, and lolloped through to fall on the bed.

Can't sleep. Too much pain. Lie still, concentrate on the pain, try to make peace with it. He pinned it down to a throb in the centre of his brain. There was a metal, medieval helmet contraption clamped on his pulsating cortex and the demon was tightening it. No point taking sleeping pills or paracetamol, they'd never stay down. (He wasn't a great believer in drugs for medicinal purposes anyway). Again, but passionately, he cursed himself for not eating and tried to relax the bone-snapping tension in his neck. No joy. After half an hour of twisting and turning he got back to sleep. It was a deep, dreamless sleep but the powerful demon pulled him all the way back to consciousness only two hours later.

He paced the flat, tried to look out the windows, but he was unable to stop anywhere. His thoughts, vague memories of the night before, another discomfort. Lurking shame; what had he done? Made a fool of himself, no doubt. Can't remember, hazy recollection of a ludicrous political argument with Right-on Rob. And did he make a stupid pass at someone? So much fallout. It's never as bad as you think. Actually sometimes it is. Sometimes it's worse. He remembered that phase when he was such a troublesome drunk he kept a card with the number of a florist delivery service in his wallet; he seemed to need it twice a week for apologies. One time he even ended up sending some flowers to a barman.

He drank water so he would have something to puke up in a few minutes, so he would have something to do. He puked, repeated the process twice and, exhausted, got back to sleep after much contorting. There was an occasional few minutes of consciousness, but he didn't properly wake until 3.15 p.m., a beautiful sight on the clock.

The room reeked of alcohol filtered through guts, bowels and sweat. And there was a sweet taste in his mouth. Relief. It's the aftermath of the biochemical battle. The demon is in retreat now. He had noticed how he often had a relapse after a few hours. It was like a peak in the battle, it lasted a few minutes and was dizzying and terrible. It was the demon having a last desperate push for his soul, before retreating. After that he was definitely on the mend. He figured he had slept through it today.

Now, moving will still be hell, but got to try some water. Got to speed up the demon's retreat. Water stayed down. He ventured an Earl Grey tea. Damn. Puke. Right, just have a bath, to wash off all the fumes, well, mainly to just let twenty minutes go by. After bath, still unsteady, bit dizzy in fact, water again. Stayed down. Good Fifteen minutes pacing about, trying to get body back, make it behave, function, keep willing yourself well, it'll come, Earl Grey again, not too strong, excellent, staying down. Filter coffee after another fifteen mins. Cereal straight after. It's all staying down. We're home. Codeine pill, staying down, just the job.

Finally, time for the demon's last rites: phone to arrange to go out drinking. Don't bore yourself by promising to leave off the drink.

'Hangovers are the most amazing things,' declared Rich. 'Such profound pain, the purest hell. And it goes so fast. Ever thought about how strange that is? I mean that pain, it's much worse than say the flu but the flu stays around for days. In fact a hangover must be worse than fever, or the plague, it must be much more painful. Like when I got malaria and dysentery, it was awful but not as hellish as a bad hangover. Even when I broke my arm, the first hour was as bad as a really bad hangover, but I don't know if it was worse. I didn't cry – and I have cried during hangovers; you feel so put-upon.

But a hangover goes in a few hours! My arm was in plaster for five weeks. Just six hours ago I wanted not to exist; I was living in hell. I mean you'd think that amount of pain, you'd think it meant death or a prolonged illness, but no, it doesn't. You're better soon. God really took the piss with hangovers.'

'Gosh, Rich, you're so deep,' said Simes. 'Any drugs?'

'Nah, still too delicate for that.'

'But you'll want them later?'

'Possibly some powder. But we must go and eat. This day has been shit.'

'Dick wants us to go with him to pick stuff up.'

'Dick? Oh "Dick" is it now? Do you mean the man we have hitherto only ever referred to as Sick Dick?'

'The very same. Anyway he said if we go with him – he's in the bar, somewhere at the back, I think – he'll give us a free gramme of posh.'

'Oh great, forty per cent Persil, forty per cent baby laxative, twenty per cent that isn't even fucking there if you bother to weigh it and three molecules of cocaine; and all we have to do is risk our lives in some crummy estate to get it. Correct? We must eat.'

'It's only Pilton, thirty minutes there and back. Look, Rich, it'll be safe, it's only seven o'clock.'

'Of course, how foolish of me. They don't slash faces before eight. I forgot. And of course we both speak Radge Cunt so well. Listen, we must eat. I shouldn't even be drinking before a good meal.'

'We'll be fine with my Glasgow accent.'

'Bullshit. They hate Weegie as much as any accent, maybe more. Are we meant to be protection? Is that a joke?'

'You can have some of my posh, c'mon, I've already agreed to go.'

'Fine, I'll use your posh to wash the bloodstains out of my jumper.'

Rich was talking tough and sarcastic, as ever, but his tone was hangover-weary. He was resigned. Simes suggested they get it over with. They downed their beers and went to find Sick Dick. When he saw them approaching he finished off his lager. He looked unusually straight, and nervous.

'Right, lads, I'll go and get the car. It'll take me ten minutes, what d'you want to drink?'

'Two Pils lagers,' said Simes. 'Nothing!' thought Rich, but he went along with it. They stood with Sick Dick's friends, not saying much. Rich wondered why some of them couldn't accompany Dickhead to Piss-awful Pilton. Probably not close friends; drug dealers don't have close friends. The group was awkward. Rich smirked. Sick Dick's friends were suspicious of anyone who was a friend of Sick Dick's. That's how it goes with dealers. Simes and Rich drank up fast and went outside.

Simes lit up and mused: 'What is it about visiting an inner-city council estate to buy drugs that makes one feel contaminated?'

'Dunno. Better question: what kind of drugs dealer drives a Mondeo?' enquired Rich.

'A clown. He's quite edgy tonight, don't you think?'

'I hope it's because he's straight. I hope it's nothing to do with where we're going.'

'Hmmm. DT''s, I'm sure.'

Simes sounded worried. Rich turned to look at him. Christ, he is nervous too. It's like three kittens going to talk big in the lion's den.

'I went to a proper estate dealer's place once before, two years ago: it stained my psyche forever,' said Rich. 'I've refused ever since. Dunno how you face them. It's where you and I part company. I can wait, go without, whatever. But if you want drugs you'll do anything; you'll fly to Kabul and fight the Taliban for them.'

'Yeah, but who goes for weeks without them? Who doesn't feel like them for ages at a time?'

'I go without for most of the week. And I never have cravings, like you.'

'Oh yeah? And you never overdo it either, do you? Not like that time you couldn't sleep for three days.'

'You're sounding like a woman, a wife.'

They watched in silence as Sick Dick pulled up in his Mondeo on the other side of the road. He signalled that he would do a U-turn to pick them up.

'At least I'm not a poof. Scared of the Taliban, honestly, you little shirt-lifter.'

Rich could see Simes wanted to ease the tension. Fair enough. They were in this together.

'Actually I'd rather face the Taliban than drug chiefs in Pilton,' said Rich.

'Right now, me too.'

They climbed in and Sick Dick tried to affect casualness, as if Rich and Simes often accompanied him on such sorties. He passed them a can of Carlsberg each, lit a joint and put a Massive Attack CD on the stereo. Rich, in the back, raised his eyebrows. Sick Dick had taken so long to bring the car round because he was rolling a joint. That's why he and Simes had had another drink. And now old Sicko was giving him another. He needed it like he needed herpes. 'Shouldn't take long lads,' grinned Sick Dick. The sweat was visible on his cotton shirt. He was detoxing all right, but he was also nervous, very nervous.

After fifteen minutes they were rolling up in front of a dismal housing block. The houses were mostly boarded up and vandalised, except every couple of doorways along there was a satellite dish on the wall. There was no traffic. The opposite block seemed more occupied. A few bodies leaned out of its windows. One woman looked at Rich as the car crawled by. Her pale reddish hair was greasy, her expression challenging. Rich mused; that lined face, designed by and for shouting.

A couple of brats played in the overgrown green below her. Their easily heard voices made the scene seem quieter, adding to the creeping unreality. The weather too; it was so calm it was as if the elements had been cancelled this evening. It felt like a film set.

By now the car had stopped beside one of the satellite dishes. The speed at which Sick Dick had slowed revealed he wasn't sure which doorway he wanted. He wasn't on familiar ground. Rich got a bad feeling. A rottweiler walked by, on its own. That must be an omen, he decided. He still felt fragile, only now he felt drunk too. The alcohol had raced through his empty system. His hunger was going. He did not feel like leaving the sanctity of the car. 'Let's drink up first,' said Sick Dick, obviously in no hurry either. Then he forced some conversation out of Simes.

Rich gazed out the window at the depressing nothingness. This was the second version of hell today. Normally he actually enjoyed the final phase of a blow-out. This should be the post-hangover daze; that lovely, quiet euphoria, a celebration of the demon leaving, just the drained body, dry and high. In that floaty state, he liked to stay purposeless, and just people-watch. He did it today, for a few minutes when he walked to the newsagent for fags. He recalled seeing a young woman in office clobber, striding by in a rush, she looked worried, he had wished he could ease her worries. It was always the same: in that weak, contented state he felt kindly, like giving and receiving affection, he felt it's what you should be doing all the time. Now he wished he had retained the residue of that gentleness, but he had washed it away with the drink. Still he spared a thought for the office woman, wondered where she was now, what her house was like, if her hassle was men, kids, money, boss, health, parents or parents' health? Similar things get us all.

For him, right now, drink and drugs were the hassle. Alcohol would have dissolved his native wit. He wished he had grounded himself with proper replenishment, not just a bowl of Frosties; he was making the same mistake as yesterday. He badly wished he had his wits to face the rubbish that awaited. In fact he wished he had his wits so he hadn't agreed to come. Sick Dick indicated it was time to get out, and then muttered: 'It can't have looked good sitting here all this time.'

'In here,' he said, as they walked away from the car. He led them into a darkened close. Long-rotted foodstuffs and stains of urine streams made it rank. The stench of soured souls, thought Rich, to be feared. He regarded a hypodermic needle at the bottom of the stairs. 'That's uplifting,' he said. The other two ignored him. They trudged up one flight. It was the door of a serious dealer: reinforced with steel and at least three locks. Rich wondered who fitted these things. Was there an ad in the *Evening News*? 'Selling illegal drugs? Call Gangster-helpers!'

A wan youth opened the door. 'Yeah?'

He sounded like he couldn't care less what Sick Dick said in return: 'We're here to see Mac. He's expecting us.'

'Yeah, Dick innit?'

'Aye.' Old Sicko was speaking Radge Cunt. Anyone adopting an accent, in any circumstances, always a bad sign, thought Rich.

'Best come in then.'

They breezed in to the detrital dump as if this was a polite, social call; always the comical pretension to the deal being a minor part of a pleasant visit, an afterthought, as opposed to the whole point of the detestable contact. Another, bigger weed appeared from a doorway at Rich's elbow. This one may have aged before his time, from drugs and the stress of dealing, or he may just have been older than the first one and born even uglier. Rich nodded at him as nonchalantly as he could.

'Dick?' he asked.

'Nah, him,' Rich sounded laconic as he pointed, but he was furious Sick Dick didn't seem to know anyone here at all.

'Right Dick, through here,' said Mac. 'Why don't you two jist wait in there?'

Why don't we indeed? mused Rich, as if that was merely a suggestion. They went through to what was deemed to be a living room. More like a dying room, thought Rich. It had no furniture save for a television and a few wooden chairs, the like of which belonged around a cheap kitchen table, a very old one.

An electric fire heated the bodies languishing on them: three guys and one woman. Another woman, a girl really, lay on the floor, nearest the telly. All five were watching a travel programme featuring a Masai game reserve.

'Awright?' said the biggest guy, trying to make Rich and Simes feel at home. They were hovering just inside the door. The had barely received a glance from anyone.

'Yeah, fine,' said Simes.

'What ye up tae tonight?' asked the big guy. Christ, it's as if we're all mates, thought Rich. Sure thing, the bond of drug-taking, you can stick it where the monkey stuck its nuts.

'Just a quiet one, a couple down Broughton Street probably.'

'Oh aye, the auld Phoenix?'

'Probably end up there.'

'Here, help yirsel'.' He gestured at the sideboard where a slab of Tennents lagers lay opened.

'Cheers,' said Simes. He picked up two cans and passed one to Rich, who felt it might be an offence to decline.

Great, thought Rich, four beers down and still haven't eaten.

They all seemed happy to learn about the Masai quietly. Rich relaxed slightly. The girl on the floor spoke, with a surprisingly sweet voice: 'It's so dirty, so depraved!' Nobody responded, but Rich looked over at her. She didn't turn round, the back of her brown bob was steady. He afforded himself a chortle inside: '*They're* depraved! You mean de*prived* anyway, like your language skills.'

Soon after the girl's comment one of the men lifted his jacket and left the room without saying anything. He exchanged a knowing look with the big guy. It slightly unnerved Rich. Then the woman muttered to the big guy. It was blatantly conspiratorial. The big guy nodded. She reached inside her pocket and took out her works. Oh Jesus, thought Rich, she's going to shoot up.

And she was. The other guy, wearing a black jacket – indoors and near the fire – glanced round at Rich and Simes. His expression wasn't friendly. The two were standing behind the chairs, still hovering near the door. Rich was very conscious that you couldn't bolt out of this flat, not with that front door.

The woman was seated at the end of the row, just a yard from Rich. She poured a tiny mound of greyish heroin on to a small soupspoon and poured on a little vinegar. Then she heated it with a Zippo. She was getting down to business fast. Rich tried to fix his eyes on the Masai wandering through the Kenyan bush.

The guy in the jacket said something. Rich didn't catch it. He looked over at him and the guy repeated himself. 'Ye dinnae mind Jean.' It was an order, not a question. 'No probs,' Simes answered. 'Aye, awright then,' said the guy, his threatening tone still intact. But the voice itself? Like a slow, low reptilian moan from the back of the throat, the tongue reluctant to get involved in communication. Rich had heard that depressing noise before. Shit, the git had already shot up before they came in. God, they had walked in while this shower were having a shooting-up session. Maybe that's what the other guy left the room to do? Christ, bloody junkies, they just can't wait.

The woman looked as intent as a scientist on the threshold of alchemy. The heroin liquefied. Shit, thought Rich, needle will be next. In no sense or shape or form could he bear hypodermic needles. He had fainted once at the sight of the doctor injecting him. It was visual, nothing to do with the tiny prick of the needle. Since that occasion the mere thought of intravenous vaccination had been known to influence Rich's choice of holiday destination. She pulled out the needle and put it on her lap. The prospect of that metal going into her flesh made him shudder. He checked himself, and was glad nobody saw him wince.

She pulled back the plunger and the needle sucked up the liquid. The spoon was rested delicately on her lap. Rich didn't move. He was trying his best to not be there. She tore a cigarette upart and placed the spongy bit from the filter on the spoon. It soaked up the remaining liquid which was then sucked up into the syringe with the needle. It presumably kept out all the junk and dirt that the heroin would be cut with. 'Why did she not use the filter effect from the start?' wondered Rich. 'Christ, I don't want to know about these things; I don't want them to exist, not in my world.' He started glugging back his Tennents, which he normally loathed.

Her raised arm was in his line of vision. What could he do? Say something? 'Excuse me, wretch, but your crass drug-intake is intruding upon my anthropological learning, so give it a fucking rest, bitch!' He resolved to not look at her any more.

But he couldn't stop glancing. She had wound a bootlace round her skinny arm, just below the elbow. That's clever, thought Rich, use the really fragile veins on your forearm. She was tightening it by pulling on it with her teeth. But she was struggling. Pulling the tourniquet meant moving her head to the side and then she was having to peer out the corner of her eye to see where to stick the needle in. You'd have thought the stupid cow had done it often enough to get it right. She swivelled round in her chair. Rich could see it coming. He tensed and prayed and tried harder to not be there, but it came: 'Could ye haud this?' she asked him.

Why couldn't she have asked one of the others? Or Simes? He had injected before, a couple of times. Why did he have to be standing so close? There is so much space on Planet Earth and he was landed here, beside this shrivelled ghoul. And this was some kind of test, some kind of way of including him, dragging him down to their level, letting him know he needn't think he was better. And it worked, because he had no choice. Mr Jacket was glancing over. Rich nodded. This was going to be harder than either of these junkies understood. He remembered again the time he fainted at the doctor's. Oh God, please not this time. He would 'haud' the fucking lace, but he wouldn't watch.

She offered him her puny, bony arm. How revoltingly feeble, like there is no flesh to sink the needle into, like it could hit bone. He shuddered again, stifled it, took hold of the lace and held it tight.

She was smiling. Yeuch, it isn't just the anticipation of her heroin rush, but that scrawny face is flirting. Rich felt sick enough already from the thought of the needle and all the unwanted booze in him. He smiled back. Mr Jacket kept looking over. Christ, why is he not relaxed? Heroin makes you all laid-back and woozy, or at least it did the few times Rich had taken it – when he had sniffed it that is, no way would he ever be a jagger, like this scum, not even once. Sure, heroin has come a long way from its scuzzy skag image and in some circles, especially in London, it was acceptable to sniff or smoke it, but he was all for that last taboo, which still stood, and which maintained that one doesn't inject, one simply doesn't. It was society's way of not becoming full of useless fuckwits like this; Christ, it was society's way of surviving.

Imagine a world peopled entirely by this shower? One is a surplus. Hang 'em all.

He held the tourniquet tighter and the woman's face – more like a hollow-eyed skull with dead skin stretched over it – grinned again. She stuck the needle into her arm then pulled it out. 'Haud it tight!' she snapped. He worried the queasiness upon him might be slackening his grip and he pulled it tight. He was very aware she was sticking the needle in again, but this time his eyes were staying firmly fixed on Kenyan vistas. No loss of face, she couldn't see where he was looking.

Good, she seemed to have stopped stabbing. He glanced down without moving his head. Oh God, he looked straight back at the Masai. The needle was in her flesh but blood hadn't shot into the syringe. That's what's meant to happen, isn't it? Then you've found a vein? He wasn't sure. She pulled out the needle and went at it again. Rich knew what she was doing and kept watching the television, concentrating on not loosening the tourniquet, not feeling faint, not thinking about her flushing gunk-ridden heroin into her disgusting, tabetic body through the metal she was stabbing into herself.

The television commentary was about how, among some Masai, men were considered weak if they did not beat their wives. 'Jesus Fucking H Christ, bunch of savages, the Victorians were right!' thought Rich. Some young Masai warrior was arguing that a landmark ruling against a wife-beater should never have been allowed to reach court, that it wasn't a matter for the law, and wife-beating was something which the people would address themselves. Nobody in the room commented.

The woman, Jean, the Thing, seemed to be taking an age to find a vein. 'C'mon,' thought Rich, exasperation now fuelling him and possibly preventing him from fainting. 'You do this all the time; you must have a vein working; you're alive and functioning, unfortunately for the rest of the world.' He glanced down at her again, and shuddered again, still no blood in the syringe.

The needle was too compelling; he angled his face so she couldn't see his eyes which he closed. 'Aye, awright then,' she said. He opened his eyes, blood had shot into the syringe and was mingling with the heroin. He stared, frozen. 'Aye! Awright!' she said again. Still he stared. He had just grasped her meaning when she got impatient with him. 'Ye dinnae need to haud it now,' she said, as if to a mentally retarded child.

Rich let go and the lace dangled on to her lap. She started pumping the mixture into herself. He realised that obviously you don't start pumping in until the tourniquet is relaxed. He stepped back and looked at the television, then, after a few seconds, back at her, still pumping. He could only see her face from the side but it was enough to tell that she was smiling, a huge smile, as close as such an ugly face could get to beatific, like a religious fanatic who's just been laid by the pale Galilean himself. Of course heroin takes about three seconds to kick in, if you're mainlining.

He tried not to see the needle but he was aware what she was doing: emptying it and filling it up again and emptying it back in: she must have done it three times, they're called flushes, aren't they? Three flushes and she's going for a fourth. He'd heard that junkies get a kick off the needle. Imagine, the fucking idiots get a buzz out of that. How can she do this? It's a Freudian field-day, penetrating your flesh for a thrill, and then that bloodlust, you need to find blood with the needle, and then you kickstart a change, deep down in your very being, you become an arsehole, all the time sexual penetration becomes less interesting, less desirable, less possible, true junkies' sex urges go. That's probably more of an issue for guys. Women, like Jean, insofar as she merited the respectful label, could probably open their legs and take a cock, and she would probably take any if she was desperate for heroin and the guy offered her a hit in return, but she wouldn't be fucking, she wouldn't *be* there: she was always far away, down the other penetration path.

She smiled at him and Rich smiled back, but wished the stupid bitch had found a vein faster. He took a huge swig of lager to try to relax and get his mind off junkies and back on to the Masai. She leant back on her chair. She looked like a grotesque doll with those steady faraway eyes and that big inane grin on her thin lips. She was gone, imagining they were all having a fantastical time together, experiencing some higher truth or some such bollocks.

Rich looked back at the television. The Masai were going through a rite of passage called Eunoto, whereby men went from warriors to elders. Rich determined that he would learn all about Eunoto, he would be there with the Masai, on the sunny plain, utterly arid but for a few lonely trees with wind-flattened tops, hundreds of men jogging around it, all wearing red and carrying bark-stripped staffs instead of spears to symbolise their new status. They've to stop warring, plundering neighbours' cattle and shagging prepubescent girls. They have to marry, procreate and come into fulfilment. 'Now that you are an elder, drop your weapons and use your head and wisdom instead,' the voice-over translated. Sounds like a good idea, thought Rich, wish somebody would kick this lot into maturity.

His boozy melancholia promptly dispersed as Mr Jacket and the big guy exchanged words, in low voices. Rich knew he was being discussed. Now Mr Jacket turned to the girl on the floor in front of the telly and spoke openly; 'Ye wantin a wee hit?' The girl nodded and he crossed over to her. Out came the works. He started to mix the heroin and vinegar on a spoon, then used a cheap lighter to heat it from below. Rich watched a Masai council. He tried to tell himself this was nothing, they do it all the time. But he worried they would all regret shooting up in front of strangers. And it would be his and Simes' fault, of course. An argument could break out. The room was tense. Why can't everyone just watch the bloody Masai?

The girl hadn't yet injected when Sick Dick returned, looking and sounding relaxed. 'Oh aye, beer, eh?'

It was a bit too familiar. Everyone looked round. Mac took an executive decision to sanction Sick Dick's comment; 'Aye, huv yin'. But the mood was definitely getting ugly and Sick Dick hadn't helped. He noticed his *faux pas* and tried to compensate with a loud, polite 'Thank you' which emphasised the tension. Mac handed round fresh cans to everyone who wanted. Rich took one. If he had to endure this he had to drink. Nobody talked while the two prepared to shoot up. Rich stared, almost glared, at the television, determined to enjoy the Masai doing their jumpy dance thing, determined to stay in that programme, but he couldn't concentrate; he was too irked by the pretensions to sociability. He just kept thinking, 'For Christ sake! We've got the drugs; let's get out of here!'

Then it happened. Jean keeled over. Thumped to the floor. Everyone turned. Rich and Simes stared in horror. Mr Jacket raced over and tried to shake her. No response.

'Right! Wir takin her tae the bath!' he shouted at Rich and Simes. The two men looked at each other not knowing what to say, before setting about helping Mr Jacket pick her up, an arm each while Mr Jacket held both legs. 'That wey!' he shouted. They turned left along the hall. 'There,' snapped Mr Jacket. 'Fuck's sake, thirs the toilet!' They turned to the right now and the big guy, following behind with the others, turned on the light. 'Ower the side, in the fuckin' bath!' Mr Jacket shouted as if somebody was objecting, though nobody was.

They set her down in the squalid green tub. She hadn't responded to being moved but she was still breathing.

'Git a hairdryer oan her face!' said the young girl.

'Ur ye fuckin' silly?' shouted Mr Jacket, his manic eyes flashing hatred at the girl, who slunk off. Rich felt nervous, like the situation could explode more yet. It was obviously Mr Jacket, not the big guy, who ruled in here after all.

'Maybe we should call an ambulance?' said Simes, visibly shaken.

'Git tay fuck radge, who the fuck ur you?' Mr Jacket's voice was a low snarl.

Mac and the big guy started arguing and then agreed to pour water over Jean's face which was at the opposite end of the bath from the taps. Rich felt it was his fault for putting her in the wrong way round. Her feet and calves were getting soaked but the body remained resolutely limp.

'Yous cunts, jist go,' said Mr Jacket.

The big guy nodded at Rich. Neither he nor Simes could think what to say. They didn't want to leave Jean with these callous bastards who were only worried about their hideous little den being disrupted. For fear of that, this woman might die.

'Look, we could take her with us,' volunteered Rich.

The guy who had left the room shortly after Rich and Simes arrived had reappeared behind them in the bathroom. He looked at Rich: 'Fuck off, you total wanker.' His voice was quiet and self-assured. The way he emphasised 'total', savouring what should have been a glib insult, it caught Rich's full attention. This was a man prepared to fight without notice, a man given to violence. He looked Rich in the eye, calm and sneering. Rich looked back at Jean's body.

Mac spoke sternly: 'Jist go, she'll be awright, she's done it before.' All three saw they had no choice but to leave. They walked past the living room to get to the front door. The girl had returned there and was finishing off the preparations to shoot up. She glanced up at them. They looked horrified. Her expression said: 'And what the fuck do you ponces know?'

There was nothing they could do. That lot could have them killed if they called an ambulance. Rich kept telling himself during the drive back. Then Sick Dick, back to his cocky self, said it: 'Nothing we could do, I'll phone later to check the lass is all right.' He sounded downright cheerful. He'd got the gear, to take and sell, life was just dandy. He could have had the human decency to feel like a heartless bastard, or even just try to sound concerned, but oh no, not old Sicko.

Rich looked at Sick Dick's eyes in the rear-view mirror. Pupils wide and flying. Already on powders. Maybe he found that drama a great buzz.

Sick Dick could sense Rich and Simes' unease. 'She'll be fine, you heard them, she does this. Here lads, told you, free gramme, there you go, that's posh, but I've got good whizz too, there you go, another freebie.' He handed Simes a second wrap from another pocket.

'What? You don't want to take it home and cut it?' said Simes. His tone was snide.

'Nah, already done that in there.' Sick Dick smiled back.

Normally it was taboo to even hint at the brazen dishonesty of a dealer to his face, let alone tease him, but for this trip Simes and Rich were honorary members of the dealing fraternity and Sick Dick was letting Simes off because he knew the poor lads were a bit fazed by that junkie nonsense. Rich hated it. That world they just dipped into; it was always there, never as far away as you want it to be, and never as alien as you want it to be. And until they discovered if Jean had died or not, they hadn't really left it. Sick Dick had better ring to check. And if she's dead, well, they were going to have that on their consciences for life. Maybe he could get charged with manslaughter for helping her to shoot up? Maybe he deserved it? Christ, he needed a drink, several thereof, now.

In the pub, Rich and Simes could only talk about Jean and their evening's misadventure. When they spoke Jean's name, it seemed imbued with the significance of an old and treasured friend. Between Jean and the cocaine buzzing them through the beers, they were one tense pair, waiting for Sick Dick to return from wherever he was and phone about Jean. Mac was a big league dealer, he would have a jazzy mobile, so Sicko needn't bother with any excuses about getting through. He had rung already today for drugs so he could ring to see if a woman died, to see if they were implicated in a manslaughter.

'If she's dead, we're fucked,' declared Rich. 'That lot will implicate us to the police, maybe even genuinely believe we're responsible, maybe look to batter us.'

Simes nodded. 'Shower of psycho-junkies, no doubt. Want some coke?'

'Cheers,' said Rich taking a dab. 'Christ, you can't beat the psycho-junkie experience, can you? Nothing quite saps you of life with the same efficiency.'

'Tell me about it. Feel like I'm ageing a month every five minutes. Can't stop picturing Jean.'

It was the same, if not more so, for Rich. Jean, proffering that lifeless limb. Jean, the grotesque doll sinking into a coma right in front of him. Jean, the bundle of bones lying awkwardly in the bath. No amount of cocaine and alcohol and chaining the fags could wipe her from his mind's eye. He tried to review the situation objectively: 'You know, cocaine, all uppers, they're a way of borrowing energy from the future. Tomorrow we'll feel slow, burned out, emotionally fragile, physically weak, all that crap, that's the payback, and tonight we've withdrawn that energy from tomorrow's quota only to bloody squander it on some stupid junkie.'

'Yeah, we should be well-fuelled sharks.'

They paused, trying to be reflective. Rich broke in seconds: 'But that woman could die! What can be more worrying than death? And there will be fallout, of some nasty sort, I just know it. Here, give me another dab.'

If only he could hear Jean was fine. This cocaine, he had taken about five generous lines, but given that his lager intake was absurd and his food intake was zero, it was damn fine cocaine. By all rights, he should have collapsed several drinks ago. He didn't care about food now, didn't care that he was making the same mistake as yesterday, didn't care about anything but that stupid, junkie bitch whose tourniquet he held. Jean, the grotesque doll proffering that lifeless limb. Jean, the woman collapsing into a coma right in front of him. Jean, the bundle of bones lying awkwardly in the bath. Bloody Jean.

They stewed until ten forty-five, when Sick Dick returned, only half an hour late, pretty good for a dealer. 'It's fine, lads, already called in the car, no coma. Seriously, I've got her number, you can call her yourself tomorrow. Mac said she was rabbiting on about Rich, saying she felt bad and embarrassed and all that. Went on about you more than her sprogs.'

Rich felt relieved, but not released, not yet. The information would need time to do its job. Suddenly he stepped back from himself and saw the anxiety Jean had caused him and Simes. He was livid: 'She's got kids! That's a fucking outrage. I'll take her number and her address and I'll phone a social worker about that bitch. Kids! That means the disgusting wretch has been shagged, I feel like puking. I don't give a fuck how the snivelling selfish junkie feels about me, so long as she didn't die. Come to think, maybe it would be better for her kids if she *had* died. Social workers couldn't find a worse parent!'

Simes was surprised at the outburst. The two men had talked in hushed tones all evening. 'Chill, man.' He smiled tentatively.

'I know,' said Rich, aware he had ranted. 'It's just you know, why should we have had to feel bad? I mean, Jean, she crossed the line, her, herself! Fucking smackheads, crackheads, speed-freaks, stoners, alcoholics, the bloody lot of them, it's the same with all junkies, all classes, all races, all ages; their drug comes first, before kids, before good manners, before princi-ples, before anything can be done, their moronic fix is needed first. That's the difference between junkies and users, like us: junkies need drugs to operate, or what they think is operating, but us, we never forget it's just for escape.'

'Sure Rich, but calm down. It's over. We're out of that squalor now.'

'It's not about squalor! You know, I tell you, junkies see the squalor too, it's not just the rest of the world, but the fuckwit junkies think they know a higher truth, just because they know how good it is to be on drugs' – Simes' eyes rolled upwards – 'And if they just stay on them they can believe they are above such petty concerns as squalor, kids, all other people, the law, and filth, pride, decency, dignity . . .'

'You're ranting again, mate, but you're spot on,' said Simes. 'That said, you're ranting because you're on drugs, you know.'

Rich contemplated his own intake and smiled. He felt a bit stupid, but so what? It had been a hell of a day, dragging him along into drugs and drink; you create patterns in your life and they hold you.

Junkies should be guillotined, he concluded, and staggered off to the toilets to steady his walk with another line of that damn fine cocaine.

'Anyone can fall in love here,' said Jemima.

'Sure.' Fiona shrugged and inhaled from her joint. Excellent Thai grass.

'And I didn't really. He was just more backpacker trash. I'm not sure I want to hear from him now anyway.'

'Sure.' As Fiona exhaled she realised she should be more reassuring. 'Don't feel bad about it.'

'I don't.'

'Sure you don't.' Oops, sounding sarcastic, agony aunt hat back on. 'Why should you? If he just wants to hump and dump women that's his problem, his inability to enjoy a relationship. After all he was obviously besotted with you.'

'What do you mean, hump and dump?'

Oops again, thought Fiona, she's not ready for a reality check. I must make a note not to mix drugs and the counselling of delicate girlfriends.

'Not hump and dump, no, that's wrong, I'm being simplistic.'

'Exactly, it's complicated.'

Fiona managed to nod wisely and sympathetically, while thinking that if she got any more stoned she might say something she regretted, like 'Face it Slackpants; you've been had. Again. Third time this trip. What's so complicated?' which would probably move things on, but might damage the friendship. Beside it's a shame for Jemima. Imagine being born that stupid.

She passed Jemima the joint and started rolling another. Neither spoke. Soon Fiona lit up and gazed across the South

China Sea. She fell into a reverie about swimming naked at night, in phosphorescence; basking in an oval of electric blue light, carrying it far out into the inkiness, out to sea.

Then she fixed on a huge tanker sailing past and thought about how little phosphorescence there is in these dirty waters, or anywhere near this dirty town, and they are only here because Peabrain got dirty with an Italian. They must leave Surat Thani. This is a dirty experience . . .

Her train of thought was abruptly terminated. 'Maybe his letter will come tomorrow,' said Jemima.

Aaaaaargh! His letter hasn't come all week because his letter doesn't fucking exist. They had hung around this dump for six days, pretending that they wanted to stay here anyway, but knowing full well nobody has ever wanted to spend more than a day in Surat Thani. When will the penny drop? It was a drunken one-night stand on a beach. And he's buggered off. He is a bloke. That is what blokes do. It was nice of him to talk to her afterwards since they hardly said a sober word beforehand. And it was bloody stupid of both of them not to use a condom: that's what they should be discussing.

'Maybe,' said Fiona. 'Any discharge?'

'What? What do you mean?'

'I mean, oh Little Innocent Speckle of Angel's Breath, have you got VD?'

'Of course not! Why should I have VD?'

'Well,' Fiona sounded like a nursery teacher. She was stoned now. She started swaying as she switched into song; 'Let me tell you 'bout the birds and the bees/And the flowers and the trees/and a thing called . . .' She switched into serious science lecturer, 'gonorrhoea, or more likely chlamydia, from the Greek I believe, Khlamus-udos, and containing sixteen strains, all infectious diseases transmitted via genital contact and common among young people given to conducting sexual pairings when' switching to street slang 'outta der fuckin' box' back to science lecturer, 'aka the celebrated *modus operandi* of the dirty little slapper. Now Jemima, did you take notes?'

'Just because I had sex doesn't make me a slapper.'

'Of course not, you adorable thing.'

'Well, don't call me a slapper.'

'You tell him honey.'

'Him?'

'Yes, Mussolini, the Italian git on the beach what shagged you last week. You don't remember?'

'His name's not Mussolini and he didn't think I was a slapper. He liked me . . . Do you think he thought I was a slapper?'

'Oh, I see, ah, you should have said, I thought you were older than fourteen. Jemima, you are the sweetest thing that ever existed. I'm sure you fart Anais Anais and I'm sure there isn't a man on this planet who deserves the pleasure of you' – Fiona was doing a mock-frown; Jemima tensed, waiting for the put down – 'But this is not complicated. He possibly did like you. He also possibly thought you were a slapper. The two are not mutually exclusive. And he doesn't care either way. In fact he would probably rather you weren't a slapper. You see, you being a slapper makes him feel less special, so on balance you're probably correct, he doesn't think you're a slapper. But not because he is a supersensitive lover or a highly perceptive judge of character, but because it suits his ego for you not to be a slapper. That's blokes, it's all about them, not you.'

Fiona cut herself off there, she knew her patience was evaporating with the grass and she was picking on Jemima – who nobody should ever pick on – because she was keen to leave Surat Thani. She whimsied on inside to herself about men, bloody men, the reason they were stuck in this revolting town. What does it matter if Mussolini thought Jemima was a slapper? What does he know about it? We've all got it in us if we feel like it. Men are so clueless. They don't even know they like slappers, in fact they need them, without slappers they wouldn't get laid. If women didn't drink, get desperate, get careless, viz and to whit get slappered, the world would stop: that's why we've all done it, guys don't know we have, their sweet little sister that they think no guy is good enough for, their betrothed, their mother, their every lover, they hate the thought, and when they hear a girl is a slapper they hate it because they haven't had a bit of that action, a bit of her, her soul, and if we didn't give them hope, if we didn't behave like that they would always have to behave decently to get laid, and that could halt the evolution of our species, and how did men and women end up in the same species anyway? I'm not always sure that we should have. Oh God it would be so much easier for smart girls like me if dumb girls like Jemima made the buggers earn it. I remember Tanya Rowles, had one boyfriend for five years, had one one-night stand, married the next guy; she said people said she missed growing up, she thought she had caught too much of it, with just three sexual partners; I'd like to say she was one smug bitch, but she wasn't, she was smart and kind, one happy chick, I really liked her, but then at the opposite extreme there was Samantha Hearne, total slapper but also really nice, and very intelligent, and . . . Fiona was distracted by Jemima, who was staring at her. In fact Jemima was looking right into her eyes. Good God, Jemima looks deep in thought, if that's plausible, and she was just rambling, stoned, she really shouldn't have spoken to Jemima like that: what exactly did she say? Why has Jemima worked up this head of steam?

Jemima spoke slowly, as is her wont. 'Now you are being really simplistic. And I don't want to be like you, you might think you're smart, but you're cynical.'

'I think not. I'm just intelligent, an affliction since birth, but OK, maybe I am cynical too.'

'You have no faith in anybody except yourself because you're clever. You're always lonely, so don't give me lessons on love.'

'Love? So you loved him now? You spend one night on a beach, half-cut, fully-stoned, his possibly-infected semen dribbling down your thigh for sand to stick to, and it's love?'

'Why are you picking on me? Are you jealous? Don't pick on me. You know I look up to you when it comes to being clever in arguments.'

Jemima's eyes were wide and enquiring. She wasn't being bitchy, just stupid.

Fiona said: 'I'm really sorry for picking on you, I love you, as you know.'

Fiona thought: No, *Ma Petite Bouquet de Fleur* I am not jealous of you pining miserably for a slimy piece of Mediterranean butt while possibly incubating a serious venereal disease and becoming distressed over the brutal truth which your loving friend is kindly revealing to you. No, my Little Jar of God's Nectar, I'm not jealous of you.

'But you are jealous I did that?' asked Jemima.

'Jealous that you got humped and dumped? No, you gorgeous and sexually overgenerous goddess, bizarrely enough, I'm not jealous. Are you stoned?'

'No, no. I mean are you jealous that I hoped not to be humped and dumped, as you so crudely put it? You know, that I still hope about things? Like not being humped and dumped? I don't think it's right I should be lonely, you know, but you just expect to be lonely, so you are. Sorry, I didn't say that very well.'

'Didn't you?'

Fiona was thrown. Jemima doesn't often probe. She looked into her friend's eyes again. Still they were big, innocent pools, inviting her in, still no hint of hostility. She just meant the depressing big insult she had somehow uttered, between her words. Only she meant it as curiosity, maybe even concern. Very Jemima.

'I'm not lonely, I just want to love well, not waste time.'

'Practice makes perfect,' Jemima smiled.

'That's the best excuse I've heard for being a slapper.' Fiona smiled back. 'Can we leave this shit-hole now. If we get a taxi back to the hostel, we can still catch the ferry out to Samui.'

'One more day? Please?'

'Why?! Sugar-Pie Darling, you could wait a lifetime.'

'I won't feel properly slappered until I've waited a whole week.'

Jemima was laughing. Fiona smiled affectionately. She knew she wouldn't laugh at herself in such circumstances. She had long seen off such innocence and would never get it back. Yes, they would wait another day, for Jemima no problem. They'll have a quiet night, get up early and check the mail as usual. At least it comes early, and they can have the rest of the day to ponder moving or not, again.

The next day Jemima woke Fiona. 'I've been to the post office. No letter.'

'Oh well . . .'

'But he sent a card, really!'

Fiona was still half-asleep but awake enough to be pleasantly surprised by Mussolini's epistolary effort, small though it was. At least it meant they could now leave Surat Thani.

'Read it, you'll love it!' Jemima was twinkling and tingling; adorable but a bit lively before breakfast.

Fiona picked up the big card, clenched her eyes, opened them and examined the tiny scrawl.

'Hi, it's Joseppi here, except that my name is not Joseppi. It's Richard, I'm English (actually half-Welsh) but after Simes and I decided to pretend we were Italian to you and Fiona, I just couldn't take it back because you were so trusting and never picked up on any of our mistakes. If I'd admitted it you would have felt like we were taking the piss out of you. I felt so much like a worm after we had sex. Weekend before last I almost drowned – don't feel sympathetic; I don't deserve it; I fell off a boat stoned – and have been feeling calmer and more thoughtful since then. I realise it doesn't matter, in the vast scheme of life, that I deceived you, but I think you should know I really did think you were lovely, an absolute treat to meet. I'm in Wales – my mother's wedding (no joke though I do feel like a bastard; my mother is remarrying) but note my Scottish address above, that's where I'm contactable. I have a (very on–off) girlfriend, but please get in touch if you want. I hope you do. And I hope you are well. I also hope someone is honest with you and can enjoy and appreciate you in a way that I stopped myself from doing. I regret that. You have nothing to regret. It's a lucky man who ends up with you.

Tons and tons of love and precious memories,
Rich (Richard Ross)

Jemima waited until Fiona finished reading and grinned like a child who's been handed a big candy floss. 'God, imagine, what is he up to now? Who is he?'

'Let's see now, it's 7.00 a.m. here so it's 1.00 a.m. there, so he's floating around some Edinburgh pub or club or party, lying to some other girl, but I'll give him a point for the postcard, that was straight.'

Jemima laughed: 'I feel nicely slappered now.'

Fiona regarded her: 'None of them will ever love you as much as me.'

'I know. They've got a lot to measure up to. I don't make it that easy for them. I'm not as stupid as you think.'

'Right, Slackpants, we're leaving Surat Thani. And fuck Mussolini, I mean Rich, we're leaving, we are!'

'We are, and I already fucked Mussolini, you mean Rich,' said Jemima, jumping onto the bed to tickle Fiona, who shoved her off. But Jemima, physically far stronger, jumped back on and invaded her ribs properly. 'And I need to be bossed about by Miss Misery Guts, do I?' Fiona couldn't stop laughing. 'Sorry Fi, you cynical cow, can't make out a word you're saying . . .'

B ack in Edinburgh, lovely darkness had shrouded everything. Rich relished the mood: people feeling vague and spontaneous, flying on alcohol and drugs, though it was really only him. To think that less than an hour ago he was worried about Jean, a stupid junkie who nearly OD'd, but hey, she hadn't, and hey, he didn't know her anyway, just held the tourniquet on her weedy, wasted arm while she injected, big deal, she asked him to, he never wanted to, he never wanted to be in a room with her, he never wanted to be on a planet with her, not his fault, and not a problem any more, because he knew she had pulled through, and his spirits were soaring, that junkie business, all gone, oh yes, and thanks to his two foreign friends, Charles, from Bolivia via West Africa (probably), and Mr Holsten, an unusually jolly German, he was tickety-boo all right, just the job and ready to use that fin thing. Now, where's the prey?

Well, how about that? She is here. Right on cue. But no, wait. Now Rich wasn't much of a one for remembering things – the previous evening was often a stickler – but he remembered this woman, very clearly. He had seen her only twice, ever; that long dark hair and those strange dark, blue eyes, a memorable combination, but not as memorable as the way she made him nervous. Why? He was having trouble thinking. Right, he had never talked to her but both times he had been dying to. Something had held him back. And it was bloody doing it again. But now, she is almost right by him. He felt too pissed both times before, he felt too pissed now. Bollocks.

What's that about? He talked to women all the time pissed. He got pissed in order to do it. What's so scary about this one? It's not as if she's the most beautiful he's ever had, she may be completely stupid, she may just look interesting because he's on class A drugs. Many dull things look interesting when one is on drugs. Rich reminded himself he was indeed on drugs; he believed that if you just remind yourself, regularly, you don't do anything too stupid. But he should tread warily. She's with Holly and her friends, she was the other times too. It was at least six months ago he last saw her. Weird, he had really clocked this one to remember that. She's not around often and at this moment she is virtually within whispering distance; it's now or never. This is as good a chance as he's ever likely to get. What's the big deal? It's not as if he hasn't been red-carded a hundred times before. What does it matter?

'Hi, have I met you before?' asked Rich.

'No, I don't think so.'

'No, I didn't think so either. But I feel it's always best to check. Don't you?'

'That must be up there with "d'you come here often?" '

Love her voice, as precise as her eye contact.

'Sorry. I couldn't think of anything to say and felt like talking to you. I'll bugger off if you like.'

'What do you want to talk about?'

'Oh, I was thinking of Plato's *Republic*? Post-Romantic faith in originality? Or Occam's razor if you want to get obscure?'

'What's obscure about medieval monks? William of Occam was a star in his day. And why try to hide behind intellectual superiority if you want to talk to me?'

Fucking brilliant!

'Sorry, just don't know what to say. Eh, can I buy you a drink?'

For Christ sake Rich, how clichéd and awful are you trying to be here arsehole! Concentrate.

108

'Yes thanks, but I'm leaving soon.'

'Yes. Yes I mean of course. It's closing soon. Sorry I have been drinking all day, against my will.'

'Against your will?'

'Really. I know that sounds like bullshit, but it's true, it's too tricky to explain . . .'

Shut the fuck up Rich. Just shut the fuck up. Go buy some drinks before you make even more of a fool of yourself if that's possible.

'. . . I'll get the drinks. Another red wine?'

She nodded. Rich could not recall wanting to be served so fast. He was petrified she would leave. When he returned she thanked him and smiled. He smiled back, uneasily, unworthily.

'Sorry about my pretentious philosophy references.'

'Shame. I'm rather interested in Plato's Republicanism, I think it's vastly underrated.'

'Really? Well, actually . . .'

'I'm kidding. I don't know much about philosophers, just happened to know about Occam's razor.'

'I don't know much either, I think I was just being a creep by trying to agree. Sorry. Our relationship is two minutes old and I have apologised, what? Four times? Sorry. Oops. Five.'

'That's OK. I like apologies from men.'

'Eh, are you from Edinburgh?'

'With this accent?'

Oh, good one, arsewipe, you really are keeping your cool tonight.

'Of course, sorry – aaaargh sixth time, look I'm not a creep – where are you from?'

Nice accent, but it's always the voice that counts; faintly husky, but excellent articulation, very girlie, sounds like a stuck-up twelve year old chainsmoker, and you don't get many of them to the pound.

'A village in Wiltshire.'

'Oh.'

What do you mean 'oh' numpty-face? Like you know it well?

'Whereabouts?'

'Near Salisbury. Where are you from?'

'All over . . .'

Please tell me I didn't say that.

'. . . Well I mean I've lived in England and Scotland all my life, sort of fifty-fifty here and London in the last few years, but a while in Spain before then, and a little while in Ireland. I'm half-Welsh, Half-English and, eh, that's it.'

Ground, swallow me. Did I go on a dullness course recently?

'I'm English.'

'Yes, you are . . .'

Talk sense numpty.

'. . . And what do you do?'

'I work in the travel industry.'

'Oh, interesting.'

'Really?'

'Well, I don't know, actually.'

'The industry is dull. The travel is fun.'

'You get to travel then?'

She just fucking told you that, you charmless little globule of discarded, festering chewing gum.

'Yes.'

Get your act together man.

'Look I'm just going to the toilet. I'll be right back. Please don't go away.'

She looked nonplussed. She had taken about two sips of her wine. Why should she be going away?

Rich didn't feel he had time to put out a line and he fell into a panic again that she would leave. The floor was flooded, the cubicle was disgusting and the door wouldn't lock. Christ, normally this place was in good nick. Right, oral it is. He filled his gums with several lines worth of cocaine and left, not even using the toilet, which he needed. He hurried up to her looking frantic.

'My name's Rich. What's yours?'

Christ, need some beer, tingling something awful, mouth totally numbed. Rich started glugging back his lager at a ridiculous rate. He worried about washing the cocaine into his stomach. The woman watched him, her smile broadening all the time.

'My name is Lee-Ann.'

Now she was laughing. Rich couldn't figure why. Had he been so crass? He thought he was being fairly straight with her, he was too zonked for bullshit. The tingling in his gums was wild. He took another mouthful of Pils. Oh no. No. No. No. And yes. Classic amateur mistake. He had been pouring drink down the front of his numbed mouth, right on to his light blue French Connection jumper.

It turned out to be a good icebreaker. They talked a lot. He admitted he had taken 'a little cocaine'. She almost never touched drugs. Simes joined them for a quick drink and dutifully slunk off like a good wingman. Rich didn't fancy his chances, but believed it would be rude not to try. 'Time's about to be called, so I'm heading now for a cab. Would you like to join me for coffee? Neither of us have work in the morning.'

She laughed instantly. It took Rich a few seconds to analyse what he had said.

'Sorry. I do mean coffee. Honest, we can keep it to that. I didn't mean to suggest you stay the night.'

'Sure you didn't. Forget it right now. But I'll come back for coffee, I'm not tired. It will just be coffee, in fact herbal tea if you have any?'

111

'Eh thanks, I mean yes, herbal tea.'

That is to say we can get the taxi to stop at the all-night garage. No, wait, I had an Earl Grey earlier, that should do. Will Earl Grey do? Maybe she wants Rosehip? Or Camomile?

Something like that, don't think I've got any, the garage won't have any either, just Earl Grey, shit. And what about milk? There wasn't much left after that cereal, but, no, she probably won't want any milk in herbal tea, right, got that sorted, Earl Grey'll need to do. Wait. Rich, you are panicking about types of tea. You are losing it. She doesn't care that much.

They didn't talk much in the taxi. However back in the flat, Rich realised she was more drunk that she seemed in the pub, but still, she had a force-field round her. Anyone attempting to enter will be blown out, sharp-style. His touchy-feely-cokey mood was not mutual. For once he had been almost completely honest when chatting up (except forgetting to mention he had a girlfriend, but who ever remembers that?) But no way was she going to crack. That's where honesty gets you.

Fuck it, let's close the night with even more alcohol.

But first, while he boiled the kettle for her, he drank lots of water and forced a banana, a yoghurt and some cereal down his throat (dry, in case she wanted the dribble of milk; he hadn't fully subdued that beverage panic: that's the thing with drugs, the thought goes but the feeling stays). He went through to the living room to check and, to his surprise, she said she would join him in wine. This evening – this whole hellish food-free, drink-driven day infected by scary, proper junkies – might actually end his way.

His hope was dashed, at least momentarily, on the rock of perception. 'This is what you do, isn't it? You pick up women in bars and bring them back here, and when she says she'll take more drink you think "whey-ey, I'm in!" You're a bit practised and obvious. And I'm only drinking to make me tired. Sorry. Don't worry. For such a sleaze you're quite charming.'

'Eh, thanks. I think. I'm always being told I'm obvious. I'm always obvious. And tonight I'm drunk too. Mind you, I'm always that too.'

'I bet you have a girlfriend? But it's not going very well?'

'Ten out of ten. She lives in London.'

'Ah, long distance. Pseudo-commitment.'

'At least I'm honest.'

'Yeah, as far as it's appropriate. I don't mind. Some people can put great store by honesty. But often it's a way of being selfish and self-referential, and annoying or hurting other people. I think the idea of honesty is often childlike in its simplicity.'

'Hey, you sound like you're the cheating kind.'

'As I told you in the pub, I have no boyfriend. Remember? You were dying to find out. And I have been unfaithful only once in my life, six years ago, for two days when I was twenty.'

'Oh. I've not been so good.'

'Really, you surprise me . . .'

She is a curious character. And clearly has the good taste, or at least enough sobriety, to keep away from me. Got to concentrate; she is worth tuning in to. Her body, all vigour, no slinky-sexy stuff, yet frisson is great, I'd love to touch her.

'You know Rich, I know you think this is all a game. I bet you think life is all games.'

'No, I don't.'

'Hmm, I bet sometimes you meet certain people with the guts to take things seriously and you see your own cowardice?'

'Oh, that's a bit heavy, a bit clever, but yes, some truth there, as you well know, I'm very obvious. But just to smart women. Most women, most people, they're stupid, totally stupid, the rise of Nazism's no mystery to me. Hey, why do you keep picking on me?'

113

'Don't mean to, just chatting, and showing off. Guys like you, so easy to see through, especially when your defences are down, like now, because you have had all that cocaine and drink, I mean you're never off the job, are you? You're worse than my brother. Let's see: what would be the normal procedure to try to get me into bed now?'

'Eh, OK, well in this situation, where physical contact has not been established, by now I should be asking all about you, unless you are on drugs or are the show-off type – which *you* are – and in both cases you won't shut up so it's easier in a way. But assuming I have to draw you out, well, after that, after I've been all sympathetic about your childhood and your parents' divorce, your dreadful ex-boyfriend about whom I make wise noises and after I've smiled sweetly at your sentimental memories and you have confided about that problem with your girlfriend and I've furrowed like I empathise something painful, and I have successfully steered you between maudlin and frivolous and cross-referred back to earlier comments to show I am sincere and paying close attention, after all that, when you have come to believe – or at least hope – that I am a caring, listening kind of man, then I think we would dance, yes, sort of jokily. Then I think I would invite you to stay, without even going for a kiss first, in your case, I think.'

'So you patronise the shit out of me in other words?'

'Eh, hmmm. That might seem like the intention but I often end up genuinely interested if someone has had an interesting life or can talk about their experiences interestingly. It's sort of in spite of myself, I suppose.'

'And then you ask them to dance and then stay, just like that?'

'No, I ask casually, incidentally, you know? God, I'm so used to doing this I can't describe it . . .'

'A-ha! That's part of your technique! I saw it earlier, pretending you are being unusually honest. You're still trying.'

114

'You're being paranoid. But maybe right, OK, force of habit. Wouldn't you be offended if I weren't still trying to bed you?'

'Seriously, it's a waste of time. But tell me how you'd ask me to stay.'

'Right, you're very relaxed and a bit drunk, but crucially, you still have to be interested in me, so let's pretend. By the way, it's interesting you're still here. Did you know it's because you have a brother about the same age? Yes, women who have brothers, big advantage, much more relaxed with guys. We're less otherly. Isn't that a good word for it? "Otherly"? Childhood sharing: the die is cast; colours your perceptions for life. As you can no doubt tell I had a sister.'

' "Never trust a man who has no sister, he'll cling to your breast, so only know him" – The Go-Betweens, an old Australian pop band. And so true. It works both ways. I remember listening to those words when I was eleven and thinking they were very funny. By nineteen I thought they were incredibly wise. But I think the ones without siblings of the opposite sex maybe find it more exciting with the opposite sex, that otherly thing? No?'

'Dunno, but that song you like, do you attract the cling-ons?'

'Mm, often.'

'Well, I'm never clingy.'

'Really?'

'Honest.'

'You promise?'

'Honest. I'll expect nothing.'

'You sure?'

'Yes! You can stay. Afterwards it's your shout. Seriously, whatever you choose.'

Lee-Ann laughed. 'You really are *never* off the job! I'm not staying. Do. You. Speak. English?' At first Rich was annoyed.

But soon he raised his eyebrows and smiled. He had walked into that. She was stylish. She was something.

'So Rich, in that alternative universe where you are in with a dog's chance in hell of sleeping with me, what happens next? You were saying? If you're not too out of it?'

'Yeah right I say some bollocks like, "Why not stay, you know, just to crash; we don't have to sleep together", to make it easier for you to agree. And then you say, "OK, but just to sleep" and you look at me sternly, as if you would never stay with such a recent male acquaintance on any other terms, heaven forbid. And I nod, in a small, of-course sort of way. So then you wonder that maybe I'm not that bothered about sleeping with you which of course faintly outrages you and makes you want me to want to sleep with you. And this sort of pulls you into the idea too, assuming you were swithering. And you wouldn't stay otherwise.

'Alternatively, you are completely confident that I want to sleep with you – and you should be by then, I mean I am *so* obvious, as you like to point out, but some women aren't totally sure, it's weird, self-esteem problem or drink muddling them up usually, and once in a while you come across true innocence, whereby they genuinely believe you only want to sleep beside them, got to be careful with those ones, can waste hours trying to get round them – anyway, once you're sure, I'll still manage to plant a teasing little doubt in you, once we're in bed.'

'You! No way! You're far too . . . *obvious.*'

Rich thought about that. Lee-Ann was wrong. The cocaine was doing its duty. He was fairly focused and energised now. He badly wanted to disprove her, and have a go at turning her on in the process. He was an expert on the stand-off after lights-off.

'Oh yes I will,' he announced. 'By taking ages to test the waters once I've put the lights out. By then we're lying in bed, breathing quietly, trying to remain very still. Some time

116

passes. It becomes significant if you move; the other has trouble not responding. This intensifies as you notice it. Pretty soon if one twitches, just ever so slightly, the other instantly just *must* scratch their nose or something. And they *must* know if that movement you made means desire or discomfort. And therein lies the inevitable. Supposing you had decided against sex, you still want to know about that movement. You have to know. And the harder you try to lie still – to prove your entire consciousness is not infused with the other person's presence and your curiosity about their arousal – the harder it gets. The communication becomes electric, your brain is buzzing, every moment charges it more. Soon, just the faint sound of breathing becomes significant, and then you worry your breathing is too loud, or too fast. And your heart, its beating, is that deafening? You think it would be best if you could pretend you were dozing off but you are nowhere near dozing off; couldn't be more awake with a ton of amphetamine fuelling you. Jesus, what to do? And still the tension rises. Sex has now floated across your mind, as you know, and quietly settled into it, as you do not know. You see, you are already having sex. All your hopes and dreams and fears and worries that exist in the rest of your life, they're on hold. You are just here now. That is sex. Think of the tension which suspends you, your yearning for catharsis; you're having forcplay but you don't know it.'

'Mmm, and all that comes after not looking at me while I undress, right? Just to my underwear, of course.'

'Of course.'

'OK.'

'What? Don't start teasing me again, I know you won't stay.'

'Oh, good line of attack: try to challenge them to stay. But we both know you've no chance. What I meant was, if your druggy little brain can take it in, we'll do the dancing bit. I feel like dancing.'

'Really? OK, well, after this amount of drugs, and this being about seduction and fun, the best way is to cut to the quick. So I ask you to dance alone. And strip. I love it.'

'Oh do you now? By dancing I meant we just danced, you know, both of us, in clothes.'

'Oh, come on, you're a show-off and you love to tease, think about it, go for it. Don't worry, the planets won't fall out their orbits.'

'You are kidding.'

Her voice was playful, not outraged. This conversation, it feels like a ritual. Good God, would she? Oh that body.

'Oh yeah, I mean I would be so shocked at a woman sexily undressing herself. And I am sure no man has ever seen you naked. Go on Miss Tease, Miss Tease With Ease, that's what I call you in my head now.'

Strange, Rich asked so soon, but then she really is a show-off tease – and no less wonderful for that – so why not? She's taking time to reply, she is melting, oh yes.

'I pick the music, and I think I'll stop at my underwear.'

She is going to strip. Miss Tease has leapt over to my CDs and is rummaging through them. And she is going to strip. Fucking hell, I'm in. Miss Tease. Stripping. There is a God. This nightmare day is about to end like a dream. Miss Tease. Stripping. Got to play it cool.

'I'll just get more wine.' Rich sauntered off as if it was perfectly normal behaviour to striptease for an acquaintance of three hours. Even by his own high standards of sleaze, this was fast, usually took five hours between meeting and stripping, actually it usually didn't happen, let's be honest, but still this was scarily fast. Is she really going to? It can happen. He recalled Simes meeting a woman for the first time at a party and fucking her within minutes: drink and drugs, anything might happen in that maelstrom. He recalled a most bizarre one: sleeping with a girl in the afternoon, he had only met her in the park two hours before, when he was all hungover and fragile: she had warmed to his vulnerability, and she was rebounding. So bingo. And no alcohol involved that day. But this? This was an odd one too. Lee-Ann is a control-freak. She does what she wants. And she wants to do this? Wow. Is she really going to do it?

Lee-Ann shouted through to the kitchen: 'Lady Marmalade, "La Belle", has to be.'

Yip, she's gonna do it. Yipee. Think how long these things would take if drink wasn't involved.

Rich had been negotiating, spiritually, with the concept of not drinking. He loathed it. In truth he had a sneaking respect for arranged marriages. All those sensible parents choosing partners for their young and stupid offspring, all that responsibility and expectation given you before you've even seen her body, sometimes before you've even seen her. Christ we decide to have sex when we can hardly walk or talk properly, let alone think sensibly. Praise be to the great God Alcohol. It lets people like him away with so much. Without that magical potion we might find the right person and miss all the fun. And women might put him in his place more often. But this, Miss Tease With Ease stripping, this was living.

She turned off the pause button as he entered the room. She had already turned up the volume. Immediately she started swaying her hips, standing right in front of the old fireplace, facing the couch which they had been sharing and he now sat back down on, barely able to believe she was actually going to do it.

She had wiped all expression from her face and was concentrating on swaying, on enjoying dancing. She met his eye, the blank face faintly sultry now, and then she looked away and started to dance about properly, moving her feet. She didn't need his encouragement or approval. This woman had decided she would strip and that was that.

119

Her movements were confident but careful; she wasn't flamboyant, no strutter, far too controlled to just let it all hang out. She was one of those who existed in isolation, she wasn't in the room at all. She was stripping, that's where she was, nowhere else.

She's proud of her body – and well she might be: curvy but compact, vital but not frenetic. A true show-off, she sort of wears it rather than lives in it. And she wears it well. Very well. Very sexual and sexy, and still not even taken a stitch off. A natural tease, straight into the part; automaton sex object. She just knows how to do it.

At the first chorus she widened her legs and ground downwards stroking the inside of her thighs, still writhing her hips in circles, flicking her head from side to side, her loose, knee-length skirt riding up her legs. No tights, shoes kicked off before she started. She ground upwards, swivelled round so her back was to Rich and moved her arse in small circles while unbuttoning her dark blue shirt. Then she flipped her head backwards and rolled her shoulders, sticking near the beat. The blouse fell away from her neck to hang halfway down her back, a drape.

He could see her flesh now, surprisingly dark, almost Mediterranean, supple but firm. She turned to face him, her expression still sultry-blank, that faint pout, not a trace of shame, sex itself. Her black bra had no frills or lacy bits, it was stark and neat, like her dancing. She slipped out of the shirt then looked away and ground down to her hunkers again, more vigorously this time and lower. She mimed along to the chorus 'voulez-vous coucher avec moi, ce soir?' Her skirt was riding higher up her thighs. She opened her legs more, then abruptly halted the peep show and shot up, twirling round at the same time, so he could now see her pulling the zip on her skirt down at the back. All the while her arse was swaying. She pulled her legs together, her arms in the air and the skirt fell to reveal her gyrating arse. Then she unhooked her bra and turned to face him, holding the loose bra to her breast with her left hand, the bra-straps dangling by her sides. A couple of little dancey steps towards him, a dead-eye glance from those blue jewels, and it was dropped.

Next the arms were waving high again, to show off her small utterly unsagging tits, with small brown nipples. This was a woman in full bloom. Her skin and her body, like her blue eyes and her black hair, they didn't match yet went perfectly. The skin tone was Mediterranean, the body an upright non-pear, more Northern European. She was a mongrel, a beautiful freak, captivating. She started writhing towards him, waving her arms in front of her as if gesturing to him to come to her. Rich recalled that junkie creature, Jean, offering him her arm earlier. God, so far away now. That bony, track-marked, feeble limb and this succulent flesh, in the one day.

She knew the song was nearly finished, the fade-out was starting, but still she hooked her thumbs into her black briefs unhurriedly, and edged them down, taking a few seconds, all the while wiggling her hips and looking him in the eye, defying him to be vulgar enough to leave her eye for her cunt. He did it. She smiled. As the music faded out she opened her legs, and just slightly, lightly stroked the front of her pubic hair. It was a sensual fraction of a second, a visual image that would stay with Rich for some time. The music finished. He clapped.

'Wow!' he said, and meant it, but he couldn't think what to add to that, too turned on for polite pleasantries.

'Did you enjoy that? I did,' said Lee-Ann. For once she looked self-conscious, but just for a moment. A quiet insight intruded on Rich's arousal: she is actually very self-conscious, just manages to hide it normally. He smiled at her vulnerable nakedness, no longer led by lust – though that was still there – but by unexpected tenderness.

'Eh, yes, very much so, yes, eh, very erotic. Very, very erotic. You have a great body, great dancer, what can I say?!'

'Thanks. Your turn.'

Rich laughed nervously.

'You really are very sexy,' he said.

'Hmm. Your turn.'

'Ha-ha.'

She was putting her skirt and blouse back on, no underwear.

'Choose your music.'

'Look, ha-ha, I'm kind of drunk and . . .'

'I'll get more wine. I want a last glass. We need to open that other bottle so you've got about two minutes. I want the music to start when I return.'

Oh Christ. Talk about someone having you by the balls. It would be rude to refuse after she'd done it. And even more imperative, just now she will stay and if he refuses she might get petulant and clench up. Oh Jesus, help. Think fast. He had been here before. No, wait, he hadn't. When he had been forced to do a reciprocate strip for Natalie, it was totally, completely, utterly different. Natalie was fun, a regular bed-mate, that is to say, *not* terrifying. But the same thoughts went through his head then. What can you do? Bed was by now a certainty, right? So what is there to hide? But still, he couldn't dance with the control and relish of a Lee-Ann. In truth he wasn't that confident a person. Last time he did an old funny song, Jonah Lewie's 'In the Kitchen at Parties', which he sort of mimed along to. But that was different: Natalie was a fellow party animal, she dressed and stripped again, twice. Lee-Ann scares him, she makes him nervous, she just does. He remem-bered that she always had, even before he talked to her tonight. Shit.

Same song again? No. Something surprising and powerful, not too difficult to dance to, or he'd just look stupid, some-thing energetic but not a dance track, too monotonous. So what? What boxers was he wearing? Oh no, those bloody silly purple ones. He had energy and a certain charm to his dance but that was it. His body was fine, small boned, very little fat *et cetera* but really he just wasn't comfortable doing a striptease. OK so he was a hypocrite, expecting that show from women, but Jesus, women laugh and shriek at male strippers, whereas guys do get turned on, they're that dumb. Oh shit, just pick a song, any song, no, a short song, a sexy song, no, couldn't live up to it, so not any song; but do give a show. Oh shit.

Dimmer, switch the dimmer down more, yes, good plan! Chakka Demus and Pliers, 'Tease me', that's the one; fun, honourable sentiment, and about stripping, sort of, and with that cute miaow sound. More importantly, it's short! Isn't it?

Lee-Ann walked in as Rich was loading the CD.

'Just coming,' he spoke assertively.

'Just turning the dimmer back up,' she spoke more assertively.

Rich smiled. She really was something. She really was worth making a fool of yourself for. And here goes.

Rich started reggae dancing in an exaggerated way, then he switched to mimicking rap strutting, doing that rolly slow punch using the whole forearm and sticking out fingers at odd angles. He was parodying and enjoying it. He put on mean mutha' expressions even though the music was gentle and earthy, not urban at all, apart from the rap invocations.

Now he mimicked a pseudo-coy striptease artist, fluttering his eyelids and then turning his back towards Lee-Ann while looking over his shoulder at her, sultrily. She was laughing. He was encouraged. He moved his hips gently and lifted his jumper up and over his head. He twirled round to face her in one step, pouted at her, absurdly, and threw the jumper away. She laughed more and clapped. He had his shoes off. And he figured there is simply no sexy or amusing way to take off one's socks. He leant down, holding her eye while moving his own eyebrows up and down quickly, suggestively, as if he were a woman being knowingly desired, while he got hold of his socks. Then he recalled how an old-fashioned professional might pull of stockings. He switched tactics and put his right leg up on the arm of the couch, pouted again, and swayed while slowly pulling his sock down. Then he looked at her meaningfully, switched legs and pulled down the left one slowly. Lee-Ann was in knots.

He undid his jeans, made feminine circles with his hips and then pulled them off macho-rough. He adopted male model poses as if he was showcasing his lurid purple boxers. He did a little catwalk stride up and down in front of her, pausing at each turn to strike a pose and indicate the boxers with his hands.

Next he took off his loose T-shirt, as if it were tight, inch by inch, like a lycra bodyhugger around a torso bursting with muscle, as opposed to his own lean frame. Lee-Ann watched and followed every joke, laughing and drinking.

Now it was down to his boxers and the song was approaching fade-out. She did it, after saying she would leave her underwear on. He didn't want to do it, but it seemed churlish not to. He copied her: thumbs down the side, no wait, pull back up, the music rang out on cue – 'tease me, tease me . . .' – he did it again, down to the bottom of his pubes, and back up. This was good therapy, preparing for the full monty. Go for it. He turned round, back to her, pulled them down, wiggled, they fell to the floor, the music was fading and as he birled round to face her he discreetly tucked his penis between his legs which he then crossed so that when she looked to where it should be, there was just a pubic mound with him bent over it, bowing to signify the end of the performance. Lee-Ann beamed at him and raised her eyebrows questioningly. He smiled back, relaxed his legs, stood up and let his penis flop out. He wasn't hard, far too self-conscious, probably a good thing. Then he swiftly picked up his jeans and put them back on.

Lee-Ann was still smiling and giggling when he sat beside her.

'That was lovely,' she said.

'Glad you thought so,' Rich replied, relieved it was over, but surprised that it hadn't been more trying, and feeling extremely happy to have amused Lee-Ann. 'More wine?'

'No, I've got to go, it's getting late.'

'What?!'

'Yeah, sorry about that . . .'

'But, one more glass? You can stay, eh? I thought you might want to.'

'Oh, just to sleep of course?'

'Whatever you want, It'd be nice to cuddle you, we don't have to have sex, I mean I thought that would be good.'

'You mean you thought I'd stay because I stripped? Cuddle? You didn't mention that tactic earlier.'

She was smiling as she put on her shoes. Rich was panicked and confused. You can't strip and leave, one doesn't. Does one? Christ, this one does. She had picked up her underwear and was stuffing it in her bag, and now reaching for her coat. Rich was gawping, trying desperately to think of something persuasive to say. She spoke first.

'Don't worry,' she said. 'I'll get a taxi easily out there.'

'No, you can stay. I mean, why don't you stay? I mean, please stay. Look, we can just talk more . . .'

'Bye.' And she was heading to the door. And Rich could think of nothing more to say to stop her. He just watched, perplexed, as if this wasn't real, it just couldn't be. He heard the door close and was devastated. She hadn't even offered a phone number or email address, and he had been too flummoxed by her leaving and too drunk to think to ask. She was gone. And she didn't live in Edinburgh. He had just seen all of her and now he might never see any of her again. From unalloyed joy to killer frustration in ten minutes. Shit.

After a few seconds a smile built on Rich's lips. Soon he laughed out loud. Then he spoke out loud, in his empty flat: 'Nice one!'

Tuesday, 16th May

I need to add final details to a story I have been writing –
unknowingly – for a long time. The first entry will be
almost exactly two years old. I have to word search and cut
and paste bits of my diary together, from since that time. It'll
take hours, but it must be done. I'll just pick out relevant bits.
I'll not edit. And I'll not dare try to understand.

Wednesday, 6th May

When does love come? I watch people; I am a compulsive
diarist and story gatherer. I feel like I spend my life trying to
learn. And other women seem to be born knowing about
love, like Amaranta. She marries Josh on Saturday, it's her
hen night tomorrow. She glows, smiles and is fearless. She
doesn't expect to dwell in bad relationships, so she doesn't.
People like me expect it, so we find it and we wallow in it. I
know you find what you're looking for, in some sense, I've
learnt that. It scares me.

Amaranta found Josh, always an intelligent livewire, but he
drank too much. Now he doesn't. You just know it came
naturally. She never had to nag him. He is hilarious, always
telling stories against himself, and a good listener, the only
person I know who is as good a listener as me. And unlike
smarmers, he remembers things; asks you again weeks later.

127

They make it look effortless. Both are energetic and passionate, but together they are serene. When they got together something was completed. You can sense their life ahead. It will be a good, successful life and after one dies, the other will die younger than they would have.

Grief will reap the last one in early. Weird thought: you look at their relationship and envisage it ending with a shared headstone. Even then it won't end. Their bodies will rot into each other and feed the earth together. In some sense they will be together forever. How does love like that come?

Amaranta knows, instinctively. You know or you don't. You are her or you are me. She doesn't have to make all these notes and try to learn, and mostly fail. Yet she does know about bad times. She once told me that for twenty months, before Josh, she had virtually stopped having periods. She was so uninterested in men and sex that she worried she had no hormones. She said, 'Now I'm a vampire's dream every month. And I can't get fucked enough.' She looked luminous as she said that.

Thursday, 7th May

This evening Amaranta walked into the pub for her own hen night, asked everyone to be quiet and placed a fawn sheet of A4 on the table. Then she said: 'That is a letter Josh wrote me today, when I was at work. He's left me. All I know is what is in that letter. I don't know where he is. Do any of you know?'

Silence, then a few incredulous 'eh?'s and 'what?'s. Amaranta nodded slowly, not taking her eyes off us. Her lovely brown eyes were rock steady. It looked like some kind of mania. But when she spoke again she was terser, running out of self-control: 'I need to find him.'

We were really struggling to take this in. Was it a joke? Amaranta and Josh were getting married next Saturday. We had been discussing her dress. The shock wave wouldn't recede. Amaranta closed her manic eyes, tensed her face, opened them and nodded at the printout. We started reading, gingerly, so badly not wanting this to be real. The paper was headed with their home address.

Amaranta,

My love, this is hard for me and I know it will be harder for you. I am sorry, beyond words, but I have left you. My stuff is outside in my car and in thirty minutes I will be out of your life, driving far away from Edinburgh. I won't return for months, maybe years, until the fallout from me doing this has cleared. Even then I can't imagine wanting to live in Edinburgh again.

I cannot marry you since I am still in love with Ali. It is no lacking in you. I think you have taken me as far away from her as any woman could. You deserve somebody who can love you completely, not somebody who is grounded in the past. In my heart I have never got over her, not for a moment in six years. I am going to ask her to leave Jamie and be with me. I doubt if she'll say yes, but it would be weak not to try, just as it would be false to marry you when I'm yearning for her.

Above all, I apologise for leaving it close to the wedding. I think it had to go that way. I think I hoped – sometimes assumed – I wouldn't feel this way. I suppose I wanted the momentum of all the wedding arrangements to carry me further away from Ali. It hasn't. As it approaches, the prospect of marrying you feels like an honour being bestowed upon a pretender. It would be cowardice and laziness for me to go through with it.

I have cancelled the church, minister, marquee, hotel rooms, cars, chauffeur, video, photographer, caterers, microphone hire, make-up girl, flowers, favours, place-name stationery, organist, tailor, ceilidh band, bar, DJ and honeymoon. We lose the deposit on the honeymoon, caterers and wedding cake, and on the hotel which your parents paid. I've posted a cheque to them. I've sent cards to some guests but I've done an emailshot for most of them. It's underneath this file. I'm afraid you have to press send. If I sent it now I would be inundated with hassle while I'm slipping away.

The flat, furniture, any mutual possessions and whatever I've left behind is yours to keep or get rid off. I've put six months of my share of the mortgage into the joint account, which I won't use forthwith. (I took out a bank loan to do this.)

Do not waste time looking for me. Nobody will know where I am. I don't ask for forgiveness. I do ask you to get on with your life, as fast as you can, as soon as the anger and grief have subsided. If I could I would take the pain and bear it for you.

You are wonderful and you deserve to be fully loved. I wish I could be that man. I am crying and my heart is breaking for both of us.

Josh

After we read it Karen spoke first, like an animal growling. 'It's as well he's gone to ground. God help him if I meet him.' Everyone was glaring as they thought about Josh.

We were all about to rip into him but the look on Amaranta's face halted us. She didn't want our venom. She wanted us to track Josh down and let her deal with it how she wanted. And, God knows, this was her call.

We reasoned somebody must know something about his plans. We used the six mobes we had between the eight of us and the pub payphone to call half of Scotland and quite a lot of London.

On the phone Ali confirmed he had asked her to come back to him. He rang her about 3.30 p.m. She told him he was insane to suggest it after all this time, that he was being sentimental and was hysterical with pre-wedding nerves. She shouted at him to get back to Amaranta where he belonged. If he just stayed she wouldn't mention the call to anyone and it would all be OK. When she said, 'I'll see you at your wedding on Saturday,' he hung up. She had dreaded this call all evening. She seemed almost as angry as us; 'He's as bloody useless as ever. Tell Amaranta she's worth more.'

Other than Ali, only his family had heard from him, about 5.45 p.m., just over an hour before. He had sounded calm. He said he was disappearing abroad for a few months and would ring to let them know he was fine. He apologised a lot but it had cut no ice with his mother. She too had dreaded this call: 'I thought he might have come to his senses. I don't know what he thinks he's playing at!' Afterwards they had 1471'd. It was a payphone near Tollcross.

An hour of interrogations later – including his brother in New Zealand, where it was almost six in the morning – we ran out of people to phone. Amaranta looked particularly disturbed after the calls she made to her and Josh's joint Visa service and twenty-four-hour bank. There were no bookings and he had tried to take his name off both accounts, but was told to write in. Amaranta said she could sense he had posted the letters already.

Nobody knew a thing about Josh's plans. He had organised this well. He meant it.

We could feel him slipping further away as we sat there, down some motorway, or into an airport perhaps. The frantic phoning had given Amaranta hope; everyone having ideas and offering facile reassurance. Now she didn't say anything. She sat there, biting her lip, still trying to keep herself together.

We all shushed each other to hold in our spite. It felt like being in a coven, but lynch mob would be more accurate. We had witnessed every women's nightmare come true, and for one of the best among us; so loving she didn't share our bile. We couldn't think what to say.

I imagined the hell of the years ahead; the hurt returning each time she thought it had died, the fear of never trusting anyone again, perhaps really never trusting anyone again, the feeling that it's all her fault, the nervous terror that comes with that, the creeping bitterness and all the sleepless nights as she cried herself raw. I imagined that this minute, as she sat there in front of us, it was all starting to etch its way into her pretty features.

She spoke quietly. 'I thought the same as Ali, that he was being sentimental. The past doesn't matter. I know this was meant to be. But maybe I just wasn't enough for him'

Everyone objected but she wasn't hearing anything.

Friday, 8th May

Josh rang this evening. My heart skipped a beat but I kept my cool – at first. I knew this was delicate. He could hang up any moment, and he will have 141'd. I opened gently: 'Josh, honey, what are you playing at? Why don't you just come back for the wedding and this will all be laughed about in the best man's speech. Don't be embarrassed, people will understand, they'll be glad you're there, you could . . .'

'Listen, Denny, I need a favour. Forget the wedding. It's cancelled. Are you alone and can I trust you?'

'Yes I'm alone and of course you . . .'

'Denny, we've known each other a long time. Don't patronise me. I know you're angry.'

I exploded, called him a wimp, a sentimental piss artist, a

selfish egomaniac playing God with a lovely woman's life who he clearly doesn't deserve but he'll get what he deserves if he ever sets foot in Edinburgh again, it's the talk of the town and people hate his stinking, worthless guts which I for one would happily tear out *et cetera* . . .

He waited until I ran out of puff. 'Denny. You are someone I trust. I need your help.'

I asked him if he had a clue what he was doing? He said, 'No . . . Just got to get away . . . Got to get away . . . from all this hurt.'

'You caused it!'

'It's not that simple. Trust me.'

A few of the menfolk in the company have been saying that. Arguments have broken out, invariably partner against partner, as any man who dared show any modicum of understanding whatsoever to Josh got it in the neck. But it made me think.

Mike, who had only met Josh a couple of times, said, 'Would you have admired him for going through with a wedding when he wanted to marry someone in the congregation? You know he cared deeply about Amaranta. What is he going through?'

I still thought Josh was pathetic but I had slightly softened to him before the call, but only slightly, and it felt like a betrayal of Amaranta and our girlfriends.

Josh said he didn't know what he was going to do. He had decided to bail out only three days before he did it. He'd had a lot of organisation to distract him until two days ago. Then he drove off. He hadn't been able to look beyond that point.

Now he was in limbo; left one existence, didn't have the faintest idea how the next one would go. He wanted tomorrow to be gone. Only then would it fully sink in that he wasn't marrying Amaranta. I began to feel sympathy for the bastard.

He and I have a small history, of course, just drunken flingette stuff really. We never mention it, nothing to say about it, I suppose. But now it seems significant, I think, because I have agreed to help him.

I am the only person in the world who knows where he is. He's in Manchester, where he's a complete stranger. He's about to sell his Renault and fly to Greece 'for God knows how long'. He's got his computer with him, three thousand pounds from the loan and he's going to set up on the island of Santorini. He's never been there but he liked the look of it on *The Holiday Programme*. He's flipped.

He insists that as a website creator he can work from anywhere. He wants me to keep him posted about Amaranta, check she is OK. He will ring every 3–4 weeks and set up a new email address in a week.

Before he hung up he said something curious. 'Things aren't quite what they seem. Bear with me.'

Tuesday, 1st September

Josh's third call. Bad as ever. Amaranta is still cut up. I saw her yesterday. She was worse than she was last week. She cried endlessly, blaming herself for being so stupid as to fall for Josh, then blaming herself for not being enough of a woman to take him away from Ali, then blaming herself for being such a cry baby, then blaming herself for giving up (only good sign). Always blaming herself.

'Sometimes I cry calmly,' she said. 'It's not always hysterical. I feel like someone has died . . . The really bizarre thing is I keep wanting to talk to Josh about this problem I have. Even though he's the problem I still want to talk to him to find out what I should do. Isn't that funny? I miss him so much it's made me mad . . . Why doesn't he contact me? I would forgive him. We could set another date. It was meant to be. He is on some mad trip. He must come back to me. I wish I knew where he was ... The doctor's put me on antidepressants. I know I'm pathetic and clichéd going on about it, but nothing else matters to me ...'

It's less than four months since Josh left, but to listen to Amaranta it could be less than a week. People have mostly stopped talking about it. They still have sympathy, but now it's tinged with pity. Karen and I still call round on her. I'm the confidante therapist, Karen is the party-girl distraction. Curiously, Jeremy also calls round. He would have been best man at the wedding, Josh's best friend since they were ten. And he is falling hard for Amaranta.

He is extraordinarily different from Josh: stolid, determined, serious and a very rich property developer. He is also very good-looking, with beautiful bone structure, an elegant gait, thick, blond wavy hair and a quiet, enigmatic manner. But he's distant. He left Amaranta's today with me, and invited me for a drink.

He is famously uninterested in relationships and hardly even does flingettes or one-night stands. But now, in his thirties, he is doing some picking, he is going for Amaranta.

'I think what Josh did was shameful,' he said, and it rang out like 'I think I'm rather virtuous.'

'Who doesn't?' I asked. 'I'm sure even Josh thinks it was shameful.'

'But Amaranta, she doesn't, she thinks he made a mistake, she is so sweet she would forgive him if he came back.'

I could see his frustration. It must be infuriating for someone so committed to Project Amaranta. I told him: 'The way into Amaranta's heart is not to insult Josh, her anger will come and go, it's too personal to share in. I know you're interested in her.'

'Who wouldn't be?' he shrugged. It was more like hands-up. 'Except that idiot Josh. He was always too flighty and volatile, even at school.'

'You're sounding like an old man, Jeremy,' I laughed.

He laughed too: 'I know, I am careful, but you have to be careful, especially with people like Amaranta, such a loyal, decent, pretty, intelligent person. No wonder she is so popular.'

He didn't say sensual, perceptive, passionate – Amaranta's true allures. And popular? Think for yourself, decide for yourself, but I guess when you love someone you throw any compliment that comes to mind at them. He clearly wants me onside in his battle to get her. He wants to be her hero too, can't blame him for that, but he is a little too keen to show up his best friend, and a little too quick to insult him. Also, never catch someone when they're down, once they're up everything changes.

Maybe I'm picking on Jeremy? I feel loyal to Josh. But the prosaic truth is Amaranta needs to be taken away from Josh. Jeremy must be a good thing. It's just so sad and unnecessary. God, Josh is one stupid arse.

So now I feel like a traitor to Josh as well as Amaranta.

How would she feel if she found out I'm in touch with Josh? What would people say? He assured me he would never let anyone know we were in contact at this time, whatever happens in the future. He better not. Christ, I'm trusting a man you can't trust to turn up for his own wedding.

Wednesday, 2nd August

Josh sounded low on the phone. He cares more about Amaranta than himself. He seems to have given up on Ali, never asks a word about her. He just drinks and parties in Perissa, a holiday town. He hardly wakes during the day, except for a few hours on his computer.

He must be lonely, he had already emailed earlier:

Greetings Denny,

Carving a wonderfully shallow life out here. It still revolves around the black beach, but I no longer sleep on it; taken a cheapo apartment about 200 yards from it. The sand is black because the island is volcanic. By eleven in the morning it is too hot to walk on; you have to run over it from your beach mat to the sea. I work or drink every night, never sleep until the morning. I often walk down to the beach for the dawn; sometimes you see bums go up and down in the soft morning light. It looks more romantic than that sounds.

Miss you tons, thanks for everything.

Josh.

Amaranta has had a good month. She knows from Josh's family that he is OK. (He won't tell them where he is; he knows they would tell her.) She came out twice in the last fortnight. She drinks too much now. She wants to go back to work, says it will stabilise her. Her doctor says she's not ready.

Friday, 1st September

Josh rang tonight, drunk, and asked, straight away: 'Have Jeremy and Amaranta got together yet?'

I hadn't told him about their relationship. He just knew. Weird. I decided to come clean about helping Jeremy. After all, Christ knows why Josh deserves any consideration. Why do I feel so loyal to the bastard? Why do I feel sorry for him?

'No,' I replied. 'He takes her out a little now. He's very patient. He said to me she is too vulnerable, it would be too easy and it would be a rebound. It wouldn't work. He's waiting until she's ready.'

'That's good,' he said. 'She deserves that.'

'What's good about it?' I wanted to scream. 'You guilt-laden fool. She wants you, and can't have you because you are a complete arsehole, so she takes your best friend instead!'

But I didn't say anything. He's been down for months. What's the point in making him feel worse?

Wednesday, 23rd December

Earrings. So often it's earrings. A green one under our bed. Not mine. I confronted Mike when he got home. He shrugged innocently but turned red. I could feel his palpitations. It was pathetic. Mike and I are pathetic. No rage this time. No revenge cheating. I booked a weekend away. I'll see Josh, smile and pretend everything is sweet in my world, like my heart isn't in a hundred pieces, again. Mike thinks I'm going to a conference (starting three days after Christmas? Pillock).

Sunday, 27th December

In Santorini. Bizarre but brilliant seeing Josh. His hair is long, his face tanned and he looks all muscly and healthy. He really has carved out a new life. He shows it can be done. You are never as stuck as you think you are. And this isn't the facile drinking-and-shagging life that got him through summer. Now he spends two days of the week on an archaeological dig ('I really live in the past now, sentimental old me') and another two days building the website for the dig ('the past being stored up for future use; anything but the present for me').

It was just warm enough for an outdoor meal tonight. Over coffee, I listened to him rambling about the ancient Cretans. Watching his animated face, lapping up his innocent enthusiasm, I couldn't help feeling sad. Why does Amaranta have to be deprived of this joyous man? She deserves him.

I said, 'I'm sure you'd fit in well with Cretans,' and he laughed.

'I love the eternal things they tapped into. All that psychology stuff, which you are into Denny, we think it's all inside, these ancient cultures put it on the outside. They threw it into stars and stories. The god Dionysus gave Ariadne – who would become Queen of Crete – a jewelled coronet when they married. Now it's the constellation of stars, the Northern Crown.'

'Yes, you would like that myth, the one where Ariadne is left stranded on the beach in Naxos by Theseus, the man she has saved and loved and expects to marry. But it all works out fine for her, doesn't it? So it's OK.'

The mood between us tensed. He asked nervously: 'Is that bad of me?'

I felt like a brute. Of course it wasn't bad of him to want Amaranta to be with a god and become a queen. I collected myself. After all, what business is it of mine? Why does it still upset me? I said, 'Of course not.'

He added, in a mutter, as if to himself: 'Mind you, Jeremy's no god.'

He says he loves the winter, got fed up with the intense heat: 'Though of course there are less backpackers from Northern Europe to lay.'

Now he spends his nights reading, and drinking less. The local Greek boys know him and never bad vibe him, like they do with lots of English guys; both groups are competing for the foreign women (numbers problem; Greek women generally don't party). The Greek Casanova-fighters are called something like 'karmakis'.

He is also learning Greek. He has no plans to come home. 'This is home,' he declared, triumphantly. 'I'm moving to the other end of the island, to the capital, Ia, in a few days. It's resolutely Greek with few tourist facilities. Moving mainly for the sunset: it's one of the best in the world. The huge orange ball doesn't sink beneath the horizon, but beneath an invisible line well above the horizon. It really is that strange, like sci-fi, very epic sci-fi. Everyone gathers at the clifftop in the evening to watch the sunset, to pay homage to the magic. The ancient Greeks will have gathered there too. Also, I'm going to go to the nudist colony when the weather gets better. It's incredibly unsexy, an oldish crowd. You don't feel lecherous; no point when it's all hanging out. Nothing tantalising at all, but you get a great all-over tan.'

All this boyish passion, such contrast to Jeremy. What an odd pair they must have made as best friends. Yet both ending up falling for the same girl. I asked how he felt about Amaranta and Jeremy.

He answered with a grin: 'Still just want away from it all. Ancients, naturism and sun will do the job. Drink and Nordic slappers were never going to get me far.'

Is it that simple? Can you really just leave your past behind? Why can I not leave Mike?

Monday, 28th December

Josh has a romance kicking off, with Chrissie, an archaeology student from Athens and 'a latter-day Greek goddess,' apparently. They teach each other language 'and much else' (wouldn't have thought such an infamous slag as Josh had much to learn in that area) but they only see each other two weekends a month. And it didn't stop him having sex with me last night.

I really though we wouldn't. The lights were out and we were lying on our backs in his double bed, wearing knickers and T-shirts, looking at the clear sky – so busy, so inspiring, no wonder the Ancients felt philosophical – through the skylight. We were talking astrology, myths and space travel, like a long lost brother and sister, I thought. He placed his hand on my thigh. It was an unambiguous request and it felt inappropriate. I let it lie there a few seconds, and was surprised to feel myself getting turned on. I rolled on to my side to face him, his hand slipped off, he turned to check my reaction and I started kissing him. Then it all got vigorous, groping each other, wetness and hardness, full on, straight away, unexpected abandon, oral sex, dirtily, my finger in his bum, and him making me come with his tongue and then more pulling, even some biting, two needy animals fucking hard, like dogs. I felt relaxed after, like a weight I didn't know was there had been lifted from my shoulders. Revenge truly is sweet.

But it never works for more than a few hours, or even just minutes. Tonight my anger with Mike has receded, sadness is filling me up and I look forward to seeing Mike, the man I love, and need, despite what we do to each other.

I wonder, did I really think Josh and I wouldn't have sex? Did I maybe even suspect he and I could revive our old flingette? Maybe turn it into a relationship, and thus I could escape Mike? Or did I come out here for a revenge fuck to keep Mike and I going? I only know for sure I wanted that sex and didn't know it, let alone understand why I wanted it. And Josh? It's all wrong. He's not as relaxed as he says. That wasn't casual sex, that was desperate sex.

Monday, 29th March

Got an email from Josh. We have the most private friendship imaginable, and I like tapping into his strange life, yet it always makes me sad. Amaranta deserves Josh. Lovely Amaranta, a man couldn't ask for more.

He has enrolled to study Classical Greece at the Open University. He can get videos sent out and fly to England for exams. He also runs an English language class and still does archaeological websites. I feel his life is not real, as if it's all just a game since he left Edinburgh.

Friday, 7th May

Amaranta rang; down. It's the one-year anniversary of Josh leaving her. She has been in tears all day. She says she has come to love Jeremy during their six months together, but she hasn't stopped missing Josh. Lately she thinks Jeremy has been building up to ask her to marry him. Some days she thinks that would be wonderful but for the last week or so, with the anniversary coming up, she keeps imagining she sees Josh in the street. It's back to where she was last October. 'I don't feel angry, I just want to hug him and cry. Sometimes I do cry, but it's when I come out of it a second later and realise it's not him.'

Saturday, 8th May

Josh rang to ask how Amaranta had taken the anniversary. I told him. 'Shit,' was all he said. It's the anniversary of the non-wedding tomorrow, I reminded him. 'I know, gotta go, Denny, hope you're well.'

Friday, 20th August

Amaranta's been on good form for weeks now and today she was very happy. She said she has decided she will definitely marry Jeremy, but not until he gets up the guts to properly ask. She was being her old, romantic self. I felt oddly upset. She was different now; ground down, a crushed flower. She had aged too quickly. I remembered twenty months ago when Josh asked her to marry him; her glow must have been visible from the moon. At least she can still glow a bit.

She says she won't marry for many months. 'I want time to arrange an even bigger bash than Josh and mine.' She spoke as if it had happened. In some ways, for Amaranta, it was a bigger event for not happening. Moreover Amaranta mentioned her and Josh's non-nuptials while smiling; moved away from that time at last. Yet still, I found that sad, which was eerie. But she seemed comfortable; 'Jeremy, he's a sweetie, but he still needs to loosen up a bit.' And she giggled in her adorable, girlie way.

Rang Josh to tell him. I agreed to tell him everything. He wasn't in. I checked my email later and he'd written to say he had gone away for two weeks with Chrissie, to Akrotiri, a major archaeological site on Crete. Apparently he might become the website bigwig for Crete as well as Santorini. Maybe he'll marry too and stay there?

Thursday, 9th September

I told Josh about Amaranta. He said that was good. He hoped Jeremy would make her happy. He said he had also thought about marrying, but after the last time he realised he'd better wait and be sure. I laughed and agreed.

Sunday, 12th December

Amaranta fixed a date to marry Jeremy: May 29th next year. I do wish I knew Jeremy better. I admire his resolve in this fickle world; never getting fed up with Amaranta's trauma, never going astray, never doubting his own love, always wanting to be there for her. Amaranta said she would like to invite Josh. She'll tell his family to say when he phones. She said he never rings on a land line but they have worked out he's in Greece.

Thursday, 16th December

I rang Josh to tell him about Amaranta's wedding date and his forthcoming invitation. He said it would stir old and bad feelings if he went, which was strange. Surely it would help put things to rest? He said he'll visit them some time after.

'Anyway, what about that coven you told me about? Do you remember?' he was laughing.

I told him not to worry; everyone is fine. Amaranta has got over it and that's what counts. He still didn't want to come to the wedding.

Saturday, 29th April

Odd, rather ominous, moment tonight. Josh was about to hang up when he said; 'Do you remember when I first asked you to keep me posted on Amaranta? I told you things weren't what they seemed?'

I did remember. It stuck with me. He said he would explain what he meant in a letter in a few days. He would be sending one to Amaranta too, which he hoped would make her feel better. 'Email won't do.'

Tuesday, 2nd May

Josh's letter arrived. There was a short note:

> Denny,
>   Please find an old, sealed letter within this letter. Open it: as you will see it is a printout of a letter I am sending to Amaranta, posted with this. Her sealed letter is, like yours, addressed to myself in Edinburgh and postmarked the day before I bailed out, two years ago. I did that to show I was being honest now. Read it and you will understand. I did three. The third copy I am keeping. And never intend to open. Now that really is me being sentimental . . .
>   Josh

Curiouser and curiouser, but with a little trepidation. I opened the letter. The sight of the fawn paper and letterhead chilled me. It took me back to that night two years ago when I saw Amaranta's heart break in front of me. It read:

> Hi Amaranta,
>   You can tell from the postmark that I wrote this about two days before I slipped out of your life. You are marrying Jeremy.
>   I send you this now, purely to prove a point and as a token of congratulation. It was always him you really loved. I'm not the jealous type and didn't know how to deal with your mutual attraction. I was wrong to pursue our relationship. I hoped yours and Jeremy's burgeoning love would die. I will have waited for the news about your wedding. The news will have released me.
>   I have never wanted Ali back. I will ask her – I know she'll say no – in two days just to back up the story which I will use to leave Edinburgh, an old story by the time you

145

receive this letter. What is it? A year? Eighteen months? Two years? Whatever, I know you will have been in my thoughts every day. Hopefully you will have nestled in comfortably by now, just part of the dailiness.

I have never wanted anybody but you.

And I never knew what it meant to want somebody until you. I remember once, after you told me about your perfectly acceptable though not likeable past (it never is, I learned that at nineteen), you said you worried I might see you as used goods. You even used that old-fashioned phrase. I looked at your worried face. I didn't know what to say. Afterwards I often wondered what you were thinking. Regretting revealing so much about your past to me? Embarrassed? YOU seeing yourself as 'used goods'? Ashamed of the men you had slept with? I never worked it out. I knew it was one of those kind of insecure things, but never knew which one. It made me smile, for days afterwards. As if I could see you as used goods. I hate any man that's not been good to you but at the same time I want to shake his hand and sigh with relief, 'Thank God you didn't care or didn't try or got it wrong. Whatever, mate, thank you for letting Amaranta slip through your hands. Moron.'

When you are that in love it means everything. Without the other you have two choices: new life or death. I will have a new life by now. I will have drank and travelled and immersed myself in something, and I will have forged a new life. Hopefully I will love again too. I wish you and Jeremy all the happiness and luck and love in the world.

    Josh

Rang Josh immediately. The answer machine said he had gone to Turkey to look at ruins for two days. Asked him to ring as soon as he got in. I no longer think he should come to the wedding.

Thursday, 4th May

Had a battle on the email with Josh:

I didn't like your letter. You're being a smartarse. You have distressed Amaranta enough in the past, and you are interfering with her feelings now.
  Denny

The letter will ultimately make Amaranta feel secure in what she is doing. I waited until Amaranta and Jeremy's relationship had time to grow, until marriage was imminent. If I had sent the letter shortly after or before they got together – which I considered – it could have impeded them. Amaranta and Jeremy might have felt foolish, manipulated, predictable, if I sent it too early. It could make it seem like their relationship took place at my behest, in my shadow. So I kindly left it as long as possible, to let their relationship flourish.
  Josh

Why bother sending it – unkindly – ever?
  Denny

For Chrissakes Denny, let me win a little. I lost the love of my life. I resigned her to my friend who she wanted more than me. And I pretended that wasn't happening for dignity's sake, including theirs, and for the sake of their relationship. I said it was all about me and made sure I wouldn't be any problem for them. If I made a fuss they would have tried to stay away from each other to prove I was wrong. They might have succeeded. So let me just be a smartarse now. Let me

score this point. It's not going to derail the wedding. Amaranta thinks she is the only one to know anyway.
  Josh

I understand that. I'm a proud person too. I'm hurt you never told me the truth, you fucking stupid male. Anyway, I think you may have blown your invite to the wedding.
  Denny

Get with the programme, honey! Amaranta's wedding? Me? Is that invite from Hades? If I die and go to hell Amaranta will be there declaring vows to a face that's not mine.
  Josh

Jesus, where has he been at these last two years?

Monday, 8th May

Josh rang after only three days. I couldn't figure why; we just chatted as usual. He was just about to go off the phone when he blurted it out: 'Wasn't going to tell you but I'll be in Scotland next week. I'm not really going to St Lucia with Chrissie. Don't let anyone know I'm in town. My Dad's ill and I'm going to visit him. Hopefully he'll come and visit me after.'
  Shame about the circumstances, but it'll be great to see my secret friend!

Friday, 12th May

Hell could break loose. After Josh saw me (lovely; thin, even more tanned, funny as ever, bit edgy being back), the cretin went for a walk along the Water of Leith. Donna McBride saw him, said she didn't know he was back. He tried to play it casual, made out like it was no big deal: yeah, he was here for a few days, just seen Denny for a drink, catch you around. She is not a close friend but she's close enough: Edinburgh is small. I'm a wreck waiting for Amaranta to hear.

Saturday, 13th May

It's happened. Amaranta rang me, distraught. 'Why didn't you tell me?'

'He just rang out the blue and invited me for coffee, asked me not to tell anyone. I was going to tell you.'

'I can handle it, you know that. I want to see him.'

'Look, tomorrow, a bunch of us should go for a drink, including you and Josh. How about The Dome, 8.30 p.m.?'

That was the easy bit. It took me half an hour to persuade Josh it was all his fault and he had to show up. I've drummed up five others. It's going to be ugly, I can sense it.

Sunday, 14th May

It was ugly, but we all missed it. I had to find out from Josh on the phone twenty minutes ago.

Amaranta walked in fifteen minutes late. It was eerily like her hen night. We were all already seated. She stood before us. Everyone shifted a little and went quiet. She wasn't taking her jacket off and she obviously wanted to say something. A shard of ice ran through her polite request: 'Josh, could I see you alone for a little while? Outside? Just the two of us?' He shrugged and stood up.

For the rest of the bar it was as if they often talked, as if those weren't the first words between them since he left her two years ago. But we all caught it. 'Nice tan,' she said as he put on his jacket. She might as well have said, 'You're dead meat.'

They walked away side by side, looking strangely relaxed.

Outside she said they should go to All Bar One, across the street and along two hundred yards. He nodded. They got across the street and that was as long as she could last. 'Stop, wait,' she said. He turned to face her. She flew at him, screaming and clawing and punching.

He tried to deflect her blows and step backwards. He stumbled into a van and she was on his face, still screaming that he was a bastard, a cunt, a wanker and so on. Some bouncers rushed over, from Whynot? night club across the road. They missed what happened and instinctively grabbed Josh. She paused while they pinned his arms to his sides. Then she launched at his face again.

Another bouncer pinned her, shouting, 'For Chrissakes, what the fuck are you playing at?' They both agreed to behave sensibly and go on their way.

The bouncers were hardly halfway back across the road when Amaranta started bashing at Josh's head. The bouncers ran over again, angry this time. They told him to go while they held her for a minute. He agreed. She shouted: 'Be in All Bar One in five minutes Josh.'

He had been sent off in the opposite direction from the pub. He felt compelled to show up.

He had a little blood on his face. When he arrived she said: 'Go and wash, I'll get the drinks. Still bottled lager?' He nodded.

When he came back, she said: 'Drink up fast. We're going to Angie's.'

'Angie's? Who's Angie? What for?' Bar the shouting with the bouncers, they were the first words he had spoken to her.

'Don't worry; she's out. I asked her for keys. Her flat is

handy and I thought this might cause scenes.'

'Look, Amaranta, there's no point in this. Do you want me alone so you can attack me?'

'Probably. Drink up.'

They didn't talk. They drank quickly and then she led him to Angie's second floor flat on Queen Street, still in silence. They weren't through the door when she launched at him. He managed to shut the door and grab her hands. She agreed to calm down. He relaxed his grip. She caught him a huge scratch on his right cheek. (She is left-handed.)

She wouldn't stop coming at him. Eventually he hit her back. It made no difference to her. She just kept flying at him. He grabbed her hair, pulled her down to below his chest and shouted at her: 'I'll keep you like this for the rest of the evening if you don't stop it. Now grow up!'

She just waited. Slowly he eased her face up. She had a left hook planned: straight at his right cheek. He jumped back. She was in with both hands.

He grabbed her again, threw her to the floor and spread himself over her. With enormous effort, he eventually managed to force her arms out and kneel over them. She tried to use her legs to kick him. He grabbed her hair and pulled her head back on to the floor. She lay still and stared up at him. He let go of her hair.

He was drained. She wasn't. 'Let's stop this,' he said.

'I'm only getting started,' she replied.

Some time passed. He caught his breath. She didn't seem to need to.

'Ciggie?' he asked, intended as a gesture of reconciliation. She nodded.

'I'll get off you and get us both one. OK?'

She nodded. He got up. She jumped on his back but he was ready and hit out at her shouting, 'Christ, you'll get the neighbours!' She kept coming at him, arms flailing, body wide open and easy to hit. He hit her a few times. She seemed to feel nothing. He felt bad.

'Amaranta, this is getting boring!' He shielded his face and cowed down into a corner. She started kicking his body. She was wearing solid, flat shoes tonight, she had badly wanted to do this.

After a few kicks he grabbed her foot, slowly tipped her over and ran for the fags and lighter which were in the pocket of his jacket, discarded on the hall floor. He got them but she was on him, pulling him back to the floor and digging her nails into his ribs. Taking a few facial blows, he eventually pinned her arms with his legs again. Exhausted, he lit a cigarette for himself and one for her. He had to hold hers for her. There was no way he was releasing her arms.

He managed to reach for an ashtray that was on a small semicircular table for the hall telephone. They didn't talk. She just glared at him. After they finished smoking he said: 'Now, if I release you, are you going to act your age?' She didn't take her eyes off him as she nodded.

'Fine, well I'm not releasing you. You're lying.'

She shrugged, like it didn't make much difference to her.

'Amaranta . . . I'm sorry.'

No response for several seconds, maybe as many as twenty, just her staring into him.

Then she howled: 'How fucking dare YOU leave ME!' and started to cry.

'I'm sorry.' Josh started to cry.

'Sorry for yourself!'

He was crying more than her already but he managed to say: 'Probably. Sorry.'

Then he couldn't stop crying for a while. He wasn't sure how long. He glanced at her face every so often. It was tearless now; just that angry, accusing stare burrowing into him. He kept crying, occasionally sniffling out 'sorry'.

After however long it was, she said: 'Well you've lost me! You're not creeping back in at the last minute.'

'I wasn't trying to . . .'

'Bullshit! You send that letter just before I get married! You show up here and pretend you are annoyed at being seen! You pretend you don't want to go for drinks when all the time you're dying to see me! You don't fool me, even if you have fooled yourself for two years you pitiful, selfish, jealous bastard!'

Josh kept crying, more and more.

After an indeterminate time he got off her and she didn't stop him leaving to go home, still crying. But she came out to the stairwell and shouted after him: 'How does it feel to have been asleep for two years? Hope you had a nice rest, bastard! Rip Van Wanker, that's you, you stupid cunt . . .' By then Josh was slamming the door at the bottom and rushing away, shocked, not by her violence or out-of-character crudity – they were as nothing compared to his own regret.

Monday, 15th May

Josh called round. His face is a mess. He's booked an early flight back to Greece, leaving tomorrow: 'That's home now, even though Chrissie and I broke up. Ia is home.'

I made a comment about his face and he said; 'It's funny, I don't want it to heal. It's my last real contact with Amaranta.'

'Certainly is contact,' I smirked.

I had to ask and I tried to be light-hearted: 'What was it, Josh? Why did you think she always loved Jeremy more than you, before she did, before you made her? You arse.'

He didn't smile. He walked over to the window and stared out over north Edinburgh, across the Forth river and to Fife on the other side. That view feels like Scotland spread before you on clear sunny days like today. After a long pause he spoke, his dark shadow standing in front of that view, which he continued to look at.

'Some things shouldn't be said. They can't be unsaid, no matter how hard you try to redefine what you meant. Amaranta said one of those things, two years ago.

'We used to tell each other fantasies, for fun, to tease and turn each other on. This night after sex, about two weeks before the wedding, Amaranta said she had been fantasising about Jeremy fucking her while we had sex. We never talked about people we knew like that.

'I knew they got on, but it had often made me uncomfortable; she seemed to look up to him. He's a steadier man than me. When we were younger I was the exciting one, but as adults, I often felt a little inferior to constant Jeremy, who never makes scenes or fucks up like me. I didn't say anything back to Amaranta. I couldn't. She would say I was taking it the wrong way, or worse, deny she said it, or whatever; it would just make me angrier. But I couldn't get it off my mind. I was sure she fancied him and I couldn't fancy anyone. I could appreciate that some women were attractive, and maybe I would flirt when I was drunk, but I couldn't sustain any real interest in anyone else. It was a wonderful feeling. I loved Amaranta, completely. For the first time in my life it had been that simple.

'After a few days I didn't feel close to her. I was drinking heavily, brooding about it. Earlier today I was blaming it on the drink, but I know it wasn't just the drink. Maybe it was me and the drink? That's the problem with blaming alcohol: you drank it, yourself, your fault, your decisions and mistakes. Whatever, I got this notion that it was as if Amaranta had planted a bomb, and I had to detonate it, or it would go off itself when I wasn't expecting it. Running off to Greece was my way of doing that. I wanted to see what survived, what relationship survived. Theirs did, but then I didn't give ours a chance since I was thousands of miles away. Mad, I know.

'The most terrifying thing about being back is now I think she told me that fantasy because she found it amusing back then. That doesn't help me.'

I was shocked. His regret was painful, just to be near. And it was obviously inconsolable. He'd blown it all right. That regret would be there for years, maybe forever. Eventually I found the right words: 'Josh, honey, you really are an arse. That doesn't need to be unsaid.'

He smiled, for the first time all evening, and said, 'I know.'

Tuesday, 16th May

Tonight, at last. It's 4.30 a.m. This one finishes as dramatically as it started.

After Josh left here last night he started walking back to his folks' in Merchiston, intending to get a taxi at some point. Jeremy had phoned Josh's parents wanting to talk to him. They said he was here so he had waited outside my flat to see Josh alone.

As Josh cut along Rose St, Jeremy approached. Josh turned round and caught Jeremy's fist on his left cheek. Blood flowed immediately. Jeremy pressed on with both fists. Josh fell to the ground and laughed. Jeremy started kicking and shouting: 'Wanker! Think you can just step in and out of people's lives. Well, here's what you'll get! . . . Think you can hit Amaranta, you sad fuck!'

He kept kicking. But something had loosened Josh's euphoria valve and he couldn't stop laughing. He wasn't sure why. It was the second time he had been attacked in two days. He really didn't care this time. Maybe it was Jeremy that was funny. Vacuous, prettyboy, patient, facile Jeremy, all hot under the collar, very funny. He lay there, getting beaten up, yet feeling superior.

After a minute or so, of insults and kicks, Jeremy accepted Josh wasn't going to fight back. He walked in closely and Josh grabbed his foot and upended him. Jeremy thudded to the ground as Josh got up. But Josh didn't capitalise on it. He just kept hold of Jeremy's leg and looked down at him, wriggling on the ground.

Josh laughed again, then spoke; 'And what does fighting me prove? Eh, hero? That you love her more? That you're a better man than me? I know if I let you up, you could batter me. Wow. What a guy. Feeling a little bit desperate, are we? Don't worry, dickhead, it's you she wants. Maybe it's that cute little Roman nose of yours. You obviously appeal to her shallow side. It's certainly not your asinine character. You're as much fun as a wet fish, but not as sexy and intelligent. But hey, you're safe. Hear that? You are safe. Guaranteed dull. Self-absorbed, witless, tedious, but safe. Be clear about why it's you she wants, cockcheese.'

Josh was astounded at his own vehemence and unselfconsciousness. It felt great, liberating. Jeremy didn't answer, maybe didn't hear. He was livid and intent only on battering hell out of Josh. He squirmed and writhed, vigorously, endlessly, to get up, but Josh kept a tight grip and twisted his leg painfully. Josh also seemed able to absorb any number of kicks on his side from Jeremy's other foot.

After a couple of minutes, Jeremy stopped kicking and said: 'You wanker. I'll fucking get you.'

Josh smiled. 'Gosh, ain't you fascinating?'

Josh had already seen two police uniforms approaching at speed. When they arrived he explained that Jeremy attacked him because Jeremy was a very pathetic individual who was insecure in his relationship. Josh looked arrogant but plausible, especially with his battered face.

Jeremy normally never lost his cool. He had no training for this. He couldn't get it back. He shouted and ranted to the policemen about Josh leaving Amaranta at the altar and hitting her last night and so on.

A look of boredom descended on the police. They could see immediately that neither Josh nor Jeremy were a threat to anybody but each other, and they couldn't be bothered doing them. Josh understood this. One told Jeremy to shut up or he would be arrested. Josh shrugged and gave Jeremy a sly wink. Jeremy punched him. The police grabbed Jeremy. Everyone looked at Josh. He had a huge grin on his bloody face. The police told Josh to leave. Josh went to the wire with a cheery 'Bye bye, saddo.'

The police hadn't even taken Josh's address. He knew they would just hold Jeremy in the street until he calmed down. Josh walked all the way to his folks' home. He said, 'I felt more alive than I have done these last two years.'

He rang and told me all this before work today, at 8.00 a.m. At 2.47 p.m. at work I got this email from Amaranta:

Denny,

This is the last email I will send from this godawful office. I'm leaving. At lunchtime I went round to Josh's and told him to take me with him to Santorini tonight. I'm genuinely doing what Josh originally pretended he was doing; abandoning somebody at the altar for an ex. Isn't life terrifying?

I know I have to do this. Josh and I are meant to be. I couldn't marry Jeremy now. It would be wrong, even cruel to him, since my heart wouldn't be in it. I wish I could help him. He will be bitter, for a while.

Strangely, I don't think he will be surprised: we stayed up all night arguing about Josh, me defending the man I've cursed for two years. I think we both knew we were really arguing about me leaving Jeremy for Josh, but neither of us voiced it. Jeremy went to bed about six, I never joined him. I had already left him. I realised, but waited until lunchtime to be sure.

Josh said you called him an arse; best explanation I can think of, too. Everyone gets to suffer because the arse was jealous. I asked him if it was worth it? What did he get out of these two years, which we'll never get back? He said 'a good tan and some great bruises'. I do love him. But I don't know if I could marry him. I don't know if I could trust him. Basically I don't know if we can get over it. We're going to discuss it.

Amaranta

Discuss what? Where to have the shared headstone?
I can feel her glow from here.

'Got a light?'

'Yeah . . .'

'Me too. Useful, aren't they? You know, when you want a cigarette.'

'Very funny.'

Oh, sulky, sulky. And probably thick as mince, methinks.

'Sorry, it was just a way of saying hello, I wasn't meaning to take the mickey. You looked bored, so I thought I'd say hello.'

'Yes, well, I'm not bored.'

Quite, how could you be with your manifestly brilliant wit? Love your see-through top. Is that a Wonderbra? Or have you got great tits? Scrumptious bum. Yum. Oh, I do enjoy a pert posterior. Wish you'd climb off that stool, and let me do a full, slavering survey.

'Honest, I didn't mean to offend. Look, can I buy you a drink?'

'I've already got one.'

Shit, should have checked.

'Yes, but it will run out and then where will you be? You can die of thirst waiting to get to the bar in here. I could queue now and by the time I get served you will be absolutely parched and perfectly primed to enjoy your next alcoholic beverage. Budvar, is it?'

'Look, it's a tiny queue, I'm meeting people here, I just want to be left alone until they come. OK?'

Fine by me, you little dullard. God help your friends having to suffer your company.

'Sure, didn't mean to harass you. I hope you have a nice evening.'

And die of AIDS.

Simes didn't care. He was so amused he almost swaggered back to Rich.

'You know, Rich, some people have no sense of humour.'

'You mean she never fell for your crap?'

'That's another way of putting it. She's a misery guts; more your type. Why don't you have a crack at her?'

'Because I'm discerning.'

'You're discerning? You're dreaming, Slapperman. By discerning you mean you don't shag blokes, right? Or kids?'

'Unless they're cute.'

'Oh, but of course, got to make an exception for cuties, be rude not to. Male, child, you name it, cute is cute and much respect thereof. Animals?'

'No way, not unless they're really cute. I tell you now, there is no way I'd shag a sheep, absolutely no fucking way, man.'

'What if it was a total cutie? With a pert little woolly bum and sultry big eyes?'

'And a tight wee cunt?'

'A virgin.'

'Maybe I'd think about it.'

'I don't know, Rich, I guess you're right: you are choosy. Wee Sulky Drawers there, though, quite tasty, sure you don't fancy a crack at her?'

'Dunno, not really bothered these days.'

'You're not still banging on about your London stripper?'

'Something Denise said: me nearly drowning, might open me up to love. And I do keep thinking about Lee-Ann.'

'Jesus, and this is before you're drunk. Look, face it, Shallowpants; you keep thinking about her cos you didn't get to fuck her. Keep them off to keep them on, always works. Now get an E down you, get your fin on and have a crack at that delectable little nightmare over there.'

'Don't know if I can be bothered.'

'You mean you don't know if your chances are zero, zilch, nil or none at all? Wimp. You're scared to have a crack at her. Quite right.'

Simes figured ecstasy might embolden Rich enough to chat up Sulky Drawers, but he wanted Rich to move fast before her friends came, or even worse, she got drunk, loosened up and let Rich in. They swallowed one each, but Rich frowned. 'Dunno,' he said. 'E's crap for sharking anyway. Makes you think everyone's in love with you, when it's you who's in love with everybody.'

'Yea, coke's better, it just turns you into an arrogant prick. And a little arrogance goes a long way.'

'Yeah, lets you handle the blow-outs. You must find it very useful, Simes.'

'Not me, matey. I know what it is to be a true shark; you get ten blow-outs for every hit. And you care not for one of them. The strike rate doesn't matter, just the number of hits. Among men, that's what separates the shark from the jellyfish.'

'Really? That's just as well you're so mentally prepared because this isn't your night.'

'Oh ye of little faith. I'm unstoppable tonight. Hey look, another loner. Lone women are weird, they look vulnerable but they are aware of it so they play tougher, don't you think?'

'Probably. But weirdos are your speciality. Now get your fin on and go and give me a laugh by making another fool of yourself.'

'Yes! I'm your man!'

Simes sidled over in the most obvious way he could. The girl looked round at him. He smiled and before she had a chance to reject or reciprocate, he turned his head ostentatiously; as if she'd caught him and he was trying to look innocent. He moved closer. She rolled her eyeballs. He caught that. He puffed and spoke irritably, 'Oh, OK then, you can talk to me.'

She looked round at him. Key moment: she smiles/talks or glares/ignores.

'Pardon?'

Christ, is this Thicko Night?

'It's all right. I've decided it's OK. You can talk to me.'

'Oh. Can I?'

Oh deary didums, got my work cut out again.

'Indeed you can. I honestly don't mind. Really.'

No response. That's the worst. Even a put-down is better. At least that's fun, something to take away and laugh at.

'Maybe I don't want to talk to you.'

Progress. I think that tone was 'try a little harder' rather than 'die, dickhead'.

'Oh, but you do. You must. The next few minutes, or hours, shall pass. It falls to us to talk, to make life interesting. That time could pass so emptily, this is our chance. Otherwise you will have sat here and I will have stood over there, and we will never get that time back. Oh, it would be such a tragic waste of time, such a missed opportunity, and there is nothing so sad as a missed opportunity, don't you think?'

'Really.'

'Oh, most definitely. Have you ever thought about how little time we have? About the terrifying brevity of life, about . . .'

'You're a bit pretentious.'

Schemie alert, schemie alert.

'No. I'm very pretentious. In fact did you get the filmic reference in my monologue.'

'No.'

'There's nothing so sad as a missed opportunity; Woody Allen, *A Midsummer Night's Sex Comedy*.'

'Haven't seen it.'

162

'Doesn't matter. After all, what does Woody Allen know? He sleeps with his stepdaughter. Would you like a drink?'

'No thanks.'

'Would you like me to fuck off and die?'

She shrugged.

'Just to fuck off then? I don't actually have to die?'

What's this? A smile. She is quite cute. Pretty-petite face, very delicate wee features; it jars with her body, it's not ethereal at all, very vital. Nice tight, tit-hugging top, I like that on a woman.

She paused, then shrugged again. Simes gave up.

'OK, I'm gone, you missed your chance. What can I say? You get one kick at the ball in this life, next thing you know you're dead. *C'est la vie, c'est la mort, au revoir.*'

Simes waltzed off, then sashayed up to Rich. 'Oh yes, matey, it's going well tonight.'

'Sure thing, the chicks just love you man. Was that you having to fight off another? Oh, Simes, how boring for you.'

'OK, Mr Wimp, how's about you get your fin on?'

'And here it is. Now watch: you might learn something.'

'It's OK. I already know how to get a knock-back.'

'Just look and learn, loser.'

The ecstasy hadn't taken much effect on Rich. He was thinking fast but not too fast; plenty derring-do but no crassness yet. Just to astound Simes, he moved in on Sulky Drawers. He didn't have a clue what on earth he was going to say.

'Hi.'

She stared and gave a limp smile. It was sarcasm incarnate.

Shit, she has 'No Entry' stamped on her forehead. Inspiration!

'Sorry to bother you. I noticed earlier that my friend Simon was on your case. Sorry about that. He reckons you're a cold fish just because you didn't feel like talking to him. I said he was being arrogant and that you can probably be very friendly when you want, so I thought we could wind him up by pretending to be all friendly now. What d'you say? We give each other a big smile and I go off to the bar to buy a drink. We'll just talk for a few minutes, pretend to exchange phone numbers and I'll go back to him.'

Sulky Drawers looked at Rich's open, hopeful face. His sense of fun was infectious. A small smile was forming on her face. It was a good wind-up, and that other guy had been a creep. She had time to kill. Bloody useless friends were half an hour late, probably drunk.

'Well, you're a good friend.'

'I am, I love him dearly, but I love taking the piss out of him too. He asks for it; he's too pushy with women. Oh, go on?'

Sulky's smile grew, slowly, but acquiescently, eventually a warm beam. She was rather fired by the idea. Rich smiled back and turned to go to the bar for drinks. He winked at Simes.

Simes was astonished. He definitely saw Sulky Drawers smile. He sidled up to Rich at the bar; 'What the fuck did you say?'

'I'll explain later. But there's not much point, mate. You've either got it or you haven't. Better dash, don't want to keep the lady waiting.'

Simes was impressed. Rich was worthy opposition. Shit taste in women, shit taste in music, shit taste in everything (except wine, paintings and best mates) but worthy opposition on the sharking front.

'That was hilarious. Simes came up to me at the bar – I'm Richard by the way, what's your name?'

'Elaine.'

'Nice name, from King Arthur of Camelot, isn't it? Angli-fied form of classical Helen, of Troy. Anyway Simes said "what the fuck did you say?" He is totally confused.'

'You two do this a lot then?'

Now try to sound innocent.

'No, we're not sharks, just both single for the first time in years.'

Always a good line, that and 'wanting kids some time'.

'I'll bet. Do you usually do better than him? You're more attractive.'

Hey, what a girl! Would you like to repeat that? A hundred times? In front of Simes?

'Do you think so?'

'Well, he's better looking, but you've got a nicer manner.'

Bitch.

'Thank you, but to be honest Simes probably gets more women than me. He tries harder and there is something about him that attracts women. It looks to me as though he's too domineering, even faintly bullying, but they love it. I don't get it. But he's not a bad guy. He always says he doesn't understand why any woman would go with him. He doesn't analyse it in case if he found the reason then he would become all self-conscious about it, and it would kill the attraction.'

Always look like a loyal friend. Women don't like bitches. Just like none of them ever think of themselves as bitches, good God, no.

'Well you can tell him he's too glib. It's obvious he doesn't really care. He makes you feel like you could be anyone, you would have to be stupid to fall for all that full-on eye contact and constant chirpiness. You can see right through guys like him. You can always spot sharks like him.'

Hey, harsh judge, they barely spoke. But bang on.

'He's too a-lot-of-things. And that's true about him not seeing a woman as special. I think it makes it dull if the woman senses she could be anyone, that the guy is only interested in a one-night stand or fling. I don't really see the point for the guy either. If it's definitely going to be such a

small deal then what's the point? What's there to get excited
about?'

She's buying this bollocks. She's looking straight at me, all
ears and faint nods. Expand your theme man, come on,
you've got this pish on tap.

'Even for me as a man, it kills the frisson if it doesn't feel
special. I mean even, if say it just worked out that way, as a
one-night stand, then that's OK, but it's more fun if you don't
know how it's going to go, you know, it's just more exciting if
you're open to whatever may happen.'

'Do you always want to sleep with a woman on the first night?'

Are politicians liars? Does Chris Evans need a kicking?

'Not necessarily, guys can want time to sort of catch up as
well, you know, to sober up, to see how we feel, you know
what I mean?'

Because I bloody don't. Shag first, think later. Christ, I'm a
guy you daft bint.

'Oh yes, and I suppose you are always sincere?'

Nice one, take it on the chin. Go on, Rich, laugh as if you
are having a moment of self-realisation.

'Ha ha, no I guess I can be just as bad as Simes sometimes.
But I honestly like seeing a woman as special, it's much better
if you have that feeling, though you can't force it. And I'm
not scared of commitment, I want kids some time. Don't look
at me so suspiciously. I'm not saying I'm desperately looking
for kids, or a relationship but, you know, it is actually possible
for a man to be interested in relationships.'

Especially one that last nine hours. Your eyes are great:
creepy-starey. I'd love to look up at them as you impale
yourself on my cock.

'Oh, there's my friends!'

'Boyfriend?'

'No, but I want to go and be with them, sorry. Let's swap
numbers, or emails.'

'Yeah, good idea, let's do it for real, not just for Simes' benefit. Buy hey, if you've got a pen don't take it out. I just must ask Simes for one.'

Rich nipped over to Simes, put on his most gleeful smirk and asked for a pen.

'Oh, she's red-carding you? And giving you a false number to shake you off.'

'No way, matey. And I think you know it.'

They smiled at each other. Simes was glad Rich was coming back for more sharking. Rich was glad he pulled off the wind-up. He knew he would tell Simes some time, not tonight though.

As Rich returned, he felt slightly uneasy, noticing that Elaine had been watching him, carefully. Now she handed him a business card and smiled: 'There you go, email me if you like, I'll leave it up to you. You're fairly full of shit, but maybe we can be friends.' Rich was taken aback. She winked at him, climbed off her stool and walked away, clearly feeling good in her see-through top.

Simes pegged Anna for a bitch the minute they met. Her opening words were a lie. 'Can I help?' she asked, angling her face coquettishly, looking ever so serious and concerned.

She was standing in a black housecoat and a deliciously thin white night-shirt. She could help him all right, she could help him enormously. But not right then: how could she help carry in Jim's stuff from the van? It was bucketing down outside. He answered airily, 'Nah, it'll just take us fifteen minutes, not worth getting dressed.'

He couldn't take his mind off her while he fetched in more boxes. The insincere offer was fine. You could write that off as politeness. But that look, 'I am a really nice and caring, sweet person': it was false, so false it was funny. Simes knew the type well: 'You'd better buy into my pose if you want to so much as talk to me.' It was demanding and self-regarding and immature and damn sexy. You just wanted to puncture her false airs with your cock.

Conveniently Jim had marked 'LR', for living room on several boxes. These were mostly books, so they were heavy, but Simes carted in every last one of them to get more looks at Anna. There she would be, all curled up on the sofa, straining to smile and looking extremely irked; all this to-ing and fro-ing, a major inconvenience to her telly-viewing.

No matter that Jim, the man she professed to love, was about to begin living with her. No matter that he wanted to move to London and was only stuck in Edinburgh because she hadn't found a job in London yet. No matter devotion.

No matter love. No matter anything but Sunday night's costume drama on telly. Selfish as well as false. It just got sexier and sexier.

He had had it out with his mate Rich often enough. 'Simes, you are fucking clueless,' he would announce, in his over-stated way. 'Every time you fall for a bitch, you think you are going to hump and dump her; it's going to be easy because you don't even like her. And, every time, you end up half-married to the insufferable sow and I have to listen to her for weeks in the pub. By then it's all gone fucking totally insane. You never liked her at the start and now you like her a wee bit, but you have to chuck her since – of course – you don't like her enough for the slavery she demands. You feel all guilty, you become a mopey pain in the arse and then, eventually, you ditch the bitch. And feel like a cunt. Let me reassure you: you're not a cunt. You're fucking stupid.'

Rich had a point. Something like that had happened three times in the last eighteen months. But there's no getting round it: bitches are sexy. You want to fuck them; more, harder. And it's enslaving. It's a trip, and like any drug, while you're on it, you can't get enough. But this one is different. Rich is wrong this time. Anna is taken, so no possibility of drifting into a relationship situation. She is perfect. She is me-me-me! writ large; false, transparent, needing pricked, penetrated, that kind of thing. It would be simple. Simes wanted her. Splayed beneath him.

Simes called round on Jim a lot over the next couple of months. He was a recent acquaintance, a curious case of instant fondness. He had been quite surprised when Jim asked him to help flit. Simes had felt grateful for owning a van. He was sure Jim wouldn't have asked him otherwise, and it was nice to help such a decent guy.

Mostly they bonded over chess. They were very well

matched. Simes' game didn't seem to deteriorate with wine, but at the start of the evening Jim was the marginally better player, almost unbeatable with white.

Each time Simes came round, Anna would express no interest in him. She had gone from dubiously bright hellos to small smiles of acknowledgement to ever-vaguer nods to acting like he was invisible. Oh, just sexier and sexier.

Simes tried to put her on the back burner. He tried to ignore the sullen-faced self-absorption which he wanted to violate. He tried not to get sucked into that sexy swirl of moodiness.

But he knew he was spinning into it. He sensed those strange moments, and realised she was actually very conscious of his presence. He was surprised; they seemed to speak to something inside each other.

One night he decided to go for it: 'Anna, I know you hate doing wee architectural jobs, but could you possibly come round to my place and give me some advice?'

'Mm.' Anna didn't do magnanimity.

Simes lived in a mews cottage with a sizeable garden. He wanted to discuss extension options. He could no more afford an extension than he could a private jet, but Anna wasn't to know that. She agreed to come round and look at his property the next day after work. Anna in her charcoal two-piece office suit, that'll do nicely.

After the visit was arranged, Anna asked who was winning at chess. Jim answered: 'Simes, with black; one for the diary.'

'I'm better at the Sicilian, I like a knight that charges in. He tries to face me down by developing his queen; always a mistake, I corner her.'

Jim heard only literal fact in Simes' words. Simes thought how nice it might be to live in Jim's naïve world.

'The trouble with Simes is he hates facing the Scheveningen System. All the new variations lose him. Good old-fashioned Sicilian, that's about his stretch.'

'And Ruy Lopez, anything with a Latin name, always more fun, more adventurous, more romantic than your dry Nordic and Slav openings. I'm an old-fashioned guy, and proud of it.'

They all smiled. Anna watched for a few moves. The feeling was cosy, except Anna was absorbing Simes' concentration; the way she was careless with that black dressing gown, slipping off her legs all the time, most endearing, it was hard not to sneak glances, those lovely firm thighs. Simes almost got caught with an obvious fork. Anna sauntered off to bed to read saying, 'Goodnight, chess bores.' It was only half-playful.

The following day Simes got up sharp, tidied his cottage and had a productive day working. 'The prospect of sex,' he mused, 'brings out the best in a man.'

She arrived at five thirty, looking impatient and distracted, as always, but beautifully attired in that charcoal two-piece. He asked if she had had a bad day at the office?

'No worse than usual, I suppose. I'm dying to leave.'

'I think all offices are shit. Sometimes the small ones are OK, maybe. Usually the bigger, the worse. It climaxes in the corporate nightmare. But let's face it, all offices are crap; office politics, office paranoia, office gossip, office desks and chairs, office coffee, office parties, office anything, except the clothes. They're sexy. They're uniforms, designed to convey power and capability. And power and capability, in the final, evolutionary analysis, is about being sexy, don't you think?'

Anna smiled but didn't rise to his flirtatious compliment. 'I don't even like the clothes; they're uncomfortable. Did you have a bad day at the office?'

'Not at all. I'm the manager, I'm the junior, I'm the secretary, the slacker, the workhorse and the MD. It's a very democratic office. Come through and see.'

Simes led her through to his workshop. It had been a Georgian scullery and still had period character: massive sink, visible piping, big pulley and windows too high to see out. It still felt like the engine room of the house. Paintings and frames were stacked everywhere. It looked organised and was well-lit.

'Why do you frame pictures?'

Simes shrugged. Nobody had ever asked him. 'To avoid offices, I suppose. It pays well if you're good, and I am. I've got a good reputation, anyway.'

'But there's not much to it? Don't you want to paint?'

'I'd love to, but I'm not good enough. It's frustrating. Maybe one day I'll be better, but just now I would have to be one of those jokers doing abstract bollocks because I can't really capture a likeness or convey anything powerful.'

'I like abstract art.'

'Oh? I guess some is OK. But I suspect it's mostly emperor's new clothes, you know, like some famous critic said: "a product of the untalented sold by the unprincipled to the utterly bewildered."'

Anna smiled. 'Jim said you and your friend Richard were the most opinionated men on earth. Is picture-framing art?'

Simes grinned; fair call from Jim.

'In a small way, yes. The frame is the link from the physical world into the aesthetic world of the picture. It separates the picture off and at the same time gives it a place in the real world. It has to be the right kind of frame for the picture, in order for it to do that, to give it its place. It's a simple but strong aesthetic.'

Anna was amused at Simes' seriousness about his dumb job. They gravitated through to the conservatory and looked out at the garden, which Simes tended. Most of it was in virtual darkness but in the middle a rectangle of grass escaped the brutal shadows of the tenements and high garden walls. It was golden, and the tall bamboos at the west of the green streaked it with long, wavering lines of evening shadow.

'Nice, eh?' said Simes. 'When those shadows come I know it's G'n'T time. Like one?'

Anna acquiesced, in her inscrutable way. Simes went to fetch the drinks. She remained in the conservatory watching the shadows dance on the rectangle. When he returned she said that the effect in the middle of the garden looked like something in a frame, and it was beautiful because it was framed perfectly. She stood very close to him. He could smell her perfume now, not one he recognised. Her blouse touched his bare arm. For one sensitive instant her arm stroked his. Simes thought about that. Sober, people are almost always aware of any body contact. Sometimes they pretend not to be. Sometimes it's to throw it back to you.

Gently Simes held her hand. She didn't squeeze his, not at first. Then she did and pulled away straight after. She turned to him, smiling. 'We shouldn't do this.'

'Do what?' Simes smiled back.

'Carry on like this. You know what I mean.'

'It's just the sight of you in that suit. Does something to me, something very . . . very . . . very . . . nice.'

Anna laughed, very happily. She was glorying in the attention. 'Let's just be friends,' she said.

It wasn't a red card, just yellow. This game could have some time to run. Simes knew the trip. As a shark, you get a bad reputation. Without even knowing you, women decide they hate you. You're a membrancer of past hurtings, a demon, soulmate of other demons, like the guys who hurt them in the past. You only have to reveal honest, nice sides of yourself and it throws them. It has a bigger impact than with guys they expected to be nice. They feel confused, as if they've misjudged you, even wronged you. That's where we are up to with Anna.

The next step is they want a bit of that attention that every other girl seems to have had. And in their case, of course, they will be the one that tames the shagger in you. Piece of piss. Except Anna wasn't fully biting, she wasn't in a position to; she was engaged. She needs friends more than fuckmates but she just won't stop striking fuck-me poses. She is natural shark bait. He had watched her in the flat: leave-me-alone moodiness (and you might just have asked her the time) and give-me-attention flirtiness (sometimes when you are already giving her your undivided). You never can tell what bitches might do. They might well fuck inappropriate people. Their mood was crucial.

Back in the workshop, Anna brought up the fictitious extension. Simes toyed with coming clean but missed his moment. He let her ramble on too much about extending the workshop and found himself joining in. It would cost £15,000, minimum, even with his builder mates doing a sidey. Moreover, she doubted he would get planning permission. 'Hmm, I'll put the idea on hold,' Simes shrugged, and ushered Anna through to the lounge where he fixed more G'n'T's.

Anna decided to show Simes her and Jim's holiday snaps which she had picked up at lunch-time. She flicked through them herself, passing them to him individually, including one of her naked in the bath. She joked about her tits looking like fried eggs. They did rather, but still, nice pic.

When she had gone, Simes smiled to himself, thinking how Anna loved to flaunt her lack of inhibition. He wondered if it was for real and he looked forward to finding out. While bodily fluids had, sadly, not been traded this evening, there had been some chemical happenings, some flows of some quiet sort.

Simes had to wait three weeks for his next opening. Anna had the day off and needed his services, or at least his van's services. He agreed, through Jim, to drive her to Thistle 'N' Spice, a furniture importer on Barclay Place. The bitch was buying a table. Of course it was made of teak or mahogany or some other hardwood wrested from the beautiful jungle.

On the way Simes asked Anna how she felt about the environmental impact of hardwood trading. Did she know it took teak trees seventy years to mature? That in imperial times they became crucial in shipbuilding, but now they could all be saved, if it weren't for furniture buyers? Did she know that an area of 100 square metres around a felled tree might degrade to uselessness in days? Did she feel anything at all for the death of the mesmerising rainforest?

She didn't reply. She just asked if Simes minded her smoking. She already had a lit cigarette in her mouth and she was winding down the window. She seemed to be asking only out of interest. Rainforest? Is that a pop group?

What would it take to get a bitch like this going? OK, jibing about the rainforest was never going to be the way into her knickers. He drove on in silence, thinking about her placid non-response.

He was aware he had never seen Anna really enthuse about anything. He remembered the time Jim booked them a surprise holiday to Cuba, she had had to force herself to be bubbly. Simes had been surprised at himself that day; it was her, not Jim, he felt sorry for. Dozy Jim missed her falseness and was happy. But her, unable to look forward to an exotic holiday with her lover, that was a genuine shame.

After they dropped the table off, Simes suggested lunch. He did if offhandedly, knowing she'd say no. But Anna shrugged and nodded. It wasn't exactly 'give me your loverod now', but it was a start.

They went to Bar Napoli on Hanover Street. It was utterly unromantic: full of office types, lots of loud, proud voices and big, quasi-hearty business laughs, all rebounding off the tiled floors and bare furniture. It was a racket. But Simes would not be thwarted: intimate chat was on the menu.

They both went for Bolognese from the lunchtime special and he ordered a bottle of white wine, carefully choosing a non-Italian label. 'Italians,' he tutted. 'Great for reds, but still struggling with whites.'

'I thought you were having red meat,' said Anna without looking up. Her tone announced uninterest in whatever he ordered. She just wanted to point out that Simes had ordered the wrong colour for his meat dish, so he needn't bother making posey remarks about wine.

Simes said nothing. He caught the put-down and didn't protest that he loved wine and was never happier than when he was abroad roaming and tasting in vineyards. But let the bitch win, it meant more to her.

When the wine arrived Simes felt rewarded. She downed a glass almost instantly. Excellent. It oils the rusty urges, glides you bedwards, slips you into slapperdom. He was a great believer in getting women drunk. He was male, after all.

Straight after she put the glass down, Anna snapped the tension, 'You know, Simon, I do know about the rainforest. But it doesn't help to go on at me. I just saw the table and liked it. OK?'

'Sorry.'

He knew for sure to leave the rainforest out now, but what did Anna want to talk about? Herself, maybe? No, Simes reminded himself, that's not a particular trait of bitches, just of humanity, at its dullest. And like most of humanity, Anna was surely the type that talked not so much about themselves as about the person they wanted to be, and they looked to you, the innocent, victimised, bored shitless listener, to confirm their trite self-image. So then, what about thoughts and opinions? Did she have any? Buried among all that neurotting and scheming? She was very intelligent, he knew that. Books? She did read a lot. But no, intellectualism wasn't her thing either.

He decided to shut up until she talked. She's bound to feel uncomfortable with silence eventually. Tense minutes passed.

Simes spoke. He said he'd better go and get change to feed the meter.

Outside he wondered if Anna habitually, even unconsciously, did this sulky routine to get attention. He couldn't imagine anyone being interested in her if they didn't want to fuck her. She always looked impatient, like something was bugging her. It was sexy, but not attractive in any other sense.

As he walked back he unexpectedly caught sight of her through the restaurant window. Her gaze was fixed on the middle distance. He stopped walking, to watch her some more. He felt as if she was far away, through that glass in another place. She looked lonely, framed in the window like a sad picture. He resolved to talk when he got back in.

'Van's been towed away.'

'Has it?'

'No, just wanted to get a reaction out of you.'

'You weren't saying anything either.'

Christ, she really was a tense one. He decided Anna was nervous but clueless about people. Funny how those two traits were normally poor bedfellows but in Anna they fucked liked pigs.

With hope fading fast, Simes ordered more wine.

'Sorry, I hope you don't mind. I often drink in the afternoon, then not at all in the evening.'

Anna shrugged, said she'd like more wine too. They talked about relationships. Anna had a few pet theories, mostly clichés, but dogmatically held to. Flirting, frisson and sex – the stuff of life for Simes – were conspicuously absent.

Simes was losing his will to steer the chat somewhere interesting. He had tried to enliven her, she was a bitch, this was all you got.

'I like that song,' said Anna.

'Oh yeah, "The Ballad Of Tom Jones," best thing Space ever did.'

178

'Dunno, I thought "The Female of the Species" was great. Remember that? From years ago.' She started to sing in a funny, deep voice, 'The female of the Species is more deadly than the male . . .'

Simes laughed. 'How true. But then . . .' Now he started to sing, in a troubled, serious voice. 'Woman is the nigger of the world . . .'

'Ah yes indeed but . . .' She paused, struggling to find an appropriate song. Her face lit up and she switched to aching soul. 'No woman, no cry/No woman, no cry . . .'

'Oh quite, my dear, that's because.' Simes had his song and his high voice ready. 'Only women bleed . . .'

'A-ha, as I'm doing just now.' Anna laughed. 'Yes it's lonely being a woman. In fact, "The only man who could ever reach me/was the son of a preacher man , , ," '

'Oh you have to watch for that stuff, because . . . "Love is the tender trap . . ." '

'Tell me about it; "The things we do for love/like walking in the rain and the snow/when there's nowhere to go/and you're feeling like a part of you is dying . . ." '

'Oh no, Anna! Not 10cc? You cannot remember 10cc?'

Anna put on a whispering voice. ' "I'm not in love/so don't forget it/it's just a silly phase I'm going through . . ." '

Simes burst into a Beatles song, A World Without Love. 'Please, lock me away/ I don't care what they say/ I won't stay in a world with' . . .10cc.'

' "I saw four faces/four men/four brothers from the gutter/they looked me up and down a bit/and turned to each other . . ." '

They talked about pop and classical music. Turned out they had remarkably similar tastes. Simes didn't have to pretend. Brief bursts of song punctuated the chat. They were amusingly poor singers but both of them knew it and mocked themselves by overdoing the dramatic intonation. Both also courteously awaited their turn to sing, thus allowing the other to halt the game if they got bored.

As he drove her home, Simes sang, ' "Homeward bound/I wish I was/homeward bound" but I have to run you first . . .'

Anna sang straight back at him, ' "Ah gotta go home/home, home/gotta go home . . ." '

'My God, Boney M. How d'you know all these old bands, you're way too young for them?'

'Hey, you brought up Simon and Garfunkel! My parents used to play them all, well, my dad, they drove my mother up the wall eventually. It amused her when they were happy, but by the end it always got on her nerves. He stopped playing them, but I'd started playing them.'

'Pop music,' said Simes. 'The soundtrack to our lives, whether we want it or not. "London Paris New York Munich/everybody talk about pop music." '

By now he was parking outside Jim and Anna's. He decided to give Anna a kiss on the cheek, just to establish some kind of friendliness. He undid his seatbelt and leaned across the long, single seat of the van. He realised he would love to kiss her on the lips, but of course he didn't dare.

Suddenly he felt stifled. He was aware that Anna knew he wanted to kiss her lips. She didn't move towards him. He felt embarrassed. He worried he might blush. He was very conscious of all the mess in the van. His mind raced: Anna can see I want to kiss her; Anna can see I want to fuck her; Anna finds nothing sexy in me; Anna is bored by me; Anna is kissing my lips.

It was the most exciting kind of kiss: deeply desired but not expected at all. Slowly Simes asserted his tongue, and explored her mouth. It lasted just a few seconds, tongues always moving slowly, deliberately, challenging each other to prove their commitment to the kiss. Their bodies moved into each other only a little.

Afterwards Anna smiled and got out the van. She didn't invite him in. She didn't say anything. It seemed she just wanted to stop kissing, so she did. Simes drove home over the alcohol and speed limits, happily fazed. He sang, 'She had kisses/sweeter than wine/mmm hmm sweeter than wine . . .'

Simes hadn't intended to go to the party with Anna and Jim, but when Friday came he had nothing better to do.

Once there he regarded Jim and Anna. He was struck by how she was socially nervous, yet utterly untroubled about being there with both her fiancé and a man she kissed behind his back just two days before. She is Jim's girlfriend; it must mean something to her?

Convenience for the passionless bitch? What drove her? Hot and cold, as if it was all the same, her blithe manner constant throughout as she moves from one meaningless mood to another. You just want to break it, to get to her, with sex. That's the beauty of sex, it gets to everyone, including detached bitches.

What does Jim see in her? Christ, he hangs on her every word. He certainly doesn't see a sexy bitch. He thinks she is lovely and – this is the best bit – 'so honest.' Simes loves it when Jim says that. Ah, the power of love. Mind you, his type are easily blinded. He is one of those good people who simply can't see when others are subtly evil. He needs big signposts – I'M BEING NASTY AND SELFISH NOW – before he believes it. Badness isn't part of his world. He just wants to get by and is grateful for what he's got. He's a clueless sap. And one of Simes' favourite people. Not that that stopped Simes wanting to fuck his bitch fiancée.

At the party Simes wandered out to the patio. Next thing he knew Anna was beside him. Just wandering too? Like that day in his mews, she seemed to be standing very close. Did she know she was near him? Did she know he had half an E kicking in? She was about to find out.

He slipped his hand into hers. She squeezed his hand. He felt warmth. Is Anna drunk? She doesn't do warmth. She's just bored, likes doing this near Jim, the thrill of stolen affection, but if it needs these circumstances, then it's contrived affection. Is it that simple? Is Anna unhappy in life, yearning for more, reaching out in some frustrated way? Whatever, it was nice to touch her flesh.

He touched her flesh a few more times at the party. She backed off if he pushed it, but hands and subtle strokes were permissible, and reciprocated. When Jim or anybody else was about they talked as if they often talked, as if they were good friends. Strange thing was it didn't feel put on.

At some point Simes got stuck talking to a man who cared about the Dow Jones index. He made his excuses and went to the toilet. On his way upstairs he mused: it was a pleasant, quiet party, but he was getting bored. The people were nice enough, the décor amusingly terrible; a rented flat, not a home. It all felt transient and carefree, which he liked. But there was nobody to hit on.

Then it occurred to him: he wasn't sure if he would be at ease hitting on a woman in front of Anna. Maybe it would have repercussions with her? Arouse bad feeling? Voyeuristic feelings? She would be amused? Too amused? Forced? Jealous? Sneery? Hmmm. How did this get to be an issue, albeit a faint one? The bitch is here with her fiancé.

By now he was in the toilet. Here he took against the flat. 'Why is that every sodden flat party you go to has a toilet seat that won't sit up without the aid of your knee? This greatly diminishes the pleasure and relief of a well-needed pee, goddammit.' Simes was just finishing musing and peeing when the door rattled.

'Hold on.'

'Is that you, Simes?'

'Hi, Anna, just coming.'

He quickly flushed the toilet, did himself up and opened the door. The toilet was still flushing when he spoke. 'Just about done; washing my hands.'

It was true; he was washing his hands, something he never normally did after peeing. Anna, just inside the door of the tiny toilet, seemed to be desperate. 'Just a mo.' He sensed this was an inappropriate time for flirtation, but he couldn't resist adding, 'You can go just now if you like.' And she did. Just like that. With a look on her face that was knowing and sheepish.

Simes took his time washing his hands. He only glanced and smiled at her twice. He worried she would feel insulted if he left, not that he wanted to. The splashy, low sound of a woman peeing finished and he couldn't bear to look her way; it would be so obvious he was waiting for her to stand up so he could regard her body. She pulled up her trousers, buttoned them and walked out. Simes was annoyed at himself for being too gutless to look.

Over the next few weeks there was less flirting, more blunt touching and a couple of stolen kisses. Sometimes she rebuffed him, sometimes she made it clear she was keen for it. This is surely bound to end up in the sack. The notion will take the moody bitch one day.

But then there was a break. Jim and Simes had both been too busy to hook up for over a fortnight. When they did, everything changed.

Simes went round to their flat and Jim greeted him excitedly: Anna had finally got a job in London and his brother had found them a flat down there. Jim was ecstatic. He would make a packet in London as a freelance computer programmer – he already had the offers – while still taking several months off each year to bring up the children they planned. Anna's office were only making her work two weeks' notice so they would be gone by the end of the month.

Simes could see instantly, now that Anna was going, that he had come round to liking her. And still she had bitch appeal. He felt disappointed, predictably. He was surprised to also sense release.

'We should go out for a farewell meal, the three of us: you're one of my few friends Anna likes.' Jim laughed, not seeing Anna's intolerance as an indictment of her, but rather as part of her sensitivity, her aboveness. Jim shouted an invitation up the stairs to Anna. She was just in from work and didn't seem keen, but then she didn't do keen. She relented, they cancelled the chess and headed off to The Tapas Tree on Forth Street. Simes was happy for both of them, particularly Jim, the kind of guy who deserves good things.

Anna would join the ranks of the ones that got away. (Funny, it's actually them who stay with you.) Now that he probably wasn't going to find out, Simes was convinced, more than ever, that Anna would come into her own in bed. In was where she belonged, what she was born for.

The meal passed uneventfully, everyone in good form. Then Simes snorted some coke in the toilets and decided to persuade both of them to indulge.

'It'll be a wee treat for you. And this is good stuff, well, good by Edinburgh standards. London is wasted on you pair. One of the few good things about that outsized toilet of an excuse for a city is the quality of cocaine. And you pair will not even take advantage. I despair.'

'I'll take some just now,' said Jim. 'Just to indulge you.'

'Don't feel like you have to,' said Simes. 'It's expensive. I want you to enjoy it.'

'I'm sure I will. I'll try anyway.'

Jim went off to the toilet. Simes smiled at Anna. She seemed less enthusiastic but decided she might as well join in.

'I'll just rub it into my gums, I don't mind that tingle.'

'I quite enjoy a wee tingle myself,' said Simes, in a mock Carry-On voice. 'OO-er missus.'

Anna was tired and wanted to go home, but she smiled pleasantly. She looked quite dreamy to Simes.

Jim returned full of largesse. He insisted on footing the bill, as payment for the coke. Simes suggested they come on with him to The Basement bar, to hook up with Rich and a few others, maybe make a night of it? Po Na Na nightclub later?

Anna was dead against it. She had come almost straight home from work and didn't feel like going out in these clothes. Both men flattered her, Simes declaring her 'officely babelicious', Jim laughing in his doting way.

They managed to get her up the street to The Basement, her whining all the way. Jim's largesse was increasing with his cocaine absorption. He insisted he get the round in. Simes nodded over at Rich, who was with John and Wills. Then he found himself alone with Anna. She still didn't look too pleased about being there, but she smiled and raised her eyebrows as if resigned to going along with it.

The music was loud so Simes leaned into her to speak. 'Well, I definitely won't be getting you into the sack if you're in another city. Pity. You're a helluva babe.'

It just slipped out. Coke-fuelled? Whatever, it was clearly inappropriate given the grim look on her face. Damn, he had wanted to sound conciliatory, complimentary. He had been trying to make her feel good. Bloody drugs muddling him up.

'What?' said Anna. 'I can't hear you.'

That's a relief, thought Simes. But should he risk saying it again? A voice inside warned, 'Don't!' He repeated it anyway. What was so harmful? It was just acknowledging his feelings, which she already knew full well. It kind of tied things up, ended the pointless non-affair.

Anna didn't say anything in response. Jim returned with the drinks and they joined the others. The noise was too much for a voice to carry through a whole group so the conversation became fragmented. At some point Anna and Jim slipped away. Simes never saw them leave but when he noticed they'd gone, he felt uneasy. How could that have offended her? They had joked about sex umpteen times. Another line of posh and he didn't care.

Two days later Jim phoned to say he was really hurt and pissed off about what Simes had said to Anna.

The fucking bitch had fucking told him. For Chrissakes, why?

Simes tried to collect his wits and deny all charges. He suggested Anna picked him up wrong. It rang out hollow. Jim believed her. Simes found the expression 'at sea' announcing itself in his head. He really didn't know which way to turn. He said he couldn't remember. He said he couldn't imagine saying something so crass. But Jim could imagine it. Simes could feel himself sinking. He blamed his loss of memory on the drugs, he blamed his comment on the drugs. He was drowning in embarrassment. He was making it worse. And Jim, so sweet, clearly thought this was a huge betrayal of friendship. He had stewed about it all weekend before confronting Simes. But Oh Christ, he thought this was a big deal. If he but knew. Jim listened to Simes panicking. He sort of humphed, unsatisfied, but managed to say 'see you' in a non-aggressive way.

It was all so Jim; a short call that left Simes reeling. It was dignified, and crushing; much worse than somebody who comes on all fisticuffs and pride. Why the fucking hell had the fucking bitch fucking told him?

He rang Rich, and insisted they meet in Maison Hector immediately. Rich agreed but sounded exasperated. Simes was looking for answers. As far as he was concerned there weren't any. She was a bitch; he dabbled, he got burnt. It wasn't a big drama, except to sappy Jim.

Simes got to the pub sharply, ordered a bottle of Chablis and downed a glass in less than a minute. He poured another and tried to organise his thoughts while he waited for Rich. He shuddered and wished Jim and Anna dead. He felt contaminated by their world; her falseness, his going along with it.

He knew he was picking on Jim now. He knew Jim was a good man. That's why this tiny thing mattered so much to Jim. That's why it mattered, period. That's why he, Simes, felt embarrassed and terrible.

His guilt had to compete with his fury. Anna, what a complete and utter total bitch. Why distress Jim like that? A chance to play the delicate flower for him? A pseudo-confession? Whereby she convinces herself that it was all just Simes harassing her? Maybe that. Maybe then she can think, 'There's no need to bother telling Jim everything, it was all just Simes harassing me.'

What had he done to offend her? Had he looked too flip? Like wanting to sleep with her was just a joke that didn't matter? No, surely not. She knew the rules. Her and Simes were two of a kind. They weren't saps with high morals like Jim. Of course Simes was looking for a lay. But of course he had come round to liking her, too. And of course her type might take a whim and go for it. They both knew the game. Why had she broken the rules?

Rich arrived. Simes told him the whole story, carefully explaining how hurt Jim was by Simes, how embarrassed Simes was with Jim, how awkward things would be between Jim and Anna and how his fucking fury with Anna was the only straight card being played. She stressed out her future husband and ruined a friendship for no good reason. It was all ugly.

At the end Rich paused thoughtfully, then asked, 'You do know why she did it?'

'No! Of course not. Do you?'

'It's obvious. You dragged her to a trendy pub in office clothes when she didn't want to go. You both did it, as a team. She is selfish and moody, she's not wearing that. So, just on a whim, she wrecked the friendship, that was her intention. Evil bitch.'

Simes thought about that for a few seconds. 'Christ, I think you're right. That shallow. I'm going to tell Jim the truth. Friendship's fucked anyway. He'll realise that soon.'

'Don't be stupid, Simes. You can't do that.'

'I bloody can. Stupid bitch thinks I don't have the balls for it.'

'Well, I know you have. But you still can't tell him. Think about it.'

Simes furrowed his brow for a few seconds. Then his face yielded to frustration and he snarled, 'Fuck!'

'Exactly. She would deny all charges and he would believe her. Or worse, she would put the harassing spin on it. I suspect she could even get him to feel sorry for her. He thinks she's the most honest thing since Jesus. Imagine the pain she's been in, keeping this from him? He's such a sap he would end up thinking he's lucky to have a woman another guy fell for. It goes on and on. With bitches like her you can't win. She writes the part that suits her. She gets right into it. Leave the poor sod alone. He's distressed enough. And he's got a life of shit coming up with that selfish bitch. Pity him.'

'But I feel like she played so dirty. I want to up the ante. All this fuss, Christ, she and I know that comment meant nothing. She and I know it all meant nothing, never even had sex.'

'I doubt if she thought much about the fallout. She doesn't think of other people. But she didn't break the rules. She just won the game. Be grateful you are not in her league for malice. She is a truly selfish bitch.'

'But I know I'm more like her than him. And I know which one is the good person. I always remember the way she bought that table; she did exactly what she wanted and then felt sorry for herself. As if the rainforest dying was a terrible hassle for her, because people might bring it up.'

Rich smiled. 'You're as angry with yourself as you are with her. Look and learn matey, or bitch appeal will be your downfall. But this one doesn't matter. It'll be a good pub story soon. Pretty funny, I have to tell you. You're too hurt to see it, yet.'

'I'm not hurt. And I can see clearly, it's just I can see through Jim's eyes and I'm getting a good view of my vile self and vile Anna. We're both selfish and thoughtless.'

'No, you're not so bad, you have limitations, you wouldn't want to hurt without good reason. Also, you and Anna shared something private and, at times, delicate and trusting. It was unusual for both of you. Now you feel like a trusting fool. Angry with yourself. It'll pass.'

Simes smiled. 'It's passing already.'

'Then spare a thought for your former friends. For Jim and Anna it won't pass. It's something ugly and unfinished for them to carry now. For her it takes its place in the vast array of duplicitous acts she forever strains to rewrite and forget. It is tiring being a bitch. But his baggage is the worst. This doesn't really belong in his ingenuous world, but it's there now, a presence from you and Anna's reckless world. He'll never see it, he'll never know the truth. But something will be uneasy, some detail will never seem quite right. Maybe, one day, he'll wonder why the incident stayed with him?'

'You mean figure out the truth?'

'No. He knows that already. I mean, *face* the truth.'

Saturday, 3rd June

Mike's father died today. I told him I didn't give a shit. He looked shocked. I was quite shocked myself. He started to say, 'Denny, you shouldn't . . .' but his voice faltered when he looked into my eyes. (Dismissive contempt; my forte since childhood.) For a moment we were both in a black play; him needing his lover to give him some love, me buggered if I could be bothered. Not a very pleasant play.

They've been expecting the old flaky to die for the whole four years I've been with Mike. But still, I should have been kinder. Unfortunately I could only think, 'Great, my cheating boyfriend will have to go to his mother's tonight, so I won't have to have sex with him.'

Not that it's difficult to open one's legs. On the contrary: I can lie there composing a mental list of things to do tomorrow while he pants and thrusts and has a seemingly nice time. Men don't want to know how much women can disengage during sex, i.e. completely. And women don't like to think about how often they do it. Hardly surprising; either way it doesn't make you feel special.

Usually I get into it, almost in spite of myself, but lately I've been thinking about sex. I've been remembering a long, long time ago in a faraway life when a really good seeing to was bliss. Contentment and excitement would merge into one and flow through me all the next day. Now some mornings I wonder where that thin stuff dribbling down my leg came from.

191

And worse, now I'm crude about sex. I'm angry, and anger and crudeness are holy bedfellows. I know that my anger, like all anger, has nothing to do with you rightly judging someone who's wronged you. Anger is you failing and *flailing*; you were taken in, you trusted, and now you are lost, it's hopeless, all you can grasp are crude, contrived, base certainties. You have become a pathetic creature. But since the world turned wet we cannot accept that. Heavens above no, now we *always* have a good reason for our anger. It's your mum, your dad, society, your cat, widgets, anything but you being reduced to a useless arse. Ancients understood anger better. The word arrived here from Old Norse, but it originally comes from the Greek, *agkhone*, and it means choking. You, the angry person, are choking. And you kind of know it.

I hate sounding like a therapist. I hate *being* a therapist. I hate our poor-wee-me culture. (Come to think, I hate the way I start so many sentences with 'I hate . . .') But what I hate more than anything about being a therapist (funny how that word splits into 'the rapist') is the unyielding faith everyone has in the nonsensical notion that we always have fine reasons for whatever we feel and however we behave. I know it's bullshit. The philosopher who said 'beware of reason: it leads you astray' was wise. I see the evidence every day, but I listen to their reasons. I'm well paid not to say, 'Just get a grip, you self-obsessed pudding,' or 'Shut up about your mother, you're a forty-three-year-old man, for fuck's sake, and chop off that childish ponytail while you're at it' or 'Keep your knickers on, slut, and you'll be fine,' or 'Have you the faintest idea of how stupendously undignified and dull you are?' or (the inner scream occurring at least once every day) 'Fucking grow up!' Oh, I could go on for days about the things I don't say. So I hate my job, I hate my relationship and I hate the way I behave, but I don't want to hate myself. And that's getting tricky. When I'm like this, when I'm angry, I am the cornered animal hissing and spitting at Mike and writing furiously fast to get away from where I really am, but it doesn't work for long. When I sit down to write, the blood cools, eventually. It takes anything from ten minutes to two hours, but it always happens. And then I do hate myself. That sensitive man's father just died and I thought 'Great, fuck you,' or rather, 'Great, not fuck you.'

Shit. Better stop writing. Easier being angry. More wine, please.

Five hours later. Went and had sex with Aaron. He was fucking me missionary-style and I was easing into the oblivion – a cinch after all the alcohol (still a bit drunk) – but then I glanced at his face and found myself staring. The contortions were beguiling; not unamusing and not unlike a gargoyle, his twinkly brown eyes closed tight and the normally loveable laughter lines seemingly bespeaking agony. With each thrust his wince tightened then eased, tightened then eased; very painful, quite painful, very painful, quite painful. An image of a gargoyle having a large, wiry brush jabbed in and out its bum sprang to mind – I'm sure it's expression would have been the exact same – and I couldn't stop seeing that image. I tried not to giggle. I closed my eyes to get back to my orgiastic fantasy (well, orgiastic except I'm the only woman there of course) but all I could see was a gargoyle being rogered, first with a toilet brush, then a pine branch, then a hedgehog on a bamboo stick and then I couldn't help it, I started giggling.

Aaron caught me. Oh dear. Men think women are emotionally delicate between the sheets, but giggle at a man having sex and you find out what touchy means. Aaron wasn't too bad; he pulled out, smiled defensively and went soft. He went hard again and finished the job soon after, very pointedly from behind, very aggressively, very pleasurably.

Before he resumed we laughed about his expression, agony and ecstasy registering the same, namely comical ugliness. Aaron said opposites often meet: 'Tears and laughter intercept each other; the way you might get an attack of the giggles at a funeral, or cry when you've been laughing a lot.'

I hope I don't giggle at Mike's father's funeral. 'Mike's father'? Why do I keep calling him that? His name was Al, I knew him well. My diary is full of emails we sent each other.

God knows I had tried hard to hate him – after all he had cheated on Debbie, his wife – and I'm bloody good at hating. But Al had secret weapons: mature insight, reservoirs of empathy and irresistible magnanimity. It's all so clear now he's gone. He could defuse, nay destroy, my puffed-up pride. But for the first year or so I insisted on that little ritual wherein I tried to pretend we hadn't taken to each other the moment we met.

I would make a barbed comment, some supposedly caustic gem wrested from a turgid TV drama like: 'Isn't it interesting how the cheating male starts out feeling unloveable and then makes that a palpable fact?' Then I'd sit back, feeling smug and Al would meet my lacerating wit with silence. 'Ha! That told you, you cheating father of a cheating son!' I would think. Then the silence would evolve and come into its own. It took me a long time to accept that silences can be irritatingly eloquent.

Slowly it would become obvious that this was – yet again – not the silence of the flummoxed, not at all. This was a particularised and very peaceful silence, one reserved strictly for my previous barbs. It would sort of prop my barb up, as it were, suspending it in time, such that we could all analyse it at our leisure, and contemplate the twisted bitterness from where it seethed. Embarrassment would creep up on me and, with perfect timing, Al would puncture the mood with conversation. He never intruded with banalities, he always spoke

194

meaningfully, asking after a suicidal client, or whether my mother was feeling better, or whatever, always resetting the agenda. The mood was conciliatory, even loving. He was the wise old man unburdening me of hot-headed pride. It galled me, but I grew to relish the pleasure of being corrected and simultaneously cared for. Al is the only person who could ever do that with me.

I said as much to him on the email, long after I had given up trying to hate him. He replied with sarcastic insults, in order to pay me a huge compliment: he said he didn't know what I was talking about, that he thought I was the most offensive person he had ever known and God knows why he tolerated me; 'I can only guess I'm desperate for grandchildren or going senile or some such.' Such panache. I'll never have the pleasure of that intimacy and easy confidence again. He had never mentioned grandchildren before, didn't want to pressurise Mike or me, I guess. But it should have been obvious. He loved life. Life, period. It didn't have to be his own. And he loved me. Al, our relationship – like everything else – simple and clear once it's over. I can tell it like it is, easily now.

He never mentioned his looming death on the email. The only time he alluded to it was the few times he said to Mike, 'You don't want to die with regrets,' always in ho-hum tones as if it were an obvious profundity rather than something he was in the process of doing. But they both knew what he meant. It chimed with his other fatherly refrain: 'You don't appreciate her enough.' Then he'd smile at me, gently teasing Mike, but meaning it too.

He said it a lot, trying to press the point home, hoping his son wouldn't break the heart of the love of his life. He knew something had gone wrong between Mike and me, but Mike never wanted to tell him how bad things were. Al was dying and took pleasure, perhaps even strength, from

Mike and me being together, and Mike no longer being a philanderer like him. Even I didn't want him to know his son was just as bad as him.

And just as good too.

I miss Al.

Sunday, 4th June

Mike staying at his mother's again tonight. I wish he was here. I want to make amends, cuddle the poor guy. His father died and his shit girlfriend went out for a fuck.

Had a bottle of wine, wee brother phoned, high as a kite, as ever, or at least trying to be, much like me, got to try. Sometimes can't pull it off. Pillow beckons. Temazepam time.

Monday, 5th June

Mike still not here. Aaaaaargh!

Funeral set for Wednesday morning, only slot they could get this week. Mike doesn't care who isn't able to make it at short notice. He says Debbie is a mess and doesn't need lots of wank well-wishers coming along just because Al was a big shot doctor and they want posh points for associating with his corpse. A bit tense, methinks.

Apparently Al specifically asked to be buried in Warriston cemetery, one of the best places on Earth. I had to stifle tears when Mike told me. Immediately I recalled Al's voice and words: 'Not a bad place to decompose.' We were walking the dogs through the cemetery, admiring all the Victoriana, as we often did. And then another moment came flooding back; the time I told him Mike and I had made love in the cemetery. He had laughed and told me I was a 'gorgeous, shameless flirt' and not as original as I thought; 'Debbie and I did that decades ago!'

Al and I had so much more to talk about. Some people you just don't run out of conversation with. I'll go to Warriston Cemetery and commune with Al, regularly, until I lie there and rot myself, beside my mentor. (Imagine: a conceited cow like me had a mentor, but of course was too conceited to notice at the time.)

Mike's coming home tomorrow, thank God, I really want to see him. He must miss Al more than most men would miss their fathers. There is no tinge of relief for Mike. Al was never a burden; totally *compos mentis* to the end and magnificently stoic. I want to be there for Mike. Poor guy has never had to cope with death. He can't even cope with life.

I'll drink myself to sleep. Maybe meet Mike and Al in dreams.

Tuesday, 6th June

Mike rang, very curt, said he might as well just stay at his mother's again since he has to be there in the morning for the funeral directors. In other words, 'Sod off, heartless cow, I don't need your particular type of solace!' Christ, why did I say I didn't give a shit?! I do. I was thinking about sex when the (expected!!!) news came through. I just blurted it out.

I'll surprise him in the morning by being every bit the sweet Denise he fell in love with. But tonight is beyond frustration. Think it could be a two-bottler, at least. Want to work things out. Being near death makes you review your life – rather than your self, which is invariably dull anyway. I'm so aware tonight that the stars will shine,, the tides will shift and the earth will spin, as they have to, and they still will if I die right now. Death is my, and everyone's, only certainty. Frankly it's an outrage, to the ego.

Back to reviewing my life. I'll need a therapist. I'll be my own therapist, my own honest (gulp!) therapist, cutting to the quick the way we therapists never do: 'Now Denise, how did you get to be a self-deluded, sour slut who has to cheat before you can mourn the passing of a good friend?'

Oh, I don't know! The widgets made me do it.

'Yesss . . . But still, being a therapist who loathes her clients, despite knowing some are lovely, surely implies, via any branch of post-Freudian non-misogynist psychoanalysis, and indeed even on a simple, observational Gestaltist basis, that you're an insufferable bitch?'

A man's fault! That's it. Not sure which one, but yes, definitely some guy. Give me a mo, eh, let's see, eh . . . Ronnie! It was Ronnie! After I lost my virginity to him he fell asleep, just one hour later! I've never got over the callous brute, boo hoo.

'Yesss . . . But don't you want to get back to being sweet Denise?'

That sappy bint!

Actually, yes I do. Funny, when I met Mike I thought I'd got there. I thought I'd be sweet again. Love visits innocence on you. And, alas, blind ignorance. But I can recall – and, even now, relive – falling in love. Age twenty-six, intelligent, detached, always observing, thought I'd sussed it all. But I was the watcher of the skies who never saw the dawn coming. Nothing would ever look the same again. I hadn't known I had been waiting for it until it happened, and by then the waiting was over.

'Hmmm. How touching. So your whole life was just waiting to get to this wonderful place? Shame it turned out to be hell.'

But I can never regret falling in love with Mike. I like the way we all think we are so smart but we don't know diddly squat about anything when love kicks in. There is no warning and you have no chance against it. Even if it all goes wrong, I will have that humbling, comforting awe for life.

In the years immediately before Mike, I had been wading through what I used to call the mire. From the viewpoint of a sincere therapist – yes, I was one too once – the mire is interesting, anthropologically speaking. We unmarrieds sink into it, unknowingly, in our mid-twenties. By then we've learned to drink; we've learned to take drugs; we've learned to pull; we've learned you can get away with sleeping around; we've learned that nothing is important unless you let it be important and we've learned that everyone else is as desper-ate as ourselves. It's all one big level mêlée. And, of course, we are mature enough to handle the bruises.

'What you've really learned is how to be lonely and do damage.'

OK, if brevity means so much to you. But this mire thing, it engulfs you. By your late twenties you're wallowing in it. It's allowed now; you can brat the years away until middle age. The mire has room for thirtysomethings, even fortysome-things, it's always there, welcoming in anyone who thinks being single is exciting; anyone prepared to think like a nineteen-year-old and behave accordingly. All are welcome at the big, illusory party.

'And you, Denise, think you're above it. Surely no wallow-ers are more ridiculous and sluttish than those with a partner, yet you're there, putting yourself about?'

Give me a break. Do I pay you to hear the ugly truth? No. I pay you to tell me I'm tickety-boo. So take it easy with the honesty, bitch. The mire is tricky. And yes, I am there because I am lonely. I always have been. Why the fuck else would I be interviewing myself on a computer? Why the hell else would I have ended up in the mire?

'Sorry, slut-queen. I understand. It's not your fault.'

Quite. The mire is out to get you! The mire is in pubs, clubs, parties, offices, television, friends' flats, your relationships,

eventually your mind, everywhere since being young, irresponsible and vacuous was sanctioned. Not quite sure when that
was? The 1950s, perhaps? Has a small mire been growing ever
since the movies decreed that teenagers are interesting (which
of course they aren't)? I don't know. I just know something has
gone wrong and we all party on borrowed time and the years
slip by, quietly and unremarkably, while we jade. Is that a verb?
It ought to be. It's what we do for years. We brat and jade. But
hey, we're taking drugs and trading fluids so we're never being
boring, yeah right.

The last vestiges of my youthful hopes shudder and crumble when I think about what I – OK? I, I said, not society –
have put me through. I remember the nadir of my experience
in the mire. It occurred just the year before meeting Mike. I
went back to this guy's flat, drunk as you like, and he forced
me to have sex. I was too out-of-it to resist, I was too out-of-it
to talk. I never even tried to stop him. But he and I knew I
didn't want sex. I lay face down on his couch as he pulled my
skirt up, yanked my knickers to the side and fucked me. I lay
there thinking, 'I deserve this'. It felt like punishment, perhaps even vaguely gratifying punishment, though only
vaguely, I didn't enjoy it. Explain that. I certainly don't think I
deserved it now. Bastard.

'Sorry to hear about that.'

Thank you. I made it up. Simple truth is he raped me. But
I can't be bothered with the guilt and trauma of that defini-
tive word, so I gentle it up, and slip in a little anger to infer
there's no denial.

'Even sorrier to hear that.'

Thank you again. However, having skilfully avoided that
trauma, I found one-night stands more disillusioning. You
see, I wasn't watching for them. I didn't notice at the time
that they were confusing me. During my sojourn in the mire I
had four, a mere four: that is, less men than I've had since

Mike and I started cheating on each other, a phenomenon which Mike started of course, and that is a fact which must be restated each time our infidelity is mentioned. Every time. Every single time. Always 'he started it', like in the playground, like 'It's not my fault'. Comprendez?

'Only too well. Back to the one-night stands.'

Well, each time I went in with my eyes open – I didn't care, I just wanted sex and expected nothing.

'Your bull is boring me. You just wanted sex and expected nothing? Not your style at all. Is only the last bit true? Was nothing all you dared expect? Let's see: are those memories always fondly recalled? Tinged with anything? Such as feeling like an abused slapper?'

Perish the thought, I usually do. These are post-liberation times and we don't do vulnerability in the mire. It is old-fashioned to feel used, and it is weak to pine, so one doesn't, one simply doesn't. Now we women get to be scorned but aren't allowed the fury. Mind you, I'm confident I would rather gouge my eyeballs out with a plastic teaspoon than go out with two of those guys. But the other two? I really don't know. I never knew them. And I do know I would have liked them all to have tried a bit harder afterwards, like tried at all, like phoned more, like phoned at all. Two didn't ring once.

However, looking back now, the two who phoned were more depressing. There was Daniel, the married man. He was kind, attentive, and adored his wife and kids – but he still had (great) sex with me. He was the biggest bastard; completely comfortable with it. Like I say, he even phoned, though just once to say hello; a teasing titbit thrown from the sanctity of marriage.

'To the grovelling hound who sucks so good.'

Hey, there are nicer phrases, 'delights in fellatio', that kind of thing, OK?! But he didn't even offer an affair (which I still feel I deserved an option on). What disturbed me about

Daniel was the way we didn't disturb each other at all. It was as if we had sex without touching. We were casual sluts, we knew it and we didn't care. I never even diarised it.

Then there was Colin, 'call me Col' – after all it's such a long name, it really needs to be abbreviated. He was absurd, so hilariously serious about anything to do with women. I laughed at him all evening then got drunk and went to bed with him. It felt comfortable. Until we got into bed, that is; he was hopeless, I was still laughing. He asked a thousand times what I wanted. Eventually, between sniggers, I said, 'to go to sleep,' and he gave a stupid speech about how he respected that. Funny at the time, but not later; again the desultoriness gnawed at me, and he kept phoning, which recalled it. He must have phoned a dozen times, and he respected my every excuse until I asked him to misplace my number. In fact he respected that too. Colin respected everything any woman did to him because the poor lad didn't respect himself. If you don't like yourself how can you expect anybody else to like you?

'Quite. Look in the mirror and visit that emptiness.'

Fuck off. You don't understand. I thought Mike and I were leaving the mire together. But we've hauled each other deeper and deeper into it, with our infidelities. And you're right; the mire is not suitable for couples, they're the cheapest ones in it and so I don't like myself because I can't understand how we got here, so give me a break.

'You and Mike and the mire, on and on you go, bla de boring, bla. My God, woman, you're dull. You know that you find what you're looking for in life, you're always saying that, character is fate and so on. You must have expected this.'

No. I always thought Mike and I would be different. At the start, he reminded me of the time before the mire, before the guys who fucked my eyes wide open, when I still believed in innocent love.

Back then, in my early twenties, I saw the mire ahead and

was determined to avoid it. I mostly had those bizarre monogamous relationship things then. But they ended in failure. I guess I was beginning to despair before the mire, so I tumbled in. I had nothing better to do.

'All relationships end in failure, otherwise they wouldn't end, silly cow. Bitter people define the relationship by that final, bad taste.'

I appreciate that. When I got together with Mike (and mistook the world for a benevolent place) I looked back at all those years shared with those four very different men, when I was young and could trust, not because the guy was or wasn't worth it, but because you just do before you enter the mire. I stopped seeing them as a waste.

Back then the mere mention of infidelity made my stomach churn. I never snogged anyone else, not even behind Stevie's back, though he was the one I always knew for sure was temporary. I knew he would be temporary because I didn't care when he mentioned ex-girlfriends. Oh for the days when it would still crush to think your lover had been with someone before you. Woe, to find that a hellish nightmare.

'Hmm, somewhat different to the open-to-the-drunken-public beds you all do dirty stopovers in now, eh, slut?'

And how. 'I like to do it this way,' 'Sorry, used my last condom last week,' 'Oh, didn't I shag your best friend last year?' 'Nah, my sister actually.' And no offence taken. We're far too learned to feel special.

'Innocence is retrievable. You can't feel it just now, but it is.'

Lying bitch.

'What are you like? Al dies and you prate on, not about Al, or even Mike, but about your own pathetic loneliness. Are you in denial or are you such a self-obsessed slut you just like talking to yourself about yourself? Have you nothing to say about your lover who just lost his father and whom you aren't there for?'

Pass. I can't bear to think about Mike and me in this situation. We are too separate.

How about this definition of love (Rilke, I think) which I read the other day: 'Two separatenesses meeting and greeting each other.' Mike and I have had a few days off. Maybe tomorrow we can be like that.

Wednesday, 7th June

We were standing over Al's grave. Everyone else had gone and Mike had asked me to stay on with him, after telling the driver of the hearse to wait. Apart from the driver having a fag, two hundred yards away, there was nobody to be seen. It was sunny; lots of dappled beauty and quietly proud gravestones, and crosses, urns, statues and mausoleums, things I love. We both looked away from the headstone, across to the old, overgrown part, where all the artistans lie rotting. It was originally a cemetery for artisans. I looked at an obelisk sticking up through the bushes and thought about how artisan was a good word for Al; an artisan has one skill, and Al's was nurturing life. Perhaps that's why he was a good doctor. I was about to say something to that effect but Mike spoke first: 'I haven't actually been sleeping at my mother's, just going over there during the day. I have been spending the nights with a woman you don't know. I think we should break up. I love you but we screwed it up and shouldn't waste any more years.'

I pulled back from him and stared. It was one of those planned speeches, but delivered without tension, just something simple that had to be said. His eyes met mine, fixed and sad. They were even soothing, like his voice; all calm conviction and no hostilities. He kept looking at me, watching his words sink in. I guess a few seconds passed. I didn't explode, implode or anything. I didn't even ask her name. It was as if I was expecting it.

Mike wasn't leaving me any choice, but he wanted me to agree, that was clear. It wasn't that male thing of demanding you see sense and don't make a scene. He wasn't nervous at all. He was doing what needed to be done and was going through with it, however I responded. And he was being caring, worrying for me, how I would take it. And standing there I could see it. He wasn't thinking of himself. There was no shock for him. He had left me before he said it.

I seemed to be watching us in that graveyard, looking at each other. The man, being right, and resolved – brave, like his father – and tender; feeling just as sad as the woman, who can love properly and wants to, and at that moment she understood and appreciated him as he did her. I had hoped we would share the sadness of Al's death, but we did better; we shared the sadness of our own lives too.

I think I nodded when I eventually replied. I definitely said 'OK.' Mike didn't express relief. In fact the muscles on his face tensed, as he successfully fought back tears. We both knew to say nothing. Words might break the spell.

When we reached the car Mike asked if I wanted to be dropped off before he went back to attend the funeral tea. I said I would walk. He nodded. We didn't say goodbye and could not even look each other in the eye. Even that could break the delicate spell. It already had four years of desire bearing down on it.

When he left, I contemplated a walk in the graveyard. Then I decided it would be wiser to say goodbye to Al than give myself time to brood. I spoke quietly to his headstone, 'Al, I would have been privileged to have your grandchildren, but it's not going to happen. Sorry. Thank you for wanting it so much. Miss you, always will. But you know that.' I managed to smile, my eyes tried to well up, but I strode out to the road and concentrated on hailing a taxi. Time enough for tears when I've got through this bit.

I will pack up my things and leave the flat tomorrow, before Mike returns. I know it can't be this easy. But for now I will cling to the truth of that moment to get me through what I know practically must be gone through. I will keep telling myself; our futility was as profound and real as those gravestones around us. We've both known for years, but loved each other too much to face it. It wasn't just cowardice and sloth keeping us together, as I secretly feared. It was yearning; innocent hope struggling against all the odds and evidence. I'm sure I won't always be able to see it that way, but for now I can, and it helps a lot.

Last night had been a good night. Well, he hadn't made any scenes anyway. So Rich was determined not to obsess about Lee-Ann today. He went off to read the Sunday papers in Indigo Yard with Simes. Hangover wasn't too bad, his big sister, his comfort blanket, Denise, was going to join them, and it was sunny. It would be a lovely day. People were squinting and smiling, wearing sunglasses, parading their flesh, pallid early summer stuff, but still signifying the season to make whey-hey.

There were lots of couples in the bar today. Or at least Rich's eye could only alight on couples; their warmth and ease together, even the groups seemed largely comprised of couples, mostly reading the Sundays. Rich wondered about all these couples. Maybe they're going to pick furniture later, or going out for a romantic meal, before facing a week at the office? How boring.

Still, on an anthropological level, they are cute, can't hear them, they look wordless, or like words don't matter; just wee, weakling, unhairy baboons playing with their wee, weakling, unhairy, baboon mates. That smartly-dressed pair, reading the broadsheets but looking stupid, like people do when they play a Gameboy, as if the game is controlling them, programming them, that moronically absorbed expression; maybe hungover despite the neat look? And yet, they bask in each other's presence, they look so much more comfortable than loners. The smiley girl there, nodding like a dotard while he rabbits away, gesticulating with his hands, his paws, trying hard to amuse her. And the sleepy-looking, trendy ones, he keeps plying her with orange juice, watching her drink it very intently, not yet down off last night's uppers methinks, and worried his wee baboon isn't going to be able to play today. The tall, lanky guy trying to read *The Sunday Telegraph Magazine*, his tiny girlfriend keeps interrupting him, he just lets her, smiles, knows it's gibber, she knows it's gibber, gibber it is, but he answers patiently. And that black woman to the left, she can't stop glancing up at her man, lovely big eyes, can't concentrate to read, he winked at her as if to a child, acknowledging she's being restless, childlike. And the older couple opposite, hardly talked or looked at each other, thought they weren't getting on, old worn-out beasts, but when they talked their faces lit up, still, after all those years. All these couples, babooning away together. Being in a couple isn't so bad.

Sunlight was streaming in through the glass roof and imbuing the round, hard-edged tables with an unfamiliar, soft glow.

I'm not going to think about her. I'm not going to think about her. I'm not going to think about her. I'm not going to think about anything else. Oh God, I need her.

Rich was shocked to feel his eyes welling up.

'You okay?' asked Simes.

'Just a bit bleary mate,' said Rich, brightly. 'But not really OK either. You see, I want to go to Ikea.'

'Hmmm. What do you need?'

'Nothing. I just want to go to Ikea. With Lee-Ann. On a Sunday. For a particularly crap piece of furniture made by some silly Swedish name and replete with unintelligible instructions. Then I want us to take this cumbersome item, which we can't afford and don't need, back to our home and make a cock-up of setting it up. I want my life to be that boring.'

'Yeah, right. Well I'm not sure Ikea is open on a Sunday. And if you sift through your memory banks you will notice, under 'addresses', that you don't live with Lee-Ann. So, whose home would you take it to? And how would you get her to go to Ikea with you when she won't even answer your hundreds of calls?'

'I've stopped phoning her so much.'

'Just once an hour now? Stalk them into a relationship, that's the way; never fails.'

Rich shrugged, picked up the *Sunday Times* and sought out his horoscope.

Simes read the latest 'My Cocaine Hell' interview with a celebrity. They were his favourite form of journalism. And this one, with a model he had never heard of, was a classic. She really thought she was fascinating for being unable to handle her drug intake and checking herself into an expensive clinic. Remarkable. Unwitting mirth dripped from every silly syllable. He contemplated a compilation book, 'Inane Wretches Of Our Time'; he could go and interview them all and get the exact same self-absorbed quotes and make the stories as repetitive as possible then market it tongue-in-cheek as a cure for insomnia, the blurb would run 'better than Temazepam!', some would threaten to sue, instant controversy . . . Rich interrupted his daydream: 'Simes, have you ever thought about the moon?'

'Never off my mind mate.'

'Well, you should think about it, you know, especially when you're doing your wee garden.'

'Why? Is that what the Lord our God, Lee-bloody-Ann recommends?'

'No, well I don't know, but you should plant leafy vegetables when the moon is waxing, and root vegetables when it is waning. And it is inadvisable to plant tubers other than on a full moon.'

'And when should I buy a new lawnmower?'

'Seriously, I've been watching the moon this cycle; there's been a lot of clear nights. It's fascinating.'

'I'll take your word for that. You don't have to elaborate, no really, you don't.'

'You know it disappears for three days, waxes, is full for three nights, wanes, and disappears again? And that's just the way it is. Disappears tonight.'

'Hmm, so it'll be too dark for my 2.00 a.m. gardening shift then?'

'But it's sort of like a woman, with her moods, and how much you can get of her, and then she shines; you get all of her and it's worth it.'

'Ah, the Lee-Ann connection! Very interesting.'

'Just a thought.'

Simes frowned and peered right into Rich's eyes. 'Jesus, what are you on?'

'Reality, for once.'

'Well, we better get you back on to sensible class A's, before you bore some poor girl to death. I've been thinking we could go bungeeing in France this summer? Any space on your credit cards. I want a tan.'

Simes regarded his and Rich's reflection in the shaded part of the glass door. Despite his own strawberry blond hair, which the season had already lightened, he tanned better than brown-haired Rich. 'Shame the way you get those freckles in the sun, the way your hair frazzles and you only go golden, never brown,' said Simes, running his hand through his own flop of hair, which needed a cut. 'You must get awfully jealous?'

'Mmm. You know, it's funny with dangerous sports, I mean, not that bungeeing is really that dangerous, but imagine if the worst happened and you died, then that wouldn't be fair on your lover. I mean, I don't think I'll go hang-gliding any more.'

'That's very interesting Rich.'

'Hmm, worth thinking about.'

'Yes, indeed, after all it shows you're truly insane because you've never gone hang-gliding.'

'I know, but I keep meaning to.'

'Oh, my God. Look, would you get out of your Lee-Ann, fantasy world? That's what you mean when you say 'your lover' isn't it? Bad news; she's not interested in you.'

'She's seen me twice.'

'Yes, she has. Twice. In seven weeks and after seventy thousand phone calls. Oh, she's hot for you! Listen. You check every pub you go into, in case she's there; never mind she lives in London and is only up here four days a month. She looms over your every so-called thought, which leads to some funny utterances, and I'm not meaning 'you're witty matey'. You really care about her, I understand. You are planning your life around her, I know. It's cute to watch, but I tell you, it's also sad matey, because she doesn't want you, it's very sad, you are a sad man, a mopy, miserable, sad man. Now, about bungeeing?'

'I'll be fine when I get her.'

'Watch my lips: she, viz and to whit, the female personage known as Lee-Ann, is bereft of amorous desire for thyself, the man they call Richard, for that is indeed his name. Now, to matters of significance: bungeeing, and did you get the coke?'

Rich shook his head and looked away. He knew Simes was right. He didn't care about being a sad man. He cared that Lee-Ann didn't want him. All this waiting, maybe it's not waiting, maybe she will never come round to him. He stifled a tear and felt angry with himself.

Simes looked at him piteously. 'Look, it would just be the usual disappointment if you got her. Six months down the line; her unsatisfied and on your case, you trying to wriggle out the relationship, cheating, what have you. It's always the same.'

Rich shook his head. They both returned to their papers. Simes glanced at Rich; not reading his paper, staring into the middle distance, that glaze he spends so much time behind now. He would be thinking about Lee-bloody-Ann of course.

Looking at her face, I can see her as a child. Wish I'd been there, growing up near her, her life unfolding with mine, intertwined; all the gradations and startles as she went from child to woman, under my skin from the age of five, though neither of us would know anything of the future; we would be unable to imagine being married, we would be unable to imagine being nine. Fascination with her, it would have defined my childhood; this pretty, seemingly unattainable creature I would feel lucky to be in the presence of. Her, aged thirteen, looking over her shoulder to smile at me unexpectedly one winter's morning, her breath in the air, such small images would foretell our later life together. Sometimes I would be watching her from afar, always on her side though; protective, outraged on her behalf; other times I would be privileged by her confidences, sensing her vulnerability; initially a shock, she seemed to complete, higher. Then loving her all the more for it, wanting to assuage her pain, which such a magical girl shouldn't have to endure, one day realising it is not a girl but a young woman beneath that dull uniform, still unable to dare believe she could ever be mine; by late teens unable to bear the horror that she might not be. All that time circling towards her, distractions only real until I see her again; unawares, she would puncture any interest in any other, pulls me right back in, nobody else could come close to this constancy and depth, intricately constructed over years. This solid desire would be as a real as the physical world, more real, the physical world mere echoes of what I cherish; her, this lifetime's purpose.

You can't get that in the modern world. There are no constants from childhood; it's hard enough keeping in touch let alone sharing the years intimately. Now it's the vagaries which get to be the constants; urban anonymity, moving about, the sense that there are always more possibilities, maybe better chances, a life half-lived while we wonder what we are worth, what we want, what we can pull off, how we feel, how we should feel, are we missing the glamorous party which television tells us is on?

Beside the child in her face, is the old woman. I can see that too. I can see her in middle age, smiling across the table, enjoying her guests; or being immersed in a book, maybe one I loathe, we'd tease each other; or her marvelling at some wonder in Tibet, we'd always go on adventurous holidays, especially once the kids were out of the way – am I really thinking this stuff! – or her worried about something, I'll soothe her, solve what I can. Please God let me be there for her ageing.

'So how are my little Casanovas?' Denise had come in and crept up on them.

'Hi Denny,' said Rich.

'Hey, Denny!' said Simes. 'How are you?'

'Top of the world. I'm going to Thailand for ten weeks; loved you guys' pictures of it, leaving in three weeks.'

'Excellent plan,' said Simes.

'You OK for cash?' asked Rich.

'Yeah, sold the car. Only ever used it for runs at the weekend with Mike, and we hadn't even been using it for that for months.'

Simes and Rich could hear Denise hurting through her forced flippancy about her relationship. Rich wondered if she wasn't trying to shed all reminders of Mike. Denise felt them analysing her and spoke brightly: 'So what have you pair been up to? Lowered many women's self-esteem lately?'

'Nah,' said Simes. 'Anyway he's not a Casanova now, he's a lovesick little Romeo, remember?'

'Of course. How could I forget that some poor woman was experiencing the nightmare of his sole attention?'

Rich wanted to broach the subject of Denise's relationship breakdown. As he watched her self-consciously seat herself, he thought how she would never tell him if she was OK or not. Did Denise ever lean on anyone? So determined to be self-contained, a real sweetie wearing pantomime armour. She had been there all his life, one constant, the only one.

'Seen Mike at all?' he asked.

Denise didn't flinch. 'No, but we talked on the phone last week, sorted out a few more things.'

Rich smiled and nodded faintly. She returned the smile and shrugged as much to say, 'I really don't understand a thing about how I feel about Mike and me, but I'm getting by.' Rich looked at her clear, green eyes; not drinking much, good. He noticed her brown hair was freshly cut, as short as it had ever been, but still halfway down her upper-body; looking after herself, another good sign. You observe Denise and glean what you may, even as her brother, no point expecting her to reveal.

Simes was aware of the tenderness between the two. He knew Denise never talked about her private life, yet gave good counsel to everyone else. He decided they ought to discuss Rich's insanity; 'So what are we going to do about Romeo here?'

'Oh, my little brother? My useless little drinker, my self-indulgent little hedonist, it's all gone horribly wrong, eh? No resources for dealing with this love thing, have you? Not just a laugh any more; oh dear!'

Rich wasn't amused, or even interested.

'Why do you think she doesn't want me, Denny?'

'I don't know why anyone *would* want you.'

'Seriously Denny.'

'Seriously Rich.'

'Oh Christ.' Rich rolled his eyes.

Simes spoke: 'You know what he wants to do? He wants to go to Ikea. With Lee-Ann. He thinks that would be fun. Is he the saddest man alive or what?'

'What's so great about this Lee-Ann?' asked Denise.

Rich shrugged.

'Is she pretty?'

Rich shrugged again. Simes said, 'Good stripper apparently.'

'What?! She's a stripper?'

'Nah, normally she's a travel consultant, but your perverted wee brother turned her into a stripper for a few minutes. That's what she did, didn't he tell you?'

Rich groaned; 'Simes, shut up.'

Denise laughed. 'No, go on, Simes, do tell.'

'Well he got Lee-Ann back to his flat one night and persuaded her to do a striptease for him. That's his trip, you know? But then Lee-Ann got dressed again and made him do a striptease too. And then she left, just like that, in the middle of the night, not so much as a by-your-leave, not even a teensy weensy peck on the cheek! Pretty witty, you have to admit.'

'I like her already! But, silly little brother, you sure you're not just annoyed about the one that got away?'

Rich's fury came out as a choked snarl since he couldn't shout in the peaceful bar: 'Look, I don't give a fuck about her stripping and I don't give a fuck about the ones that got away. They can all go away. I just want to go out with Lee-Ann. Get that! It's not a fucking crime. And I don't understand why she doesn't fucking want me. So if you two have anything helpful to say then say it, if you think it's funny then fucking bully for you. I don't.'

Denise and Simes just stared for a few seconds, aware that he was on the verge of tears. Simes shifted awkwardly. Eventually Rich swallowed and spoke quietly: 'Sorry, the whole thing is just wearing me down.'

There was another short silence during which Denise continued to watch Rich. She had never seen him in love, not really, caught up in drunken melodrama and maybe in loving relationships, but not really in love. Little pillock probably thought he had been in love, he'll know otherwise now. She had always said it would be good for him to have his heart broken, but now that it might happen, she just wanted to cuddle him and shield him from the hurt.

'Don't worry so much,' she said, trying to sound reassuring but looking perturbed. 'You're not as bad as you think you are. I don't know why she doesn't want you. You're my wee brother, I don't know why every woman doesn't want you. So I'm not the one to ask. But you haven't failed with her yet. What was it like when you met her afterwards?'

'Eh, same both times; bizarre. But the first time was the worst. I thought maybe I wouldn't be so interested after all, that it had been the drink and drugs, so I stayed straight for three days before meeting her. The moment she walked in I knew I wanted her. So I very impressively clammed up and started to sweat. But that's the bizarre thing; it felt like I was already going out with her, seriously, but obviously I couldn't behave as if I was, so it was awful, stifling, that's why I couldn't talk, and I couldn't get drunk, no matter how much I drank, so tense, for me anyway. I was useless, boring, nervous, don't blame her not wanting to see me again.'

'She knows how you feel about her?'

'Oh yes, that's clear. I doubt if I have a shred of dignity in her eyes.'

'Sometimes you have to start out as a fool. It's honest, a basis.'

'What?! Well it's not working. What do you think I should do Simes?'

'Dunno. I think you're insane actually. I mean wanting to go to Ikea, you're losing it.'

Rich smiled; 'Nope, me and Lee-Ann in Ikea. That's the way it should be.'

Denise was still regarding him thoughtfully. 'Not sure it's your fate, seems very organised. You have a restless soul, should have been an artist.'

'I am. Copywriting is art, if you care for that term, that cover for all manner of crimes, and anyway I'm not saying it has to be all organised or all anything. I just want to go to Ikea with Lee-Ann. Is that so weird? Is it too much to ask of this awful life?'

Simes fell over the edge of frustration and into the abyss of despair. Rich really meant what he said; the lunatic dreamed of going to Ikea with Lee-Ann, as if Sunday furniture-shopping with one's partner wasn't on the ninth level of Relationship Hell, when she has you alone and pinned for the day and you've been drunk the night before, just to add to her litany of misgivings.

'Right!' said Simes. 'C'mon Denny, we're all off to bloody Ikea. I'll be Lee-Ann. Rich, I'm going to show you how crappy it is going to Ikea with your partner.'

'What?' asked Rich.

'Look, you want to go to Ikea with Lee-Ann? Well, imagine I'm Lee-Ann. Imagine we've been going out for, say, six months, and we've moved in together and I have decided we need a new coffee table. And you, unlike every other man in the world, are happy to be trotted off to Ikea on a Sunday when you should really be sitting quietly nursing your hang-over. I'll show you it's shit.'

Simes picked up his Camel cigarette packet and silver Zippo lighter. Then he stood up and put them in his jeans pocket. 'Help me here Denny; let's knock some sense into this shell of a man.'

'OK,' said Rich. 'It'll be practice for when I get her.'

Simes' mouth was wide open as he shook his head at Rich.

Denise was grinning: 'OK boys, let's go. Let's see if Ikea with Lee-Ann is so great or so bad. I'll adjudicate. Let's get a cab.'

In the taxi they worked out the rules. Rich insisted Lee-Ann wasn't bitchy, moanie, demanding or bad-natured. 'Oh get real, visor vision,' said Simes. 'You're looking down the love tunnel.'

'Yes, Rich,' said Denise, sternly. 'She's not perfect; if you expect her to be perfect you are putting too much pressure on her: it's a form of bullying, nobody's perfect.'

Rich was delighted that Denise still talked as if he was likely to get Lee-Ann. However he frowned as Simes outlined the scenario; 'Listen, it's Sunday, so you're hungover and I, BEING A WOMAN, have whatever the opposite of sympathy is when you're hungover. Also I saw you drunk last night and, BEING A WOMAN, I see this as great material for bringing you to heel and I don't give a Yeti's breakfast for your embarrassment and pathetically fragile, big ego. Furthermore, I didn't like the way you spent most of the evening talking to that pretty girlfriend of mine, the one you lyingly say you don't think is attractive. Got that? Point is, I'm NOT in a good mood with you.

'Furthermore, we've been going out six months, right, so obviously during that time we have had a few arguments and I, BEING A WOMAN, have memorised your every nasty remark to twist round, pull out of context and use in evidence against you later, like today. OK?'

Rich looked to Denise for help. She shook her head. 'Nope. All good stuff. Any more Simes?'

'Oh yes, I've got the full feminine stockpile. Decimation awaits. A-ha! A personal favourite this: I have become aware of your financial ineptitude and, BEING A WOMAN, I see that as empirical proof that you don't care about me, about us, our future and so on. What's more, although I deny that I care what my family think of you – which is, naturally, that you are a waste of skin – I wish you would make me proud just once, just bloody once! Of course I say that but, BEING A WOMAN, I actually mean I wish you would make me proud of you all the time; in point of fact I wish you would make it your entire life's work.'

'All that's no problem, DARLING!' said Rich, signifying the beginning of the game and fixing an angelic smile on his face. 'I will make you proud. Trust me.'

'Why should I trust you? You let me down all the time.'

Rich looked to Denise. She shook her head and said: 'Allowed.'

Rich looked back at Simes. 'I'm sorry honey, I'll try to keep it together.'

'Oh yeah, like stay sober for a whole three days and think you're the bee's knees for it. Even though you're a tense pain in the arse to be around. And that's another thing; I hate the way you paw me in bed when you're drunk.'

'I'm sorry DARLING. I really will stay straight and I'll take it easy, don't worry, and don't get on to me until I have failed, c'mon now, be reasonable.'

'Oh, that's just so typical of you. Trying to turn it on ME!'

'Sorry DARLING, I didn't mean to. Really, I love you and agree with your criticisms, really, I do.'

'Oh yes, you're always so contrite when you're hungover! But only then.'

By now the taxi was pulling up at Ikea, and Rich was paying. Both men were entering into the spirit for the main event; loaded with righteousness and gunning with I'll-show-you petulance. They strode into the huge, airy space, with fast-paced certainty. It was busy. 'Christ, people really do this on a Sunday,' said Rich, regarding all the couples.

Again, he was in Couple Land; he could hardly see anybody else. Even the family with two girl tots in cute, orange jumpsuits were just a couple; the kids were the fruit of coupling. Couples, that's what it's all about, couples everywhere.

'Yes they do, Rich!' said Simes. 'It's called being normal, sober, responsible, caring, building a home, a whole new world to you no doubt.'

'Well, frankly, yes, DARLING, it is somewhat unfamiliar, but I'm trying to change. I like it.'

'Oh, do you now? A wee change, is it? You like getting drunk with your pathetic friends, that's what you like. Anyway they're not even friends; you're all just bonded by drinking, you hardly even know each other, not properly.'

'I don't know about that, sounds old-fashioned, and untrue. Guys do have to be sensitive to each other, in some ways more so than women, since we can't expect each other to be explicit about our feelings. It's self-serving and unob-servant for a woman to assume guys are, by mere definition, emotionally unsophisticated and only capable of lesser friendships.'

Rich was chuffed and quite surprised at the eloquence of his little stance. Simes looked to Denise. Her eyebrows were up in surprise too; her little brother was obviously feeling a lot. 'Allowed.'

Simes looked back at Rich: 'Don't snap at me. And don't call me self-serving.'

'Sorry darling,' said Rich with a smug smile. 'Do you like this?'

They had strolled towards two coffee tables. Simes regarded the one Rich was indicating and said, 'And that would fit into our spare room? A modern, metallic, coffee table in a room full of old, wooden furniture?'

'Sorry, honey, you have better nesting instincts than me. I didn't think, just thought it looked OK, you know?'

Simes harumphed in despair. 'Yes, no doubt your friends would agree.'

'Would you stop going on about my friends? What's your problem with them.'

'That prick Simes!'

'Oh.'

'I can't bear him.'

'Well, give it time. He is surprisingly kind.'

'Yes, to the brewery industry.'

'Granted. But he's OK. He is always nice about you.'

'Pah. Only to you since he knows he has to be. He can't stand me either.'

'How do you know that?'

'He is a boyfriend's friend who is single. What is less interesting than a woman he can't hit on but still has to be nice to, constantly, even though she deprives him of his sharking partner?'

'Oh, you are cynical.'

'No, I am a WOMAN, a realistic one.'

'By saying that, you say more about yourself than Simes, since he wouldn't . . .'

A voice interrupted them. 'Hey, what you doing in here?' They looked about for a second then saw the small, dapper figure grinning: it was Ruaridh, an old friend of Simes', with his model boyfriend, Pete. 'Hey, hey,' said Simes. 'They're letting poofs in now?'

'Indeed they are, though I hear they have an issue with drunks,' replied Ruaridh. 'What you up to? Sharking in Ikea? Desperate days lads.'

'No, not on the pull. This one here's been pulled; pulled on to the path to hell. He's in love, apparently.'

'That's good, surely?'

'No, no, no. She doesn't want him, must be afflicted with taste or sense or something. And I'm trying to show him that's lucky.'

Simes introduced Ruaridh and Pete to Denise and told

them not to interrupt the lesson. 'Follow me,' he ordered. 'For I will prove that men have an inverted learning curve when it comes to womanhood; repeatedly they go into relationships expecting approval, forgetting that what she will give him instead is guilt. They've been there before, it was awful, but back they go again, and again, and again, one of witty evolution's little malices.'

Ruaridh raised the stakes; he had a mischievous sense of humour and his boyfriend had a quick laugh. It had now become a proper performance, with an audience.

The three followed a few paces behind, giving Rich and Simes enough space to play the isolated couple.

'What about this one then?' said Rich, indicating the second table, a slatted wooden affair.

'What about it? It's horrible.' Simes did exasperation very well.

Rich looked at the table, frowned and turned to Denise, Ruaridh and Pete. Denise looked at the table and said, 'Allowed.' All three nodded.

'There's one over there I think,' said Rich, indicating twenty yards or so further up the aisle.

'Oh, so suddenly you know Ikea, do you?' asked Simes.

'No, just saw it, DARLING,' said Rich.

They walked along. Rich put his hand on Simes' back, and said 'You OK darling?'

'Hmmm,' Simes sniffed back. 'Don't touch me.'

'OK, sorry.' Rich spoke immediately and brightly. Simes realised he had walked into that one. They arrived at the table. Both men were aware that the entourage had mysteriously grown to seven or eight, but they pretended to be uninterested in it.

'It looks sort of feeble,' said Rich.

'Yes, that glass top, just the sort of thing you might stumble into drunk.'

'I have hardly ever broken a thing drunk. I just think it looks sort of flimsy, insubstantial and too delicate among all our OLD WOODEN FURNITURE, DARLING.'

'Hmmm, at least it will be easy to carry.'

'Hardly a reason to purchase something we'll have to live with. *I'm* not feeble, I can carry a bloody coffee table.'

'Don't swear at me!'

'Oh sorry, forgot that was a one-way street.'

'Quite. My prerogative.' Simes stuck his nose in the air. They grinned at each other, for a moment not a parody of a couple, but a good-natured couple parodying themselves.

'Actually, are you so sure you can carry a coffee table? You're not exactly a keep-fit fanatic these days.'

'I go to the gym, play football a bit, swim when I get the chance, come on!'

Rich turned to Denise, who was puzzled. Rich was definitely a few points ahead, but would he still be going to the gym?

Ruaridh spoke: 'No, no and no again! You straights are shocking; the way you just let yourselves go. And the men are the worst! I don't know how the women let you get away with it. After six months you're slobbed out on the couch: unshaven, inattentive, probably unwashed, you're sitting there, mesmerised by a peurile game show and you still assume you are worth being with.'

Rich was irked: 'You mean we are not mincy, youth-obsessed narcissists!'

Ruaridh came back at him: 'I'd sooner be a youth-obsessed narcissist and still fanciable after six months in a relationship than smelly Mr Blubber taking root on the couch. Six months; you have probably now put on weight, definitely forgotten aftershave exists and generally learnt to make her feel about as exciting as pond life. A Cup Final enlivens you more than she does.'

'Bang on, Roo!' crowed Simes.

'Allowed,' said Denise, as some smartly dressed woman nodded enthusiastically at her side. Her tubby lover, also standing beside Denise, was frowning. 'Sorry Rich,' continued Denise. 'As a woman, I'd rather face someone who wants to look young than a pigged-out egomaniac daydreaming his lazy life away on the couch.'

Bullshit, thought Rich, as if I'd do that with Lee-Ann.

'You're right again, DARLING,' said Rich. 'I'm going to the gym later. I have been getting really out of shape, haven't I?'

He turned to Ruaridh. 'And what about her? After six months, letting herself go?'

'No,' said Ruaridh, flatly. 'That's a myth, men are the worst.' Denise nodded.

'Right,' said Rich. 'About this sodden table? What do you think, DARLING, HONEY BUNCH, SWEETIE-PIE, my PERFECT little COOCHIE-WOOCHIE-WOOCHIE, eh?!'

'Now, now, no need to be sarcastic. I'm just trying to help you.'

'Oh yes, if a woman criticises she's trying to help you, and therefore help the relationship and therefore being all caring and nurturing, but if a man criticises then it just shows what an uncaring, insensitive git he is, correct? Exasperation: copyrighted by women.'

'Temper, temper. Anyway, that table isn't very nice.'

'I like it.'

'You would, honestly!'

'I do. Honestly.'

'Well, you buy it. But I don't know where you are going to put it because it's not coming back to our flat.'

'That's very reasonable DARLING. Thank you so much for considering my opinion and debating the aesthetics of that glass coffee table with such precision, perception and patience.'

'What's the point? You're clueless. There's another one further up.'

Simes started walking up the aisle. Rich followed, exclaiming loudly: 'Yes, that's me; Mr Clueless! Mr Beneath-Arguing-With! Mr Hopeless! Amazing I survived before you, isn't it?'

His theatrical antics were attracting more attention and the entourage was now about a dozen strong. Rich noticed one giggly couple of strangers, particularly.

'It is actually . . .'

'Yes, incredible, got to thirty all on my Jolly Jack Jones, amazing!'

'No. You turned thirty. You got to nineteen.'

'Sure thing. And now you are helping me get to thirty. Thank you so much. Be lost without you.'

'You would be.'

They had arrived at the table, a chunky wooden affair with small, hand-painted tiles inserted near the edges of the surface.

'Women always think that!' declared Rich. 'They really believe you couldn't survive without them; that you're so impractical your life would simply fall apart if they left you. Oh and then you'd be sorry! Oh, you'd know all about how bloody wonderful they are then, wouldn't you? When they'd gone, you'd appreciate them then, eh? Oh yes, that would show you! Listen. I like that table. I like my life and I'm with you because I want to be, not because I can't survive without you. I can. I did before. Now don't put me down.'

Simes turned to Denise. The entourage was so large it was expanding automatically as others joined to see what the fuss was. 'Allowed,' said Ruaridh, and Denise nodded approvingly. Simes was flummoxed. He heard Rury explaining to another couple: 'They're pretending to be a couple, the smaller one's lovestruck; some woman who doesn't give a toss for him.'

'Calm down,' said Simes, loudly. 'I just didn't like that table. What about this one?'

'Whatever you think, DARLING,' said Rich, also loudly.

Every burgeoning of the audience emboldened both men. They were certain it was the other who was talking clichéd rubbish.

'Oh, take an interest, would you?' said Simes.

'No. Frankly I cannot give something I do not have in my possession to give. And I have lost interest because you are in a mood.'

'I'm always in a mood, I'm a woman for Chrissakes. I love being in moods. I live to be in moods! Moods are the stuff of life! Moods ARE life!'

Rich smiled; 'Of course, sorry, it's probably me, bit hung-over, drank too much last night.'

'Yes, most unusual. And how interesting you were too. I'm sick of it.'

'Lighten up; it was Saturday night, only time I've been drunk in a while.'

'Lighten up! You get drunk and I take it seriously, but the problem's mine?! Honestly, I need to *lighten up*! Oh, do I now? It's you who needs to be more serious!'

'Seriousness is the province of the pompous.'

'What? Stop complimenting yourself. Seriousness is what you need.'

'Nah, seriousness is for self-important posers; people who think if they just seem earnest that proves they are important. Take politicians, tedious windbags always being morally indignant and outraged and more-concerned-than-thou, always being serious in other words, as if that proves they're right.'

'I'm not asking you to become a politician, just to take things more seriously!'

'Seriousness is pretentious . . .'

'Oh, change the record!'

'Do you really want me to take myself seriously? Really? To behave like a bloody actor? To take my every puerile thought seriously, to bang on about me me me non-stop?'

There had been chortles, 'here here's and murmured remarks from the crowd but now someone spoke out. 'Hey, I'm an actor!' '

Rich glanced at the crowd, saw a small, smiling man, and thought; 'Jesus, they're never ashamed of it.' Everyone was watchful, waiting to see how Rich would handle this sidewinder.

'Typical!' bellowed Simes. 'Offended somebody again. And this is you sober!'

Simes had been brief. He was throwing it straight back to Rich, who was foundering. He was now a designated big-mouth, about twenty faces said so. Nothing he could do to change that. Only one way out: rant on and win the argument.

'Well, honestly, actors prove my point. They are *so* serious about their trite craft when, really, their job just entails being good at pretending to be somebody they're not, good liars in other words, a dubious art and nothing to take too seriously, but the attention-seeking pretty prats think they're bloody fascinating, as their ridiculous seriousness shows. Oh yes, seriousness is the key; whether it's facile thespian arm candy or any other peabrained peddlar of drivel, you shall spot them by their seriousness. They will be the ones serving up banal thoughts and banal selves as serious matters, assuming that then we'll all take them seriously. Seriousness is the refuge of the bitterly average and the self-deluded. I thought you would expect more of me?'

He didn't glance at the actor, didn't want to encourage the limelight junkie to speak up. Simes was frowning at him, thinking, 'Entertaining little bastard.' Rich smiled back, sweetly.

Simes changed tactics and laughed. 'Ha ha. You're right, DARLING. I shouldn't get on to you. Why don't we go home now and you can paint the hall, you know, like you have been saying you'll do for several months.'

'Weeks, DARLING.'

'No, no, we are dealing in WOMAN numbers. Gripes work in multiples of reality.'

'Well, I've been busy lately . . .'

'Yes, I know, you're so busy, *so* busy, busy, busy, all those urgent appointments, with bottles of wine, bedclothes and computer games, I understand. And you know what else? When we go home, just for a completely *un*serious, laugh-a-minute treat, I'll show you how to work the dishwasher! You know that big, noisy thing that sits in the kitchen corner? It cleans dishes. No really, it's such a hoot, you'll love it, not serious at all!'

Rich laughed good-naturedly. 'What an excellent idea DAR-LING. You're right anyway, that table isn't very nice. Let's go.' Simes had missed his chance for bust-up and singularly failed to shake Rich out of his Lee-Ann fantasy world.

'We could try Habitat?' said Simes.

'Disallowed!' shouted Denise and stepped between them. 'Performance finito! And tonight's Oscar goes to . . .' and she held up Rich's hand.

The crowd cheered and clapped. As Simes and Rich bowed, Simes noted a few people smiling approvingly. 'Bloody couples, the lot of them,' he grinned at Rich.

The audience dispersed and Simes headed off into town with Ruaridh and Pete for coffee, partly to give Rich some time alone with Denise.

Rich felt proud. It had been a fun game, played with surprising passion, because it wasn't just a game, it was a hint of what might be. But for now it was back to being a mopy, sad man. He and Denise went into the store's coffee house. It was full of couples, but wasn't the world?

Denise fetched the coffees and returned looking pensive. She sat down opposite, without looking up at him, took a sip of coffee, carefully placed her cup back in the centre of the saucer, and began.

'You know Rich, working as a therapist you see a few things starkly, not least of all the vacuous nature of most psychology of course, and how little it ever helps anyone. You realise how little we all know about life but you also get to glimpse some insurmountable truths. You see them more often because people bring theirs for you to look at.'

Rich listened carefully. Denise never ever discussed her work.

'In my consulting room, there is a small wastepaper basket and a box of tissues on the coffee table beside it. Sometimes people cry when they come in. At the end of some days, I have a bucket full of tissues, a bucketful of tears. There may be tears of sadness, letting go, a calm sound; or tears of grief, very pure, a distressing wail; maybe tears of regret, releasing the stress valve, the tired face recognising, yet again, this familiar flow of tears while simultaneously managing to experience the pain anew; or tears of loneliness, the quiet pitiable sound of the worn-out, ground down to hopelessness.

'And there are other kinds. But the worst are those tears of regret. All the others will pass, they'll take their toll and they may take time, but only true regret is definitely forever, until death releases you. It can be so terrible that you invite death in, to release you. Suicide can be unknowing; just shaving a little time off your old age by withering your will to live with these implacable worries. People do it, all the time.

'What is really frightening is that the state of regret is very nearby. People move into it casually, uncaringly. One simply has to do something wrong and irrevocable, and then notice; that's all. Even amid the terrifying beauty of tears of pure grief, there is a flower of regret. It's regret that keeps the pain alive; wishing you had loved her more nights, taken better care, gone on more holidays, not shouted, tiny things testifying to a pain that has a life of its own, which dominates your life.

'Most people have some regrets – except psychopaths, the terminally pointless and Edith Piaf – but they are negotiable, learning experiences, counterbalances to hope and happy memories, just part of daily life. Unless you are predisposed to spending time in the dull, broody, spaces, they are insignificant. I'm talking about true regret, which is rare and different; it's not a nagging feeling you can sometimes ignore. It is there, every minute of every day in everything you think and do, and colouring your dreams too. And it's hard to imagine, let alone anticipate, until it is already haunting you like that, but try to anticipate it. It's love that causes true regret, you know? Don't acquire it Rich. Don't spend your life agonising over that small phrase, 'If only!' All your precious, spiritual energy, absorbed into an unwanted, unchangeable past, defeating you. Do you understand?'

'I think so,' said Rich. 'But what are you driving at?'

'God, do you need it in semaphore? You are in love. Don't spend the rest of your life wondering 'If only I did this . . . If only I did that . . .' Know you did everything you could to get her. And that will probably mean getting her. It often does. Love is that unfair. If love's demands aren't met, it mutates into true regret. Use the charm you just showed off through there at the coffee tables, send her flowers, be available any time without being too obvious about it, accept she doesn't feel like you feel – yet! Use your wits, work it out, stop dreaming and make plans, get a grip on your nerves when you do see her, maybe accept you look like a fool to her just now so you can only go up in her estimation, I don't know, just do whatever you have to do to get her.'

'Do you really think I can get her?'

'Don't even debate it, you sappy wimp whining about your miserable, little, seven-week effort. Understand this, you thoroughly modern, lazy, self-indulgent, complacent, little brat: you might just be getting started. Be prepared to wait, more weeks, months, don't rule out years, not until she's married someone else. Understand that, or you might as well stop bothering and start regretting right now.'

'Denny, that's putting a lot of pressure on me. I find it terrifying enough . . .'

'Shut up moaning. Moaning is preparation for failure. Hang in there. Get her. Don't be a faint heart.'

Rich shrugged. Denise glared. Rich nodded.

Wednesday, 30th August

Hurt my knee today, rather badly, but it didn't bother me. What happened afterwards did.

I got off the boat, from the Thai mainland, at Tapan Yai, which means Big Beach; just a klick in length and host to a bar, restaurant/house, about a hundred beach huts and far too many stoners. I waded ashore cradling my rucksack in my arms. I was struggling to put it on my back when I keeled over and grazed my right knee on the thigh-high wall that runs round the restaurant porch. It had what looked like a gravelstone surface, full of tiny sharp points which shredded my skin. I wanted to ignore it and not make a fuss. But there was a lot of blood running down my leg, and I knew it could get infected, from the grit. Also there were a few frayed bits of skin dangling, hideous.

Everyone said 'Mama' will sort it, 'nona problema'; 'Mama owns all this'; 'Mama's great', and so on. I got a bad vibe from these travellers, lazy, drugsy crowd. I already wasn't keen to meet their matriarch, but I was astounded by the chilling apparition which manifested itself. Mama is of indeterminate age; middle-aged or perhaps old and guileful. She had no warmth at all, was utterly false. I disliked her on sight and I disliked her relationship with these backpackers. A contract of lies; she gets to feel popular, acceptable, I bet her own kind can't stick her; and they get to feel like they belong here since they know a local, big deal. She's an outcast, and rightly so! She's a witch.

233

She took me through to the kitchen and started ministering to my knee with a wet cloth. Then she started tearing off the loose skin and picking out bits of grit, putting her nails into the exposed areas, scratching at the tenderness, and smiling – not that Thai smile, that policy of serenity; this was quietly passionate glee, very fixed. At one point I had to scream to get her to stop. She looked up at my face, to see when she might continue. Her eyes scared me, they were glittery black and utterly opaque. I let her finish, as if I was her plaything.

It really troubles me that I did that.

Friday, 1st September

God, I am one stupid woman! I had been told not to go into the jungle alone. The Thai barman warned me yesterday: 'Green tree snakes, deadly. If you are alone, get bitten, nobody to carry you out.'

I was wandering, aimlessly, down at the empty end of the beach, just wanting away from all the bloodshot eyes and faraway faces about here, and Mama. I was only vaguely thinking about visiting Tapan Noi, the small beach just a klick up the coast. But there was this unmanageable outcrop of rocks in the way. Coming up against the rocks made me determined to get to Noi. How bloody-minded is that?

The tide was in. I probably had the strength to swim round the rocks, but looking at all that water, just a few hundred yards out, terrified me. Those depths, that volume, I've got goose bumps recalling them. (Will I always be scared of the sea? I wonder if anybody notices that I never leave the shallows?)

By contrast, the jungle looked lovely, a horizontal green strip in a panorama, all dapples and shimmers, big sky glorying above it and inviting white sand below it. Of course it occurred to me that this was merely the impression from where I stood, from the edge of the sea, the dreamy sea, dreamy, that is, until I contemplate going into it. So jungle it was.

It was fearful from the start, just a few yards in and full of shadows, dark, enclosed, another realm altogether. I thought I would just have to get ten yards above the rocks that led to the outcrop between the beaches, but the line of rocks stretched far into the jungle; higgledy-piggedy things covered in thickets, impossible to get through.

So I followed the only trail, so tiny I wondered if it was a trail or if I was just imagining it. I followed it in until the jungle was all dark hues, browns and bottle greens, which I didn't mind too much, but then black patches became frequent. The path went up a hillside then wound through all these gullies where I couldn't hope to glimpse the coast.

I tried to make myself smile, thinking how all I needed was a red riding hood and the scene was perfect; escaping through the forest, from Mama witch and her tribe of degenerate trolls. But I didn't smile. Tree snakes were on my mind. I was staring at every bush and tree, expecting to see a horrid green serpent sliding down to bite me. I was also trying to track every rustle, no matter how small. I wasn't sure how far I'd gone but I was terrified and wondering whether it might be wiser to go back to Yai or if Noi was now nearer. I already wanted out, anywhere, when the snake appeared on the path.

Out it slithered, not from any of the trees which I had been watching so warily, but on the ground, my domain; lurid green, no stripes or patterns, just a living length of green evil and poison. Its head was hideously large, about twelve feet in front of me and it was raised off the ground, with its tongue hissing about, as if licking the atmosphere, tasting my terror and readying to lunge. But its size struck me most: huge. Five, maybe six feet and very thick. Soon the head/neck was swaying further above the ground and the coils were slithering about behind, but to no great effect. I thought it wasn't coming towards me or moving in any direction, at first.

Then I realized it *was* moving towards me; I must have been so focused on it alone, that I had lost all perspective. It was slowly traversing my way with that grotesque sideways sashay. Still, I just stared, hypnotised. Its head suggested it was aware of me but it swayed so much from side to side scanning across me and to the spaces beside me. I think it was creepier than if it had just stared. I thought maybe it looked like it was in a state of trance then I thought it looked demented. I had all this time to think, since I had frozen, never done that before. I became aware that I had frozen and started forcing my legs to step back. They were rigid with the tension. I moved a little into a bush, flinched, convinced I had moved into another snake's lair, but I didn't turn round, couldn't stop watching the snake in front, redirected my steps on to the trail and inched away. It didn't accelerate, but it kept up that horrible writhe and head-sway.

I edged round the path out of its sight then ran. But I soon stopped, shuddering and swallowing and scared to go on. I was convinced I was surrounded by snakes, in some sort of big snake pit that was difficult to discern.

I had run over a small rise. I clambered back up it, to glimpse the shoreline. Yai was much further away than Noi, just 500 yards away and the jungle cleared a hundred yards before that. There was a massive, straight stick beside the path. It looked propitious. I picked it up and started pounding the ground to scare away animals. I don't know if it works, but I had to invest faith in it, before my heart gave out. I progressed very slowly back to where the snake had been, creating veritable earth tremors for all I was worth. It had gone. I went on, at the same speed: step, thump, thump, peer, thump, thump, peer – every shadow and object for ten metres all around, checked, I prayed – thump, thump, step. It was laborious. Each thump resounded with the enormous strength of my fear.

I had heard that leeches are attracted by vibrations and race along the branches of bushes to pounce on the passing source. If true, then I was probably luring every leech on the island with my thumping, but I didn't care.

The reverberations from the stick were bruising my hand (still aching). I only realised this at the edge, as I stepped onto sand. My body managed a slowish breath and I realised a snake couldn't leap out at me now; the sparse reeds poking up through the sand wouldn't hide it.

I looked at my watch: 3.05 p.m. It had taken me fifty minutes to cover a distance you could stroll in fifteen.

I was lowering my wrist after glancing at that time when I saw something large and black moving, just inside my field of vision, to the left. I looked over at the edge of the jungle, dread mounting. It was an enormous, scaly reptile, on top of a rock, about twenty feet away. I don't know what it was – a monitor lizard, or an iguana, one of those dinosaurish things – and I didn't know if it belonged in the sea or jungle. It was over four feet including its long weapon-like tail. It just watched me. I stepped over the last blades of greenery and started walking down the beach, feeling that black creature's eyes burning into me. I imagined it was glowering: how dare you come into the jungle! My thumping heart agreed with it. I imagined it was Mama's animal spirit.

I was sweating and wanted to swim. I also wanted to wash the leeches off. I stopped at the water's edge to inspect my legs; could see three on me. The one on my left calf looked like a tiger leech: dark, huge, with tiny, livid stripes running along its back. This wee bastard had turned dark red and huge, bloated from my blood. The yellow stripe on its back was a few millimetres across in the middle now. I couldn't bear to wait for it to finish filling up and drop off. I pulled it off. It replied with that nippy bite-sting thing, big time. Greedy sod. The other two came off easier. I took my shirt off, dreading more; they sometimes manage to do a bottleneck squeeze through thin fabric in order to get to flesh. None there. I waded in and checked beneath my bikini. One on the side of my left leg. Made me shudder, washed into the sea.

Got out the water quickly, still tense. I tried to slow down walking, as I neared the huts and hammocks. The sight of a few people, lounging about happily just up ahead, was calming, but I was still thinking of all the snakes, scorpions, reptiles and crawlies in that jungle; that jungle just there, paralleling me all the way up the beach. I wanted a beer, or a joint, and I don't really like grass. Anything to knock me into somewhere else. Opium? Fine, I'd take a bucket thanks. Then I saw Noi at close range.

After Yai and especially straight after the jungle, it was a vision of peace; just a dozen people dotted about, one in the bar/restaurant, a few scattered along the beach, one swimming, two reading, everywhere tidy. It glowed with contentment.

I passed close by the wall of the first hut, and glanced at the porch. There, less than five feet away, was a Western Buddhist standing on his head on the floor, utterly still and unsupported by walls. I was startled, then impressed. I wondered how long he had been like that, and why his orange robe didn't fall down to reveal his tackle. I've come across Western Buddhists before; they come out the monastery all calm and cleansed, oh sure they do, except for those dirty thoughts that have been fermenting during weeks of celibate sobriety, like they do, quite fun.

I must have been staring. He waved and shouted, 'Be lucky!' I became self-conscious. It was as if he knew I needed luck. I shouted back over my shoulder anyway, 'Thank you, I need some.' I walked on vaguely wondering if that sounded needy and if he might come up to the bar to look me out.

I think I wanted him to seek me out, it must have been his voice; open, excitable, giving. He wasn't that good-looking. I saw him clearly, if upside down. I wondered how I looked to him, in my long white T-shirt? Just covering my black bikini bottoms? I felt grateful for my good legs and long dark hair. I hoped he approved. I thought how funny it would be to go up to him and tell him this T-shirt is see-through when wet, as if I could ever carry that off.

That tiny bit of contact helped my mind get away from poisonous creatures of the forest. My wee brother said I should make sure I have a 'liberation fuck' when I'm away. Grubby phrase, but he's probably right. As long as Mike is the last man to have been inside me I will feel that little bit more beholden to him, and I'm here to leave him. Anyway, no sex is a bad, bad thing. It just is.

At the bar, I ordered a small and beautifully chilled can of beer, assuming I was calm. I drank it in about four big gulps, and in less than two minutes. It was embarrassing since I had already sat down. I couldn't go back to the bar already, even though there was only the laid-back barman in the place.

'That was quick!'

I turned, startled. The monk had all but followed me up the beach. Now that's what I call keen. I like a man who tries. Men think they are constantly trying to get sex – they're not: they don't try hard enough; they're just constantly thinking about it and wanting it. Shower of lazy wimps.

'So have you been lucky?' he grinned.

'Probably depends on whether you turn out to be an irritating pest or an interesting guy?'

He beamed instantly, confident and amused.

'Your lucky star just glimmered because I'm absolutely fascinating. Take my word for it, don't make me prove it. Please. I'm Darren.'

He extended his hand.

What is sex appeal? It's terrifying. This guy was not special, maybe slightly small, shaved head and eyebrows for God's sake, positively insectile, and an Aussie, flip as you like; and I felt like I could fall pregnant just looking at him. His intense eyes? His voice; calm yet playful? Quick wit? I don't know. No reason. Frisson is not a reasonable thing. The more of it there is the less you can understand it. Just buzzes through you, filling you up, nicely. I'm not complaining. He was my Prince Charming, my reward for making it through the forest.

I shook his hand; he was firm and relaxed.

'I'm Denise. And I'm afraid you are going to have to prove that.'

'Damn. I'll need to buy you tons of beers until you are too drunk to notice my dullness. But given the speed you drink, that should just take quarter of an hour.'

'Oh, that was me savouring and sipping.'

'Ah, Scottish.'

'Nope, just got the accent: half-Cornish, half-Welsh, full-on drinker. Now be interesting.'

'I'll try but I spent a month in a monastery. Head's clogged with the Noble Truths and all that.'

And pornographic fantasies too, no doubt.

'So tell me a Noble Truth?'

'Nah, they're just for thinking about, not drinking beer with.'

'A beer-drinking monk? Isn't your body your temple or something like that?'

'I think that's why I left the monastery. Felt like some abuse. Fancy another? Have you got fourteen seconds to spare?'

He went off to get beers. This was good: teasing and self-deprecation, the lifeblood of flirtation. It comes or it doesn't. I watched him, very aware I was already turned on. I thought about how sexologist types always say it takes a woman longer to get turned on and turned off than a man. Bollocks. We just take more things into account, we sense the whole situation. Men just think, 'duh, woman, sexy woman, duh, please fuck me, duh.' Once the situation's teed up though, that last little factor – the right man – can click you on like a light.

Maybe I felt like celebrating life after a seeming brush with death? Maybe it was the relief of being away from Yai?

As he strolled back in his cartoon robe, I was coming down with a bad attack of the sexual righteousnesses; always happens when they're not gorgeous. 'Who do you think you are turning me on? You should be bloody grateful. And of course I can have you! Don't pretend you would contemplate rejecting me!' *et cetera*.

We embarked on one of those traveller conversations, exchanging philosophy and personal information as if we were intimate, when we are really trying out re-inventions of ourselves. He soon punctured the chat with that very description of how clichéd we were being. He said it with a laugh, wasn't snide, was intelligent, marvelled at things. You know when you've met a good one, you meet so few.

'So what will we talk about Mr Interesting?'

'Why we are here?'

'That's Noble Truth stuff and traveller tosh, surely? We might as well start talking about Garland's *Beach* and how we're just so above all that behaviour but incidentally I'm just back from the northern Moluccas where they have never seen white people and everyone kept touching me as if I was an alien or a god. Me noble savage. Me intrepid explorer. Me spiritual bla bla. Or we could start quoting from *Apocalypse Now*? Or drone on about how much we relate to the locals?'

He smiled. 'Wasn't meaning that so deeply. Just meant why you and I have come to Thailand. But you are so right about those pat chats. It's funny because Westerners manage to avoid learning anything about Thai culture. The Thais play it that way. Thailand has the Theravada school of Buddhism, it's not as free and easy, and pick and mix, as say, the Tibetan school. It's really rigid, much more didactic, more codes than concepts. Take all this sex industry, Westerners actually believe the Thais have relaxed moral codes. Those poor girls are shunned for evermore by their families, who possibly sold them into the trade, and probably happily accept the money the girls send home.'

'Ah, so you've been investigating the sex industry? Bit of a testosterone buildup in the monastery eh? A wee bitty barrier on the path to Nirvana, was it? Transcendence tricky when you're full of frustration?'

He blushed a little and smiled. 'Of course I haven't gone to prostitutes. No chase, no fun, no buzz, no point. Might as well just masturbate.'

It was getting pretty close to the bone, and just three small beers in. I was watching the tide going out, lazily. If it went out enough I could wade through the water, round the outcrop of rocks, but darkness was only a couple of hours away. I was not going back into the jungle. I started to tense. I didn't want my hand forced. I wanted the choice. I worried that if I was forced to stay I might end up declining sex and looking like a tease, an uptight attention-seeker. But if I had to stay and did have sex, it might leave me feeling cheap.

I explained my fear of the sea. He listened, sat back and frowned, as if working up to a question. Then, whoosh, tropical downpour. Never saw it coming, blue sky then rain lashing down, everything drenched instantly, a shroud of whiteish grey over people running about, laughing, and still swimming. We watched in silence, occasionally smiling at each other. It only lasted for one cigarette, exhilarating. Sun came back out, storm would be unmarked half an hour later.

Afterwards he said: 'So it's not water you're scared of? You liked the storm?'

'Of course, just the sea. Couldn't get through life being scared of water! It's the lack of a floor out there, away from the shallows.'

'So, why are you on a beach. Again, why are you here, in Thailand?'

'I like the beach, can mess around in the shallows quite happily. If I'm being honest – and we always are in these travellery conversations – like hell! – it was to get away from a relationship. Broke up a few weeks before I left. Been here a month, just wanting time and distance to do their thing. Nothing else works.'

I'm sure he took pleasure in discovering I was single because he had to turn his face all serious – to hide it.

'Sorry to hear that. Why did you break it up?'

I was complimented he assumed I broke it up.

'I didn't. He did.'

'Sorry.'

'No, it was a good thing he did it. I wasn't interested in keeping it going.'

'Really?'

Still touchingly surprised that I was chucked.

'Yeah, if I was I would have chucked him, that's how to keep a man interested.'

Darren smiled. 'But it clearly meant a lot to you. You're out here to get away from it.'

'I know, I thought I was interested, funny how things pass, it's passing all the time. I'll feel fine, some day soon I hope.'

'Was he a bad guy?'

'No.' I really thought about what to say next while Darren did a sweet nod with his bald head, while frowning again, as much as to say 'Of course, as if you would fall for a bad guy!'

I continued: 'He was lovely. We just brought out the worst

in each other. So I want away from him and the person I became with him. Just the usual, I suppose, which makes it seem more tragic and trite at the same time. Why are you here?'

Darren scored a quiet point here. He knows relationship chat is the way to engender intimacy, especially when the man gets to be all pseudo-sympathetic about a past disaster, but he knew I wanted to move the chat on and he didn't stall it there in order to patronise me.

'I'm here to get religion.'

'Why?'

He shrugged and spoke unironically: 'Looks nice.'

'Did you get it?'

'Not really. I've come to the conclusion that religion is tied to the land. You can't just come out here and take it on: you're not *of* this land, you can't just wear it like a tan. I mean look at the clothes, this robe, it's just not my colour. Westerners are too pale for these swathes of rich colour.'

I was watching the tide. It was out now and would turn again soon. I have a perverse interest in tides. It happened after something my wee brother said made me aware of them and I had a nightmare about being caught by one. I can almost marvel at them, but still, the sea, all those depths, shifting about, shudder. There are two high tides and two low tides each day. And they don't have to ebb and flow to the same level. The levels are said to be caused by the distance between the earth and the moon. But anything being said to 'cause' the eternal tides is a worthless inference. The tides just are. They are as unmoveable as the moon.

While Darren was watching me watch the tide, he decided to go for broke. We had already had the now-or-never line 'I'm off tomorrow, flight home booked.' And the availability: 'No steady girlfriend, no unsteady girlfriend either, come to think.'

'Why don't you stay on for dinner?'

He managed a spontaneous, off-the-cuff voice. But I had already thought it through. I can't handle one-night stands. I used to kid myself I could. Well I can handle them, I never make a fuss, but that's just pride, truth is I usually feel used or needy, and sometimes I get to feel both. I guess I'm just not that cool. And I can't buy into the wistful, ahh-if-only sanctifi-cation, setting it up as the great love foiled by star-crossed circumstance, the perfect relationship that never was. Dream on. He got his rocks off and you thought it was you he cared about. Duped again.

'No, I think I'll head back, thanks.'

He smiled. I thought he was capitulating, felt miffed. Come on Darren, bit more desire please. Ah yes, that's better, just regrouping for another attack, good boy.

'Yai is really awful!' Ooh, gearing up for a big rant. Bit desperate. Very good boy. 'I called in there. Too many people. A crowd. And a crowd is always stupid and usually evil. All crowds. The bigger the crowd, the dumber and scarier the show. Think of the Nazis. Would never have worked without crowds. Imagine Adolf to Eva over a quiet candlelit dinner: "I've been thinking, babe, really enjoyed that little foray into Czech politics, what say we invade Poland? Oh what the heck, let's just take on the whole sodden world, we're bound to win, and hey, let's throw in a holocaust, haven't seen one of them for a while." '

I wondered if he was trying to keep the talk going until the tide got tricky. Another hour or so might clinch it. Maybe he knew the next low tide wasn't for twelve hours. I appreciated the effort and smiled. He knew what the smile was about.

'True,' I said. 'I feel too old for that crowd. Actually you just made me feel too *wise* for that crowd! Thanks. They are a shower of wasters.'

'So spend more time up here? Don't worry about the tide.'

'Ah, but the tide is important. Here I am measuring the

time it takes for the tide to shift, yet once we measured time in terms of tides. In fact time and tide come from the same ancient Germanic root.'

'Excellent, imagine it was ancient times, and I invite you to stay for a mere one more . . .?'

That would take us to early morning. Still, it was a poetic way of pleading.

'Thanks, but I'm going back now. Hey, I think I'll move up here tomorrow. Maybe I could get your hut? What time are you leaving?'

It was beautiful: he caught the finality of my decision to leave and sounded exquisitely pained as he spoke. 'Seven o'clock boat in the morning; only way off this beach.'

'Oh well ciao, was lovely meeting you.'

I got up to leave. He extended his hand, noble in defeat. 'You too,' and he smiled to show he was good-natured about such matters, which I didn't doubt anyway.

Wading round the outcrop was bad. I had to concentrate on the embarrassment of turning back if I failed in such a simple thing. Then I thought how it's not as bad as the snake, and then I thought of water snakes and the story of this one guy who jumped into a river in the jungle, got bitten instantly and had to be helicoptered out to hospital. They say the snake would have fled if it had a chance, he probably landed on it with no warning. I started splashing and kicking about to scare anything that might be in the water. The shelf dropped steeply and I was chest high, still ten yards from the tip, I didn't know if I could bear to swim, that's my real nightmare, not being able to touch the floor instantly, when I want, I hated the silt streaming through my sandals, testifying to a shifting floor, moving with the depths, but it was better than the thought of the depths without it. I teetered on, my heart pounding, and I cursed Darren, for keeping me so long – just half an hour earlier and I would have had a guaranteed floor – then it levelled a little, I made it round and bolted up the other side, splashing wildly. Got back, had a beer immediately, calmed down quickly and been writing all this since.

It's good to have had a day worth recording. It's now eleven thirty, the dance music is blaring away, the beach has got busy, people arriving for the full moon party, though it's not for a week. Why do they bother? Half the people on this beach are so out of it they could be alone in a blackened cell watching a light bulb for all they know. I feel trapped here. The music accentuates the feeling, and so did the difficulty of getting off the beach today. And it doesn't feel like home to return to. Everything seems portentous since I arrived on Yai. All the gaunt expressions, shards of glass from beer bottles protruding in the sand, the police boat circling the bay daily, my scabby knee healing so slowly, Mama still witching about, that mad snake and the monk. But I'll be on Noi from tomorrow.

I sat down to write about the experience of the snake, mainly. But now I don't care about the snake. So there is a demented serpent slithering about in the jungle. Big deal. But the monk? He's on my mind. Monk? Who is he kidding? Mind you, he visited some spiritual peace on me, felt like I had all my levels of consciousness restored. Here I feel stifled, like I exist on one tight band. And I'm lonely. No good at approaching people. They always have to make first contact. I'm useless.

Thirty minutes later. I realise I made a mistake. And for once I want to admit it and deal with it before it's too late. I want Darren here. To hell with this oppressive place. And to hell with my pride and fear of one-night stands. I want Darren. And I want him to give me my liberation fuck.

Ten minutes later. Just phoned the bar on Noi from our bar, and insisted the barman go and get Darren; I pretended it was an emergency. He was asleep, up early after all. I just invited him for 'a drink', but he knows. After his momentary pause – during which I didn't regret asking and I didn't feel nervous, just excited, I could sense delight registering with him – he spoke as if it were a normal invitation: 'I'll be there. I always say there's nothing like a long midnight swim to whet the appetite.'

So right now, as I write, a good man with no eyebrows is swimming through the South China Sea to be with me, through that long, fearful high tide. I'm being lucky.

Rich all but clicked his heels as he jaunted up the street.

Tonight, after one full month of exhausting effort, he had been granted an audience with Ms Lee-Ann. He had earned this. He had called her just three times this month. Just three. It was a record. It had been tough. He had experienced physical strain NOT calling her. He had pulled his painfully tensed hand back from the phone on several occasions. He had started to dial her number, slammed down the receiver and screamed; 'Jesus! Have some pride, man! Be cool!' This is a process so self-evidently uncool it leaves you bereft of pride. He had done it six times. His pride was now six times removed. He had left the house and gone for walks in dismal weather to avoid the cajoling phone. He now knew the colour of everybody's curtains on this street. Fascinating. He particularly disliked that lurid green at number forty-three. He had rung her answer machine during the day, knowing she would be out, to get a fix of her voice. And he had endured feeling like a pathetic pervert for it. He had lived for one month with those eleven digits emblazoned on his mind's eye, burning into every thought. But he did it. He phoned her merely thrice. He thus managed to imply that he might not be a maniac and might even have a life – two dubious truths.

His mind turned to the phone call: 'When she phoned me, it was, no wait, I think I'll say that again. She Phoned Me. Yes, SHE MOST DEFINITELY PHONED ME!' He remembered it well. How could he forget his glass-splintering shriek as he regressed to being an overexcited three-year-old! 'Oh hi!!' It earned him an 'Are you OK?' He may have recovered when they discussed meeting up. Mind you, the few other times they had talked about meeting up, his diary had been one big window, and therefore a rather unnecessary item, so maybe she didn't fall for 'hmm, I'll just check [rustle, rustle, in the phone book]; that *should* be all right, let's see, ehhh? . . . Yes, that's great.'

This was on Wednesday. She rang to suggest tonight. Two days; not what you would call respectful notice. Rich knows she's not terribly interested in him yet (he always adds yet), thinks he's beneath her (and he agrees, but the whole world's beneath her). He guessed either somebody blew her out at short notice or she's curious to see if his ardour has faded as he hasn't phoned much. Merely a trifling matter of mild amusement, for her. But it gives him the chance to pretend he might just have cooled off. But he'll need to stop grovelling and creeping and gawping and sweating and apologising and snivelling and wincing at himself for being himself. He needs to stop that anyway, before one of them pukes.

He'll not expect too much from tonight. She has already said she has to leave before midnight to hook up with some girlfriends for a club, viz and to whit, don't even *dream* I'm coming back to yours. Fine. But if tonight goes well he won't have to stand another month of NOT phoning; they can have weekly chats, just weekly – he knows not to push it (but if she wants to ring in hourly, that's fine). Actually, being realistic, now that she's phoned him, he will spend most of the next month looking at the phone, thinking, 'Come on then, for Christ's sake, ring!'

She was there already! He had kept her waiting. On a street corner. Damn. Calm down, she's probably been there less than a minute, he was on time.

Walking towards the person you love is always special. Knowing you will soon be with them, in fact already are with them, but there's no interaction to think about yet, nothing to distract from the perfection of their presence. Lee-Ann is standing in isolation on an early Autumn evening. Black trouser suit, trees far behind her, colourful leaves, turning in the season, small breeze, probably blowing her long black hair a bit, but he's not close enough to see that yet, low sun, she's facing east to avoid it, perhaps thinking he's coming along that way, she's just waiting, nothing more, to give him some time. She's seen him, smiling now, the last touch. Rich wished he could live forever in this moment, feeling the long-forgotten promise of childhood, restored. He wished he could tell her that.

Will she ever see herself as his future wife? He was astounded every time he used the W word. Generally, he sacked friends for getting married, a simply mad thing to do. But he wanted to marry – nearly there – this woman.

'Hi honey,' said Rich, and kissed Lee-Ann on the cheek.

'Honey?'

'Sorry, I just use that word freely.' Stop being a creep! She's just joking.

'How are you?'

'I'm good. Waiting long?'

'No, just got here. Late meeting dragged on, didn't have time to go back to Caroline's to change.'

Apologetically, Lee-Ann indicated her work gear, the trouser suit, blue, silk blouse and black brief case with shoulder strap. Like Rich cared. She had her blue eyes, her long black hair, herself, she could wear pyjamas for all he was interested.

'No worries. Place we are going is up here.'

Hey, I avoided being a creep there.

They crossed the cobbles of India Street, over to the east side, to walk up the black of Heriot Row. India Street was wide and quiet and graced by some of the most beautiful Georgian façades in Edinburgh, or anywhere. Rich thought how he would love to live here with Lee-Ann. He could feel the stifling nervousness creeping up on him: I wish we were going out. I can't function until we do. Right, no self-consciousness. Enough already!

'Tell you what Lee-Ann; I would be so much more comfortable with you if we were going out but I know you don't want to go out with me, that's fine, no worries, don't be embarrassed, I'm not, I have no pride when it comes to you. But I was thinking: what if we *had* gone out? Then I might be comfortable with you. So let's go out from here until we reach the end of the block? Horrific prospect for you, I understand, but we all get over relationships. It's just a matter of letting go. Moving on. Confronting the issues. And realising that your partner was actually rather annoying anyway. So we'll just hold hands and have an amicable break-up at the corner. Then I might finally be relaxed with you. OK?'

Lee-Ann laughed, and blushed. 'OK.'

'Jolly good.'

Rich held her hand, confidently, and they walked on in silence, Lee-Ann smiling sheepishly, Rich feeling good, looking casually about, for all the world like a happy lover taking in the evening glow, which he was.

They grinned at each other a couple of times. As soon as they were past the edge of the building, Rich dutifully released Lee-Ann's hand.

'Oh, am I chucked?' Lee-Ann spoke flirtily but Rich knew not to push it.

He spoke sadly: 'Afraid so darling.'

'That was the smoothest relationship I ever had!' said Lee-Ann.

'Oh, I don't know,' said Rich. 'I thought we hit a rocky patch just after the lamppost and frankly your moods were getting to me, I mean I know I drink too much, but to be honest in the latter stages I found you a real killjoy and I never really got over the way you looked at the guy by the parking meter. It really hurt me, you know? But at least we can still be friends.'

Lee-Ann laughed. 'Yes, we can avoid the period of bitterness, normally essential to the subsequent emergence of a friendship.'

'Quite. That terrible time during which you have to wonder: "will we be friends? I'd like that, I mean I'd like the forgiveness. Don't actually want to see much of her, mind you." '

'Indeed: "Can I forgive him for wasting my time? Damn, I'm going to have to, for the sake of pride and social ease. Bastard will think he's OK. I'll make bitter jibes every so often, remind him he's a shit." '

They turned left along Heriot Row and right after two blocks, up to the brasserie on Hanover Street. Rich played the misogynist, really just an excuse to show off his insight. Lee-Ann registered everything but gave nothing away, as ever. Rich had got used to that. You don't fall in love with Lee-Ann for ease or to get reassurance, he had decided. You might get approval about intellectual matters. She'll even let you programme her a bit, but beneath all that, unless you are a conceited fool, you will never be sure what she is thinking about you. A lot of guys would run a mile. But most guys are wimps.

Just outside the brasserie, they ran into Julian, a very serious academic acquaintance of Rich's. 'Sorry mate, in a rush, taking my ex out for dinner,' said Rich. 'You know how clingy exes are?' He shook his head in a defeated manner. Julian looked shocked at his rudeness. Lee-Ann laughed. 'I'll ring you next week,' said Rich. 'Ciao for now.'

They went into Dix-Neuf, a bright brasserie. It was like an upmarket continental café, quite intimate and mature; all seating. Rich had thought it through carefully: quiet candlelight with other couples would be too pushy, the rowdy pub would be too tense and a standard Italian/Chinese/Indian not special enough. Not much of a calculation, but it had taken him a full day of neurotting to figure it out.

They sat quite far in, but in view of the big window front and away from the music. He had called in during the afternoon to pick the table. He ordered a mid-price Chablis – having resolved to fall between flashy and cheapskate – and then he indicated the boisterous Jekyll and Hyde pub opposite: 'Simes is in there. Hope you don't mind but he wants to drop in, just for one drink; has important personal news he wants to tell me face to face.'

'Of course, fine. What do you think his personal news might be?'

'Dunno. Quite intriguing, since Simes doesn't have a personal life. Unless you count quarter-baked pseudo-relationships, debts that could finance a small African nation and an intermittent herpes problem.'

'That bad?'

'Believe me. It's one of the reasons I love him; he makes me feel adequate.'

'Aren't you? What's the pattern in your personal life?'

'Don't know, I can never see it clearly, been too drunk, too into floating, I'm bored of it, I want a personal life with a pattern. A pretty pattern. Paisley maybe? What do you think of Paisley?'

'I think it's a historical town in Southwest Scotland which was probably prettier in pre-industrial times.'

'Me too. I'll pick another pattern.'

'Don't have a pattern and worrying at thirty? Decided you better settle down while somebody might still have you?'

'Nope, that's for cowards. And women; biological clock and all that. What's the big pattern in your personal life? You are terribly unrevealing.'

Lee-Ann smiled: 'I know, it's part of my pattern, keeps me looking interesting when I'm not. My pattern is crystal clear; never close to anyone, admired by everyone. I get acquirers, not lovers.'

'That'll teach you to be so damn pretty!'

'Well, my brother gets it worse. He's better looking?'

'Who is he?' asked Rich. 'Brad Pitt?'

Lee-Ann glowed graciously.

'Hold on, see, you're going to talk about your brother, rather than just straight about yourself. It's weird. Most people love talking about themselves and it's so boring: "I'm interesting" or "it's a shame for me", that's all they're ever really saying, but you, you never talk about yourself. Go on. Tell me you're interesting or it's a shame for you.'

'Neither would be true. But let me tell you about my brother. He's not good at being close to people either, so women project all this stuff on to him. He is so pretty, and now he makes a lot of money, so they live in a fantasy that he is their ideal man. They just decide he is this and that, whatever their complexes, insecurities and past baggage inspire. Paradoxically, they are often adoring of him, and *they* find that gratifying; he doesn't, they actually aren't taking him seriously. So he gets the selfish side. Often the plain selfish type; the vain kind, looking for the trophy and status but blithely assuming they are being loving, because they care so much about this relationship, but the relationship is all about them, and their *decisions* about what he is like, not about observations or understanding of him. They often pull grand traumas on him; fantastical tosh. Now he's thirty-three and swithers between hating himself for being so difficult to get to know and despairing of women for being so selfish, for stopping off to live in what should be passing infatuation, initial attraction. It's probably more his fault, but he's lovely, I feel sorry for him. Now there's the burden of beauty! You see, that usually happens to women.'

254

She poured wine rather than look at Rich. He smiled. That wasn't a shot across the bows, it was a broadside blast at him. And it was way above the waterline yet missed the masts entirely. Now she brought her replenished glass to her lips and looked at him.

'You want a response?' asked Rich.

She nodded, in her inscrutable way. Rich swallowed then felt surprisingly and completely calm. He paused and looked at her. She met his eyes. He spoke breezily.

'You are the long-forgotten promise of childhood, restored. I have nothing in common with your brother's inadequate lovers.'

Their eyes stayed locked for a couple of seconds, then Lee-Ann reached for her wine again. Rich moved the conversation on, as if that remark were unexceptional: 'So what is your brother going to do, about his communication difficulties? Sounds tricky.'

'Eh, I think he might change yet, I mean, I think he wants to . . .'

The conversation stayed on other people's relationships, as Rich's words fermented inside Lee-Ann, to what effect he couldn't hope to tell.

At one point he broke her off: 'Sorry, just seen Simes, coming this way, hmm, an hour early. He's got Paul out, I didn't know, his oldest friend from school, lovely guy, but this is the first time he's been out in weeks, got beaten up, was scared to go out; Simes has been coaxing him to come out for ages. Simes big brothers him; he's not like Simes – dark things happen round Simes, regularly, but he's so confident and capable he survives – but Paul's very quiet, shy, serious, no drugs or sleeping around, big shot lawyer, international area. They're an odd pair together. Here they come. Oh, court case came up last week, thug that battered Paul, some guy called Willie, got off.'

Lee-Ann turned round to see them and smile. Rich felt comfortable. They looked good walking towards him. He had asked Simes to look smart, and he was astoundingly well-groomed, in a fresh, white shirt, smart brown trousers and expensive dress shoes, no less. That greasy mop was newly washed and looking foppish. Paul looked like he was putting on a good show, strolling casually, not being nervy. He was a small, unassuming guy, with a self-contained manner and sharp, boyish features, especially his ever-twinkling eyes and aquiline nose. Rich found himself feeling very tender towards Paul, the last man on earth who would start a fight, or give any offence.

After introducing Paul to Lee-Ann, Simes sat beside Rich, facing the street. Rich noticed Simes was keen for that seat, Paul had been making for it. Odd, what did it matter? But Simes spoke breezily: 'Bit mobbed over there, thought we'd do you earlier and head down Broughton Street.'

'No probs. So what's the personal news you had to tell us?'

'A-ha! It's a biggie and a goodie. You know Christina, the German girl I email?'

He was addressing Rich but the company was supposed to listen. 'Yes,' said Rich, a little worriedly. Simes was clearly in mischievous mode, thought Rich, as he watched him pour himself and Paul some wine. Rich knew too well where this chat usually went. Christina's relationship fell apart a month ago, and she and Simes, both being shameless, had been having phone sex and sending each other umpteen emails a day, sometimes attaching naked pictures of themselves. They were even photoshopping them into each other. Christina would use Simes' pictures to create a silly image of him giving her cunnilingus and he would reciprocate with her fellating his absurdly magnified, and strangely unherpetic, cock. They had got round to anal, whips, handcuffs and God knows what else. They had met for one evening ever. In Paris. Drunk.

Both were exhibitionist slappers, as far as Rich was concerned, and he prayed this wasn't about to be an update on their latest cyberkink.

'Well,' said Simes. 'I got you a present this afternoon.'

He reached into his pocket. No, thought Rich, just no. He cannot produce a pornographic mockup of him and Christina. He simply cannot.

Simes pulled out a British Airways ticket folder and flicked it down on the table in front of Rich. 'Don't open it yet? Guess what it is?'

'I think the wrapping's a bit of a giveaway. But OK, eh . . . it's a CD!'

Simes laughed. 'Correct! A paper CD which will allow you to visit me in Germany, where I shall be living from Monday – indefinitely!'

Everyone stared.

'Eh?' said Rich.

'Yes, you heard right. Berlin for me, folks!'

'What?' asked Paul, who clearly hadn't been told earlier.

'Yesterday Christina got me a contract in a gallery belonging to a friend of her family, just three months at first. Thought I might as well go. Starting on Tuesday. Moving in with Christina on Monday, drive off tomorrow. You've got money Paul, come any time. Rich, check the ticket.'

'Of course it will all probably fall apart,' said Simes nonchalantly. 'What chance do her and I have? Two loudmouth, show-off hedonists together? Bound to be a disaster, but it will be fun trying. Now go on, check the ticket.'

Rich was shaking his head. 'Eh, no, it's OK. I'll visit. Have you thought about this? You only found out yesterday, did you say?'

'Yeah, hadn't thought of it before, chance came up. You know I had been thinking about that time you fooled me that I'd got a woman pregnant, and all that nonsense

257

chasing that bitch Anna, I mean do I know I need to grow up, been drinking on borrowed time, as Denny always says. And I like her. It's a challenge for both of us.'

'This is growing up? Looks like the impetuosity of youth from here, mate,' said Rich.

'Yeah, probably, best I can manage though. But check the ticket, have a look, just want to be sure I got things right.'

Since Rich had recently become aware that there was nothing in his life of the faintest import, he saw no reason to check the dates on the ticket. Of course he could take a few days off to visit; he was freelance. God, visit Simes *living with a woman?* That should be interesting. Simes had never done that before. His idea of fidelity was not shagging his lover's sister (too often). His idea of 'going out together' was living in separate countries and meeting once a month for passionate, needy sex. 'Going out' meant having an excuse to walk away from one-night stands as in, 'aah, if only I were single . . .' And Germany? He can't speak German. Can he?

Lee-Ann asked: 'How is your German?'

'She's great! Cute as you like, real sweetie . . . Oh my German language, ahh, that, hmm. Pretty good actually. *Ich bin ein Berliner!* There you go, that's it all used up. Just kidding. I can talk quite a bit of German: Munchengladbach, hamburger – no, sorry, that's American – blitzkreig, heil Hitler, Sturm Abteilung, Panzer, Stukka, Schutzstaffel, Kaiser, Schlieffen, Luftwaffen and eh . . . well I think that ought to about see me through, bound to make lots of nice friends with those words. Oh, I can also name lots of good German wines. I reckon I'm home and dry on the linguistic front. Well, maybe not dry. But Rich, you got to check the ticket!'

'If it makes you happy.' Rich opened the folder to inspect the ticket. There were two, both returns. One was in his name and the other was in Lee-Ann's name.

Simes continued: 'Now that gives you eight weeks to

arrange. I don't want to hear any excuses.'

Rich smiled: 'Of course not. Thanks.'

The two men exchanged an intimate glance, redolent with goodbye.

'Don't mean to talk down to you, mate,' said Rich. 'But I think you ought to be careful with Christina; you don't really know her, you might be doing a lot of projection?'

Simes grinned and shook his head. 'Nah, I'd never work in a cinema; lousy wages.'

Simes elaborated on his plans and Paul got up to go to the toilet. Simes continued talking, but watched Paul leave the table and the moment he was out of earshot his voice went down to a whisper: 'Had to leave the Jekyll and Hyde early, that bastard Willie is in there. Does Lee-Ann know the situation?'

Rich and Lee-Ann nodded. Simes continued.

'He's only with one other guy, won't start anything just now, but we had to leave or Paul would imagine he can't leave the house without coming across Willie. I told him Willie wouldn't want more trouble with him. But I reckon the creep would torment Paul if he saw him. And he may have more mates arriving. He's definitely a pack animal. They read out all about Paul's trauma in court, really humiliating. But Willie didn't recognise me. I sat quietly at the back during the case, so I sneaked Paul by him without Willie or Paul noticing. It was nerve-racking, could have set Paul back: this is his first time out in three months. He's still getting taxis to and from work every day. When the verdict was read out, Willie and his mates cheered in court, and smirked over at Paul, really terrifying him.'

Simes sat back: 'Now, to matters of a more immediate nature. Any drugs?'

'No,' said Rich, 'Haven't had any for over a fortnight.'

Simes turned to Lee-Ann. She picked up her handbag and

gave a conspiratorial smile, while making to open the bag:
'I've got some really wicked . . . Feminax?'

Simes and Rich laughed. 'Phew, too strong for me!' said
Simes. 'I've got some speed, but I hate speed. Had some
anyway of course. Want some?'

'No thanks,' said Rich.

Simes turned to Lee-Ann, out of politeness, he didn't
expect her to say yes: 'Speed?'

'Yes! Thirty-seven miles per hour. Speed?'

'Sixty-one miles per hour. In third. You never touch drugs?'

'I take coke occasionally but I'm one of those sponging
women who never actually buys any.'

'I buy lots.'

'Would you describe yourself as an addict?'

'I'd love to! Hey, I'm an addict! Fucking A! I get to indulge
my desire for drugs and feel sorry for myself at the same time.
Oh, this addiction lark is a wheeze: no personal responsibility,
wonderful! Our affluent society offers the time, money and
technology to take drugs, but we're too selfish to be grateful;
we want victimhood too. Pah.'

'So addiction is what? Media bullshit?' Lee-Ann was
amused.

'Yeah, I remember the story of one junkie who used to sell,
or sort of lease, her three kids, just wee kids, all under ten, to
a paedophile bunch for the afternoon, to get money to pay
for her crack. I mean, how did she feel when she picked them
up? Why is that selfish bitch walking the streets? She blamed it
on her habit and got a light sentence, but lots of people do
drugs and wouldn't do *that*. It becomes an excuse for being
irresponsible.'

'Tasteful little story, Simes,' smiled Rich, who recognised
that his friend was indeed speeding.

'Oops, sorry, guess who's speeding? Just angers me all that
though. If you want proper drug deaths, ruined lives and

long-term selfishness, alcohol's your poison. Think road fatalities, wife-battering, liver failure, career disasters, bankruptcy, heartache, crap sex and many, many, more. If you want to witness the drug problem, don't read the papers, just look out your window at closing time to watch the human flotsam and jetsam drifting home with frazzled brains to further neglect their lives, like I do. Until I go to Krautland ver vee shalls bee having orderz! Organized livez! Vis zee leeteel Kraut babe zaying "no Zimes, zat ees eenufs! Only vun glaz of zee wine a day of zer shallz bee nein kinky nookyz for you!" '

Rich and Lee-Ann smiled.

Paul had returned. 'I was just arguing about drugs with him earlier,' he said, with a grin. 'I said drugs are a huge problem, not a health thing, but they make people boring, all drugs. I mean people take them to feel interesting, not to be interesting.'

Rich and Lee-Ann smiled again. Rich wondered if Lee-Ann noticed how in unison they were, how couple-y they had become, how wonderful this was.

'You don't even drink much Paul?' asked Lee-Ann.

'No, not at all lately. Haven't been out for a while.'

Lee-Ann nodded, understandingly. For all her own secretiveness, she had that trusting air that opens people up.

'I suppose Rich told you?'

'What happened? How did you get beat up?' Again, she pitched her voice just right, not over-concerned or patronising but serious, and keen to hear the story.

'Well, I was just waiting for Simes. He'd nipped round the corner for a pee. This guy who I had never met came up, with his friend – called Willie and Joe but I didn't know what then – and said I had been talking to his girl in the club. And it was true that Simes and I had been talking to women, well more Simes, you know what he's like.'

261

'Not really,' said Lee-Ann.

'You don't want to,' said Rich.

'Well this guy – and I couldn't see how it was his girlfriend since she wasn't with him – just hit me before I could say anything. I was drunk and I've never been in a fight in my life, so he was smacking me all over the place, and then Simes heard and came running round. But he was drunk too, he was shouting and he tried to hit Willie, and the other guy, Joe, laid into him. We were both a mess by the end, only lasted a minute, not like in the films, bodies are really fragile.'

'You were unlucky,' said Simes. 'Willie was a bigger sadist than Joe.'

This was bullshit, designed to make Paul feel better. Simes had tried to put up a fight and been made to pay for it. Willie had come over to join Joe kicking Simes on the ground.

'I know it happens,' said Paul. 'But it still shocked me. As if my nerves were let loose and won't go back into their slots.'

'Mm,' Simes nodded. 'I felt really traumatised, had to force myself not to think about it or it would scare me witless.'

More bullshit, mused Rich. Next evening Simes was in the pub: 'No time for any of that trauma nonsense! Don't you think my bruises look rather manly?' But after a couple of days he realised the state Paul was in and dropped all that.

'Yeah, I think I'm too weak about that,' said Paul, whose social skills and confidence had clearly sunk to zero; he had one topic of conversation, but at least he was realising that. 'I think about it all the time, and I give myself lots of time to think about it, by abandoning any social life. Don't think I've handled it as well as Simes.'

Simes addressed Paul directly but gently: 'I told you before; it was different for me. I *chose* to get into the fight so I never sensed that threatening loss of power in my world, the terror you felt, that still haunts you. For me, I just lost a fight.'

Still bullshitty, noted Rich. He talks like he is a fighter – not good vis-à-vis Lee-Ann who knows how close he and Simes are – but he isn't. Been in two or three mind you, in the seven years he had known him. (Rich couldn't remember the last proper fight he was in himself. Surely one or two since school? No?) Anyway Simes had admitted to Rich he did feel that threatening loss of power during the incident with Willie; that's why he knows to use that very phrase.

'Isn't it different for Simes?' asked Lee-Ann. 'Him and Rich, they live the low life, out and about being drunk and sleeping around, taking drugs. They've seen things, heard things, just sensed that horrid animal milieu more; a few incidents involving themselves I shouldn't wonder. Simes would be more primed for it, in so far as one can be. I think it's always traumatic.'

So Simes and himself live like horrid lowlife animals? thought Rich. Fair call.

He enjoyed the confident way Lee-Ann didn't glance at himself or Simes, to check she was allowed to put them down. She had assumed lover's rights.

Paul was listening to Lee-Ann intently, so she continued.

'I was a care worker, a holiday job, and got to know this really sweet middle-aged man who had become agoraphobic after he was beaten up. Two youths attacked him – a very frail guy – in broad daylight in the middle of a busy street in Brixton. Nobody came to help him. He remembers them banging him down on a yellow car bonnet at the front of traffic lights. He looked through the windscreen right into the eyes of two other young men in the car, watching, but they ignored his plight, never got out to help him. Nobody did anything, the two guys were very violent, laughing as they shoved him about and tore off his glasses, stood on them after he begged for them back. He thought if he begged they might be satisfied breaking them and would leave him alone. He hates that memory particularly. After they smashed the glasses, they punched and slapped him a bit. He got up off the road, where they left him, and staggered to the pavement, bleeding and gasping for breath. The youths, still laughing a short distance away, decided to come back and hit him more, just kept hitting and teasing him and shoving him from one to the other as he stumbled up the street. At one point he tried to get into a chip shop and the owner said he was in "a fight" – a small, middle-aged man attacking two large youths? – and shoved him out. The youths laughed and hit him more, until they were fed up. As they walked away one said to him, "you boring old cunt!" That always stayed with him; such a non-specific put-down, he was just nothing to them, not even entertainment after a few minutes. When I met him, four years ago, the story was ten years old and he hadn't left his house in all that time. It was heartbreaking. Just a sensitive man, never knew what plain evil was like. You can't dwell on it. Got to think of the good things.'

'That's tragic,' said Rich quietly.

'I think it's probably depressingly common, if a bit extreme,' said Lee-Ann. 'Willie sounds different, he mentioned a woman. Men who resort to fists so readily are bad communicators, not good with women, or at least not women worth being good with. Basically, they're frustrated, failed, jealous animals.'

Simes spoke. 'Yip. Watch them down the Cowgate on a Saturday night. It's not guys with women who're barging along the pavement or calling out aggressively. It's the losers.'

Rich also concurred. But he was too busy being impressed with Lee-Ann to bother speaking. Good chat, good eye-contact – they always go together – and so good with Paul, a complete stranger in a tricky state. She engages caringly, no problem.

Then something strange happened. Simes, who had been looking out the window, said he didn't have change for

264

cigarettes and couldn't be bothered messing around with the machine. He would just nip out for a pack. It was true that there was an Oddbins up to the left, but Simes turned right. Discreetly, Rich picked up Simes pack of Camels. Half-full. Oh no. Rich's heart started thumping. He had to think fast, keep things smooth.

'I'm just nipping out for cigs too,' he said, and left, straining not to run, in case the other two guessed what was happening.

He got out onto the street, his heart thumping even harder as he walked past the window. Then he bolted down towards the traffic lights, a hundred yards ahead, where Simes was. Before he got to Simes, he shouted. 'No Simes!'

Simes turned, a manic gleam in his eye. Willie and his friend were waiting opposite, not to cross to Simes' side, but to go on downhill, across Queen Street and on down to Dundas Street. It was dark now, but this area was well-lit.

Simes said nothing, then slowly steered his stare away from Rich and back across the street, towards Willie. He was lined up at the traffic lights to parallel them down the hill rather than cross over just now. His resolve terrified Rich. 'Simes, you don't attack strangers in the street, got that!'

'Why not Rich?' He didn't turn to look at Rich, just kept watching across the road. His voice was loaded with purpose, at once excited and controlled. 'Besides, he's not a stranger to me.'

'Simes, don't sink to their level. We've talked about this before. Now come on, all that "you spill my pint?" "you talking to my girl?" We're above that!'

Simes' charged tone of voice continued, along with his lack of eye-contact. 'Sorry Rich, I want to hit that bastard over there and I'm going to.'

Rich's palpitations were intensifying. This was beyond bad. He wanted to be back inside with Lee-Ann. 'Come on Simes, snap out of it, you've been drinking. You just said fighting was for losers!'

'Three wines. And this isn't arbitrary; losers are arbitrary. I've nothing to prove, just out to enjoy myself at that bastard's expense.'

Simes was staring at Willie, who was oblivious, across the wide road. But time was running out. The lights would change.

'You've taken some stuff Simes. Trust me! This is wrong.'

'Nah, been wanting to do this since that night the bastard kicked me about on the ground.'

'You're over it! You handled it.'

'So? Why should that bastard be grinning his way down the street when Paul's too scared to leave his house?'

Rich was desperate. 'Look, we are not as low as that. We would cross the road to avoid a fight normally, not to start one, we know it's all macho bollocks.'

Oh Jesus, this cannot be happening; street violence on the night he gets to see Lee-Ann.

Simes hadn't responded. The lights changed. Simes started shadowing Willie down the hill, from the other side. It was horribly calculating, waiting to get away from this busy part, in order to assault, for God's sake. Rich glanced at Willie and his friend, as if for inspiration. 'Look, there's two of them, they'll just batter you.'

'Nope, I'll come on all psycho and get a hit or two at the bastard. I'll have the element of surprise, and I'll run off.'

'Simes, it'll just come back on Paul.'

'I won't let Willie know why I'm doing it. It's a goodie, don't you think? Early evening, very safe part of town, pretty spooky getting clobbered.'

That manic voice. Simes still wouldn't look at him, just strode and stared either ahead or over at Willie, across the thankfully wide street. Rich was at a loss. He couldn't say, 'it should be dealt with legally,' since it had been, disastrously.

'Jesus, Simes, not when Lee-Ann's about, please? You'll see him another time.'

'Sorry mate. I won't. Not unless Sweet William here visits Berlin.'

Shit, of course. Jesus, this coil was ready to spring.

'What good will it do? It won't change anything? It's not the way to get things done. What Willie did was wrong and if you do it, it will be wrong.'

'Sorry Rich, you're behind the times; peaceniks turned out to be arseholes. I never was a good liberal anyway. And I don't think we have time for a philosophical debate.'

Rich thought Simes was about to run across the road right then, but he continued downwards, watching Willie, still never looking at Rich. Rich paused to return to the brasserie, but couldn't; he was too worried about Simes. A short distance had emerged between the two. It panicked Rich more. He raced to catch up to his place, a pleading step behind Simes.

'Simes, you've said yourself you've never seen an intelligent, necessary fight.'

Still the low, excited voice, and lack of eye-contact. 'Ah but violence is all that piece of shit over there understands. He's probably battered a few people, and will batter more. I'd be doing society a good turn by killing him.'

'You don't know that.'

Simes finally looked at Rich, briefly. His face was set, like a killer robot in a sci-fi film. No emotion, yet sneering derision transmitted through the mere gesture of looking. He knew Rich agreed. Willie was just one of those people. They both knew it.

'Simes, this won't stop him! It'll just make him more bitter.'

For the first time in the talk, Simes voice stopped being manic and distant. Now he faced Rich and was plain angry.

'So tell me what's right, Rich? That Paul becomes a nervous wreck? That a sensitive guy loses three months of his life, his confidence and the woman he has been with for four years – him and Alison have broken up over this, you know? – just because shit-head over there was in the mood for jerking off his frustration? Is that *right*?!'

Simes was nearly shouting. Rich understood he wasn't at a higher volume only for fear that he might attract Willie's attention. He didn't know how to handle this. Glaring into Rich's eyes now, Simes raged on.

'You think Paul wouldn't want to see Willie hurt? Absolute crap. He's just scared, he's just too good to dare believe that violence is the only thing that gets through to unconscionable bastards. Now face it. I'm going to hit that bastard.'

Rich was really panicking now. They were nearing the bottom of the shaded stretch. 'You're on a moral crusade.'

'Why is that phrase always an insult? Are morals wrong? It's the snide language of the spineless and faithless, the do-nothingers.'

Jesus, he's in sharp form, thought Rich. 'Simes, please? Lee-Ann's here. There's no point.'

'Oh, but there is. I have a battle plan; to give Willie Boy Paul's tram.'

Simes was talking eerily calm again. It was the sound of pure resolve. Any surprise at what he had found himself doing had evaporated. Now Rich accepted it. He stood still, helpless, and watched Simes stride on, moving away, watching Willie, just yards from the bottom of the block now. He couldn't get involved, he just couldn't, not with Lee-Ann waiting.

At the bottom Willie turned left into Heriot Row, the quiet, residential street Rich had strolled along dreamily with Lee-Ann just a couple of hours before. It was perfect for an assault. Simes started crossing to the other side of the road, a measured jog. He was going through with it all right. Rich did what he had known all along he would do. He raced to Simes' side.

Simes, the amphetamine-fuelled fuck-up, needed him. But Christ, thought Rich, I'm no fighter!

He had caught up with Simes halfway across the road. Simes didn't turn, just said, 'Don't run too hard, don't want to arrive breathless. Just keep the other guy occupied, that's all.'

They got across, and rounded the corner. The adrenaline rush was intoxicating. It was unbearable. Rich wanted to get it over. There was Willie, not ten yards away, with his back to them, fumbling in his pocket for car keys, by the driver's seat of an old, red car. The other guy, about Rich's height, chunky bugger, was round by the passenger door. Neither suspected anything. Simes strode straight towards Willie, the other guy saw him, Simes clocked this, speeded up his last few steps and spoke in a very friendly voice, 'Hey, Willie?'

Willie turned round, unsuspecting, and whack, an open face at point blank range. Blood spurted out as he slumped backwards onto the car, still facing forward. Simes was in with another punch, same right hand. Willie tried to duck, sort of moved his head to the side but Simes' concentration was strong and he packed a particularly hard punch aware it would have to deal with the side of Willie's head rather than the soft flesh of his face. Willie groaned. The other guy was coming round the bonnet, shouting, 'Hey! What the fuck . . .' Rich jumped between him and the fight, fists clenched and firing on bluff; but bluff which felt strangely real. 'Fatboy! You're mine! One more fucking step!' Fatboy stopped, and jerked from side to side, not sure what to do, but quickly realised he had to focus on Rich. One step more and he would be within Rich's range. Oh shit, thought Rich, Fatboy's charging.

Meanwhile, Willie had collected his wits a bit, and landed one on Simes face; no protest, no 'what the fuck?' This was a fighter all right. Simes wrestled him to the ground. Once on the ground, Simes realised blood was streaming down his own face. He was a livid animal instantly. He grappled Willie into a painful headlock, and started twisting him around on the ground. The idea was that Willie would resist from trying to hit and kick soon, fearful of inciting that last terrifying twist that might break his neck. It was going to take a lot of hard wrestling and twisting to make Willie still, if indeed it was possible at all.

Rich didn't have a clue what to do as Fatboy lunged at him. He pushed out a hand: it was foolish, he knew it instantly. Fatboy's bulk charged down on his lean self, through his thin arm. Rich spun backwards, past Simes and Willie, out into the road, and hit the floor on his back with Fatboy on top of his legs, grappling to clamber up to Rich's upper half and no doubt pummel his face. There was a lot of clutching from Fatboy, and wriggling from Rich, trying to back out from under this beast. Fatboy got his left hand up to Rich's face and scratched and pulled at his right cheek, drawing blood. Now Rich was panicking as Fatboy managed to pull at his nose and mouth. Rich bit his hand but somehow Fatboy managed to tear at his lip and draw blood there too. This was one undignified fight. And that was before Rich pulled Fatboy's hair.

He tugged Fatboy's hair towards his left side, to get the big lump of blubber off him. He succeeded with an extra tightening of his grip on Fatboy's thick, dark locks. It was gratifying. Rich could almost feel Fatboy's pain when he let out a horrid yelp. Rich, far nimbler, was on his feet in a flash. 'You bastard!' Rich heard himself say, as the idea of kicking Fatboy – stumbling, just half-up off the ground – crossed his mind, but he found himself pushing Fatboy over. Fatboy almost avoided keeling but then lost his balance, bang on the floor, and Rich waded in with a kick to Fatboy's back. Fatboy rolled round to face Rich and got up screaming, 'You fucking cunt!'

Rich hesitated, he knew he had wimped out of kicking him hard enough or often enough, and now he was letting him get to his feet. He made an even more foolish move: he

270

jumped on Fatboy and they fell back to the ground, entwined. Instantly, he realised this was bad. Fatboy was strong. This wrestling match would not go in Rich's favour. Fatboy knew it too and clutched Rich to him. Rich was terrified now. Fatboy was exuding cheap lager fumes, all over him, a revolting intimacy, and his podgy body could take serious punishment. Rich wriggled furiously for about twenty exhausting seconds. He was collecting unnoticed bruises and scrapes galore from the black road surface, and they were both throwing useless close-in hits but finally Rich rolled free and sprang to his feet. He had a moment to take stock, and he felt distinctly fragile.

Now Fatboy was the aggressor, wanting that wrestle, wherein he would break this little shit's bones. Rich knew it and stepped back. He got a good look at Fatboy's face, a kind of square cartoon that stated: this boy is inevitably fat, it's in the stars, though he hasn't yet reached his full potential. His slit eyes narrowed further as he got cocky: 'Come here, you wanker.' Rich, who usually defended himself with humour, got his weapon back. 'You really need to go on a diet, you big pudding!' Fatboy groped towards him, snarling, 'Fuck you, ya wee cunt!' And Rich stepped back. They were circling each other, Rich backing off and round – plenty of space in the broad road between the parked cars – with his fists alert. His tongue kept the action up: 'Oh Fatboy, don't be mad with me just because I'm the one to break it to you!' Fatboy grunted, moved forward, but didn't lunge. 'Don't get laid much, do you?' said Rich with a cheeky smile. 'Women eh? Picky bitches; just don't want to sleep with fat, smelly bastards.'

Fatboy's patience vanished. He lunged and Rich punched him in the face. Fatboy's arms withdrew from the lunge, a reflex to protect his face, but he forced them back out quickly to grab Rich. Too late: Rich had swiftly sidestepped, and leapt four yards away during the second it took Fatboy to get his bearings. 'I feel your groping technique is a little crude,' he grinned. 'No luck with men either then? Come on Fatboy, here I am. Exhausted lumbering all that blubber about? This is good for you! Don't complain.' There was no getting round it; Rich was enjoying this fight now.

They danced like this up the quiet street, Fatboy lunging at Rich every ten yards or so and occasionally giving small chase, but even he was bright enough to see that was a non-starter. Both had committed a lot of energy to the scrap by the car, and were exhausted, but Fatboy more so. Without the extra adrenaline from physical engagement, his unfit body wanted to tire. Rich was not actually threatening Fatboy with physical interaction, which might have sent the adrenaline racing again. Rich was resolved not to wrestle with this fearsome bear ever again.

In Fatboy's mounting desperation, he was making ever more inadequate lunges, collecting the occasional punch and a lot of tauntings and not-too-forced laughs from Rich. Fatboy reciprocated with mindless swearing. Under the artificial streetlight, Rich had time to muse that he might be in the most unfilmic, unskilled and utterly embarrassing fight ever in Edinburgh. Neither of them had yet produced a single motion that could be called stylish.

'Tosser, come here you wanker...' lumber lumber. 'Thought about the F-Plan?...' dancing backwards. 'Tosser, you fucking coward!...' lumber, lumber, lunge, sidestep and back. 'Hookers? Nah, you'd make them puke...' lunge, punch. 'Cunt, you fucking little cunt!' 'Wow, you're witty. Ever thought about stand-up?'

At one point they were dancing round a small blue car, Rich in full flight, talking snootily; 'Spend your hard-stolen money down the docks, I'll warrant? Do you know what warrant means, you thick oaf? Been served a few no doubt. D'you do your sister?' Fatboy had just failed to grab Rich over the bonnet and now something bizarre occurred, the moment Rich would always remember and feel odd about. Fatboy said: 'Don't have a sister.' The tone was vintage grunt, but the actual phrase was the kind you might say to a new acquaintance. It was a tiny, low-key and harmless communication. It passed unnoticed at the time and didn't seem to affect the fight.

Rich led him about thirty yards up and almost back down to the red car, to hook up with Simes, obscured from view, round the other side of the car. He wanted to get the hell out of there now. This was absurd, he had come to his senses, and he wanted to be with Lee-Ann, where he belonged. Regret was seeping in already.

During most of Rich and Fatboy's taunt-and-dance routine, Simes had struggled to contain Willie in a tight lock on the ground. He collected lots of bruises and scrapes from the road surface, and his white shirt was in pieces, but finally, after a full two minutes he had subdued the more experienced fighter. Only then, when Willie had ceased struggling completely, and was lying in Simes' headlock, utterly still, did Simes speak. He did so with effortless menace: 'That's it, stop struggling Willie boy. Oh yes, I know who you are. And I know your address. Here's the picture. And it's beautiful from this side. I'll break your fucking neck if you flinch again, stop that!'

Willie did. Simes continued menacing, never sinking to a melodramatic hiss, which Willie might not take seriously afterwards, but keeping his even, keen tone: 'Good boy. I'm not going to batter you just now, not much. You're not getting off that lightly. I want you to stew first. I want you to understand that I am going to batter you every time I see you. Get that. Think about it. I'm sure you will. I will batter you worse each time. You will end up in hospital. And when you get out, it will start all over again. I'm making a lifelong commitment to you here William. Aren't you touched? You see I hate your fucking guts, you vile excuse for a man. It won't help to come after me with a team of your wanker mates. Soon as I'm out of hospital I'll be on your case, harder. The only thing you can do is kill me. And the police will know it's you, Willie boy. My friends will tell them. And, as you know, you have had a couple of run-ins with the police for your violent crimes. Oh yes, I know *all* about you. You have a big problem now: me. If I were you, I'd worry about ever leaving the house again. I'd move from Edinburgh. Even then you'll have to worry I might find you. I will be looking. I'm here for life, your punishment for being a worthless piece of shit. And there's nothing you can ever say or do to change that.'

Willie couldn't talk or perhaps was so shocked that he chose not to. Simes tightened his neck grip with a little twist and Willie let out a squeal: 'Ow!' Simes kept still, just allowed the silence to speak for his resolve to hurt Willie. He let some seconds pass then repeated the process a few times: the twist, the squeal, the certainty of that silence, on and on for a full minute or more.

Then Simes spoke again, now in a playful voice; 'You would like to know why I feel so interested in you. But you never will. You will just have to think of all the scummy things you've done and who you've pissed off. That should keep you well occupied in between my batterings. Life, as you know it, will never be the same again.'

Simes could hear Rich teasing Fatboy, getting closer, but he couldn't see round the car to what was happening. He had the presence of mind not to call out Rich's name.

'We're nearly done here mate. You? John?' shouted Simes. 'What?'

'You finished with that fat numpty? John!'

There was a pause, Rich registering the name issue, which he wouldn't have thought of himself. 'Hokey dokey – Dick! Just this obscene globule of cellulite keeps following me. God, it's ugly! Better leave before I vomit!'

Simes smiled, and sensed that Fatboy wouldn't give good chase. They were safe to leave. But he had to slightly disarm Willie, who he knew could probably fight, and probably beat hell out of him, once he didn't have the elements of surprise and fury. He released his right hand from the neck grip and quickly forced Willie's face round to meet his right fist. Blood flowed from his eye. There was also blood all over his mouth and dribbling down his chin from the first punches, to his nose. Quite bulbous features, Simes noted. He got off Willie's back and jumped up off the ground, sprightly, keen to leave while the going was good.

'We're off, John. Willie boy knows the score.'

The whole fight had lasted less than four minutes. A couple of people were watching, aghast. Simes paused to check Rich was coming his way. As Rich approached, Simes started to run too. Willie was rising and cursing, but not exactly racing to catch this pair. Rich had to run past him. 'Byeeee,' he grinned, not thinking, as he would later, that this meant Willie had got a good look at him.

'I'll fucking get you!' screamed Willie. From round the corner, Simes paused to shout back, with glee: 'Wrong way round Willie boy!'

They sped up the street and rounded the next corner, stopped and leant over on their haunches, Simes laughing between gasps and puffs. They stayed that way for 10–15 seconds. Then Simes punched the sky: 'Wow! That felt good!'

Rich was shaking his head slowly before Simes spoke, the adrenaline ebbing away, a black cloud of regret, Lee-Ann, engulfing him.

'Maybe for you,' he said.

'Come on, you got a buzz! Right now you're high!'

Rich shrugged, not denying it, but inferring, 'So what? I stand my ground: you don't attack people.'

'Thanks,' said Simes.

'Oh yeah.'

They were getting their breath back properly now, hearts slowing right down. Rich could only think of Lee-Ann and wonder if this was hellish or hell itself.

'Oh no, what state am I in? What will she think? What have I done?'

'Eh, she'll think you've been in a fight.' Simes winced.

'Oh shit, this isn't funny,' said Rich, feeling his face. 'Cut lip, shit, cut cheek, that's starting to hurt.'

'Probably some bruising to come out. You don't feel it at the time: fight-or-flight, you see, no time to bother with pain, only debilitating matters. You don't feel much pain during a fight, it's a very practical thing.'

Simes' enthusiasm and lack of conscience unnerved Rich.

'Lee-Ann. What have I fucking done!'

'We've only been fifteen minutes max. They'll be talking away, assuming we ran into someone, it'll be fine. But, eh, your face, it's a problem.'

Simes wiped the blood from Rich's face with the right sleeve of his white shirt, which was shredded and almost severed from the rest of the shirt. Rich's two wounds continued to bleed.

'Let's get back to Dix-Neuf,' said Rich, and started walking, feeling dejected and nervous. It had been going so well, better than he had dared hope, and now he had served up this classic, ultimate turn-off. How could he expect her to believe this was the first fight he had been in for years? And that it was bloody Simes' fault?

'Simes, come up with a story. This was your idea!'

'Right. OK. Eh? . . . We ran into Willie and he picked on us?'

'Transparent.'

'True. Hmmm . . . No, wait! We'll say Willie recognised me from court and from the night he assaulted Paul! That's it. And they picked on me because they thought I was alone.

276

And you came out after me – Lee-Ann will remember that – and helped me. You had no choice. Simple.'

They were at the door by the time they refined the story.

Rich cowered behind Simes, dreading Lee-Ann seeing him. Simes seized the initiative: 'Didn't get cigs, but had a full and frank discussion with Willie, no less.'

Paul and Lee-Ann gaped. 'Your face,' Lee-Ann spoke to Rich, shocked and angry. Simes tried to relax the mood with his fictitious tale of comical violence. Feeding off Simes' glibness, Paul took it well, despite Willie's involvement. He laughed when Simes told him about terrorising Willie on the ground. Simes threw a victorious look at Rich, who nodded disinterestedly. So Paul wanted Willie damaged, big deal. Blank Lee-Ann was silent. She turned and stared at Rich, regularly. He decided this was hell. Twenty minutes ago it had been heaven.

At the first pause, Lee-Ann turned to Rich and spoke sharply. 'We can't stay out with you like that. Let's go back to yours and you clean up. I've still got an hour.'

They left quickly, Lee-Ann not giving the warm goodbyes that might have been expected. They didn't speak in the street. Rich hailed a taxi. He gave his address to the driver and sat back, feeling trapped, by Lee-Ann, or his conscience, or his nerves, no, they were gone, this was numb hell.

Lee-Ann was on her side, looking at him. It forced him to look at her. He turned with an innocent, enquiring expression. She ignored it and spoke flatly. 'It was Simes' idea. How keen were you?'

Rich paused, panicked, then talked in a slightly high voice, 'Not at all! I tried to talk him out of it. I hated it.'

That last line came out uneasily. Rich hadn't enjoyed it all but he hadn't hated it all either. He had taken great pleasure from teasing Fatboy, though more from surviving.

'Had you two discussed it? Nodded or whispered when Willie came out the pub? Or did you go out to stop Simes?'

'To stop him, I swear.'

This was so couple-y it would be wonderful, thought Rich, except it was the sound of a couple breaking up.

'Hmm, you would say that,' sniffed Lee-Ann and sat back, obviously weighing up her feelings about Rich. He knew it: 'Ready to kick me out of her life. I just served up the biggest turn-off imaginable and at the most delicate time in the courting. Courting? Such a sweet old-fashioned word, implying rules, rules like: don't leave her to get into a stupid fight. Oh Christ, I am such an arse!' He was too full of self-hate to think more.

The rest of the short journey passed in silence. Lee-Ann vaguely made him feel guilty for participating in needless violence. Maybe he should feel guilty? Did it matter that much? Maybe it did? Some things, you just don't do. He didn't care about the rights and wrongs now, just what he was losing.

As they climbed out and Rich paid, it was in depressing contrast to the last time they entered this flat together, tumbling in merrily drunk four months ago. They both noted it, separately.

Inside, Rich washed as Lee-Ann put on coffee. Rich had hoped she might inspect his cuts, but she hadn't offered. Afterwards he changed his bloodied shirt and reappeared, in a similar, fresh blue one, as though trying to blot out what happened. He strolled into the kitchen as casually as he could. She was watching him, especially his cuts, as she leant her bum slightly back against the cupboards and sideboard. Her midriff was sexily silhouetted by the strip lighting beneath the wall cupboards. Her pretty face was, as ever, blank. He had lost this gorgeous creature, he could feel it as he entered the room.

But mustn't be a faint heart, keep trying, he told himself, as panic and depression fought for his soul.

She continued to watch as he crossed the kitchen floor, unsure of himself. He noticed the answer machine blinking on the sideboard beside Lee-Ann. Just for something to say, he announced he'd better check it. He pressed the button and panicked in case a bedmate had left an intimate message.

'This is a message for Mr Richard Ross. Would he please phone his twenty-four-hour banking number about his mortgage payments the moment he gets in. This is a matter of some urgency.' Bee-eep.

Rich tried to shrug it off with a knowing smile, while thinking, 'How embarrassing. I fucking hate twenty-four hour banking, never off your back. Can nothing go right tonight?' He wanted to talk about that 'infatuation' nonsense with Lee-Ann, but the mood was long dead.

'Rich, man, Murray here. C'mon with the work, man! Patrick is really on my back about you. He loves your stuff, but you'll lose the contract if that artwork isn't in his machine on Monday morning. Your words included.' Bee-eep.

Again, Rich forced his smile, thinking: 'I fucking hate bastards who work late in the office too.'

Lee-Ann had hardly moved; just the beautiful blue eyes in the blank face, following Rich's cuts.

'Hi honey, Denise here.' Finally Rich could give an honest smile, it was a relief to hear his sister's loving voice: 'My sister,' he said proudly; he was always proud of Denise. He was, of course, unaware that he was about to hear the most alarming answer machine message of his life to date.

Denise talked in a staccato voice, as if reading out a written message, but her distress was plain, and her voice was croaky; she kept coughing, sounded weak, seriously ill. 'I'm calling from Thailand. Don't be too alarmed about what I am about to say but it's important you listen carefully. I only have a minute. It's about half ten your time. Mike should be phoning you in about four hours from Bangkok. Hopefully he will be telling you I got on a flight, probably to Kuala Lumpur, in which case no worries. If he tells you I got caught, be around over the next few days, don't go out at all, I need you there, ringing the embassy, sorting out a lawyer for me, feeding the press sympathetic stories, getting campaigning stuff on to the net, and so on. Also, get as much money as you can into the Visa account you gave me a supplementary card for. If Mike doesn't phone it's gone really pear-shaped and he's been arrested too. I might be travelling under a passport that says I'm Mary Murphy. If you haven't heard anything by tomorrow afternoon, two p.m. your time, start at the embassy. They know my case but they're not keen on me. I don't have time to explain. Hopefully Mike will have left a message saying everything is fine by the time you get in. I have had a bad experience, picked on by some corrupt policemen. I'm in real shit honey.' In the space of a minuscule pause her voice cracked and she started bubbling; utterly out of character for Denise. 'I love you . . . sorry, don't worry . . . I love you, bye.' Bee-eep.

Rich stared at the machine, stepped forward and played the message again. When it finished he turned to Lee-Ann, hardly caring who she was, just stared at her. So he had blown it with Lee-Ann. So she would leave, assuming his sister is another loser like him. So what? Of course he still wanted Lee-Ann, but it would have to wait. That was as much as he could dwell on it. Straight back to thoughts of Denise. He looked away then at his watch – just after 11.00 p.m., three hours to find out what the hell is happening – and walked off into the living room. He didn't bother to turn the light on. He stopped well inside the doorway, but not particularly anywhere, not facing anything or near anything. He hardly moved his lips or any muscles on his face as he spoke quietly: 'Not Denny, anybody but Denny . . .'

Thursday, 7th September

Woke up in my beach hut at 6.00 a.m. Thought I heard something familiar: music or a sweet voice, warning me. Now I feel like someone was watching over me. I opened my eyes and there was a wild, orange ghost, flickering in the darkness, in the corner, flames, a metre high, just along from the bottom of my bed.

I had jolted out of the dream state, got to the door and was tugging at the bolt. It wouldn't budge. I kept looking round at the flames, the bed was on fire now, going up fast. I was terrified for my life before the lock clunked back. Out on the porch, daylight, a relief, but I was thinking; 'Fuck, fuck, save something!'

Ran back in. Grabbed this – the portable I'm writing on – my passport and arbitrary documents, lying on a ledge by the door. Then couldn't see: dense smoke, eyes sore and watery, and heat deathly. Dashed back out to the porch, yanked down some clothes, draped over the wooden walls of the hut (there's a gap between the walls and thatched, gable-shaped roofs), threw them down to the beach and had to jump off the porch; the flames had poked on to the roof-thatch and wisped across it as if it were newspaper. The hut became a pyre in seconds, thick, cloudy smoke belching out, huge flames being whipped far and high by the early morning breeze, sparks pinging from the wood, and strands of burning thatch riding gusts into the sky. And – the worst – this low, fast crackling noise, like an invisible, greedy beast chomping up the hut.

On the beach I watched for maybe ten seconds. Nobody around. Couldn't scream. Jumped up and down on the silent beach, my voice failing me, squeaking out, 'Fire, fire.' Felt feeble, insubstantial. There was just me, on this empty beach, with a fire gutting my hut, the rest of the world calm, ignoring me, an unimportant detail on an unimportant beach.

My hut was the first, the southernmost, of a line of fifteen huts, stretching along the beach. Another eight huts were dotted about behind the line and on the hill at the far end. I looked along for signs of life, and to the restaurant/bar twenty yards south of my hut. No activity, only the fury of my hut frazzling and the warm breeze.

I was looking for water or a bucket to carry sea water in. From round the restaurant area, a wee Thai girl appeared, about nine years old. She walked towards me, down the bar terracing, wearing only pink shorts, and staring at the flames. We looked at each other. I was thinking, 'What the hell are you doing here? Where're your parents? I need adults.' She pointed at the flames. I found myself nodding. Wee sweetie; but her calmness spooked me.

Looked back at my hut and saw that the roof of the hut beside mine was smouldering. (Is that what she pointed at?) Sparks had been blown across to it. I thought, 'Oh God, there's a couple in that hut!'

Raced to their porch. By the time I got to it, the whole roof was blazing. As with my hut, I was struck by the speed with which thatch ignites; we were all living in fire traps! Banged and bashed like a maniac: 'Get out! Get out!' My voice now effortlessly loud. Couldn't believe they weren't awake. Kept thinking, 'They're going to die! They're going to die!' Tried to open the door; locked.

I heard noise inside, eventually, the girl shouting in an

Aussie accent: 'Oh my God!' I shouted again: 'Get out! Get out!' They had their lock on the mortice; opened easily and they spilled out. We bolted off the porch. He pulled up straight and said, 'Go on! I'll grab some stuff,' and ran back.

The girl and I ran on down towards the shoreline. Then we turned to wait for the guy and to look at the two burning huts. Except that it was four burning huts. The wind was sweeping the fire along the roofs. She was shouting; 'Where can we get water? Buckets?' 'I don't know. I don't know!' Now another one – sixth along; *two* huts away from the flames – caught fire. The guy came back out and ran towards us: 'Didn't get the money belt!' We ignored him as soon as we knew he was OK. He saw us staring and turned, to watch the flames leapfrog along to the fifth roof. The inevitable fate of the fifth, sandwiched between flames, was the signal. We gasped. He said 'Oh fuck!' A shocked whisper. We had hesitated, watching and waiting, for five seconds max. Clearly, every gust, every few seconds, was carrying the fire along. The whole beach front could be ablaze in half a minute. 'Forget water, just get people out!' I shouted, and started running to the huts.

As I leapt on to the next porch I glimpsed this guy running down from the other end of the beach, wearing black shorts, thin, very tanned, watching the fires as he ran towards us; faintly comforting to see what felt like the outside world.

Thundered on the door. Didn't know if it was occupied. Tried to open it, no time for manners, locked. The guy in black shorts – Mark, I now know – had reached us. I shouted, 'Hey, here!' Perfect presence of mind, he understood without explanation, raced up, crashed the door in and hared off to do another door. There *was* a guy asleep in the hut. Hadn't even stirred when Mark crashed the door in. I had to shake him, must have been really stoned or drunk. The walls were already crackling. He woke and stared, still in a dream. I shouted 'Grab what you can!' and picked up some of his clothes and a notebook, hurled them out onto the porch and raced off to do another hut.

From then, I can't recall for sure what order I woke who up in. I think the next hut was one of two that were empty and open. I was horribly conscious that these huts were going up in the opposite direction of mine – thatch roof before wooden walls – and it meant an instant blaze, as opposed to the confined, spectral flames which greeted my awakening. I may have slept through a minute, maybe two, of wood burning. With thatch, these people had seconds to get out.

I raced along the beach past the couple and Mark who were battering on various doors. At least ten huts on fire. I saw one, clothes on the wall, glasses on the porch, locked. Bang, scream, no reply, several times. The frustration! Suddenly Mark bounced up beside me. Silent understanding again. I stood back, he shoulder-charged the door, two goes and he tumbled in, me behind him, screaming; 'Get out!' We paused for a split second to regard the room. Definitely empty. Smoke taking over. 'Crashed with someone else on the beach,' said Mark, haring off to do another hut. We were wasting resources doing one together.

There were about a dozen people running about now, exclaiming: 'Oh fuck!' 'Where's Stevie?' 'Jesus!' 'Oh shit.' 'Is Colleen all right?!' We didn't have time to instruct anyone. They were all just getting to grips with their own situation and we had seconds to finish this. The Aussie couple kept getting stuck at huts – locked and no answer – and between them only checked three. Mark and I were vaguely aware of this, knew it fell to us to race along.

I banged a door; a grunt answered instantly, and a thin, naked guy opened the door and fumbled out, trying to cover his tackle. I saw the hut was a goner in seconds. 'Grab stuff!' I shouted and leapt in to get what I could. His navy rucksack was hot to touch and I recall a red shirt spilling out it as I pulled it through the doorway, barging into him, on his return. I hared off, no time to bother with possessions.

Another hut had two girls. One, in a long, tie-dyed T-shirt, shrieked and jumped around the porch like an idiot. Felt angry with her. The dramatic brat never offered any help to anyone (and is, yet, whining over in the bar as I write). However, looking back, her scruffy, diminutive friend – in white knickers, so old they were dirty-grey, and a worn-out green, velveteen top – was probably the coolest customer on the beach. Running back in three or four times, holding her breath and thinking carefully. (Later, it turned out she retrieved more essentials than anyone; most people left their huts grabbing nothing.)

Now we couldn't check any more huts. The fifteen in the line were all blazing, walls included. Mark and I had reached the end of the line but we weren't sure we hadn't missed any in the leapfrogging. We stood together with the Aussie couple and stared for a short while, as the flames grew thicker, obscuring the structures within them. Briefly, we didn't care about our own plights and were oblivious to the panicking and rushing all around us. We were wondering about who-ever might be burning to death just yards away; someone we could have saved?

This makeshift village, our former home, looked like it had been napalmed; trees and palms from the jungle stretching up behind the orange flames; the soft morning light unfeasi-bly peaceful. It was hard to believe it was real. I had been asleep, dreaming – I looked at my watch – six minutes before, when that noise/voice/music woke me. I owe it my life, and so do people here.

After fifteen minutes or so, we accepted there was nothing more we could do. (The fire was never put out. It just burned out.) Nobody knew for sure of any unaccounted bodies and an irritating few seemed to revel in the morbid possibility. There was confusion; the previous evening some people had headed off to another beach for a full moon party and others had come to our beach to avoid the party.

We all stood now, some sat and a couple smoked, amid the salvaged possessions, which looked worthless, strewn about like rags. I glanced round: we were scared refugees in the Third World. Mostly, people didn't speak. The fifteen furnaces, so perfectly aerated by the breeze, peaked about twenty minutes later. Then the flames started to recede. The intermittent gaps in each blazing, orange block grew constant and through them we could see the foliage of the jungle; forlorn behind the watery heat haze.

After the fire, the wee buildings which survived were striking. They still looked cute and romantic, but now they also looked miraculous, for surviving so near those vicious flames. There was no in-between. The huts were completely unscathed or they were now one in a line of skeletal frames; ugly, black presences defying the dwindling flames.

It all took less than an hour from waking to looking round the frames to see if anybody had died. They hadn't. That kicked me back into the here and now, and I became aware of a tremendous pain growing in my hands, beneath the soot. We were all covered in soot. I went down to the sea to rinse. It was creepy; my fingers remained black. They were sore to rub. I went up to the big porch of the restaurant, just upwind from my hut; entirely intact. By the time I reached it, I was in a state of alarm; my fingers were agony; even without rubbing. Kathy, an architect graduate from London, who I had met the previous night, now fed me fags; she had to hold each one for me between puffs, my hands were so sore. I felt guilty for not worrying about her in particular during the fire; I just wanted to save anyone I could.

Bloody Mama showed up on cue. I moved from the beach

she stays on, but it transpires the old witch owns these huts too. Everyone was asking how the fire started. I was in tears from the pain in my fingers, but perhaps also from the shock of nearly dying; thirty seconds more sleep and it would have been at least severe disfigurement. I was less than a minute's sleep from certain death. It was unbearable to think about, and impossible to think about much else. I had been keeping that in. Now I blurted out: 'It started in my hut!'

That remark sealed my fate, but right then I wasn't to know. I thought my main concern was my sore hands.

Cabs were ferrying people to the police station to file for insurance claims. I had to wait thirty minutes for one to take me to the hospital, and then agree to an obscene fare. Kathy accompanied me and paid. I have no money, only the supplementary credit card my wee brother gave me for his Visa account. (Thank God he insisted, on the grounds that I only have one card and it could get stolen or declined by mistake. It had been lying in the bundle with the passport.)

The sweaty runt who drove the taxi was positively chirpy about the fire, bringing him all this business. He regarded Kathy and me, in our sooty T-shirts and shorts, pitifully. He chided about the careless tourists; 'Always drinking and smoking, not good.' I snapped at him that it was the shoddy *Thai* furnishings that caused the fire.

At the hospital – really a paltry clinic – I got taken after half an hour, though it seemed empty. Nobody else had been hurt in the fire. The Thai nurse looked delectable: dreamy, half-moon eyes and dark, marble skin in a light blue uniform. Born at another time, she would have been an excellent pretty ethnic in High Society.

She took my fingers and attacked them with cotton wool swabs, scraping as hard and quick as she could, while smiling insensitively. She reminded me of the time Mama tended to my injured knee a few weeks back, seemingly enjoying my pain. I had been watching that knee heal, feeling my body regenerating, casting out Mama's odious touch.

The nurse wasn't as spooky as Mama (but maybe even women forgive too much in the face of exquisiteness), but after I had screamed a few times, Kathy got worried and pleaded with the nurse to be careful. The nurse shot her a patronising glance and continued. Like me, she had underestimated Kathy. She looks small and demure herself, with her long dark hair – almost as long as mine – elegant cheekbones and composed manner. Having known her for less than twelve hours, I had no way of anticipating her big temper. After I screamed a few more times, Kathy leapt up to within a metre of the nurse and bawled in a broad cockney accent. 'Oi! I told you! Stop that! Just bloody stop it! Roight! Roight?!'

The viciousness of the snarl was astounding enough in itself, but more so because Kathy doesn't have a cockney accent. I don't know if coarse anger drew her back to an accent she had wilfully dropped, or if the well-spoken voice was deep in her and this was a technique she had picked up. Both I and the nurse stared, faintly united in shock.

Kathy was looking the nurse in the eye, like she might go for her. The nurse nodded, uneasily, if not downright terrified. I glanced at my right hand and nearly fainted. Coming off, with the black layer which she had been scraping at, was my skin. My fingers were becoming raw, exposed flesh.

I tried to breathe easy and spoke to Kathy: 'Honey, I think they're just like that here, but thanks.'

She switched from hot temper, to a sweet smile for me. Just for those seconds. She turned back to the nurse and shouted: 'Be bloody careful, you sadist! Roight?!' Eyes glaring again, jaw set, fury on tap, no ante for the nurse to negotiate with; a physical fight would be the only possible next step. Impressive.

The nurse continued, gentler, and I ignored the pain anyway; just wanted to see what state I was in when she got all that black off. It was some kind of melted plastic, I thought maybe from the casing on this laptop, but it shows no signs of melting, no smudges. It may have been that guy's rucksack I grabbed. I recalled it being hot.

I dreaded looking when the nurse finished. It was bad. My fingers were red prongs of fat inflammation, not like fingers at all; no prints, no wee lines round the knuckles. Now I could feel them tingling and hot, and simultaneously aching. The nurse wrapped bandages round them and said they would be fine in a few days. (Still agony tonight, and this typing is laborious with these bulky plasters, but must get all this down; wish I'd loaded the voice-activator program).

After much argument from me, then one bark from Kathy, the nurse grudgingly gave me some codeine painkillers. Then Kathy refused to pay the whole bill. The service charge was double the agreed price. Kathy gave her the money for the drugs and half the service charge. 'If you want to make a deal of it, phone the police, bitch! I'm staying on Noi, my name is Kathy Ligonier.' She managed to sound cockney and imperious in the one breath which, even in my detached state, was striking. Then she wrote down her name and we left. The nurse said, 'Yes, I phone police, they come see you.' Kathy shouted back from the door: 'Big fuckin' deal!' (Thank God for Kathy, the only good thing about today.)

Back at the restaurant, still before 10.00 a.m., Mama was waiting and fed us. I didn't like the way she watched me, but I didn't attach significance to it, since I didn't like Mama existing, period. Similarly, now, looking back, there was something ominous about Mama's words before we went to the hospital; 'You come back, we see police.' But that is the trouble with evil finaglers; you *want* to ignore them, to cast them out of your world. And sometimes you can't.

After the pineapple juice, fresh rolls with jam and butter, and coffee, she said again: 'You come with me, we see police.'

I felt replenished by the food and was quite keen to tell the police I almost died in Mama's firetrap accommodation. Then all I had to face was the drag of arrangements; report from police, finding fare to the mainland, somewhere to stay, money wired, contact insurance, thole their prevarications, banks, lots of waiting and phoning back. My biggest concern was could I stay out here for my last month with these gruesome hands? I walked to the car, suspecting nothing.

Kathy asked me if I would like her to come? Mama said she wasn't to come, which made me want her along all the more. I'm useless at leaning on anyone, but I had an excuse; my hands. I needed Kathy to feed me cigarettes. But truth is I find Kathy's presence enormously protecting. (Though she slightly unnerves me; she reminds me I'm full of shit. I seem confident but it's all defensive posturing. I couldn't assert myself like Kathy. I crumble just anticipating confrontation. I just don't have her sheer balls. Wish I had.)

Like the nurse, Mama soon discovered one doesn't argue with Kathy unless one is ready to fight. Kathy didn't seem to like Mama any more than me. She got into the back of the small Japanese car, poo-pooing Mama's protest with an elegant, eloquent, little flutter of her hand: 'You're boring me, I'm above remonstrating with you, weak, worthless witch.'

I smiled and climbed in beside Kathy. The car was dark blue with a plush interior which reeked of new fabric. The windows were open in the back and as Mama sped up, I went into shock. It was the sound of the air, coming through the windows, that low whooshing and leaves rustling in the wind. It was the sound of fire!

It was terrible to hear an innocuous noise sounding malevolent, like the invisible monster I heard devouring my hut. At first I thought, 'I'll never be able to travel in a car again.' Then I had a full-blown panic attack, the like of which I can't recall, though it felt familiar (something from childhood?) I turned to Kathy, 'I'm responsible for all this! All this destruction! It's my fault!' I kept saying that it was my being here which caused the fire, that it wouldn't have happened if I hadn't been here, I was the catalyst for this destruction, it really was down to me. It seemed to me that Kathy was being too simplistic to grasp the magnitude of what I was saying. When she looked at me calmly, I thought, 'She doesn't know! She doesn't understand!'

Then Kathy talked firmly about last night: how she had introduced herself to me at the bar, what we then ate, how we shared a drink with the nice Aussie couple, then went back to mine for a joint and so on. All the time I was staring at her, repeating over and over in my head, 'She doesn't know! She doesn't understand!' Then she talked about how we'd drunk a cup of tea, smoked our last cigarette on the porch as the light was breaking, then she had walked off to her hut, I had been yawning, and hadn't I gone straight to bed? I recalled using the matchbox for an ashtray on the porch for that last cig, and then throwing the matchbox into the sand, to gather when I tidied up. I was finally tuning in to Kathy and had calmed down before we reached the police station. (I would probably be more embarrassed now if I had time to dwell on it.)

Mama dropped us off at the police station about ten forty-five and drove off. We were taken at four fifty this afternoon. We waited all day in the clammy heat, sitting on the whitewash porch of that desultory little building in that poky, inland town. The only view was of a cramped household across the road. Various malnourished children mooched about the yard; people whose birthright is poverty. I remember wondering if any of the little girls might one day be sold into the sex industry.

All the backpackers from the beach were giving statements for their insurance claims. Kathy fed me fags. She had spent

291

almost her last baht. She had just enough for the taxi back to Noi. We couldn't even afford a coffee from the machine. The police were reluctant to give us water. It took a lot of persuasion for a total of two cups each during our six-hour wait. Kathy was lovely, nothing but sympathy for me, described her own situation as a doddle.

By the time I was taken into the bare interview room, I was dizzy with dehydration and depressed by the waiting. The police wouldn't allow Kathy to come in, which I didn't care about. I was so miserable anyway.

There were two policeman. One was a fat bastard, seated behind a tattered desk, with a supercilious smile; probably fancied he was Buddha with his bald head, rolls of blubber and superior manner. The other was a younger, thin guy who stood throughout, striding about, very upright and vain, with cold, suspicious eyes. They looked like a comedy duo from a seaside resort. What struck me initially was that Fatso was going to take down my statement on a typewriter. An old, black ornate one. I remember thinking that antique might be worth something; maybe you could sell it and get enough money for a cheap computer.

The questioning was aggressive. I stupidly assumed that was standard practice. 'What did you do last night?' 'Do you have insurance?' 'How many beers did you have?' 'Did you have a cigarette last night?' and such like. There was a woman translating, uninterested, a part-time local I guess.

They started on about the matchbox I had used as an ashtray. She said; 'He [Mr Vain] think maybe you start fire.' I wasn't too perturbed, assumed there was a communication problem. I explained that was ridiculous; I had thrown my matchbox from the porch, into sand, in the opposite direction from the corner where the fire started. My Vain conferred with Fatso and spoke to the translator in a diffident voice: 'He say maybe you still cause fire?' I was getting irritated but still I assumed they were merely doing their job. I asked: 'Why would I go round to the back of my hut during the night to start a fire?'

This morning and all day, I have known what started the fire. I leave my fan switch on all night. Since the generator is off, the fan is off. It clicks on in the morning when the generator is turned back on. That way, you wake up into a chilled room. Lots of people on the beach leave the fan switch on. The generator comes on at six. The fire started at six. The flames were shooting out from the corner where the fan was. There is no doubt what started the fire.

Mr Vain shook his head, and spoke bossily. The translator blandly announced: 'We arrest you.'

'What?! Arrest me?'

She nodded. I panicked; 'No, no! I almost got fucking killed.' I was on my feet. 'You *can't* arrest me. You *can't* . . .'

The translator and the policemen started chatting among themselves. I couldn't understand a word, of course. I kept interrupting to object to being arrested, agitation growing until I was screeching uncontrollably. 'What have I done? You want to arrest me for almost being killed?! You *can't*!'

Fatso pulled out his last typed sheet and the translator said; 'You have to sign this!'

I shrieked: 'What is it? I haven't *done* anything?'

The translator veered from indifference to mild irritation. It was frightening; you're a lost cause, I'm not wasting my time trying to help you.

'You have to sign this statement. Police take your passport. You under arrest. Sleep on beach, must be in hut with Katty.'

They knew Kathy's name and that she had already arranged to move to an empty hut that survived. They had kept us waiting till last. We weren't the last to arrive here. This was conspiratorial. Mama.

I stared, not in disbelief, but afraid of how far they would go. The translator thought her latest information had calmed me, and now finished her instructions: 'You come back tomorrow. Each day, you come here. Two o'clock. Police arrest you. Five thousand dollar for bail. You have insurance. Talk to insurance. Police arrest you, in cell, one week after today, Friday. Talk to insurance.'

I didn't say a word. The picture was clear. It was Thursday. I was going to jail in a week. I was being allowed out just now to arrange the bail, which they would pocket. I needed out the station, to make a plan and get help.

I looked at them. The two police stared hard at me: we don't care, we want your money, try us, we'll jail you, foreign slut. The woman didn't really look at me, just sort of watched me, from a bored distance; I'm not getting a cut, I don't give a fuck, rich, white bitch.

I had to sign to get out the station. I walked back to the desk and signed. I was thinking; it doesn't matter, with these muckle fingers, my signature is unrecognisable. As I walked back out to Kathy I thought, 'They have my passport, they don't need my signature. I'm trapped here whatever I did or didn't sign.' I was also thinking about racing off to Bangkok to tell the embassy, get a replacement passport and get out of here.

Kathy saw I was disturbed. I said we would talk about it in the taxi. I didn't want her blasting at them. I was in a daze, wanted back to the familiarity of Noi to phone for help. That said, 'Katty' might have intimidated them more than the predictable, hysterical wretch that was me. But it wouldn't matter. I've no evidence it was the fan. Those corrupt bastards can insist on a case against me, and have me banged up meantime. They are cruel enough to do it.

Rang the embassy and the emergency insurance number from the payphone at the bar. (Mama pointed it out to me, as if I didn't know it was there, but she knew I wanted to use her private phone: 'You use this! Use this, here!' indicating and smiling like she was being really kind and helpful. This predicament is not without a surreal element. How I hate that woman.)

The embassy said I must stay put. They scolded me for wanting to race up to Bangkok. The pompous oaf said, 'We couldn't possibly provide a passport for a fugitive!'

At least they have a representative, Jonah, on the island. He told me to ring back when they had arranged me an appointment for tomorrow. I was panicking, protested that my every day is precious, I'm going to jail in a week for God's sake, I have to organise things fast, can't I visit him now? Unmoved, the oaf made like I was a nuisance and he was doing me a favour letting me meet Jonah at all. What the hell is an embassy rep on a holiday island so busy doing?

The insurance company – when I eventually got through to the right guy, in Belgium of all places – said I have to get a lawyer tomorrow, recommended by my embassy, which the insurance will pay for. No reply at the embassy by then. I spent almost half of the £100 I borrowed from Kathy to establish that little. She only has two £100 traveller cheques left. I felt naked.

This evening I was the talk of the beach. I hated it. I think I'm the talk of the other beach too, probably the whole island. What for? Saving lives. No. Just for the drama I'm in now. Some of them seem to blame me. The stupid girl who jumped up and down on her porch during the fire asked, in this pseudo-timorous voice, if I was sure it was the fan? All innocence and concern. Callous cow.

Sitting round the bar, they were all going on about stuff they had lost, like photographs and personal things they bought in India. Nobody was really listening to each other. I felt pathetic for wanting sympathy and, of course, made out like I didn't need it.

Then one American guy said: 'Ooh, Thai jails; really bad. You're going to get banged away.' And shook his head like he was the all-seeing sage of the South China Sea. Creep. He had hit on me at the bar just a few nights before. His idiot Finnish girlfriend simpered, pretending to be scared on my behalf, when she knew he fancied me. She relished my situation. Thick bitch.

I said I thought I'd be OK. Then the American did get to me. Looking all serious – as if he weren't a steroid-fuelled, bicep beefcake who's barely a quarter as handsome as he thinks he is and as sexy as syphilis anyway – he told me, ponderously of course, of a racket whereby the police accuse foreign guys of rape and jail them. Then they bully prostitutes into giving statements testifying to the crime. And – punch-line – they want thousands of dollars bail. The terrified guy pays up, gets his passport back and skips country; then the police don't have to go through with a case for which they actually have no evidence, just a desperate prostitute as a witness. He finished with the uplifting assertion 'You're lucky you're out for a week.' I guess some people are just born cunts.

I desperately hoped he was making it up, but then a nice English woman said she'd heard about it too. The racket was published after some European guy went back for his trial, insisted on the court case as a point of principle, and to expose this sham. Brave man. But it didn't work. No police-man got done, even after he proved his innocence. That probably encouraged the scam.

Some of the travellers were so busy being grateful that it hadn't happened to them that they slightly shunned me, as if my bad luck could rub off on you if you got close. People can be so disappointingly selfish. They make everything about themselves. I wondered if I should have bothered saving a couple of their miserable lives. If they had died, this would have been a big hullabaloo with press; maybe too hot for the police to risk picking on me?

Now I'm being cruel too. It's getting to me. My stomach is in knots. Some of the people on the beach did sympathise with me, chief among them, Kathy. I'm sitting on her porch writing this, having left the beach early, depressed. She left shortly after, passed by me about an hour ago to go to bed. She hugged me really hard – a stranger a day ago – and stroked my back for a few seconds. Then she cut off and said, 'See you in the morning.' She didn't want to embarrass us both or be dramatic. I wasn't embarrassed. I'm beyond that, for once in my proud life. I needed that hug and if it had gone on any longer I would have cried my eyes out. I've never felt so lonely in my life.

It's about one thirty in the morning. I'm wide awake, worrying. Everyone, including Kathy, is asleep, after this morning's early rise. Our numbers are cut in half; the rest decamped to the other beach. I'm writing all this as if to make it real, to check this is really happening to me.

The sea is visible under the full moon. It comes into its monstrous self at night, wearing a sheen of ephemeral ripples, an illusory veil drawing attention to what it fails to conceal: the terror of enclosed darkness. I thought I had got over my fear of the sea last week, but I haven't.

Fear of the sea is supposed to be the fear that what we can't see is going to come and get us. Something came and got me today, and it wasn't the depths or some evil presence lurking within them. Yet tonight I hate the sea more than ever. I'm more full of fear than ever.

The blue glow from the computer screen is lighting up my face but beyond that ghostly visage, there is nothing for anyone to see or sense in this blackness, except the sound of the waves, gently dying onto the shore, thirty yards or so down the hill. Just how fearful am I? The inevitability of the lapping sounds like doom to me.

Mama is definitely a portent of doom, from the moment I saw her. I could happily throw that old witch into the sea.

Money. That's all I'm worth to these people. And it's degrading to feel hurt by people who care nothing for you. I recognise that. But I don't know how to handle it. I almost want to cry in front of them, and plead to their better natures. I shudder at the degradation and pointlessness. I mustn't give in to fear. I need my wits, like never before.

Friday, 8th September

This gets worse.

Jonah, Britain's man on the ground in the South China Sea, is an alcoholic paedophile who couldn't care if I was raped rotten and beaten to death.

He flounced off his porch to greet me, in so far as a fat sixty-year-old can flounce. He has dyed brown hair and a podgy face he tries to wear as jolliness, but is plain mean. He was wearing a pink shirt, like a short, thin kaftan, and starched, khaki shorts. I'm not one to judge by clothes but that combination announced insanity. Then came his voice, an affected pout from fantasy land, like the Raj never ended; 'My dear, the embassy told me *all* about your misfortune. I will go to the police. Straight after lunch. Do join me. For lunch I mean. And at the police station. I hear they arrest you every day. I've never heard of *that* before!'

Yet this comic book clown actually comforted me, at first. He didn't fear confronting the police, or so I foolishly believed for a happy half hour. Then, near the end of lunch – curry with expensive wine served by his maid, on silver, amid teak furnishings, no less – he said; 'Of course I can only make sure you are treated properly in jail.'

Like all manipulators, he dropped his bombshell casually.

One is supposed to not notice that explosion at one's feet. The casualness states: 'Oh come on, how ignorant to be surprised, don't make a fuss.' My heart raced a little but I remained calm, aware he's all I've got, and was polite in my protestations. In return he patronised the shit out of me.

He didn't change his clothes. As we climbed into his overpolished four-wheel, I had a bad feeling he wouldn't cut an authoritative dash at the police station. But I had to hope. His humming along to the tape of *The Sound of Music* suggested he was less than preoccupied with rescuing this pesky damsel in distress.

At the police station it turned out he couldn't speak Thai – how the hell did he get this job? What *does* he do? The police knew him. To amuse themselves, they looked him in the eye, disrespectfully, smirking indiscernibly, as only Eastern faces can. They responded to his camp now-looky-here noises with ever so slight nods, which were pointedly delayed; they so clearly wanted the caricature *ferang* (foreigner) to understand they didn't give a flying fuck what he said. But he either opted to live in his dreamworld or hoped I hadn't witnessed his ridiculing, because he walked away pleased with himself. Astonishing performance. I dare say the police are still chortling about it.

They certainly enjoyed playing Arrest The *Ferang* Slut. Fatso prattled in Thai, which he knows I don't understand. For all I know, he might have said, 'Cor blimey, do wot, knock on the 'ead, bit of a pickle what, ole mucker?' The words didn't matter. It was ritual assurance; a symbol of power being abused, with resolve. It worked. He scared me.

Jonah drove me back to Noi to make calls (didn't offer me his phone), not that I have anywhere else to go. On the way, he had the gall to insist that he can speak Thai: '. . . Central Thai, but the police spoke Pak Thai.' I could stand the stench of his self-satisfied bullshit no more. I had to assert myself somewhere. I pointed out that Pak Thai is basically just Central Thai with some Malay loanwords; hardly as different as Mon in the North, for example, oh and did he know there was a Mon-speaking community just west of Bangkok? And wasn't it fascinating that Thai script was supposedly invented entirely by Prince Ram Khamhaeng in the late thirteenth century, but 'of course you'll know all about that.' We didn't talk for the rest of the journey. Doesn't matter. That civil servant was never going to be of much service, except to little boys' bottoms. *He* should be jailed.

Furious, I rang the embassy to complain. It was horrible. A young woman called Natasha Harrison had been given my case. She gave me the number of a lawyer's firm and said they had been contacted about me. Then she said: 'I'm very sorry. That's all that is in our power to do. You must be feeling very vulnerable and scared . . .' I growled about that ridiculous old queen being a waste of taxpayer's money but Ms Harrison just washed over it. I was standing at the bar. Kathy and Mark were in earshot; I was trying to be calm as Natasha rambled on. She was using different words to say, 'Fuck off now, Jonah was your lot from us.'

As I rang the lawyer's firm, I raised my eyebrows to Kathy and Mark, but I could feel hysteria welling up inside me. They couldn't speak English. Eventually a Vietnamese assistant came on and we talked in French. He said the firm had heard nothing from the embassy and only acted for foreigners in business matters, not criminal cases. He politely gave me the number of another Bangkok firm who might help. I would have to pretend to the insurance that someone from the embassy recommended the firm.

I rang them straight away; I didn't dare pause to contemplate how badly this was going. A middle-aged American woman, Naomi, answered, checked I had insurance, said a lawyer will be here in two days and hung up. It was strangely matter-of-fact, as if *ferang* are often arrested for burning down villages. I wasn't relieved, as such, but I was able to breathe easy.

I was also able to acknowledge what else was panicking me (and this is hard for me); Mark, distant but decent, leaves tomorrow, and, much worse, Kathy two days later. She offered to stay. I said no, there's nothing she can do. But I'm dreading her leaving. I can feel myself closing in, withdrawing from everybody, becoming this pitiable victim sauntering about the beach, just waiting for the worst. Less than a week now. Don't feel I can get through this alone. Have to.

Saturday, 9th September

Woke up to a present on the porch. Before he got the early morning boat, Mark had dropped off his mobile, in a plastic bag, with a small letter.

Denise,

Use this, send me it later. It has a few hours left in it, with the spare battery. And the charger has an adapter that works in Thailand. Wish I could help you more. Let me know how it goes. I'll visit you if it all goes wrong. I'm going back to face a problem myself; getting done for drugs, court case on Friday. Shouldn't really be out the country but they never check on holiday flights. Might have to go to jail too. I really felt for you, I've never been in jail before either, but I'll be a few months maximum, and Australian jails are not as scary as foreign ones. Ring me next week if you need help, money or anything (hopefully I will have got off with a cautioning and/or fine). It was a great pleasure meeting you. You are an unusually passionate

301

person. I'm really sorry this happened to you. Keep cool
and think carefully. I wish you all the luck in the world.
   Mark

I'm so cool I promptly started to bubble.

Kathy has gone to the mainland to lift money for me. Rich
said he had a £500 limit per day on that card. Machine here
doesn't take Visa, and I can't go or I'll miss my getting-
arrested appointment. So trapped.

I really am alone today. Perhaps that's why I just rang Mike. I
felt I had to ring someone, haven't emailed anyone for a few
days, don't want to alarm people. Mike greeted me with a bright
hello, it was reassuring, but I felt such an inadequate for having
to lay all this on him. I was meant to be out here getting away
from him. He was panicked and he failed to hide it. I told him
not to tell anyone yet; don't want to worry Rich and the folks. He
offered to come out with $5,000, could be here by Tuesday. I
said no, but I might phone him again to say to wire it; he'll have
it for Monday. I need to pay before Friday to get my passport
back and the chance to skip country. But I also need to check
with the lawyer that paying is a good idea. Supposing I'm still
held here? And done in court? Perhaps they have to do me, after
taking such huge bail? Will they definitely give me my passport
by way of a sly wink to skip the country? Will they watch the wee
open ferry boats to check I stay on the island? I need to know.

Went and got arrested. Mr Vain today; very different experience from Fatso. More intense. I'm convinced Mr Vain
enjoys this, whereas Fatso is just greedy. Much more degrading with Mr Vain. Nothing personal was said, but I left feeling
shocked by our intimacy. What intimacy? What is that bond
between torturer and victim? Do I want to get on his good
side? Would I sleep with him, to try to get round him? Would
I do so knowingly, with guile? Or – being honest – is there
some little part of me that craves to serve him? Does some

part of me want to surrender entirely to him? It was strange to be thinking of sex with the man who might wreck my life, and strangely comforting. Shudder.

Nothing more to be done today. Nervously pinning hopes on the lawyer tomorrow. Got depressed at the bar. People being nice, I guess, but saying they would come and visit, bring me stuff, in jail. I got to thinking maybe a few days in the police cell would be OK, but the embassy said they normally only keep prisoners at the station for a few days while they arrange a place in a mainland prison. Unbearable. I remember my ex-lover, Aaron, telling me about a terrified woman facing jail – I remember that better than anything else about my escapist relationship with charming Aaron – and I know now the story stayed with me partly because I shared so deeply in her fear. I couldn't take prison, I'm not strong that way.

As a therapist, I've seen too much of people's raw selves not to recognise the usual mistake: confidence shattered, nothing anchoring them, they drift away into a lonely, useless, little part of their being; they stagnate, in a complex. Complexes are islands away from you and your life, away from your mainland being. You have to stay on the mainland to have all reserves on tap, and see clearly what to do in a difficult situation. I know where fear and worry can take you. But there is a difference between insight and awareness. I have the insight, the consciously contained knowledge, but still can't stop myself drifting off to a lonely island inside myself. I'm trying to hold on. I must.

June, the nice English girl, gave me a sleeping pill. I'll take it after Kathy gets back.

Sunday, 10th September

Kathy brought back some good wine from the mainland and we sat up late last night on the porch. She was determined to show me a good time. I asked about her temper. She laughed and said: 'I don't care about things. It's funny, when I lose my temper I look like I really care about things. I wasn't always like this.'

She had fallen in love at nineteen, five years ago, with Frank, who was on her course. He had suffered from manic depression and it came back. He is due out soon from his fourth hospitalisation in three years. She doubts it will be his last sojourn in a secure ward, but she is hopeful in the long run: 'Manic depression usually fades with age. One day he might finish architecture.'

I asked if she had ever broken up with him. She hadn't. She tried a couple of other guys years ago, while he was in hospital but it was 'empty . . . when he's out, it's good, it's right . . . some nights I see him laughing really manically, and not listening, and I can feel him slipping away, it breaks my heart, but I know that's not Frank, just some afflicted part of him. It doesn't scare me any more; it's just a shame. When he gets low and out of reach, it's worse; the same heartache but he's not even enjoying himself . . . I watch girlfriends going from boyfriend to boyfriend, each relationship paying ever-diminishing returns. I'm lucky; I've found the one . . . Some day he'll be fine, some days he already is.'

I asked what that had to do with her temper. 'I just know most things don't matter. I watch people being cruel and greedy. People think whatever is about them is important, they're selfish and ungrateful, they waste their lives being petty. They waste all that time and energy plotting and planning and gazing at their navels and wondering about nothing. Everybody thinks they are so bloody deep nowadays. It genuinely angers me but I only use my temper when I can get away with it: I don't like scaring people.'

I just smiled, didn't want to sound sycophantic, but I felt such love and admiration for her. She is the antithesis of selfishness, such a lucky find for me at this time. She reminded me of Mike's friend, Iain, who had lost his lover in a motorbike accident. He said similar things. I told Kathy the story. She was horrified, said that was the worst thing imaginable, his life is changed forever. She saw no parallel with her own situation. She really did feel lucky having Frank, no tragedy at all.

It was a lovely night. But it made me all the more fearful about her going tomorrow. Again, she offered to stay (and miss Frank getting out). Again, I said no. It was harder this time. I know it sounds like the most pathetic thing ever, but I love her hugging me. She knows that's how to cut through my brittle persona, and she hugs me a lot, strokes my pride away, takes me back to being a consoled four-year-old. Christ, I'm thirty-two.

It's 6.00 p.m. Fatso played Arrest The Slut today. He's too ridiculous to take seriously. Mr Vain is the man with the evil plan. I wish there was something I could do. This is so frustrating, waiting to be jailed, I feel helpless, useless, worthless. Kathy and I are going up to the bar for a meal.

Monday, 11th September

Last night was fine at the bar. Just as well I'm not lesbian: I'd be in love with Kathy. She shines even more in company: quick laugh, attentive, ever alert, intimidated by nothing. The idea was for me to make more friends for when she goes, but I just wanted to talk to her. She talks more sense than the others yet never sounds overly serious. She drips sensuality. Wish I had been as smart as her at twenty-four.

I paid her some such drunken compliment last night as we walked back to the hut. She shrugged it off saying, 'Life and people are so much less confusing when you know where you stand in love. I've been lucky.'

This morning I cried when she left. We were on the porch. I apologised and went into the hut. She followed me in and said, in her direct way: 'Sorry for what? I like you just as much as you like me. Remember, it was *me* who picked *you* out.' She hugged me again and, though I wish her no upset, ever, there was something gratifying about her eyes welling up. For a moment I felt special.

But now it's back to being a cloying wretch. And how. The American lawyer, Arnie, put it to me straight. This just gets worse and worse.

He arrived after seven tonight and is staying in the best hotel on the island, propping up the bar as I write, no doubt. I got his mobile number from the office in Bangkok and rang him. He had been here for two hours and done nothing but drink and eat. He said I had to go down to see him. 'I can't bear those revolting beaches,' he drawl-sneered.

I find him a chilling presence, but not without enigma. He has an imposing, Mount Rushmore face, addled with rigid lines that could have bespoken character but suggest wasted intelligence and middle-aged bitterness. Disastrous marriage? Career failure? Scandal? Something went badly wrong in California and he's hiding out from it, in this country, merely seeing out his days, not living any more; you come across them abroad. Disillusionment and disappointment lurking in every utterance. He's been here ten years and seems like another shyster looking to make money out of hard luck cases like me, but he's not cruel or dishonest, like the police. His curt analysis showed integrity, but sent my pulse skywards.

'I'll talk to the cops tomorrow,' he said, over a whisky or five. 'You can't trust them. We gotta phone the embassy, get them to ask the police about their intentions. If they return your passport, you skip country, but then who's gonna get done for burning the huts? Mama made a mistake running you to the cop station. She revealed she's in on it by doing that. You've sussed her right; this all might be her idea. Sometimes locals get kickbacks from cops, if they point out *ferang* for the cops to stitch up. There've been two ropy drug charges against people staying on Mama's beaches – two I found out about.'

He had done his homework. But his bald talk sounded like despair. I asked why anybody has to be done for the fire? 'It was ultimately Mama's cheapskating fault, wasn't it?'

'Who cares whose fault it was? Point is, they might be thinking they can make a bigger buck than five grand out of a burnt village. Bail may be just a starter. Who can they blame, if not you? The poor Thai electrician who fitted the electrics in the huts? No money there, no way. No, they might take the bail *and* jail you. Or leave you free to stay on Noi so you can hassle your insurance – which probably won't cover you if a criminal offence is proven – or your family. These people don't assume *ferang* are rich but they assume *ferang* have access to credit. And they're ruthless. You see?'

I was incredulous at the clarity. He downed his whisky. I think I downed mine, desperately searching for a 'but'.

'How can they hope to prove I did it in court?'

I was desperately clutching at straws now. He raised his eyebrows and ordered more whisky. He talked while the barman poured the drinks, hardly looking my way, more concerned with the arrival of his expensive Scotch than stating the obvious.

'They'll say what the heck they want in court. Mama will say she had trouble with you; drinking, smoking opium – maybe say you're a junkie. Or decadent, always taking men back – that goes down bad in court. Maybe she'll say you were told not to use the fan? Or she'd seen you leaving burning ash about? Lots of shit, who knows? It'll be no problem for them. The courts don't favour *ferang*; the middle classes blame Western tourists for turning this country into a giant whorehouse –

though it was really the Chinese who started it. If they decide on court, you've no chance.'

With his every clarification, I felt more and more isolated.

'But if I go to jail there is no reason I should ever pay them,' I protested. 'It doesn't make sense.'

'Sure, it does. Guilty in a criminal court? Makes it real easy to legally enforce reparation out of you. They'll squeeze a fortune out of you. Truth is those huts ain't worth shit. The land is worth a lot, but they've still got that.'

This was everything I didn't want to hear, yet I wasn't surprised. It was dread fulfilled. As my heart sank, yet simultaneously speeded, I became aware I was staring at Arnie with wide eyes.

'What kind of jail sentence could I expect?'

'I'll be straight,' he said grimacing and sounding sympathetic at last. 'Worst scenario, you're an old woman when you get out. Best scenario, you whip up support at home, your government puts pressure on the Thai government, the King pardons you, and you're out in a few years.'

That moment, sitting in that tacky cocktail lounge, full of middle-aged Western men hiding from their lives, and the island's better-heeled hookers trying to pose like they have a life, a long-term jail sentence became less abstract, even a likelihood.

Arnie watched me and tried to be encouraging: 'The idea of me being here is to stop you going to jail. That's our home base. Let's not panic till we see the pitch. I'll talk to the cops tomorrow.'

We talked some more, about Thailand and so on, but we hardly bonded. He recognised I wasn't up to conversation and nodded when I said I wanted to go.

Phoned Mike this morning at seven-fifty, to catch him before leaving for work. He was walking towards the Thai Airways check-in at Heathrow, said he had to be here to assess this situation. It was dispiriting talking to him. We talked as if we hadn't been out of touch for weeks and weeks, as if we hadn't escaped our torrid relationship for a minute. It seemed he might as well come out. He wouldn't let me stop him anyway. Tragic truth is I'm glad. I need all the help I can get. I would have phoned Rich if Mike wasn't coming. I hate asking anyone. Mike's hoping to catch the morning train from Bangkok and be here tomorrow evening, with the money.

Tuesday, 12th September

Saw Mama on the beach this morning. Witch said hello. It sounded like she was casting a spell. I didn't reply. Hate, pure hate, no desire for sympathy or help any more, no hurt. Mr Vain played the arrest game. Same for him. Seething hate.

Arnie went to the police after I left and then condescended to come up to Noi. I realised he's not confident; feels awkward around the arrogance of youth.

He says his Thai is competent, and he pretended in the police station that he could only speak English. They rang for their faithful translator and he heard the police talk among themselves, but they were just being cocky, saying things like, 'Bangkok big boys, think they own everywhere . . . what does the *ferang* prick think he and his city boys can do?'

Arnie says it's still impossible to see the pitch. The police told him they would give me my passport back if I coughed up $5,000. I want to believe it, but apparently 'it don't mean Jack shit.'

I protested: 'If they give me my passport then I'll skip the country, and surely that suits them? Because then they can quietly pocket the $5,000. If there's court proceedings then the money might be mentioned – I'd be bloody sure to mention it, to land them in it.'

Arnie shook his head: 'There's ways of burying $5,000, in bills; "oh we did up the station . . . bought a new car . . . got the truck fixed." Getting hold of money is the problem out here, not accounting for it to bosses.'

Everything that happens, it gets bleaker.

Arnie told me to ring the embassy, get them to ring the police station and then ring them back. It took about four calls of nagging Natasha, and over two hours. The police told the embassy they are going to jail me on Friday and ship me to a women's prison a few days later. Arnie said, 'Damn, thought they'd say that, don't necessarily mean Jack shit.'

Arnie really seemed to care now, not that he is given to demonstrating affection. 'You know,' he said, worriedly. 'You can usually guess what the scam is. But they haven't dropped a clue. You pay bail, then get jailed? It's bullshit. Five grand for a few days' freedom? But I wouldn't put it past them. You're pretty trapped here; they can watch the ferry boats. Leave it with me. Let me talk to that piece of roadkill, Jonah, and sniff about this evening.'

'You know Jonah?'

'Unfortunately. We all know the little scumbag is here, living the lazy, high life. He won't help – wouldn't know how to – but he might point me in the right direction. We need to know about the man you call Mr Vain. I could be mistaken but his bizarre name – I wrote it down, couldn't pronounce it – it's in an ancient Andamanese language.'

'What's that?'

'Group of islands, other side of the Malay peninsula, out in the Bay of Bengal, often don't appear on atlases, 'cos of their remote location, very obscure.'

'Does it matter?'

'Dunno, it's odd. What's he doing here? Visiting remote islands, that's my hobby, you see those islands are ruled by India and have a completely different culture to here. I mean, how did he get to be a Thai cop? He may not be close to his bosses. First generation immigrant? Or maybe powerful connections landed him this job? Just weird. Don't like it.'

I was pleasantly surprised to discover Arnie had interests beyond alcohol – beneath the Spillane pose, an ageing backpacker still looking for Bounty and perfection – but I suspected the Andamanese angle was significant purely because we had nothing else to note. Arnie is sharper than I first realised, a worthy ally.

He left to go to Jonah's, didn't phone first. There was a quiet understanding between us; both disgusted by Jonah. Arnie smiled ruefully as he left; 'Little shit. Maybe I'll catch him in flagrante.'

When he left late this afternoon I sat on in the bar, sipping beer, nothing else to do. Eventually my neck and shoulders untensed and I managed to take time out of dreading jail and, instead, dreaded seeing Mike.

Boat was late. Bar was quiet, between food and drink times. He climbed off and strolled through the shallows, his chinos getting soaked. His smart blue shirt, brown, leather shoulder bag and tidy, sandy hair, all looked out of place on this ruined beach. He looked like a glamorous foreign correspondent, with the blackened hut frames glowering behind him. I didn't call out immediately. I continued to watch, thinking he looked good, and was good. And I was pleased to see him. But still, it felt wrong. Why hadn't I rung Rich instead? I know that Rich, like so many degenerate brats, is mercurial in a crisis. Embarrassed to ring my wee brother for help? Maybe I felt that Mike owed me? Maybe it was habit? Through all the hell of our relationship we always cared about each other. But as I watched Mike walking towards the restaurant area, across the sand, it felt unfair on him. What can he really do for me? God, how I wished it was Kathy.

He was barely thirty feet from the terrace bar when I called out. He turned and walked towards me, with a sad smile. We watched each other not wanting to be with each other. But we hugged, respectfully. I couldn't stop thinking how you are never out of the woods as soon as you want to be; reluctant familiarity. We hadn't avoided each other for long enough to change. Defeat hung on our breath.

We ordered seafood platter and wine. There was something unreal about pointing out Mama – sitting a few tables away, doing her accounts – and saying it's probably all her scam. I outlined everything to him a hundred times. He kept coming back to the two drug cases which Arnie had uncovered, and which implicated Mama. Eventually I phoned Arnie. He said one is still in jail, and one served some of a sentence but had managed to bribe his way out somehow.

I told Mike and he made the biggest decision of my life thus far: 'Right. We're splitting. Got to get you away from where you can be jailed. The morning boat. We'll be halfway to Bangkok by the time you're meant to get arrested.'

I didn't know what to say. The idea picked me up and petrified me. I never really thought I would run. I want away from here so badly, but if I'm caught they'll really do me then, and I'll be guilty of perverting justice or whatever it is out here, even if I am somehow found innocent of arson, which I doubt. We discussed it in intense voices, both playing devil's advocate to a position, rather than feeling any real certainty.

'Mike, I would lose my one card, my innocence.'

'Won't count in court, Arnie told you. You want to believe it will. A bit of you relishes proving it, winning, getting redemption. It's a dream. They do *ferang* for drugs, that's like us jailing a driver at Silverstone for speeding.'

'And what will I do if we make it to Bangkok? The embassy said they wouldn't help a fugitive.'

'We'll strong-arm the embassy, threaten bad publicity. Maybe befriend a diplomat or embassy worker? Maybe buy a false passport? Maybe sneak you into Laos, Vietnam, or Cambodia? Tell the embassy there that you had your passport stolen.'

'How would I sneak into these countries?'

'Dunno. Pay fisherman on the southeast coast to drop us off, in Vietnam or Cambodia?'

'Great: pirate seas and tense border regions. Sounds fanciful anyway, with the Thai police looking everywhere for me. Arnie said they will try to find me. And all the police have contacts among the people whose livelihoods attach them to *ferang*.'

This went on for an hour or more, with Mike's faith and my fear growing. Then Arnie rang on the mobile. I told him immediately what we were talking about. He said he didn't want the responsibility of advising me to run off while under arrest, but he had cleared the way at the police station by saying he would accompany me on Friday with the bail. He was confident that the police believed I would show. He was hinting I should run.

Then he clinched it, while all but freezing my blood with the reason he rang: 'Our Andamanese friend, just found out, not good. He's renowned for violence, rumoured to have raped a *ferang* woman. Definitely picks on 2–3 *ferang* each year. Moved here from Samui after he beat up a *ferang* who was in for smoking grass. The *ferang*, Scots guy, got the story into all the English press out here; it became a grudge match, the police determined not to bow to pressure from *ferang* newspapers. They promoted him ostentatiously, while simultaneously moving him out here because the Thai politicos on Samui were worried he was bad for business. To be blunt, Denise, he's very bad news and will jail you if he can. They don't know Mike is here. Since he's said it, I'll say it; split. You're three days from jail. Leave fast, tomorrow, before they get edgy.'

That was it. I thanked Arnie – he never even mentioned his payment – and put the mobile down. I nodded at Mike, dizzy with petrification and relief. 'The boat comes just before seven in the morning,' I said. Mike nodded, with slow deliberation. It inspired my confidence. But it was quickly wrecked. We were turning away to pick up our glasses and we took one last glance at each other to sense this crucial moment: he looked terrified for me; lost, despite the certainty of his nodding. This was bigger than anything that we had gone through together.

Mike had brought red hair dye and scissors in case it came to this. I said no: if anyone sees my hair dyed or cut it will draw attention to us in the morning. Truth is I also found the idea defiling. I feel like I'm being bullied and compromised enough.

There was nothing else to discuss. We opted to talk about other matters, as if we were merely journeying to Bangkok in the morning as any backpackers might. Maybe it was nerves but the conversation went awry, fast.

Mike brought up his new girlfriend, Victoria. Leaving aside the degrading madness that was our relationship, this Victoria is, in literal terms, my usurper. And pride resides in literal terms. I didn't even want to know her name. I had managed to leave Edinburgh without finding out but now Mike wanted to boast about her and how she understood about his having to come out here. Sure. I bet she bollocked him good and proper. I moved the talk on to the rest of my trip. I was pleased to tell him of all the things I had enjoyed. They seemed so long ago after these six nightmare days. It was good to relive them but I felt like I was being drawn into some conversational competition with Mike, who wanted to keep things personal.

Crunch loomed when he broached our relationship. For the last few days I had been noticing nothing outside the prospect of jail. The moment he introduced the subject I was aware of the warmth in the breeze, blowing along the coast in the same direction as it had when the fire spread. Now it just had black frames to whistle through, starting with my former hut just twenty yards away. I glanced at it, still a forlorn ghost, augmented by the fading light. My memories of the good weeks, before that ghost appeared, had been revived by my own chat. And the future, jail permitting, was beckoning me forth with the plan to split. I didn't want to be dragged back into our relationship.

I was tense, but I kept thinking how Mike had come a long way so I should be nice. I said I had no regrets about our relationship. He said he had, and wished he had been faithful. Wind-up. I'm not a big one for apologies: often, with that little word 'sorry' people are really saying 'having wilfully wronged you I would now like to make me feel OK about it and, further, put your feelings to the side and proceed forthwith as if it never happened.' They want wrongdoings thrown in the same depository as accidents. I have always felt this. I don't bear grudges but pointless (false!) apologies bug me. Still, I thought I owed Mike some kindness for coming here. So I said it was OK, I regretted being unfaithful too. I skipped saying sorry.

Now he got really needy. Maybe the drama of my situation was getting to him? He started confessing things I didn't need to know about. I said it was OK, but could we talk about something else? He insisted on telling me about one last thing; a one-night stand in London, before Sarah, the first affair, the start of the torment. That was early on in our relationship. Until that final confession, the conversation, though irksome, had still sat lightly on top of the reality – going on the run tomorrow, in Thailand! – like a staid and only mildly diverting piece of theatre. We had almost avoided the rawness. But that tipped me into the abyss of those years.

I tried to pull myself back, kept giving myself the line 'I have more urgent things to think about right now!' With a shrug, I spoke lightly: 'It's done now.'

He smiled awkwardly and asked; 'Was I just always really bad to you? Sometimes I worry I've damaged you for life.' Oh the boring, boundless grandeur of the male ego, so quick to believe he is of life-devastating import, no less. His neediness was really getting to me. I was living in fear and he wanted to be told he was really a nice guy.

I forced a smile: 'You were fine honey. We got caught up in something compulsive. Hey, we'd have been wasting our time somehow. Might as well have been together.'

I felt nothing for what I said. We had finished eating. He ordered more wine. I said we had to be up early. He said we should drink, since we were both ultratense, which was true. 'You probably looked vulnerable, an easy target, for the old witch,' he nodded towards Mama.

Then I realised that Mike wasn't here grudgingly fulfilling his ex-lover role; he feels guilty about my immediate situation. I had come out here to get away from our relationship and ran into this, so he feels personally responsible. I said, honestly, that I didn't think that was the case. Though I wondered what kind of weakened spirit I was, before the fire? A magnet of fragility attracting predators? Still, it isn't Mike's fault. I got into the relationship and stayed there.

Mike looked over at Mama and said: 'I want to kill the old witch and those fucking policemen!'

The strength of his drunken passion was vaguely touching, but worthless. I had been through all that. I needed a steady hand. We drank some more and he brought me up to speed on gossip. He had run into Rich the night before he left. He smiled in pseudo-despair and said: 'He's an all-singing, all-dancing vision of ecstasy with bells on, to put it mildly. Apparently he's managed to not phone Lee-Ann, hopes to score a point for it.'

It was good to think of Rich. I was glad I hadn't dragged him into this. It will be him, not Mike, who moves to Thailand if I'm jailed.

I was drifting off, on fondness, thinking of Rich, when Mike started on about our relationship again. He saw my barriers coming down and switched to going on about how wonderful I was. It was then I saw that he wanted to sleep with me. Jesus, how predictable. I should have known earlier, just didn't want to see it. Of course, when tense, have a shag, and to hell with Victoria. I don't want one up on her. I suspect a host of women will do that for me. It felt good being beyond the realm of Mike's charisma, but I was bored; angry-bored, with his self-indulgence. Hurt.

He was gliding on to the subject of sex, rather forcefully. At some point he asked what was the worst thing about being his lover, apart from the infidelity? I said: 'You mean in terms of sex?'

'Well, yes, that, I guess.' He's doesn't do *faux-naif* very well. What was I meant to be doing here? Giving him tips for Victoria's benefit? Complimenting him on his sluttish expertise? Getting turned on at the thought? I felt really hurt now. Here I was, on the threshold of jail, and he was looking at me intently with alcohol-glazed desire, hoping to get me into the sack. Did he feel entitled, after flying all this way? Fancy himself the big hero? He hadn't rescued me yet.

'Oh, I don't know,' I said airily, selecting my insult, faintly aware I felt like being a cow; regret building before I even spoke. 'One thing I couldn't stand was the way you would never let me just suck you off, you know, like when you would be sitting on the couch and I would unzip you and start fellating you and you would always stroke my head and lift me up on to you and start doing things to me. You would never just sit back and let me do it; you would never just let me concentrate and enjoy giving that pleasure, I found it so erotic, but you always had to take control; touch me, usually undress me and give me cunnilingus, when that wasn't what I wanted.'

Remorse consumed me instantly. Such crudity. So galling. I knew I had turned him on with the image of me sucking him, and I had employed the trusty cruelty of that ego-lacerating rapier; insult their lovemaking – neither sex can bear it. Now, despite the circumstances, I have embedded all the horrid sentiments and subtexts of that comment into the next few days. Well done, Denise.

Mike withdrew, didn't retaliate, his needy talk and drunken desire swiftly quashed, bedward hints extinguished; all as intended. But I felt awful. I hadn't wanted to be dragged back into the headspace of our destructive relationship, I felt goaded into it. I don't need any shit from someone who is out here to look after me. But I still feel like a bitch. Bloody ape. If he had only known to be caring and sweet all night, then cuddled up to me in bed, we might have slept together. Thank God that theory wasn't put to the test. I'm such a wreck just now.

We came up here shortly after my pseudo-revelation. I'm sitting out on the porch. I don't even want to sleep beside him. I'll crash, clothed, when he is sound. Depressed.

But I really do have more urgent things to think about. Tonight, the biggest relationship so far in my life doesn't matter a toss.

You would never believe it possible at the time.

Wednesday–Thursday, 13–14th September

In Bangkok. Feeling fear like I've never felt. It's like an ongoing shock, something that should last a few seconds, but is there all the time, firing my body and thoughts. But I sense this situation will be over soon, one way or another. Police are looking.

Boat was nerve-racking. Before getting on, I realised Mama could tell the police about me talking to a strange, new *ferang*, put them on alert. Nobody else on the beach. Reminded me of the morning of the fire. Felt committed as I stepped into the boat.

Down the coast, saw Mama from the boat, almost let out a vocal gasp. She was on Yai, her usual beach, boat just passing. She glanced, I turned away, Mike said she just went on about her business round the bar. Boat still had to stop at another beach. Fifteen minutes, everyone who glanced a police spy. My neck was aching with tension before the boat pulled away. I noticed the Thai boatman looking oddly at Mike. He had brought Mike here the previous day. Why was the *ferang* leaving already? Out on the open sea felt better. Boatman had no phone. Two hours and we would be disappearing into the mainland.

Train less troublesome, at first. Waited outside the station while Mike bought tickets. No police about. Boarded at last minute.

Then, after two o'clock, arrest time, Mike was looking at a map and suddenly groaned. He had made an astute calculation, but too late: 'You've talked to lawyers and the embassy in Bangkok. The police know that. They know that's where you're making for. We could have foxed them by heading south towards Malaysia. It's nearer, we could have hidden out on the west coast islands; they virtually rub rocks with Malaysian islands; busy, peaceful, yachts call in, more international. We've done this wrong.'

I looked at the map feeling queasy: they'll be waiting for us in Bangkok. 'Should we get off and cut back down? Or hide out in some faceless town and get another train up or down in a few days, when they have stopped checking the trains?'

Mike thought for a bit. We were roughly halfway between Bangkok and Malaysia. 'Let's get out before Bangkok and get a taxi in. If they are posting police at every station we're already fucked.'

Mike checked the platform the few times the train stopped. Only once were there police, and they didn't look suspicious. We were in 'second class with air-conditioning'. Mike suggested we move to the crowded third class. I said no. If it comes to a search of the train, we're done, wherever we sit. He said we should try to look like we are part of a larger group and I should conceal my hands; they marked me out. I had hardly spared a thought for my hideous hands. They still hurt but they were on the mend, so I didn't care. I said they might phone the train company and ask the conductor to check for a couple, including description.

I went to the toilet, tied my hair up in a bun and put Mike's blue baseball cap over it. I also changed into smart black slacks and fresh white blouse, both non-wrinkle. Mike already looked unlike a backpacker. While I was changing he managed to engage the two German guys across the aisle in conversation. One time the conductor came through just looking at people. We both saw, Mike played his part well, quickly inveigling both Germans into conversation, as if we were all together. We were getting paranoid.

Got out at Thon Buri, last stop before Bangkok. No police. Mike pointed out the train got in twenty minutes early; police might not know. Got a taxi to Bangkok. Thon Buri is really just a suburb of Bangkok, yet so much more Thai than the capital, a lived-in, low-key place where a Westerner feels conspicuous. It's hard to believe it was ever the capital, though it was for fifteen years starting in 1767. Like anywhere, it was all the more threatening in the night. It would be dawn in a few hours. Mike astounded me by telling the driver to go to the train station in Bangkok. He whispered to me: 'We might beat the train. Want to check; it would be useful to know if the police are on our tail.'

We agreed to find a quiet anonymous hostel off Khoa San Road, Bangkok's Backpacker Central. Then we hardly talked, I don't know if the journey was thirty or ninety minutes. At the station Mike told the driver we were hoping to pick up a friend. He would go in and check while I waited. The driver found a place disconcertingly close to the station. Mike ran in, I stared at the dozen lanes of traffic, warming up already, but I barely heard all the growling Third World engines. I had a strange thought about the grandeur of the Victorian station and the romance of pitting one's wits against the police; it was an arch whim. I was too scared to revel in excitement or drama. Then I worried the police would start checking all the taxis if the train was in and I panicked, desperate for Mike to return. Couldn't see any police. Mike came back out. His face said it all.

He climbed in and said, 'Khao San Road,' to the driver. 'Swarming,' to me.

'How many? You sure?'

'It's the right platform, two at the exit, six stationed along the platform, train due in five minutes.'

Again we were silent.

Checked into this crummy but obscure hostel, this morning, after dawn. Drank wine first in a nearby restaurant, didn't feel much effect from the alcohol, couldn't eat. Felt safer in the restaurant than here. It had anonymity. Mike showed his passport here. I had to say I had lost mine; if the police check we're done, even a phonecall asking if a woman checked in without a passport. How many hostels and hotels are there in Bangkok? Could they do an emailshot? How hard are the bastards chasing me?

Separate beds, Mike's not bothered tonight. Knocked himself out with a sleeping pill two hours ago (he brought them though he loathes them; prepared well for this possibility). About to take one myself. Embassy after a few hours sleep.

Mike will go first, check it's not being watched.

Beneath the vast fear, depression. Recalled Amaranta's love for Josh. I usually think of Amaranta in terms of her monumental and well-judged act of forgiveness, but tonight I think how there is nobody out there feeling that kind of love for me, no lover to be tested if I'm jailed. Feel sad. A tragic pub story. Is that what I will amount to?

Thursday night, 14th September

Things moving fast now, and out of my control. Boat feels like days ago. It will be over by Saturday. Or jail will be starting. Mustn't dwell on either possibility. Got to concentrate, focus: my future depends on it.

Went to embassy, in hat, no sign of special police presence. Whispered my story to the guy at passport desk. His eyes went wide as if a drug had unexpectedly kicked in. Bureaucratic wimp.

Was taken through to an empty office. A young woman, Natasha, appeared. She was the one who told me that Jonah was all the help I would get. She was flummoxed. There was a note of guilt in her anger: 'Look Denise, don't speak to us. We don't want to see you. We strongly advise you speak to your lawyer before us. Legally, I'm obliged to phone the police, you know? I shouldn't be talking to you. Now you must leave.'

Felt comforted. That was probably the best result I could have hoped for on first contact. The 'shouldn't' acknowledged she was complicit already. No intention of phoning police.

Went to the lawyers, in a giant office block. Small firm but busy. Coming out the lift, saw a well-preserved, middle-aged woman leaving the office. She was wearing an orange shirt and black skirt, very well-to-do, strong air of confidence. She was making towards the lift. I said, 'Are you Naomi?' She looked taken aback; 'Ye-es . . .' Then a flicker of incredulity, as she placed the Scottish accent, and before I could introduce myself, she shrieked: 'Denise?'

'Yes.'

'What the hell are you doing here?'

I anticipated the embassy rebuff but this caught me off-guard. 'I'm here on the advice of one of your colleagues. Didn't Arnie tell you I skipped bail?'

'Oh Jesus. I'm on my way out for lunch! I can't deal with this.'

'Well what should we do?'

She fumed a bit more, collected herself and took us into the privacy of her office.

'Sit down,' she barked. 'I'll make a call.'

All she said on the phone was 'Johnny, Naomi here, can you come right over? . . . Thanks.' Then, just as brusque, cancelled lunch. Now she regarded us, muttered 'hmm' a couple of times and became slightly less agitated. 'Johnny's a very good PI. He's English, and he's got embassy and immigration connections. We'll just have to wait until he arrives. We might not be able to do anything for you.'

She asked us a couple of questions about how we got here and if the police were chasing us and what the embassy said. Despite her hostility, I could see she saw us as their firm's problem. I wondered if she worried that I might say her firm advised me to skip bail if I was caught? Bad publicity. Something – and it wasn't human kindness – had ushered us under her wing.

Johnny was an ex-pat boozer from Birmingham with a burly body, a dramatic manner and the charm of a puff adder. A fiftysomething determined to believe he was worldly and important, when he was an obvious minnow in an alien pond. He made like he was furious we were staying so near Khao

San Road: 'What the fuck are you doing there? You want to get caught?'

He told Mike to go back and get our stuff, make sure he's not followed, and bring it to the office immediately. Naomi would book us into the Hilton, where I'm writing now (amid post-imperial splendour; not somewhere police would expect backpackers).

We ran through the story again. He said to phone the insurance company from the office. I had already called the emergency line and got moved up the company hierarchy to a guy called Alain. It was the first thing that had gone really well. He wouldn't be specific but he had admitted he has the authority to release 'medical-sized funds' which can easily outstrip legal expenses.

Before I rang Alain again, Johnny blasted: 'This'll cost us thirty thousand dollars; and it has to be here yesterday!'

Had Johnny sent Mike off so I had to face that shocking sum alone? And interesting use of 'cost *us*'. It will cost him nothing. Quite the reverse.

Before Alain answered, I felt intimate with him. It had sunk in that he was the only official who had been genuinely touched by my story, and had silently intimated he would authorise what it takes to get me out of Thailand. I felt hyperconscious of everything around me, but at some deeper level a virus was fighting to assert itself. It had been all over the island. I had been slightly feverish for a couple of days and was trying not to notice. Now I could feel my throat muscles clench. I thought I was relaxing when I heard Alain's serious voice, but that's when the coughing started. Very painful ache with each cough. I pictured a red raw throat.

Alain asked: 'Can we trust these people?'

I didn't know. I glanced at them both and turned back to the window. The view was of another block. I looked down. I could see a tuk-tuk – a three-wheeled, cheap taxi; open backed like a motorised rickshaw with bicycle steering – weaving in and out the cars. A lot of tuk-tuk drivers are desperate characters: no licences, firing on adrenaline and God knows what else to make a small buck. My fever was making me unsteady on my feet. The tuk-tuk seemed too far away, too far down. I wanted to lie down in a corner, wait for Mike to return and ask him to take over and decide everything. Then I was furious with myself. I had to rise to this. I knew more about it than anyone.

Alain was waiting patiently. I concentrated hard, realising I had a powerful ally here. I replied casually: 'I don't know.' I didn't want the insurance to pay money to this crew and then things not work out; how keen would Alain be to pay out for my next escape attempt? I kept saying to myself: 'Keep thinking, Denise, you're doing fine, it's just a fever, keep thinking . . .'

He got the message: 'Where are you staying?'

Naomi and Johnny were all ears, I knew it. 'Well,' I said, still casual. 'I could call you from our hotel once you've tried to get approval? We're staying at the Hilton.'

'Fine. Here's my home number, call any time, you sound in a bad way.'

'Sure,' I said and took the number down.

I told Johnny and Naomi it was very hopeful; Alain just had to get approval. I think they both clocked that I was going to be exclusive about my contact with the insurance company. It was tense, but the destiny of that money is my only power over this pair.

Johnny went through to another room to make calls. He was gone half an hour. My fever was terrible and my throat was getting worse. Naomi and I waited in virtual silence. Mike came back, confident he hadn't been followed. I said, 'Johnny is just making some calls,' and smiled.

He furrowed his brow. Johnny came in and said he has a contact in immigration at the airport; 'Saturday before three, we'll smuggle you out, if we can wangle you a passport. Get on any flight, just you, Denise.'

Mike was appalled at the smuggling idea: 'Christ, can we not do this more legitimately? She hasn't done anything you know!'

Johnny turned to him and spoke menacingly: 'You shut your fucking mouth for the good of your girlfriend!'

Mike wasn't intimidated. He shrugged and was quiet, knowing we can review plans later. His only concern was for me. I was thinking how gratuitously bullying this pair are. They want us nervous; too nervous to protest about the ludicrous sum of money?

A buzzer went in the office. Both Mike and I jolted; you can grow so accustomed to being nervous that it takes something to remind you that you are a wreck.

'That'll be the application form,' said Johnny, buzzing the person in. 'For your passport. Fill it in as if you lost your passport on a beach.'

He looked away and lit up a cigarette, not waiting for an answer. A small Chinese man appeared with an envelope. The Chinese guy was obviously a sidekick, intimate and servile. He waited in silence at Johnny's side.

Johnny nodded at me, indicating the Chinese guy should hand the envelope to me. He said, 'After you've filled it in, take it to this address tonight.' He handed me a card. 'That's my home card – don't give it to *anyone* – I'll be out, pop it through the door. Meet here again at 9.00 a.m. tomorrow. Before you go, get your passport picture taken, there's a machine in the bus station along the street, leave all four photos with Lee, here.' Then he looked at his watch and off he swaggered, clearly pleased with his Chandleresque performance. His bossiness would have been laughable were we not entirely dependent on this egomaniac.

Did as he said.

It's now 1.30 a.m. Mike has taken a sleeping pill. We have to share a bed. He rang Victoria earlier, looked uptight afterwards. Said everything was fine. Same games. That could have been me on the other end of the phone.

That said, he is being saintly, and staying right on the ball. He assuaged my doubts about Naomi and Johnny. 'If you end up in court, you could ruin them by saying they advised you to split, and Alain would testify to their ploy for your escape too. They know it. And they're not Thai. I'd guess they're disliked, pulling in big foreign clients when they've probably only got one proper Thai lawyer in the firm. Definite fortress mentality about the pair. They don't want to see you in the dock, inadvertently ratting on them. They don't want you caught.'

I said: 'It's strange the way we both use movie words like "ratting", "grassing" and "skip country" so much now. We're definitely keeping bad company.'

Mike smiled and did his Humphrey Bogart: 'Sure baby. And the finks didn't try to get the lowdown on yours truly. I don't doubt that two-timing, double-dealing broad would pull a fast one, but she's no dumb blonde, and she'd want to suss what kind of enemy she's making. I won't be in no slammer. They're on the level.'

I smiled – it was the first humour that had passed between us – and felt nostalgia, for the fun-loving lover that Mike had been when we first met five years ago. From that high summer to this low of hiding out in the Bangkok Hilton on the run. How unfortunate. A fitting epilogue? Life can be unbearably sad.

I drew back from those feelings and said: 'But they're nervous. Immigration and police scare them. They're not totally confident. They feel boxed into this.'

Mike winced. 'Afraid so. Airport's the big test. If you get lifted I'll get straight onto the embassy, the tabloids, get Rich to do the net and make approaches to MPs. Might as well start on the King of Thailand too; his pardon may be your best shot. There are about twelve Britons in Thai prisons just now. I checked on the net; nearly all drug offenders apart from a couple of violent cases – Christ, all probably innocent! At least yours is a unique story. We won't stop until you're out.'

I appreciated Mike thinking ahead and being determined to deal with the jail possibility, but it freaked me, such a near event, if it happens. I found myself thinking of lines to put in letters and people to approach, and from there to regarding jail as inevitable. I pulled back again, to concentrate on analysing the immediate situation. Phoned Alain and asked him to be ready with the money in the morning. He said it was already set up. He wanted off the phone because he could tell I found talking painful. Thank God for one considerate and honourable person amid this rabble of shysters. And in an insurance company?! Bizarre where heroes spring from.

Actually there's not much to think about, just this fever to fend off. I'm coughing a lot, swallowing is getting difficult and I'm sweaty and tired.

Please God, two days' grace.

Saturday, 16th September

5.00 a.m. Saturday morning. Fever atrocious. Couldn't write yesterday. I keep escaping into lovely delirium, always my midnight swim with Melinda, the Amazonian Swede, a few nights before the fire, the secluded beach, she's laughing, neither of us have ever seen phosphorescence, she's kicking below the surface of the water, creating small regions of brilliant blue all around her foot, transparent, luminous in a sea of opaque black. Now I'm laughing and kicking up those clouds of shimmering light in the sea and Melinda is saying

'Watch me!' as she kicks off her sandals and swims out to sea, trailing an electric blue wake. Her body is framed in a bubble of iridescent turquoise now; a fully visible, mesmeric beauty, suspended in pitch blackness. She's shouting: 'You show me!' and I'm kicking off my sandals, swimming out towards her, thinking 'I want to give in to this sea, I want to swim in this sea.' Now I tread water beside her, I'm tingling, I am here, in the sea, right in the petrifying sea. She whips off her bikini and watches her own body, looking wonderfully aquatic. The motion of her naked legs, an even, circular rhythm, looks sexual, I think I blush, I don't know. I strip off too. We have to hold our bikinis; we're far too far out to throw them towards our sandals. We swim out – further – and loll about until we get too cold. When we return to the shallows and stand up to walk out the water, we hear Bill, the friendly scuba fanatic, booming out in the darkness, he'll be on his perch on the rocks at the end of the beach: 'Couldn't you have done that a bit nearer here?' We giggle, unembarrassed, proud, nobody else around, just blackness. 'Better luck next time!' I shout while I'm thinking, 'I left the shallows and didn't drown.'

Mustn't get delirious today. Delirium is frightening me as much as anything now. It stops me concentrating, even stops me caring. I'll care if I get banged up in a Thai jail for years. I need to write. Force my concentration. Decided to make a copy of this last week's diary on disk and post it to Rich. No time to be embarrassed. Might be in jail this afternoon. Could all go pear-shaped. Not impossible that Mike gets arrested too. Then Rich won't know what happened; has to know everything, to contact lawyers, etc. Already left a message on his machine. Hate worrying him. Friday evening in Edinburgh, he'll stay out late; hopefully Mike will have left a reassuring message, back to back with mine, before he gets in.

Getting picked up in an hour to go to the airport. Terrified. Made the 9.00 a.m. appointment yesterday. Johnny had a passport waiting for me. Couldn't have been processed on the back of my form, too fast. Either good contact in embassy or it's fake, looks fine. He said the form was to tidy up the embassy's records. Then he said he had another passport, a false one, under the name Mary Murphy. Has to make one last call this morning to see if we can use the 'genuine' one. Not reassuring.

Rang Alain in office, had to let Johnny talk to him. They argued about money. Naomi interrupted the call, as if she was a gracious person: 'I can take a cut from my share.' False bitch. It seems I'm worth $25,000. Too ill to care about degradation of being bartered about. Alain's good. He'd have authorised thirty; spineless Johnny's nerve cost him five grand.

A shocker from Johnny: 'You'll have to go to the police station for immigration stamps for that passport. Immigration at airport won't let you through without them. Airline desk might check too.'

Fell asleep in taxi on the way to police; disturbed, paranoid dreams. Woke up outside station with the feeling of the dreams, but couldn't remember them. Incredulous to be walking into a police station. Wondered if it was a delirious dream. There was a holding cell in the station; a guy cuddling his baby through the bars. I thought: 'That's where I'm going to be in five minutes when they realise I'm lying!'

Had all the right paperwork from Johnny. He was right. Minor job tended by a minion. Still shaken.

Went back to office to see if Alain had wired money. Johnny rang a bank in America. Money was there. Johnny said to go home and sleep, get smart clothes ready for the morning and borrow Mike's businesslike bag. Mike isn't to come with me today, wasn't with me yesterday. Don't like the way they cut Mike out. Bullies. Johnny will phone him after I get on a flight or am caught.

Before I left the office I asked how bad Thai jails are. Johnny, trying to be a sensitive person, said, 'Jails aren't as bad as you think ... People do survive in them.' Then he blew it by saying: 'I was thinking, we can arrange for you to take your laptop in with you.' Jesus, the man who has said, impatiently, all along, 'Just do as I say and we'll get you out!' has been preparing for the other eventuality. Very confidence-inspiring. Big-headed liar.

By then everything was blurring by, the fever was wild in me. Went to bed at 7.00 p.m., heady, nervous and tired. Hinted to Mike to join me. Wanted some warmth and sex, some grounding. Didn't take much persuasion. Thought I had withdrawn sexual affection, in that way only women can; forever, in a the-mere-thought-makes-my-flesh-crawl way. But I had given in, and it was good to be fucked. Forgive myself for it. It didn't matter. And the fact of that matters, in a good way. Like I felt when he showed up on Noi; never out the woods as fast as you think.

This is it. Bell will ring soon. Looking at timetables, the flight to Kuala Lumpur looks the best option, but I'll go anywhere. Must copy and post this. Must try hard to talk clearly and not cough all the time in the airport. Must fight fever. Don't attract attention. And if it goes wrong, try to see it coming and run. That's all I can do. Got to be strong, this is my life/my future at stake. Terrified.

Tough! Concentrate.

IF YOU'VE BEEN READING THIS RICH:

I'm counting on you. Victoria will soon pull Mike off the case. You are my best hope. The folks will be useless as ever. Don't race out here to see me until you've done all you can in Britain. Johnny's right: people do survive in jail. I will. We'll be sharing Sunday brunch in Edinburgh again one day, each other's insurance against the world, as ever. Be brave. Love you.

Yipeeeeeeeeeeeeeeeeeeeeeeeeeee! The plane has taken off. Watch out Kuala Lumpur; here comes the happiest woman on earth! It's over!

Felt good when Johnny said we can use the embassy passport, but still a paranoid wreck though in duty free. I thought the immigration contact nodded conspiratorially, in that faint Eastern way, when he handed back my passport, and then I . . . Hey! Wait. Who cares? Who the hell cares?! Not me! It's over now. Over! Yipeeeeeeeeeeeeeeeeeeeee again! And again! Yipeeeeeeeeeeeeeeeeeeeee!

That glorious moment, just a minute ago, the plane leaving the ground for the sky; Thailand and everything still racing away into the past at hundreds of miles an hour as I write. Over! Over and done! Over and out! I still like Thailand. I want to laugh. Can't wait to ring Kathy.

I wish Rich was here, I'd cry for joy with him. I've got my life back!

The fever can kick in all it wants now. These words keep spinning round in my head: I left the shallows and didn't drown. They make me smile. I'm swimming in the depths at night with Melinda framed in blue light. I can feel Mike smiling too, thousands of feet below. That was our last rites. Thanks for everything darling, especially the decision to run: good call. And goodbye.

'In future, you won't remember anything from these hours; but you will never forget that they happened.'

This was true. Later, Rich would remember nothing clearly from the time between 11.05 p.m. and 2.10 a.m., spanning 15–16th September. Oddly, Lee-Ann's statement would be his only solid memory. Other than that, there would be the moment in the living room, shortly after he listened to Denise's message, when Lee-Ann had come in and said she would wait with him, until he heard from Mike, and then she had gone to put the kettle on. But that would be a glazed memory; he had been in shock at the time and Lee-Ann's actions weren't meaningful to him. And there would be the vague recollection of Lee-Ann phoning for a taxi, at some point, which took her to the all-night garage and back, for cigarettes. But mostly those hours dissolved in a knotted stomach, manic plans, the feeling of ageing without living, nothing that could be properly recalled and relived outside the circumstances.

He had paced about, occasionally trying to settle on the couch. He talked about Denise while Lee-Ann sat still on an armchair, watchful, in her inscrutable way.

By 1.30 a.m. Rich was pacing constantly, within a few yards of the phone. However he had just sat back down when the phone rang. As he leapt to it, he banged into the coffee table but felt no sensation, still only the pain of his love for Denise, intensifying unbearably as he grabbed the receiver knowing this call mattered like no other call he had ever had. His normally low heart beat was a pulsating boom in his own ear as he skipped the hellos and blurted out: 'Mike, what's happening?'

'She's safe, everything's fine.'

Rich paused, turned and nodded to Lee-Ann, who finally smiled. Feeling his eyes well up, he turned his back on her, and concentrated to halt the flow. He was back in the room now.

He closed his eyes and spoke through a long, slow exhalation: 'Oh thank God.'

And again he wanted to cry, and again he held it in. Then he asked: 'Are you sure?'

Mike spoke happily. 'Definitely. She's out of Thailand, on a Malaysian Airlines plane going to Kuala Lumpur, over the sea right now. I saw it take off. I'm still in the airport. I wasn't supposed to come but I followed them: I didn't trust the shyster smuggling her out to ring me afterwards, and I wanted to watch, maybe jump in if there was trouble. I just confronted the shyster, told him he's a rip-off merchant and a bullying prick, and I hope he comes to grief himself some time.'

'Jesus, what happened? Aren't you grateful to him? What's all this about?'

'He's a piece of shit; wouldn't have helped if the insurance company hadn't agreed to pay him a fortune in so-called legal costs, and he deliberately intimidated Denny almost all the way through the whole thing, until he got his cash.'

'Right, tell me everything, right from the start.'

Mike told Rich the entire story, as best he knew it. Rich interrupted regularly for clarification. When he put the phone down at the end of the thirty-minute conversation he felt more murderous than he knew possible.

He told Lee-Ann about the fire, Mama, Mr Vain, the dash to Bangkok and Denise's fever. Having told it, he could imagine Denise's relief, all those thousands of miles away, in the sky right now; must be feeling great. He smiled and began to relax.

'Sorry, this must have been rather boring for you,' he said.

Lee-Ann smiled and shook her head, very briefly, then returned to the blank staring mode which Rich was now aware she had been in for some time.

'I'm not tired, fancy a glass of bubbly?' he said. 'I feel like celebrating.'

Again the merely momentary smile, and a short nod. Through in the kitchen, Rich, despite his joyous relief, felt uncomfortable about Lee-Ann. He winced, thinking of how this night had been for her. She had finally agreed to go for a drink with a slobbering fool, had slobbering fool's junkie friend inflicted upon her, before being abandoned for a fight. Then she had to come back to slobbering fool's home for a joyless tea while he nursed his bruises, whereupon she spent three tense hours waiting to see if slobbering fool's sister was being imprisoned in Thailand. He sure knew how to show a girl a good time, yes siree.

But he couldn't feel despondent: Denise was safe! When he returned to the living room, with two large glasses of Perrier Jouët 1992, he tried to share his bonhomie with Lee-Ann. 'Chin chin,' he grinned. She said nothing and drank it without taking her eyes off him. She was really beginning to unnerve him now.

He put on Doris Day's 'Move Over Darling', declaring it, 'One of the sexiest songs ever; such adult lust, such confident commitment to making love, even though the guy she's singing to is dodgy; wonderful.'

Rich had hoped to be accused of being ironic and then a conversation to emerge but Lee-Ann, still watching him, shrugged, and spoke quietly as if her sweet, husky voice couldn't actually be bothered uttering words: 'I like her too, not a great singer, a crooner, but comforting, the sound of a glamorous auntie.'

Silence. Her watching him, a frown lurking in there?

'Oh,' said Rich brightly. 'What about your friends? Remember? You were meant to go off and meet them before midnight?'

'It's OK. There was no meeting.' Her tone was uninterested. Was this getting worse?

'What?'

'I said that so you wouldn't try to persuade me to come back here.' Her loveable tones had never sounded more forbidding.

'Oh. Eh. Well, sorry to keep you up so late.'

'Doesn't matter.'

Is this anger? He was sorry about the evening, but he'd make it up to her. If she'd give him the chance, that is.

'Are you tired?' Rich asked. 'I can call a cab if you want?'

'Not tired,' stated Lee-Ann. Getting seriously economic with wordage now, thought Rich, the Ice Queen cometh.

She continued, still in a remote tone: 'And I'll stay here.'

'Oh,' said Rich, not daring to get hopeful. 'I mean, yes, sure, it's late, no problem; spare room's got clean sheets, an alarm clock . . .'

'In your bed.'

Rich paused. Still the stare and distant voice. He stared back. Confusion caused him to frown. He wasn't sure his jaw wasn't hanging open like an empty idiot's. For all his frown, which he was trying to wrestle off his face, Rich was close to ecstasy. His head reeled. He kept thinking, 'For God's sake, speak man!' At last he nodded, swallowed, and said, 'I'd like that.'

'I know you would.'

Silence. Her stare, and still him wondering what to say, how not to let this slip away. He looked from side to side and over to his CD collection, as if for clues.

He glanced back. The blank stare turning into a glare. He

smiled and looked away again. Some seconds passed. Then Lee-Ann spoke firmly: 'A few ground rules. Shag someone else and I'll kill you. I really will. Get into another fight and I'll kill you. I really will. And don't expect much from me. OK?'

Rich swallowed again, managed to affect a confident shrug, and spoke as seriously as his excited being would allow. 'Fine.'

'Really don't.' Full-blown glare.

'I won't.'

'Don't think of me as the strip-teasing sex bomb you think you met. I'm deadly boring and serious. I'm not a very happy person, never have been.'

'Sure.' Rich became aware he was nodding like a broken puppet and stopped.

'Don't expect me to have lots of friends and a glamorous life: I'm a self-conscious loner who performs in public to keep people away. And I find it stressful, OK?!'

'Fine.'

'So I won't always be feeling up to socialising and I expect you to back me in any situation regardless of how unreasonable or drunk I am. OK?'

'Naturally.'

'And that's another thing: drugs are out, maybe the occasional treat, but if you think you can handle a relationship and continue with your current lifestyle then you're a bigger fuckwit than I already think you are, which is pretty bad, I can tell you. I might as well start nagging now, so you know what you're in for.'

'Eh, yes, good idea,' said Rich. 'I mean, for when we go to Ikea.'

Lee-Ann looked a little thrown by his remark but she brushed over it. Her glare was holding steady, like a scared animal.

'Jesus, you are just going to say "yes sir, no sir, can I lick your bum sir?" to whatever I say.'

'No, no, I'm listening, I mean it.'

Rich was still a bit perplexed, a bit amused, but completely euphoric now, despite being at a loss for meaningful words.

'Right, I'm a syphilitic, bad-breathed baby killer who likes the Spice Girls.'

She was trying to lighten up. Rich frowned: 'Woah! Spice Girls, that's going a bit far. Don't know if this is going to work.'

'Have you nothing to say?'

Rich thought for a bit. 'No. No preconditions. Nothing. Just thanks. A million times over to the Nth power. Though I wish you weren't nervous that you're going to disappoint me. Just because I'm an embarrassing, lovestruck fool around you doesn't mean I have unrealistic expectations. You worry too much about that; some past problem, of people projecting on to you. No need to project that on to me. I do adore you, but I know you're a handful, believe me, it's a lot more obvious than you think.'

'But you don't know me, you don't know what I'm like to deal with, you don't know . . .'

'Lee-Ann! I didn't say I did. I'm just fated to be in love with you, that's all.'

'Well, you might not be so keen when I can't live up to all your high hopes, all the dreams you've been nurturing, they'll be soured when you see how neurotic and closed-off and fearful and . . .'

Jesus, more unnecessary proof, thought Rich, as if she hasn't got 'demanding' emblazoned on her forehead.

'Listen to yourself. You're worried I'll go off you. We haven't started and you're fearing I'll reject you. You're being difficult already, you *are* difficult, I really *do* know, but the best ones always are. And I'm not a wimp. And I am in love with you. Now please shut the fuck up and see if you can't one day love me back.'

Lee-Ann looked away and smiled.

When she turned back, he looked her in the eye and spoke in a playful voice. 'As a matter of academic interest, when did you decide on this? You weren't keen to see me; you only phoned two days ago. Somebody blow you out for tonight?'

'Another guy was going to be taking me out tonight. And he's better looking and more successful and more together than you. But I cancelled.'

'Why?'

'Dunno. Just sitting at home on Wednesday; phoned you, then him. Last week I remember realising you were often on my mind. But I didn't expect this.'

'So you decided when we were waiting for Mike's call?'

'Maybe. Really don't know. I tell you, when you came into the restaurant all cut, I was raging. If I had gone off I would never have seen you again – oh that's another thing: I've got a hell of a temper and I'm very proud and . . .'

'Yes, yes, you're the most insufferable cow ever, I *know*. So, in the restaurant you felt like we were already going out?'

'Now that you mention it, it's strange. I didn't decide about you at any time. Your ludicrous fight impacted on me, very confusingly. But remember when we met at the start of the evening, on India Street? I wasn't excited waiting, but when you appeared it was lovely, that caught me off-guard. What about me with you? When I stripped for you?'

'No. First time I saw you. Don't know when it was. Months before we talked. I just didn't know.'

Lee-Ann smiled, softly, at last. 'Thanks. Must say, I like your certainty.'

'Oh, careful there Lee-Ann, watch out, you could end up relaxing and stopping being difficult . . .'

'Hey, I know when we started going out! I kept your keys when I came back from the all-night garage, deliberately. No big deal, just knew I needed a set now.'

339

The first argument, a demeaning brush with violence, a major trauma and shared joy had already been notched up, not only in the first evening, which was obviously unusual, but also before sex. Now they stayed up until dawn, intimates talking scribble until both were yawning.

Lee-Ann was in bed by the time Rich cleared up and came through from the toilet. He undressed, neglecting to be self-conscious in front of a new lover. When they made love it was sleepy, slow stuff. He regarded her body, not as an object of desire – of course she was that anyway – but with a keenness to acquaint; the pronounced clavicles, the lightness of her stroke, the tiny, brown nipples, the dark blue eyes being fired by sex.

And that face, the old woman in there, who will emerge in time, and the wee girl, also discernible in that smile, impish, manic, passionate, smiles don't change much through life, somewhere in the spirit of that smile is Lee-Ann in her entirety.

She was perched on top of him. He had entered her casually, inevitably, there was no desperate passion, it wouldn't be the last time, but now it felt good being in there. Rich concentrated on long, deep thrusts. She kept smiling, enjoying being pleasured, for a couple of minutes, then said, 'Now, you on top.' They changed positions, he was right beside her supple body, disengaging and moving round, those limbs and curves, all the more graceful for the straightforward motion, just keen to lie down and be entered. He mounted her missionary style and, just as he got in, she put on an earnest expression and said; 'Oh, did I tell you? I never give blow jobs . . .' He smiled and raised his eyebrows. She continued: 'On first dates.'

'Aaargh! I don't want to hear that there have been other dates!' said Rich and thrust hard into her.

Lee-Ann smiled, gratified. Rich enjoyed watching her.

She writhed downwards, separating her thighs more and closing her eyes. 'Don't worry darling,' she said. Her words were bereft of intonation; they were an effort of concentration, as fucking was quickly consuming her. 'I hate your exes, they're all sluts and bitches you know.'

'Ah, jealousy! We really are going out,' said Rich between thrusts.

'I'm pathologically jealous,' moaned Lee-Ann, eyes still shut, face yielding to contortions. 'Must have just started a relationship. Oh yes, it's all downhill from here.'

'I bloody doubt it,' said Rich, through quickening, deeper thrusts.

Lee-Ann had already decided she wasn't returning to London in the morning. When the phone rang, at 9.00 a.m., Rich grabbed it off the bedside table so as not to wake her.

'Hello, you've got a wrong number. Nobody that knows me would phone at this time on a Saturday morning!'

'It's Denny.'

'Denny?! Denny, where are you?' Rich swung his legs off the bed and sat up on the edge.

'KL.'

'Well, eh, how are you?'

'I'm great! Just been to the doctor, got to rest up for a few days with this bloody fever, but then I'll go off to an island for my last fortnight.'

'You're not coming back?!'

'Why should I come back?'

'Well, are you OK? Do you *want* to stay out there? Aren't you needing to recover?'

'I'll recover out here. I'm not getting chased home by some corrupt little shit on the make. My trip's not over.'

After a few minutes of conversation Rich accepted Denise was well enough for the reproach that had been fermenting

341

in the back of his mind: 'Why did you ask Mike and not me to come out?'

'Don't know,' said Denise, and paused. 'It was good.'

'How the hell could it have been good?'

'Don't know, but it was. I wanted away from Mike. Facing that shit in Thailand together; our big deal relationship, it finally wasn't that important. And he was good, he delivered.'

'Hmm. Well, if anything goes wrong again, you phone me. Immediately.'

'I can look after myself.'

'I didn't say you couldn't but for God's sake, you just narrowly missed jail and I knew nothing about it until the last minute: it's not on! Now come on, Denise!'

'Ooooh, *Denise* is it? You are all angry because catastrophe nearly befell your big sister, and you love her so much.'

Both paused, hearing the echo from six months back, when Rich had said something similar on the phone to Denise after he nearly drowned. Neither mentioned it. Denise continued: 'Everything fine with you? How is the quest for Lady Lee-Ann going?'

Lee-Ann had woken up and become aware who Rich was talking to. She was lying on her side, stroking his back.

'Abandoned,' said Rich.

'Abandoned? Oh, Rich. Why?'

'Just no point chasing her any more.'

'Oh darling, you don't know that. Has something happened? Did you see her? And it went badly? Are you sure there's no point?'

'None whatsoever.'

'I'm so sorry darling.'

'No, it's fine, there's no point because, well, you see, I've already got her. Want to say hello?'

'What?!'

Rich foisted the receiver on Lee-Ann.

'Hello Denise,' said Lee-Ann.

Rich leant in to share the ear-piece.

'Lee-Ann?'

'Yes. That was awful what you went through. Are you OK?'

'Eh, yes. Thanks. Just got a fever. Eh, how are you?'

'I'm fine, no big dramas here, except for your little brother's disastrous life of course.'

'Of course. But I think you'll have turned the little head-case into the happiest person on earth, apart from me.'

'Feels good from this side too.'

Rich grabbed the phone back. 'Enough of that,' he grinned, addressing both women. 'You start off all sweet about me but I know you women: you'll be bonding by bitching about me within minutes. We've got years for that to happen.'

'I see what you mean about her voice, Rich. Really is like a stuck-up twelve-year-old chainsmoker. Really cute. How long have you been going out with her?'

'How long have I been going out with her? Oh let's see now; all my life! Just didn't know till I met her.'

Denise laughed. 'I'm sure you feel lucky. Remember she's lucky too.'

'Yeah, right. That's an interesting belief, in a mad, millennial cult kind of way, but I'll try to remember it.'

'God, she is *so* lucky, to have a guy that thinks like that.'

'It's good to hear you Denny.'

'It's good to hear you too. I have to go. This is costing a fortune.'

There was a short, awkward silence. 'Eh, sure, see you soon, phone again. Eh, miss you, Denny.'

'Just *miss*? I *love* you, Richard. And you love me.'